Barry B. Longyear

JUST ENOUGH ROPE

~ Joe Torio Mystery #2 ~

Enchanteds Publishing
PO Box 100, New Sharon ME 04955
www.Enchanteds.net

Just Enough Rope is a work of fiction. The contents of this work are either products of the author's invention or are used fictitiously. Any resemblance to actual persons or events are coincidental.

"Riot in Cell Block #9," lyrics by Jerry Leiber and Mike Stoller, 1953.

ISBN-13: 978-0615484129
ISBN-10: 0615484123

Manufactured in the United States of America

To the Animals
Wherever they are

JUST ENOUGH ROPE

BATMAN

At the edge of the greenbelt, Gully Raye moved between the winds and through the shadows, just ahead of his ghosts, and far from prying eyes. The sky above the landfill's working face was cobalt blue laced with peach-colored clouds driven by a gentle western breeze. The beginnings of a good day: sunny but still very cold. Special day. According to the salvaged quartz watch hanging from Gully's neck by a piece of twine, it was just before six. Morning Hill, east beyond the greenbelt screen, was still blocking the sun. The scraped dirt, the seeded reclaimed strip, and the expanses of compacted rubbish sparkled with a heavy blanket of diamonds from the late April frost.

The salvaged thermometer outside Gully's shack, hidden deep in the woods, rested at seventeen above by Gabriel Fahrenheit's reckoning. The cold was keeping the others deep within their crates and boxes packed with newsprint. It was the weekend, so the landfill crew wouldn't be out. So, until the sun appeared over Morning Hill and sunbeams reached into the woods and warmed up the winos, Gully would have at least an hour or two of prime uninterrupted picking time.

Things for his shack: plastic bags to seal his roof, Styrofoam packaging and cardboard for insulation, old canvas for window and door drapes, pots and pans, even tables and chairs. Things for his back: old repairable shirts, coats, trousers. Rinsing out the plastic laundry soap containers allowed him to wash the clothes in his salvaged plastic tub; needles, thread, scissors that only needed a little sharpening. Tools. A good Stanley all-metal claw hammer, a saw blade that would soon have a

5

good wooden handle salvaged from another saw with a broken blade. Screwdrivers, nails, screws, springs—the landfill's bounty made a comfortable man of Gully Raye. The birds made him wealthy.

The birds, snow white and primer gray against the blue sky, a blanket of harsh cries driving those images, those thoughts, far into the void.

—Luther had told him. God, they had all told him—
—The birds.

He looked at the birds.

The gulls were huddled on the topsoil rise east of the tire dump. They were facing into the slight breeze, waiting for the sun. Several of them noticed Gully and whispered to their friends. Soon dozens of white heads at a time were popping up above the crowd only to dart down an instant later, looking at him. The birds all knew Gully. They kept watching his hands.

Garbage birds and sky rats, the winos called them. They threw rocks at them, and even tried to kill and eat them. The previous July, One-eared Rocco had salvaged some small fire crackers. He'd light one, throw it out, and laugh when a gull would pick it up. It was extra funny for Rocco when, instead of killing the gull, only its beak would be blown off. Gully smiled to himself as he remembered Rocco screaming when the joint he had been smoking touched off the remaining fireworks in his crib, trapping him inside with all that warmth-retaining newspaper and excelsior. He had burned alive. Gully had called in the fire on his restored mobile police squawk, but there wasn't much of Rocco left by the time the Collier company of the fire department arrived.

—The smile. The guilt for the smile. The pain that made Rocco laugh. The battle to keep it all away. Away from his eyes. Away from his mind. Away—

Things balance out.

Gully nodded to himself. The fire fighters saved the woods. After a little knife work by the ME's Office Rocco was moved south of the landfill across Knowles Road into Digger's Field where he was stacked in cardboard on top of two other indigents in a trench and buried. From one landfill to another.

Poetry.

All of the gulls were looking in Gully's direction now and he relented. With his right hand he reached into his jacket pocket with a huge sweeping gesture. Immediately three, then ten, then fifty, then three hundred gulls left the ground and streaked toward him. He held a broken piece of dog biscuit up in the air and began turning to his left, whirling around in a slow circle, the gulls circling clockwise above him. He tossed the piece of biscuit up into the feathered ring, one of the gulls caught it on the fly, and dropped to the ground with it, immediately rejoining the rotating ring of gulls once the prize was consumed. Time after time Gully tossed pieces of dog biscuit, stale bread, dried meat and cheese up into the ring, which grew larger and larger as additional birds joined. By the time his pockets were empty, Gully was drinking in the sight of the bird formation, looking as it did like the eye of an avian hurricane, their cries deafening.

For several circuits after his pockets were exhausted, the gulls circled, one-by-one peeling away as each one recognized that their benefactor was tapped. As the circle thinned, Gully noticed something low in the bottom step of the working face where late Friday's trash had been dumped prior to Frank and his bulldozer spreading and crushing the refuse at the end of the working day. Poking out from beneath an irregular collection of flattened cardboard boxes was something that looked like the curled fingers and palm of a left hand.

Gully had found bodies and body parts at the landfill in the past. After he had found the mobile police radio and repaired it, he could call them in, and had done so until the police dispatch supervisor at the Collier Substation laid a trip on him about unauthorized use of a police frequency. Before that he had called in a human foot and a human head, five months apart, not related to each other. Much later there was the discarded body of rookie mobster Little Dog Morgan. A valuable find, too. Three hundred and twenty-one dollars in his wallet, a cell phone in his pocket, and a gun tucked in his belt at the small of his back: a nice Pocket Auto. Excellent down-filled L.L. Bean winter coat, too. Blue and green, a warm detachable hood, not much blood on it, and the

7

holes patched over easily. Big pockets. Lots of room for broken dog biscuits, pieces of bread, stale crackers, moldy cookies, dried meat, and fuzzy pieces of cheese. He knew nothing of how Little Dog or the body parts had become dead, consequently they came with no messages. There were no killers with whom to share pain and tears and outrage and nightmares. He was not afraid of this new arrival.

Half the gulls had left the circle by the time Gully made it to the hand. Human. Female. It was a left hand, palm up, and was attached to a right hand at the wrists by a one eighth-inch thick black nylon cord wrapped twice and fastened with a square knot. There was an additional loop of cord between the wrists.

Gully staggered backwards as though smacked in the face by a truck. He fell back against the next highest step, his body—his heart—aching.

Nylon cord. One eighth inch. Black.

Wrists tied behind the back.

Two loops. Square knot. Extra loop in between.

Hard to catch his breath, tension tightening the muscles in the back of his neck, driving the pains forward across his scalp. Gully, pegged in place, blinked and forced himself back for another look.

He pushed away from the wall of compacted trash, went back to the hands, and moved a sticky Martha Stewart catalog until he could get a full view of the left hand. The ring finger carried a plain gold wedding band.

Relief. He felt his neck relaxing. He had been wrong. The ghosts and nightmares had joined forces and gathered, but now they disbanded, fading into the mental mists. Safe. The puzzle of his first reaction, though, teased at Gully. He bent down and looked more closely.

Beneath the hands was wrinkled and stained dove gray cotton cloth: the woman's blouse. It was spotted with blue and orange paint. He leaned in and sniffed. Oil paint. Artist's. Still fresh. Gully squatted down to see beneath the cardboard. The black nylon cord extended from the wrists beneath the cardboard where it was tied to her ankles. Her wrists and ankles had once been tied tightly together, but there was plenty of slack now. The long bones of her arms and her legs were broken. Getting run over by a bulldozer a few times does that.

What looked like a pair of charcoal gray pants with a black leather belt and a pair of once white panties were pulled down to just above her knees, exposing her buttocks. Another problem.

Pubic hair. Blond. Problem number three.

On the right shoulder of her blouse was a blue and white patch. Eagle perched on a key. She was the one who had been mentioned on the news, which made her occupation problem number four.

Taking off his pack, Gully took the mobile radio from it, turned it on, held it to his mouth, and pressed the transmission switch. "Collier dispatch, this is Batman on tac three."

"Collier dispatch. Long time no hear, buddy. I been trying to raise you for weeks. How's your thang, Batman?"

"I got something important, Raff. You sure your boss isn't going to shut us down?"

"Lieutenant Quinlin has been brought up to speed, Batman, and she asked us to render her sincerest apologies to you the very next time you checked in. She knows now about what all you've done for the department. We square now?"

"All corners."

"What you got for me?"

"White blond female DOA dumped at the east working face of the new landfill off Collier Road. She came in a compacter truck and was here before seven PM Friday. The dozer has been over her and Frank puts the dragon back in the box at seven."

"Any ID?"

"I haven't touched the body, but I think she's the missing Books State corrections officer that's on the news. Katey Sloan?"

"What makes you think so, Batman?"

"The trash she's in is the kind that comes from Books and Friday is the prison's pickup day. Also, she's wearing charcoal gray trousers, black leather utility belt, light gray shirt, State DOC patch on the right shoulder."

9

"Everything but the song. Units are on the way, Batman. This one is heavy, my friend. The suits are going to want to talk to you."

"I can't do that."

"Stick around for the detectives, Batman. Let us give you a medal. Maybe a few dollars to show our appreciation."

"I'll make sure they find the vic, then I'm gone."

"I got you. Good to hear from you, man. Take care."

"Batman out."

Gully turned off the mobile unit and thrust it back into the rucksack. Turning back to the body of the young woman, he studied the wedding band for a moment.

The ring was wrong. Blond was wrong. The job was wrong. Lemon meringue pie without the meringue. But who insists upon meringue?

Getting down on his side, Gully tried to look far enough beneath the cardboard to see the victim's neck. It wasn't enough so he lifted the cardboard a little. There were ligature marks on what he could see of her neck: the right side and back. The mark was broken and overlapped in back. One more wrong thing.

—two plus two plus two plus—

Gully staggered back a step as his breath grew short. That had always been the problem: If this, then that. If that, then that other thing. And if that other thing—

He stood up suddenly and whirled around, his fingers reaching into his pocket to wrap themselves around Small Dog's Colt Pocket Auto. He quickly searched his surroundings, then went around again slowly, this time checking each shadow at the edge of the woods, each rise, each depression, looking for a face, a turned leaf, a sign, something out of the ordinary.

Lots of planning. They wouldn't leave his reaction to chance. What about after he called it in?

Quickly he ducked beneath the cardboard and lifted the victim's right shoulder until he could see her face. The skin was abraded. Cigarette burns. He lifted the shoulder higher. Her blouse was open, no bra, and just above her right breast were bite marks. He leaned in for a closer look. That familiar misalignment of the right canine with the right lateral incisor. Lots of planning.

10

Gully lowered the vic's shoulder and backed out from beneath the cardboard.

There was nothing Collier Dispatch could do now. Still scanning his surroundings, Gully reached into his bag and pulled out a wad of newspaper clippings. His memories. As long as he could keep them in his bag, he didn't have to carry them in his head. He leafed through the clippings until he found one only a few days old. Page twenty report on the additional landscaping and other changes out at the South River Mental Health Institute. He frowned. A line about the bridge construction and traffic jams on the way to the butterfly palace, new staff taken on: Juliana Strong, Arnold Phelps, Michael Butcher, blah, blah, blah—

—And there.

A line about a soap star, Barbara Cleveland. And that serial killer, Nathan Sunday. He was out there. Yes. And that's where they would send Alvin. That's where they would kill him—or make him kill. The bricks were being placed one after another.

He shoved the clippings into his bag and pulled out the cell phone he had taken from the perforated body of Little Dog Morgan. He indexed to the Riverview Living Center number and thumbed the call button, slightly amazed that the phone still worked. Someone out there, somewhere, was still paying the bills without reading what they were for.

The nursing home operator answered and Gully asked for room three sixteen. Two rings, a pickup, then that velvet voice with the gentle Georgia accent. *"Yes?"*

"Hey, White Sheet."

A chuckle came through the earpiece. *"Hey, Batman. You got Collier filled in yet?"*

"Not for another fifty years."

"How've you been doin', Gully? I didn't hear from you all winter."

"Still working things out, Luther. You know." So many nightmares, so little time. "By the way, Luth, Adelaide wants you to call."

"Adelaide?"

"I told her you'd call. Don't let me down, man. Okay? She really needs to hear from you. I got to go."

"Does she have her phone on?"

"Yes. Another half hour or so, anyway."

"I'll give her a ring."

"Got to go. Thanks." Gully ended the call and waited, the sounds of distant sirens making him anxious. He climbed down from the face of the compacted garbage bluff until he was on the hard-packed dirt within a hundred feet of the woods. Any further north and Morning Hill would cut him off from the Castle Hill microwave tower. The sirens grew louder. Gully moved more toward the west, still in line with the tower, but closer to the appliance dump. Plenty of good hiding places there in case he had to sprint for it.

"C'mon, Luther. *Now.*"

As if answering his plea, Small Dog's cell phone rang and Gully punched to answer. "Yes?"

"I had to wheel myself all the way down to the lobby to find a pay phone that was free. Adelaide. I haven't heard that one since we worked the Loaf." An edge of amusement came into his voice. *"Who do you think is listening in?"*

"Not sure, Luth. There's bad stuff working, though. If it's what I think it is, they may not be listening, but they ought to be. They sure got the equipment and the training."

"What do you mean? Cops?"

"Maybe. You heard about that CO over at Books who turned up missing Friday?"

"Katey Sloan. The news can't talk about nothin' else."

"She's DOA out here, partner. I just called it in."

"You sure it's her?"

"Dead sure. Look, Luth, you remember Jolene Gaye and Dena Lloyd?"

A beat of stunned silence. *"How could I forget?"*

"Same signature, exactly almost."

"What do you mean 'exactly almost'?"

"This one's got the wrong hair color, marital status, and occupational status. Strangled from the rear, too. Everything else is perfect, though, including the bite marks."

"Staged."

12

"You got it. And it was staged by someone who knows at least a little on how to do it and a lot on how to hang it on Alvin Yuker. They set up your boy, Luther. It'll work, too. The ring and the discrepancies with the ligature marks, hair color, and stuff are going to look like nothing to a jury who sees everything else that was done right."

Another silence. *"Son, you are in the headlights. The other side can't afford for you to get on the stand."*

"That's what I thought."

The sirens were loud on Collier road as the prowlers turned into the landfill's entrance. Gully thrust his left hand into his coat pocket to warm his fingers. "What do I do, Luther?"

"Vanish. Check in with me through Adelaide when you can. About what to do, I'll call Al Dockery. If there's something that can be done, he'll know what it is."

"I'm scared, Luth."

"I got the ball, Dale. Now, find the shadows. Run between the winds. Ninja detective. I'll send someone to let you know when it's safe."

"Thanks. So long, White Sheet."

"Take care."

Gully punched off the cell phone and stuck it in his pocket. As the first SRPD blue-and-white came around the north end of the green screen, Gully raced to the woods. He waited at the edge of the green belt until he saw one of the uniforms climb the garbage cliff and call out to the others. They'd found her. Gully Raye ducked into the deep woods and ran for the shadows.

THE SILVER LINE

Morning. Chilly. Numb. I was in weird places: A dimension within which all things seemed to be made of Jell-O. All new flavors, too: White, gray, black, and silver. Right arm pain. "Do you have to hold my arm so tight?" I slurred as I wobbled my head around and looked at the huge, strong, red hand gripping my upper arm.

"Relax, Joe," said the orderly. The man was big, his massive frame hung with muscles resembling sides of beef, his almost nonexistent neck supported a head resembling a wrecking ball. On his pale green fleece jacket, his nametag identified him as Brian. Orderlies at Riverside General's psych floor didn't have last names.

Brian. . . . *blessed are the cheese makers . . .*

Why is there no cheese Jell-O? Seemed important for some reason.

I had an overwhelming desire to lie down in the roadbed and go to sleep. I opened my eyes again and huddled in my tan windbreaker. Neck full of kinks. My side really sore. My brain on one cylinder. Stupid drugs. Drugs make you stupid.

Jell-O reality. Black had to be licorice. Never heard of licorice Jell-O, though. Thinning whipped cream on the lime Jell-O mountains. A big silver capsule rolling down the licorice road.

The silver-gray SRMHI shuttle bus turned off East River onto Riverside General Hospital's drive which stretched past the parking lots on its way to the portico where my escort and I waited. The distant top of Breadloaf Mountain, white with a fresh dusting of snow, a sharp wind down the west face of the mountain carried a freshening chill through the streets, which I might have

15

even been able to appreciate had I not been opiated into zombiehood . The scene wowed in and out along with my medication as I tried to figure out what flavor silver was.

"Brian."

"What, Joe?"

"These drugs suck."

"Looky here, my man." Without releasing my arm, Brian pulled up the front of his jacket and blue scrubs with his right hand revealing a strange collection of deep crescent-shaped scars on his belly. About fifty or seventy stitches worth. "See that?"

"What happen? You try to hump a weed whacker?"

"Two of us escorted a skinny little dude out to the Silver Line about four years ago. The other escort, an orderly named Gus Cosner, was bigger than me even. Our pigeon wasn't medicated at all because it was against his religion, don't you know. Well, cousin, standing right here, he made his move. Gus lost an eye and then that boy went upside my head with his bag and then went after my belly with his teeth like he hadn't had a thing to eat since emancipation. You don't even want to think about what I had to do to get him to stop." He pulled the top down over his scars. "Ever since, Code Victors on their way to the Silver Line go medicated; the more meds the better. It's easier to get putty to do what you want than a car load full of atomic ping pong balls, if you know what I'm sayin'."

"You have to hold my arm so tight? You're cutting off the blood."

"No, I'm not." Brian increased the pressure until my fingers began to tingle. "See the difference?" He reduced the pressure, allowing the blood to flow once more.

"I'm not going to run off."

"You got that right."

The public school class silver-gray bus cleared the parking lots and turned into the circular drive that ran beneath the portico. All of its windows were covered with heavy wire mesh. On its side in black was lettered: South River Mental Health Institute. It braked silently, the man behind the wheel put the vehicle in park as a shorter fellow in gray chinos and a pale blue sport jacket went to the bus's door, unlocked it from the inside, and pulled it open. He was in his early fifties with a round, freckled face capped with hairbrush thick blond hair. He had that big, wide, used-car-dealer smile. "Good morning," he said to me.

"I believe I've made other plans."

He smiled indulgently. "Are you Det. Sgt. Torio?"

"So much for anonymity."

"You're not on the bus, yet. Glad to meet you, Joe. I'm Greg."

"Enchanted, Greg," except that with my fuzzy tongue I might have said, "Shantygreb."

Greg climbed down from the bus, and after a limp handshake with me, he stood in front of Brian, took the nine-by-twelve blue envelope from him, opened it and began examining the contents. As they made small talk about the bridge construction near the prison that was jamming up traffic, I copped a peek at the windows in the silver Jell-O bus. There were three faces looking back at me through the mesh. Close to the front was a thin, mocha-complexioned man with dark eyes who looked to be in his early twenties. His head was shaved and his lips were intensely involved in a conversation with an entity who was not corporally extant. Seated directly behind him was a woman who was post menopausal with a vengeance. White hair gathered at the back, blotchy caramel skin with more wrinkles than a barrel of crepe paper. Her red-rimmed glasses made her irises appear as big as plums. With a kiss she pressed her lips against the glass, then grinned with a mouth full of really bad teeth. I smiled wanly in return and checked out the third occupied window.

Two seats behind the Grandma Klump was a sullen Jackie Chan look-alike who glared at me as he mouthed the words, "Fuck you."

"You're welcome," I mouthed back.

All three of them were wearing solid maroon tops. I wore the jeans, gray wool shirt and tan windbreaker the hangman had brought to the hospital from home. I glanced back at the hospital entrance, hoping to see Julia's face through the glass. A psych floor orderly who looked like Jesse Ventura nodded back.

"Let me see your ID bracelet," said Greg.

I faced the man from the bus, took a moment to process the request, then held up my left wrist. Greg compared the information on the soft plastic bracelet to a form from the blue envelope, then initialed the form and handed it to Brian. "It's all right that I call you Joe, isn't it?" said Greg to me.

"You can call me five pounds of Bazooka Bubble Gum, if you want."

"Is that your bag?"

"What? Being five pounds of bubble gum?"

Greg nodded at the brown duffel bag on the pavement next to Brian's foot.

"Oh. Yeah. My bag."

Greg picked up the duffel, and while Brian the nurse maintained his grip on my upper arm, Greg opened a panel low on the side of the bus, placed the duffel inside the compartment, where it joined several others, and closed the panel. As he once again faced me, Greg said, "Let's go."

Brian released my arm and said, "Good luck, Joe. Don't do anything stupid and you'll be out before you know it."

The only way I could be out before I knew it was to be either knocked out or dead. Not much point in making the observation, especially with an anesthetized tongue, so I pulled myself up the stairs into the bus, the smell of freshly mopped rubber greeting my nostrils. The door closed, Greg locked it, and stood behind me as he urged me through the wire gate that separated the passengers from the driver. There was a second cage wall and gate toward the rear of the compartment sectioning off the last six seats. Greg pointed toward the driver, who did not turn or otherwise acknowledge the attention. "This is Bert—"

"*Big* Bert," interrupted the boy who had been conversing with his friends from an alternate dimension. Neither Greg nor Big Bert appeared to notice.

"That," said Greg, "is Thomas. Behind Thomas is Geraldine." The old woman grinned seductively, her decaying teeth parted slightly, her rheumy bug-eyed gaze fixed on my groin.

"Sitting behind Geraldine is Yukiko." The Jackie Chan look-alike repeated his earlier silent message. "And the fellow on the opposite side of the bus is Teddy."

Dirty blond hair, watery gray eyes. Teddy was a bent up, shrunken down collection of angles and sunken spots who resembled a preying mantis who had been run over by an ice hockey team. Instead of pajamas he was wearing baggy tan pants and a faded orange tee shirt beneath a dirty red denim jacket. One long-fingered hand was holding a sizeable silver boom box up to his left ear, his large long-lashed eyes shut as his entire body twitched to silent rhythms.

"Everybody," said Greg, "This is Joe."

"Hey, Joe, waddaya know," said Thomas, again laughing at his own thinly spread humor.

"Hi, honey," said Geraldine, still looking at my groin.

"Fuck you," greeted Yukiko, this time out loud.

Teddy simply maintained his fixation on that different drummer. Greg pointed at the seat across from Geraldine's and I hesitantly swung myself in and sat down.

"Okay folks, listen up," announced Greg. "We have only one more stop to make. If the traffic gods are kind, we'll be home in enough time to settle you in and get you some lunch. I just want you to know that, even though the South River Mental Health Institute is a city hospital, it is fully accredited and staffed by well-trained caring professionals who have only one agenda, and that is to help you get better. Welcome to our family."

"Who's got the remote?" asked Teddy.

"Big Bert," said Thomas.

I turned back in time to see Yukiko repeat his prior invitation for Greg's benefit. Greg went to the other side of the wire mesh wall, closed and locked the gate. Once the door was secured, Greg took the rear-facing seat next to the driver and nodded at Big Bert. The driver put the vehicle in gear and drove from beneath the portico.

The blinding mid-morning sun coming in through the right-side windows singed my retinas and forced me to close my eyes. Pulling out onto the East Branch Connector, the bus turned right, moving the sunlight in through my side of the bus. With a whine and a lurch, the bus began climbing the grade up to the McCann Bridge.

I shielded my eyes and looked out of my window at the industrial park on the southeast bank of the East Branch River. The Hood Semiconductor plant filled the near third of the park. Thinking of Julia, I felt a tug on my right sleeve. I looked and Geraldine was sitting on the aisle edge of her seat, leaning toward me. Above the breast pocket on her maroon pajamas, embroidered in yellow, was: Canal Park Hospital. Sixth Floor. The sixth was Canal Park's psycho floor.

Breathily, Geraldine said, "Hi," enveloping me in a cloud reminiscent of a warm summer day in a fish cannery.

"Don't talk to me," I said. "I'm sick."

Geraldine pouted, then a deafening siren went off followed by a stitch of equally deafening machinegun fire. I dove down between the seats. Close on the machinegun fire came the Coasters singing "Riot In Cell Block #9."

On July the second Nineteen Fifty-three,
I was serving time for armed robbery,
At four o'clock in the morning I was sleeping in my cell,
I heard a whistle blow then I heard somebody yell:
There's a riot goin' on.
There's a riot goin' on . . . .
#

Holding my side, I pulled myself up from the aisle, looked around, and no one seemed to be particularly perturbed over Teddy Boom Box's rock golden oldies played at max volume with extra bass. The boom box was still perched on Teddy's shoulder. Only Geraldine appeared to have noticed my grab for Mother Earth. She was frowning and shaking her head. "Decaf time, Joe boy."

I lowered myself into my seat, wrapped my arms around my heart, leaned my head against the glass, and closed my eyes.

The motion of the bus bumped my head against the glass once, twice, then the glass softened, I drifted through it and conjured the image of Julia in her diamond dust robe as she let it slide slowly down her body to the floor, gathering at her feet like cooling wax at a candle's base. I reached for her then she faded and Miles Kieffer was standing in the door surrounded by blinding white light, fire stitching my side, Julia's face hovering above me, spatters of red as I coughed out my life—

A squeal of brakes and a lurch forward and back brought me awake. I blinked and looked through the window. A smear of cars, faded white lines on charcoal gray asphalt. A big sign warned visitors to lock their cars and to keep their keys with them. My gaze wobbled about to the right until I spied the familiar gray edifice of Books State Correctional. A clatter at the rear of the bus and I turned around.

The rear door swung open. Voices, then a charcoal-gray uniformed Books CO entered the caged off rear compartment. Burly red-faced man with a squashed nose and dark glittering eyes. He checked the lock on the door between the compartments, shook the door, then called "Clear," to his outside companions. A second corrections officer, chunky brown-and-brown, probable female, entered followed by a man so tall he had to duck his head and shoulders to enter the compartment. The tall man resembled what Dolph Lundgren would look like if the actor ever got serious about body building. He was in his early thirties, carrying two hundred plus pounds, mostly in his shoulders, and he wore a complete state issue here-I-am orange ensemble: trousers with matching shirt and jacket. His wrists, waist, and ankles were manacled with a complete set of restraint chains. Two additional COs followed him in: a sergeant who looked like a bloodhound, and a CO who resembled Pancho Villa.

Pancho pulled shut the door behind them, which was followed by the sounds of an outside lock being driven home. The big man, his head and shoulders still hunched to keep from banging into the bus' overhead, was directed to the right center seat. After seating himself, the man in orange was bracketed by the four COs, each

21

one sitting in a separate corner of the compartment, all four of them keeping their eyes on the big man in chains.

"Who's that?" asked Thomas.

I wobbled my head around and looked at him. Thomas was looking back. "Why ask me?"

Greg gave Big Bert the nod. The driver released the brake and began the turn toward the parking lot exit. Thomas changed seats, taking the one in front of me. Geraldine sat next to me on my right. "Hey—"

"Greg called you 'detective' out in front of that other place," interrupted Geraldine, making us both wince from her breath. Thomas recovered first.

"Who is he, Joe?"

"Alvin Yuker."

Thomas's face came alive. "The serial killer, right? Killed about two dozen women—"

"Three."

"Only three?"

"You sound disappointed."

"Didn't he just kill that prison guard? On the news? That woman, whatsername? A couple days ago?"

"He's been charged. The CO's name was Katey Sloan." The conversation was wearing me out.

"What's Yuker doing here?" The voice came from behind. I turned and Yukiko was now sitting behind me. "Why is he on this bus? He's the one who killed that prison guard, right?"

"I don't know. Psychiatric observation, probably. With prosecutions, sometimes—" I felt something working its way up the inside of my right thigh. I looked down and Geraldine's fingers were in my crotch centimeters from home plate.

"Get away from me!" I pulled her wrinkled old hand out of my crotch and pointed toward the opposite side of the bus. "Go on. Get in your own seat. *Git!*"

Pouting, but not breaking eye contact, Geraldine slid off the seat and backed into the opposite seat as Greg stood and looked through the wire at his charges. Thomas moved to his previous seat and became intensely interested in a blank wall that the bus was passing. A beat, then Greg resumed his seat. As the bus swung out of the lot onto Fortieth, I looked toward the

22

rear of the bus. Yukiko had also returned to his seat. Boom Box Teddy had a big smile on his face as his finger hovered over the CD box's play button.

I glanced at the very tense corrections officers guarding Yuker and shook my head at Teddy, mouthing the word *"No."*

Teddy nodded, grinned, and mouthed, *"Oh, yes."*

The finger pushed the button, the shattering siren was followed by the ear-smashing machinegun fire, and I couldn't bring myself to watch what was happening in the back of the bus. Colorful expletives, however, mixed with the lyrics as the bus joined the traffic jam before the Fortieth Street Bridge.

On July the second Nineteen Fifty-three,
I was serving time for armed robbery. . . .

I checked to make certain Geraldine was in her own seat, then looked through the window on my side at the state mental hospital perched high on the knee of Breadloaf Mountain overlooking the prison. The all white concrete and glass structure was a row of three massive octagonal towers connected with white rectangles broken by regular small windows in line with its five floors. The towers on the ends were made of glass, the tower in the center windowless.

My gaze lowered to a green Buick stuck in traffic next to the bus. In the rear window was the face of an angelic little girl. Seven or eight years old. Brown eyes, black hair, and a tasteful sprinkling of freckles. She stuck her tongue out at me and made a face. I mouthed the words, *"I know where you live,"* grinned malevolently, and drew my thumb slowly across my throat.

As the bus crept forward a few feet and braked, I slumped down, my knees against the seat in front of me, and let my head sink to the back of my seat.

"Man," said Yukiko, "look at that traffic jam. We're going to be stuck here all day."

"Too bad," responded Geraldine. "I got me a weak bladder."

I checked to make certain that Geraldine was not within tinkle range, then closed my eyes and allowed the drugs to hijack me back to Goofytown.

THE LAUGHING HOUSE

"Do you understand each of these rights I have read to you?"

I half-opened my eyes, wobbled my gaze around the room: desks, office lights, a giant fat chickadee, a young red-haired woman looking at me over the tops of her glasses, a file and a working paper before her on the desk. "What?"

"Your rights. Do you understand your rights?"

I tried to open my eyes all the way as well as get them both pointed in the same direction. The chickadee was a framed picture on a wall. I tried to focus on the young woman. Green eyes, no shield, no gun. A cross between Susan Hayward and Brittany Spears. "I don't understand. Why am I under arrest?"

She laughed and shook her head. "You're not under arrest."

"Why are you reading me my rights?"

"These are patient's rights. As a patient you are entitled to certain protections." She read from her prepared list about the Patient Self Determination Act of 1990, about the patient's right to make decisions concerning his medical care, how he could accept or refuse medical or surgical treatment, and could have and assign living wills, and durable powers of attorney—

"I can refuse medical treatment?"

"Yes."

My gaze tripped on down to her breasts where, among them, it located her nametag. "Antoinette?"

"Yes."

"Well, Antoinette, I want to get the hell out of here."

"Now, Joe, you've been committed to fifteen days psychiatric observation." She gave a sap-toting mountain of an orderly the high sign with a raised eyebrow. "That's a legal thing, rather than a medical treatment thing, understand?"

"So, I can make decisions regarding my medical care, except that I can't make them here."

Her face remained tactfully blank.

"Okay, Antoinette, what about this medication they have me on? Can I refuse that?" Except that it came out sounding like *zat*. Words containing *th* were minefields.

"What's wrong with your medication?"

"You mean, besides not being able to stay awake, perceive reality, control my lips, or remember how to put on my underpants?"

She placed her hand on the blue file folder. "Now, Joe, according to your file you had a number of violent episodes while you were at Riverside General. Trying to throw a chair through the window—"

"Didn't even break the glass. Plastic super—"

"And you attacked a man."

"Well . . . that."

"The purpose of the medication is to help keep you calm. Are you calm?"

"If I was any calmer I'd need life support."

"Once things even out for you here and you settle in, Joe, I'm sure your doctor will reduce your medication."

"So, I can't refuse medication."

"Well, sure, you can." Her eyebrows went up. "It's just that your refusal can be overruled some of the time. Here we're pretty much committed to the doctors knowing more than the patients."

Antoinette handed me a faded nineteenth generation copy of something. "These are your patient rights and your patient orientation instructions. Be sure to read them. Keep them with your room's patient handbook. Once you get on your wing, your group leader will take you through the routine. Welcome to Em-High. If you'll help us we'll be able to help you." She looked beyond me and said, "Billy? This is Joe."

Like a judgment out of heaven, a hand dropped out of the sky onto my left shoulder. I looked around and up, the office door was open and the ceiling lights were blotted out by a pasty-faced beefy-looking guy in whites who looked like the Pillsbury doughboy after eating a stack of Goodyears.

"Hi, Joe," greeted the mountain.

"What's happening, Billy."

"Take him to Dan's office, and after that, Joe goes up to Turkey West, Dan's Group. Good luck, Joe. Help us to help you." Antoinette was already motioning to someone to bring on the next patient.

"Is your side bothering you?" asked Dr. Walker without looking up from the file on his desk. The psychiatrist's office reeked of atmosphere: Antique glass-topped aircraft carrier of a desk littered with matching accessories: framed photos, paper clip dispenser, telephone with lots of lights and buttons, and a non-matching scratched gray metal intercom. A pile of files. Dark walnut paneling interrupted by built in bookshelves jammed with professional texts and journals, heavy green drapes, a painting of some Nineteenth century personality who looked disturbingly like Bill Murray frozen in the act of sucking a lemon.

"The stitches?" prompted Walker.

I sat up in the minimally upholstered client chair. With my right hand, I gestured vaguely at the left side of my waist. "The stitches pull some."

"Once you're settled in, possibly tomorrow, we'll check out your sutures. If everything is kosher, we'll take them out."

"Swell."

"I understand you were wounded with a knife?"

I shook my head. "Knife wound is on the other side. This side was a gunshot."

"Dear me," he almost exclaimed.

"Swell."

Walker glanced up at the sarcastic note. "Is there something you'd like to say to me?"

There were a number of things, so I picked one at random. "Why's the door locked?"

The director of the South River Mental Health Institute leaned back in his chair. He was a lean, tanned professional complete with white jacket and brown

Vandyke. Edward Norton playing Sigmund Freud. "The locked door is a security matter —May I call you Joe?"

"Sure. I'll call you Danny."

"Dan would be adequate."

"Cool, Dan. Puts you in a real power position, doesn't it? The locked door."

The right corner of Walker's mouth pulled back in a tiny smile. "Here we are rather committed to having the staff run the institution rather than the patients."

"Hell of a lot of commitment around here, Dan. You're committed, Antoinette is committed, the inmates are committed. Of course, we're the only ones who are really committed."

"Patients," Dan corrected.

"Patients rather than inmates?"

"Indeed. And this is a psychiatric hospital or treatment facility, not an insane asylum or nuthouse." Walker leaned forward and rested his wrists on the edge of his desk as he intertwined his fingers. "Words are important, Joe. The labels we attach to ourselves and our situations determine to a very large extent who we are and the severity of the situations in which we find ourselves. Our mission here is to help patients in the restoration of their mental health—"

"—Not to lock up the crazies," I completed.

"Exactly. By the way, we discourage the nickname *Squirmhi*. It has discomfort and drug abuse connotations that are anti-therapeutic."

"Anti-therapeutic," I repeated. The drugs I'd complained about were actually great. I could have passed anywhere as a lobotomized moron.

The psychiatrist turned back to the folder on his desk. "According to your file, you were sent here for observation after a number of violent episodes subsequent to your injuries. This latest one was while you were in Riverside General. You attacked a police captain who was visiting you?"

"Just as hard as I could."

"What brought that about?"

Why not tell the truth, I thought. "He asked for it."

"What made you think he asked for it?"

"He said, 'Joe, attack me.'"

A less-than-believing smirk. "How do you feel about that?"

"Feel? With these drugs? If Jeffrey Dahmer was in my shorts with a bottle of Heinz 57 having Thanksgiving dinner, I couldn't feel it. Numb. That's how I feel."

"Try again."

I waved a dismissive hand. "I don't remember much about jumping Capt. Dockery. Some yelling, lots and lots of medication. Couple of orderlies who hit pretty good. Once the drugs wear off, I suppose I'll feel sore. Like crap, too. Al Dockery isn't just my boss. He's also one of my best friends. We used to be partners." I leaned forward, rested my elbows on my knees, and clasped my hands together. "I guess I flipped out."

"I believe that was your therapist's diagnosis. Dr. Grable?"

"Betty."

"Let's see." He turned a page in the file on his desk. "Your father used to be the state hangman."

"Twenty years behind the knot and proud of it."

"Do you have a good relationship with your father?"

"Sure. I live with him." Walker's eyebrows went up. "Yeah, I'm thirty-four and living with my father. No I don't have an inflatable rubber doll and a porno collection of copulating gerbils."

"And?" Walker prompted.

"Well, I do have two goldfish. Nothing funny going on there, though. I do have some standards, after all." I frowned. "What did you want to know?"

"About you living with your father."

"Oh. Yeah. Okay. Uh, I moved out of my father's house when I was eighteen and couldn't wait to go to college and put as much distance as possible between myself and the hangman. I went to East Shore and stayed in the dorms. After that, into the Police Academy, into the force, made detective . . ." I looked up at the psychiatrist.

"Living with your father."

"Right. Got shot up on a case—different case—was hospitalized. Last November. Rizzo brothers thing."

"I remember the news reports."

"Yeah. So, in the hospital, I died couple of times. On top of that I'd lost my living arrangement—"

"From a cursory reading of your file, I believe the woman you were living with asked you to leave."

"Actually, while they were lighting me up with the paddles, she was busy tossing my stuff into the hall and pouring Dr Pepper all over it. Trust me on this, Doc: Don't die on your significant other. Death puts a definite kink in a love relationship."

"Your father?"

"Yeah. Pop had me move back home to help me through my recovery. I couldn't use my arm. Couldn't drive." I shrugged and raised my eyebrows. "Couldn't bear leaving the house."

I glanced down. "I got better, but in the process I discovered I didn't know my father very well. It felt important to find out who he was. Still does."

"While you were in the hospital, when you found out that your girlfriend put your belongings into the hall, how did you feel?"

"I hear the big guy never shuts a door without opening a window."

"Is that's how you felt?"

"No. I felt screwed."

"I don't know how screwed feels, Joe. Can you put it in terms I might understand? Mad, sad, glad—"

"All of the above."

"Glad?"

"Well, to be honest, doc, we really didn't like each other very much."

Dr. Dan Walker stared at me for a moment, then looked down and flipped through my file for a few pages. "Your prior hospitalization—the one last November—where was that?"

"University Hospital."

"Here it is." He smoothed down a page as his eyebrows went up. "Knife wound. Cardiac arrest. Twice."

"I was down a quart. When my heart stopped, I didn't remember any tunnel of light. There was a big fat devil screaming at me for going into that garage without any backup, but I think that was Al Dockery."

30

"Three months later," continued the psychiatrist, "in the hospital again concerning the Gentleman Killer matter. Three gunshot wounds and a knife wound that partially collapsed your right lung." He glanced at me. "How did growing up as the hangman's son affect you?"

I sat back and blinked. "We're changing the subject, aren't we?" I shrugged. "Being the hangman's son was a pain in the ass. Fights in school, shortage of friends, absence of girls, butt of teacher jokes. The whole perpetual outcast thing. I've pretty much worked through all that with Betty —Dr. Grable."

"There appears to be at least something you haven't worked through, Joe."

"I guess that explains why I'm here at Squirmhi, a crazy locked up in the nut house."

Not rising to the bait, Dr. Dan nodded toward the file. "You have the city police department's record for the number of perpetrators killed in the line of duty." He looked up at me. "Seven men dead."

"I've heard that."

"Does it bother you?"

"Not as much as them being alive and me being dead."

"How does it make you feel?"

I looked off into a shadow. The guy wanted to get serious. "I don't know, exactly," I said. "It's not guilt. It's more like anger. Anger at them for putting me in that kind of position; That something like that was necessary at all. Sadness. I know why most of them did what they did. I dream about them sometimes. A lot of times."

"Which ones?"

"All of them. All at the same time every so often."

Walker scribbled a note and leaned back in his chair. "There were two rapist-murderers you arrested who were later executed, correct? Lawrence Collins and George Pruitt."

"Yeah."

"I see that you witnessed their executions."

"Yes."

"Where do you stand on lethal injections?"

"I make it a point never to stand on lethal injections."

A beat. "Very well. Let's begin with Charlie Matthews."

"Are we going to go through all of them?"

"Just to get them straight in my head. Charlie Matthews."

I let out my breath. "The Reservoir Killer. Six or seven years ago."

"Matthews was your first killing, wasn't he?"

I leaned forward and pointed my finger at the doctor. "He wasn't a killing. He was a murderer who came in second in a gunfight that he initiated." I leaned back and attempted to cross my left leg over my right knee, but the stitches pulled.

"Back to you shooting Matthews," said Walker.

"He shot me first."

"Your partner then was Albert Dockery. Is this the same fellow that you attacked? The police captain?"

"The same. We were both in uniform back then."

"You saved his life."

"I still owe him two. Dock was my TO."

"Tee oh?"

"Training Officer. Out of the Academy, I was on probation for the first year. Dock scraped the fuzz off my shirt. Later we were partners until he got his gold shield —became a detective."

Dan studied the file for a dramatic moment, then said, "How did you feel about killing Matthews?"

"There wasn't enough time to feel anything. I was busy plugging a hole in Dock, calling for a bus, and trying to keep an eye out for Matthews's accomplice."

"Afterward. When you went home."

I frowned as I tried to remember. "I was hungry. I wanted lasagna. Meat sauce. Great slabs of hot garlic bread. Black raspberry ice cream. Must have had two liters of Dr Pepper. Then I stuck my head in the toilet and puked until my nuts ached. Watched movies on TV all that night. The usual."

His eyebrows were up. "After Matthews was killed, you were ordered to see the police psychiatrist, Dr. Hall. You walked out of the initial interview and never went back."

"Huntley Hall. A giant penis looking for strokes."

32

Dr. Walker's mouth pulled back in another tight little smile as he sat back and crossed his legs. "A year later you killed Jay Hellerman."

"Hellerman raped and murdered seventeen boys. Ate a few, too. Haven't been able to face ketchup since."

"Why did you kill him?"

"Besides the ketchup? He was holding two boys hostage in his house on Soldier Heights."

"Did he shoot at you?"

"No. He was about to kill his hostages. I prevented that."

"How did you feel about killing Hellerman?"

"Fettuccini. Got to watch a lot more movies that night."

Walker glanced down at the file. "The year you killed Hellerman, you also killed a minor drug dealer named Eldridge Coumbs." He looked up at me. "Self-defense?"

"Yes."

"The media was pretty cool toward you on the Coumbs shooting."

"They like drugs more than they like dead kids."

"How did you feel about it?"

"I'm not fond of anyone who's trying to kill me." I shrugged. "I watched almost the entire *I Claudius* series that night."

Back to the file. "Last September a year ago, you killed a sixty year old homeless man named Paul Baines. According to you, Baines came after you outside your apartment and tried to kill you."

"He did."

"There was an investigation on that shooting, wasn't there?"

"All shootings are investigated."

"According to your file, this one was investigated with more than the usual zeal. It went to Internal Affairs?"

"Yes."

"For some unspecified reason, Joe, it appears that this homeless man from down in the Zone took it upon himself to go all of the way to West Beverly to kill you, and managed to pick up a six-hundred dollar pistol for the job along the way. Do you have any idea why?"

"Why is this beginning to sound like a shooting board?"

"Events like that, Joe, all those loose ends, can leave you in a lot of doubt. Doubts can become guilt with very little effort."

"Baines came at me with that brand-new Beretta, fired once in my direction and still had the gun aimed at me when I fired back. Not much room for doubt there."

"How did you feel about killing Baines?"

"Very, very confused."

"Why?"

I thought about that. "I never got in his head. When he tried to kill me was the first time I ever laid eyes on the man. I didn't know anything about him. I still don't know why he did what he did. That confused me. Still does."

"That was when you went to see Dr. Grable?"

"Yes."

"Why?"

I rubbed the back of my neck. "She used to be a cop. She took one on the job. I thought she could help me. She did. She still does."

Dr. Walker cleared his throat and turned another page in the file. "Now, the Rizzo brothers. That was the event last November that put you into University Hospital."

I nodded.

"I'd like you to think about something, Joe. Don't answer me, just think about it. Okay?"

"Okay."

"I want you to think about the possibility that the reason you bring them back dead instead of alive might have something to do with what your father did for a living."

I sat back and squinted. "You know, Dan, they are rare. You wouldn't think so, given the state of the world, the economy, and the number of them you see on TV and working for the Department of Motor Vehicles every day, but they really are rare."

"What is that, Joe?"

"Absolute assholes. Most persons are either ignorant, misguided, brain damaged, sick, twisted, or

34

just plain stupid. There are a number of folks suffering from a touch of it: cab drivers, congressmen, but you are absolute toes-to-thatch, love handle-to-love handle, bellybutton-to-butt crack asshole." I leaned forward with just a touch of menace. "Let's get this straight, no nuts: I don't bring them in dead. Ask the hundreds of still living meatballs making license plates over there at Books. Those seven didn't make it back to the house alive because they put me in a position where I had to make a choice between their lives, mine, or someone else's. They lost."

"I said I wanted you to think about it," reminded the psychiatrist.

"I did. About a nanosecond more than the suggestion merited. Having a hangman for a father won't make you a killer any more than having a psychiatrist for a father would drive you insane. Was your father a psychiatrist, by the way?"

"No. He was a steel executive." Walker glanced down at the file, suppressing a smile. "What is your current relationship with Capt. Dockery?"

"Subject change again." I held up a hand and let it fall on my knee. "I'm in MCU—Major Crimes. Dock's the unit commander and my friend."

"Is he your immediate supervisor?"

"No. Lt. Hewitt is my field commander, if I ever get back to work."

"Winnie Hewitt?"

"Yes."

"She replaced Miles Kieffer, correct?" There was a long pause while I stared back at the doctor. "When you shot Miles Kieffer, he was your field supervisor and partner, correct?"

I moistened my lips and looked away. "Miles Kieffer died and was buried in Nineteen Seventy-one when he was two years old. The person I shot is a killer named Nathan Sunday."

"The Gentleman Killer," stated Walker.

I gestured toward the ceiling. "He's here. In a coma."

"On the Fourth Floor, Joe. Nathan Sunday put three shots in your left side and drove a stiletto into your right lung. Why didn't you kill him?"

"I didn't have to. Will Sunday recover?"

"Bone tissue was flaked off the inside of his skull and driven deep into his left parietal lobe. The bone was removed, but there's no accurate way of determining how much damage he suffered. According to the neurosurgeon's report, Sunday could come out of it and recover completely, be a vegetable, or remain in a coma until he withers away. As near as I can tell from the news, Nathan Sunday committed close to a dozen of the most gruesome murders imaginable, deceived and betrayed you as his partner, not to mention trying to kill you."

"All partnerships have their ups and downs."

"You really care how he's doing?"

"He was the best partner I ever had."

Long confused look from Walker. "Best how?" he asked.

"Smart, funny—I liked him a lot. Rather, I liked his Miles Kieffer a lot. Sunday's thing, you see, was becoming whatever you wanted the most. For a lot of people it was the Prize Patrol with a million dollar check in his hand. You should've seen his makeup. I almost bought that one myself."

"And the one you did buy?"

"I wanted a friend. A really good friend. He was all of that until he tried to kill me."

"Does it ever bother you that Sunday knew you well enough to become the friend you wanted?"

I raised an eyebrow at Walker. "You might not be a complete asshole, after all. Yes. It bothers me. A lot. My claim to fame, such as it is, Dan, is being able to read people and situations. Dock calls it my third eye. I found out everything about Nathan Sunday—why he did what he did, what he thought, what he felt. Everything in the world about him except that he was right under my goddamned nose." I leaned forward. "Is there any chance that Sunday is faking it—just lying there waiting for his opportunity to make a break for it?"

Walker smiled indulgently and gave a slight shrug. "Anything is possible, of course. It's extremely unlikely, though. However, in the event that he should ever regain consciousness, and the even more remote event that he would be functional, he is under maximum security. Up here, that's twenty-four hour lockdown under surveillance, restraints, and room entrance and egress only with security assist."

"Ought to do it," I observed.

"We've been at this awhile, Joe, and we know what we're doing. What you need to be doing over the next two weeks, though, is to focus on yourself." He glanced again at my file. "I am curious why Capt. Dockery took you into the Major Crimes Unit to work on the Gentleman Killer case when you were apparently still unstable from your experiences concerning the Rizzo brothers." He glanced up at me. "Doesn't that make you mad?"

"Mad? That Dock rescued me off the Cold Cases desk? Some free advice, Dan. Don't try and make me defensive about my unit or my boss. Get me? I'm not mad at Al Dockery. I love him. I just decked him because the sonofabitch asked for it."

Dan frowned, leaned back, and nodded toward a space above and behind me. "Billy?"

A familiar heavy hand dropped on my shoulder. "Joe."

"Hey, Billy. Long time no see."

"Let's go see Harvey."

"That isn't a pet name you have for some kind of electroshock machine, is it?"

"We call that one Sparky, same as the Texas hot seat."

I looked from Billy to the director of Squirmhi. "Sorry about that asshole thing, Dan. It's the drugs."

"No offense taken," Walker said not looking up from his next file.

Billy shook his head as he practically lifted me up by my elbow and propelled me from the room into the hall toward the elevators. "Cop, right, Joe? Under suspension?"

"Involuntary commitment for observation."

"Tough break. Most of the cops we get, even just for observation, the PD doesn't want back. They're all depressed and trying to cure it with more depressants. Do you drink?"

"Dr Pepper when I can get it."

"Yeah. Joe DiMaggio Torio," said Billy. "You nailed all three of the Rizzo brothers."

"Only two—"

"You got the SRPD's top body count, right? Seven or eight notches on your gun? Wasn't your old man the state hangman?"

I glanced up into the aether. "Mother, is that you?"

Billy raised a hairless eyebrow, then grinned when he saw that I had been joking. "Okay, I'll give it a rest."

The elevator doors opened and we entered the car. Billy glanced at me and said, "Harvey is the Dan group leader."

"What does that mean?"

"Therapy group. You just had an interview with Dan. He runs this place as a hobby in between skiing at Aspen and hooter groping on the Riviera."

"Pretty well fixed, is he?"

Billy nodded as he watched the floor indicator climb slowly. "The man doesn't even refill his bottled water from the spigot."

"Whoa."

"I like you, Joe, and I have a soft spot for cops anyway. Take some free advice?"

"The price is right."

"As long as you're here, don't spit, bleed, pee, or throw turds on staff."

"A union thing?" I asked.

"It's in the contract. And never, never lay hands on staff. That's the big sin. Everything else we understand. You want to be Napoleon, that's cool. You want to hit staff, it's Waterloo."

"I'm hip."

The door opened revealing a busy nurse's station backed up by a big picture of a scarlet perching bird with dark wings and tail. A sallow-faced man in gray coveralls sporting a white-embroidered "Norman" over his left breast pocket was pushing an automated floor cleaner that looked like a miniature Zamboni machine toward the security check door to the wing on the right. Next to the door was a small group of patients, two middle aged men, a man in his early twenties, and an old woman: my fellow passengers from the Silver Line bus. Alvin Yuker wasn't among them. They were being talked to by a very tall fellow wearing pale blue coveralls.

"Come on," said Billy. "There's Harvey."

TURKEY WEST

"As am I," began Harvey, "you are all assigned to Dr. Walker's group. Our group's rooms are all the way down at the end of Turkey West toward Half Satan." Tall, skinny, light-coffee complexion, black hair, big dark eyes with long dark lashes, and a strange resemblance to Brundlefly. I steadied myself against the security wall between the wing and the Third Floor nurses station trying to remember Brundlefly's name. The actor. Remake of *The Fly* —Jeff Goldblum. Friend of Buckaroo Banzai. Harvey directed his charges through the west wing security door where a security officer named Munroe, who looked like Jay Leno on a bad hair day, studied each one of us as he nodded us through.

Thomas, Geraldine, Teddy, Yukiko, and I stood in a rough crescent facing Harvey as the man guided us through the mysteries. Midway down the hall on the north side, Norman, he of the automatic floor scrubber, arced the scrubber to go around a smallish female patient who was sitting on the floor beneath a pair of surveillance cameras.

"The theory in this toilet," continued Harvey, "is that the patients do all the work and the staff gets the paychecks. We do our own cleaning, bed making, and therapy. We have two sessions of self-healing group therapy a day in our circle down in Half Satan. The good doctor likes to be thought of as just one of the guys and he wants us to call him Dan, so, of course, we all call him Dr. Walker. If they haven't already assigned you your groupmate, they will soon. Dr. Walker's theory is that everybody needs a friend: someone who can break through our isolation with bonds of trust and gentle support. In aid of this, you will be paired up with some

41

nut in an insane asylum who has a history of violence." He pointed a thumb toward the east. "Twice a day we all individually report to the nurse's station to get our vitals read and load up on meds. More often for certain cases. If you don't show, they will hunt you down. Any questions?"

The man with the floor scrubber reached our end of the hall, turned, wiped up a streak with a squeegee, and continued from whence he came, the machine making a damp hum.

Geraldine raised a hand. "Boy, what is this Half Satan shit?"

"Revelation sixteen, two, Sister," said Harvey, raising his eyebrows. "Mark of the beast? Six-six-six?" Harvey nodded once toward the west. "The big room at the end of the hall is Room 333. Half Satan, get it? Turkey West Commons. Before breakfast and following afternoon group, it's the recreation lounge—TV, games, magazines, you can make phone calls, whatever. Between breakfast and late afternoon, that's where the four groups on this wing meet for group therapy, except when we meet outside."

"Turkey West?" I asked.

"Yes." He nodded and faced me. "In an attempt at deluding you that you are in a Disney theme park, young nutball, our director renamed the floors at Squirmhi after birds: Chickadee, Dove, Tanager, Cardinal, and Blue Jay. They, of course, were immediately renamed Chicken, Dodo, Turkey, Redshank, and Buzzard. Those are the names everyone uses today, including staff. Third floor is Turkey, and this wing is Turkey West."

"Turkey wing," said Thomas to himself.

"Now that they have you behind a lock, Sunshine, maybe they'll reduce your medication," Harvey responded.

"Man," said Thomas to Harvey, "I am here *for* the medication."

"Where are the real crazies kept?" interrupted Yukiko. "We're just depressed, right? Bipolars, a couple of junkies, people who got fed up with the crap out there?"

A look of mock tenderness came over Harvey's face. "My, child, you are a soul lost in the wilderness, aren't you?" He held out his arms, encompassing the entire therapeutic universe. "Welcome to the butterfly palace, Moon Pie. You have finally made the bigs. This is bug barracks, the laughing academy, Happy Fucking Valley, and if you don't pass your fifteen, you'll be in blues sitting in circles until the repeal of the income tax."

He pointed at his right slipper. "Chicken Floor is where you signed in. That's administration, P.T., medical offices, treatment, surgery, staff and patient cafeteria, staff lounge, visitor's lounge, and security headquarters. Second Floor, Dodo West, burnout wards for retired hippies, drag queens, acid burnouts, flower counters, and other dements. Lots of oatmeal drooling, crying, yelling, and peeing in pants down on Dodo West. Dodo East is populated by sex fiends and perverts of various inclinations. Don't bend over in Dodo East. Turkey, the entire floor, is the unit elite, of course. We all have records of violent behavior."

"What about Redshank?" I asked.

"Next floor up, Sherlock. Violent, but they're not crying for help. They're looking for victims. Short of a mess of miracles, they're not getting out and no one cares about the insurance. Max security. The two most recent celebrities we have are both up on Redshank: Barbara Cleveland, the soap star, and Nathan Sunday—"

"—The Gentleman Killer," completed Yukiko.

Harvey pointed up. "Above that is Buzzard, Fifth Floor, also max security. Adjudicated criminally insane."

"I thought they go to Temple Glen," said Thomas.

"Business is good, Sunshine. By special contract with the State, Buzzard is the overflow for the Glen. Keep in mind, children, that on Chicken, Dodo, and Turkey, killing someone is still murder. On Redshank and Buzzard it's considered a treatment setback."

"Group?" interrupted Teddy. "Group of what?"

"Group therapy, young Burnout. We all sit around in a circle and share and give feedback and hug and cry and blow snot on each other. The only thing you really need to remember is that whatever is said in group stays there."

43

"I don't want to be locked up with a bunch of crazies," said Geraldine. "I mean, real crazies. They don't pee on each other on this floor, do they?"

"No, Sister, we pretty much limit it to turd throwing. That's a joke, by the way. If no one told you yet, do not throw turds at the staff. Even more important, never lay hands on staff. Absolutely no grabbing, touching, or hitting. Take my word for it, the orderlies in this institution can hand out a beating that can cure masochism. Everybody understand?"

"To tell you the truth," said Teddy, "I haven't understood anything you've said for the past five minutes."

"Excellent."

"What about our belongings?" insisted Teddy. "I want my CD player back."

Harvey grinned with genuine pleasure. "I heard about that little machine gun thing you pulled on the Silver Line, Burnout. Nice increase in the chaos quotient. You might want to think about using that for the Turkey Talent Show in a few days."

"What?"

"Later." Harvey pointed vaguely down the length of the hall. "Your stuff ought to be in your rooms now that the staff is finished searching it for drugs, poisoning your mouthwash, and planting listening devices in your suppositories. Anything that's missing you're not allowed to have and is probably being sold on eBay as we speak."

"What about my CD player?"

"Radios and CD players are okay. You can only use them in your rooms and out in the park. Keep them out of the hall, out of Half Satan, and out of the doctors' offices. Laptops and straight handheld computers are okay until you start throwing them. No drugs. No cell phones or wireless handhelds. Use the pay phones. During morning and afternoon group sessions the phones are to be taken off their hooks."

"Are those lines monitored?" I asked.

"Without a doubt." Harvey frowned for a moment. "There are three old group members: me and two you haven't met yet. The first is named Leila. We call her Dusty. She's been here about two and a half years and has a cleanliness thing going. If she runs her lint roller over you then runs off into the night cackling, say thanks and let it go. The other old-timer is Louis. We call him Mad Dog. You'll see why. In the few months he's been here we have learned that there is absolutely no profit whatsoever in maintaining that Victor Hugo was a fiction writer. Everybody on the same page?"

"So to speak," said Thomas.

"What?" asked Teddy.

"Excellent," said Harvey. "Half Satan TV etiquette, first come first served. If you run off with the remote we will hunt you down and squirt toothpaste up your nose. Now, does anyone know the name Alvin Yuker?" Harvey was looking in my direction.

"I know the name," I said.

"The killer," added Yukiko. "The Silver Line picked him up at Books on our way here."

"There haven't been that many chains on a man since Jacob Marley," remarked Thomas.

Harvey pursed his lips. "Alvin Yuker is slated for our group."

"Don't know as I'm real happy about that," remarked Geraldine.

"There'll be guards on him, right?" asked Thomas.

"Don't be such snobs. There are other killers at Squirmhi, and a few of them are even on this floor." He glanced at me and raised an eyebrow. "Alvin Yuker will fit right in." Harvey looked around at the faces. "Dr. Walker maintains this fiction that the group is a democracy, so he might even ask us all what we think about letting Alvin Yuker into the group. If he wants the man in, he'll call him 'Alvin.' If he wants us to vote to exclude him, Walker will call him 'Mr. Yuker.' We usually vote the opposite of what Dr. Walker wants."

"Isn't that slightly anti-therapeutic?" asked Thomas, a smirk on his face.

"You'll get lots of chances to do your own research regarding the healing gifts of Danny Walker, Sunshine. More important, however," he looked back at his sheet, "chow. After you settle in, change into your blues, put whatever you're wearing now into the white bag that's on your bed, and leave the bag on your bed. You can keep jackets, shoes, and coats and wear your own underwear, but all trousers, jeans, skirts, dresses, shirts and blouses will be held for you. The purpose of the uniform is to make you easier to spot should you go over the wire. When you're done changing we'll all meet at the stairwell across from the nurses station at eleven-oh-five to go down as a group under escort. We all eat together or no one eats, so don't be late. The food here is not absolutely repulsive. After lunch, at twelve thirty, we meet inside the commons—inside room 333—at our circle for afternoon group. You'll see a sign in each of the corners of the commons: Nance, Wanda, Mark, and Dan. Our group meets next to the 'Dan' sign. Did I say that Dr. Walker likes to be called 'Dan?'"

"Check," said Thomas. "Dr. Walker."

"Outstanding. Sunshine, room three twenty-nine. Sister, you are in three thirty-two," and so on.

My room number was three thirty. While I concentrated, trying to remember my number, I weaved my way down the hall toward Half Satan, reality still wowing in and out from the medication. Odd numbers were to the right, north, uphill, toward the mountain. Even numbers were to my left, south, down slope, overlooking the south eastern edge of the city, including the prison. I reached the young woman sitting on the floor beneath the cameras. A very young looking seventeen or eighteen, Prince Valiant haircut, dark blue almond-shaped eyes, her mouth in a tight little line.

"Found the one spot the cameras can't see, huh?" I said to her.

She turned her head, but kept her gaze fixed on me.

"Later," I said.

A dark wild-eyed man in Squirmhi patient blues walking from the direction of Half Satan glared at the man operating the floor scrubber, then looked at me, walked over, jabbed me in the chest, and said, "You'll never catch him. He has been warned off. He's made a clean getaway. You may as well give up and go home."

"Who?" I asked.

Without looking back, the man continued toward the nurses station. I wobbled around to watch him. Harvey was looking at the man as well. Harvey looked back at me and said beneath his breath, "That's Mad Dog." He pointed at the departing patient with his thumb. "He just warned Jean Valjean you're on his trail. You appear to be the relentless gendarme, Javert."

"Vraiment?"

"Bonne chance."

"Don't go crazy on me, Buckaroo. That pretty much exhausts my memories of high school French."

He laughed. "Mine, too."

I looked back at the young woman sitting on the floor. She was staring blankly at the opposite wall. "Fucking cop," she said to me.

"I'm a murder cop. The fucking cops are in Vice." I wobbled around and continued my trek toward room three thirty. "Great job, Javert," I muttered to myself. "You're here less than an hour and your cover's already blown."

UNLOVED FLOWER

The frigid water hit my face like a thousand ice needles making me gasp. Again I cupped my hands beneath the running faucet and splashed more water on my face and through my hair, on the back of my neck, trying to drive away the unremitting narcotic wooze. Straightening up, I caught a glimpse of myself in the mirror, the water dripping from my thick black hair and sallow face. Large dark eyes with large dark circles, sickly pale skin, and not quite open eyelids. "Kevin Spacey on crack."

I reached for a towel. As I dried my face and hair, I walked out of the bathroom and sat in the middle of my bed next to my duffel bag. If I closed my eyes the room began spinning around, so I didn't do that but once. I was facing the window in the small niche made by the bathroom wall. It contained an orange plastic-covered easy chair, a shallow metal clothes closet built into the left wall. Through the sealed window I could see Fortieth Street as it worked its way through the construction across the canal half a mile away, and crossed South River's main drag, Canal Street, which appeared to be jammed up for a mile from Fortieth in both directions. Lunch hour rush.

I looked at the room, checked the ceiling, the corners, and behind myself where, on the opposite side of the bed, there was a nightstand. To my right, against the wall opposite the foot of the bed was a small table and a straight-backed visitor's chair. I zipped open my duffel bag and began removing the contents. On top was a plastic bag containing a receipt from SRMHI for my cell phone, an SRPD evidence receipt in another plastic bag for the clothes I had been wearing when I had been

49

admitted to Riverside after the Sunday takedown. There was an additional receipt from SRMHI covering the shirts and trousers I was not allowed to keep at the institution.

From the duffel bag I removed my shaving kit. In it there was an additional receipt-in-a Ziploc that revealed that electric shavers, hair brushes, and tooth brushes were acceptable, but nail files, finger and toenail clippers, combs, and tweezers were not. I envisaged for a moment the rampage through the halls of Squirmhi of Trevor the Tweeze who left a series of completely hairless victims in his wake, the mother plucker.

Opening a zippered pocket on the side of the bag, I removed my obsolete model Palm handheld that had been substituted for my wireless before I had been put on the bus. I flipped open the cover and turned it on. The battery charge indicator was down an eighth. Someone had been reading the unit actively for more than an hour. Someone had been through everything in it.

My back to the door with its observation port, I pulled my shirt out of my trousers, revealing the dressing taped to my left side at the waist. Picking at the top of the dressing, I lifted a corner of the tape. Keeping tension on it, I pulled the skin away from the tape revealing the small clear plastic evidence envelope containing the expansion card. Taking the dummy card out of the back of my handheld, I took the blue plastic chip and inserted it into the handheld's card slot.

In addition to the Gentleman Killer files, there were personnel records from Books State Correctional Facility, the city's hospitals and clinics, the South River Police Force, full personnel records on Police Park Tower, Breadloaf/North Valley, and East Branch Divisions SRPD. In addition there were all the murder books on Lucinda Dobbs, Jolene Gaye, Dena Lloyd, Gilbert Kane, and Corrections Officer Katey Sloan. The last was a State Police file. There were also the records of convicted killer Alvin C. Yuker. Satisfied that everything was complete and operational, I indexed for the SRMHI staff records and called up Billy, the orderly who had escorted me to Turkey.

William Divine, forty-six, former Navy Corpsman, put himself through Breadloaf University's College of Nursing, worked as an ER nurse in University Hospital, came to work at SRMHI four years ago as an orderly.

Orderly? That incongruity even made it through the drug haze. Lt. Hewitt had flagged Billy's salary figures. Even with a glowing reference from University Hospital, William Divine had actually taken about a fifty percent pay whack to go along with the plummet in status and working conditions to be an orderly at Squirmhi. It seemed to contradict freshman economics.

Norman, who had been running the floor cleaner, was Norman Cote employed by SRMHI maintenance for the past eleven years. Before that, he had been an "aerospace technician" —a truck driver in the Air Force. Sergeant in the reserves.   Recently married. Two children from a previous marriage, both girls. Current wife, Jennifer, was a case worker at Human Services. Prior wife, Laura, had died in a traffic accident. She had worked at a daycare center.

Munroe, the SO on the wing access door, was Luke Munroe, employed in SRMHI security four years, retired uniformed patrol officer from Copper City. Divorced, no children. Security used last names. Everyone else used first names. An Item from back in the 'Eighties. Luke Munroe had qualified for the U.S. Olympic Ski Team. Downhill man. No medals but lots of knee problems.

I skipped down to the bottom and called up Daniel Walker, M.D. Oh, indeed his pappy was a steel executive. A Reston Steel heir, educated at Lanford, Julia's old high school, also a mansion in Glenn Heights. He also went to Julia's institution of higher learning, Breadloaf University. Then Harvard Med. Residency at Mass Gen. From there he was taken in by noted psychiatrist Leland Parks in his Boston practice then began his own private practice out of the North Ridge Medical Arts Center in South River. Three years ago he was appointed director of Squirmhi. And Harvey the group leader didn't like Walker at all. Of course, Harvey didn't like much of anything, save chaos.

I closed the document and removed the expansion card. After replacing the card in it's plastic envelope, I put it back inside my dressing, and put the dummy card back into the slot.

Getting up, I removed my jacket, shirt, trousers, and shoes, looked for the white bag that was supposed to be on my bed, found it beneath my duffel bag, and stuffed in the shirt and trousers, leaving the bag on the bed. I pulled on my blue hospital coveralls, zipped them up, and put on my shoes. On the coveralls, there was a dark blue label holder sewed just above my left breast pocket, and in it was a white on black plastic strip with "Joseph" on it. I smiled at that. Aunt Cella had been the only person on earth who ever called me Joseph, and then only when she was angry.

CHICKEN ALI BABA

"I thought you said the food here wasn't absolutely repulsive," I said to Harvey as I poked at the overcooked diced chicken, corn, carrots, and bug-looking peas swimming in pus-yellow cream sauce.

Harvey was on my right at the head of the table using a piece of bread to help push the gluey concoction onto his fork. "This isn't absolutely repulsive, Sherlock." He looked up at the pale yellow ceiling. "Absolutely repulsive would be late-stage lepers forming hamburger patties on the insides of their thighs. Lung cancer sufferers coughing and making up their plates at the salad bar. Spaghetti and meatballs—"

"What about this Turkey Talent Show you mentioned?" I hastily interrupted before Harvey inserted an irreversible pasta image into my mind.

"Part of therapy. Once every couple of weeks, each of the eight groups on the floor puts on acts in a talent show for staff, visitors, and any patients who aren't locked down. Usually it's only one or two from each group. Poetry, piano playing, guitar picking, storytelling, juggling, singing, whatever. Last fall Barbara Cleveland began reciting Portia's speech from *The Merchant of Venice* and took a dump right in the middle of her act. She began biting when they took her away, which is why she's up on Redshank. A pretty good act, but about a month later there was a guy in Mark's group—"

"Wayne," interrupted Louis.

"Right. Wayne. He stripped naked, covered himself head-to-toe in chunky peanut butter, and went on stage to recite a free-verse composition of his own titled 'Excrementum.' He didn't get to finish, either. Still, so far he's my favorite."

"When does Yuker show?"

"Security probably has some things left to work out. The media would have quite a roast if Godzilla killed someone here or escaped and ravaged the villagers." Harvey nodded toward the goon platoon of steroidal orderlies patrolling the cafeteria.

I sipped at my glass of unsweetened iced tea and looked around the table. Thomas sat across from me picking at his lunch. To Thomas's right sat Yukiko, then Teddy, neither of whom seemed to have any objection to the food. At the foot of the table sat Louis, who said nothing but kept mad-dogging me while his mandibles rendered the house special into a digestible soup. To Louis's right was Geraldine, who kept up a steady run of chatter at Louis who neither noticed nor responded. Seated between Geraldine and me was a Helen Hayes clone who wore what looked like a shawl of plastic wrap over her shoulders. She had a large blue leather purse on her lap and kept her right hand in the purse while she spooned sugar into her tea and ate with her left hand. Four times during the meal her right hand darted out of her purse clutching a lint roller. She would remove its protective cover then quickly run the sticky roller over my left shoulder and upper left quadrant, front and back. After replacing the cover and returning the roller to her purse, Leila would continue eating, warily checking to see how I reacted. After the fourth cleaning, I smiled at her and said, "Hi."

"Hello," she said nervously, her eyes glancing in my direction, her face aimed at her plate.

"I'm Joe. I'm new here."

"I'm Leila. I'm not." A very gentle southern accent. As she turned her attention back to spooning more sugar into her tea, Thomas laughed out loud. I looked at him.

"Thomas, I can't see how a fellow who finds as much in life to laugh at as you do would wind up in a place like this."

"He's in denial," said Harvey.

"He's full of shit," added Geraldine.

"Doesn't he looks like Will Smith, though?" concluded Leila.

Thomas's eyebrows went up.

54

"Men In Black," said Harvey.

"Loved that movie," I said.

"Which one was he?" asked Harvey. "Tommy Lee Jones's sidekick or the giant cockroach."

"Sidekick," answered Geraldine. "The big bug is now doing *Law and Order: Criminal Intent on the TV.* Vincent something."

"Vincent D'Onofrio," I added as I took another mouthful of the chicken stuff and looked around the room. The cafeteria was in the east end of the building, the dining room itself taking up the entire glassed in area beneath the second floor's east commons. There were about twenty of the yellow-topped ten-place tables arranged in rows across the room. Dan's Group sat next to the north wall with what was a great view of the mountain. The cafeteria line, all stainless steel and glass, was crowded with the next group loading up with luncheon fare, the plastic-capped and-gloved servers dishing up the food with expressionless faces. I examined the new arrivals one-at-a-time as they came off the end of the line. Julia wasn't anywhere.

"You are a policeman." I turned back and Louis was looking at me.

"A detective, actually."

"Is that a status thing?"

"Occupational. All detectives are cops, but all cops are not necessarily detectives."

"Please pass the jelly," said Leila. I handed her the bowl of plastic containers of assorted jams and jellies. She emptied the whole thing into her purse.

"I hate policemen," stated Louis.

"So, how's that been working out for you?" I inquired.

Thomas burst out laughing sending a mouthful of milk up into his sinuses. By the time he was finished hacking, coughing, blowing his nose, and wiping up his face with his napkin, Harvey and I both had had enough of the chicken ali baba. Harvey nodded toward the foot of the table. "Mad Dog is a high school English teacher." He raised his eyebrows at Louis.

"Vadalia High," he completed, "and my name is Louis."

Harvey pointed at Leila. "Dusty is a potter. Have you ever seen Glaze Leila at Five Corners?"

"Across from Gianelli's Dairy?" I asked.

Harvey nodded. "Meet Leila."

I sat back in my chair and regarded my group mate with genuine awe. "I've been in there lots of times, Leila. You are a genuine artist. Incredibly beautiful work. I bought that one black, blue, and turquoise, piece—"

"'Peacock'," she said, as though speaking of an old friend fondly remembered. She reached out a hand and took an unopened raspberry jelly container from my plate and stuck it in her purse.

"Yes. I bought it as a present for my girlfriend—" I jammed as I thought better of continuing with the saga of how Cherie Vitamante had launched Peacock at my head. I hadn't been quite nimble enough to catch it. Cherie was history, and Peacock was in a box in the bottom drawer of my bureau at the hangman's house awaiting a rainy weekend free with a jug of Elmer's.

"She loved it."

Leila looked at me with very sad, very moist eyes. She smiled timidly and rolled an invisible piece of lint off my shoulder.

"What about you, Sunshine?" Harvey asked Thomas.

"Student."

"Where?"

"Breadloaf."

"What year?"

"Sophomore."

"So, it's not until your junior year you get introduced to multi word sentences?"

Yukiko burst out with a laugh at Harvey's comment and Thomas sat back. "I can pile up verbiage by the carload until these very walls crack from sheer boredom, just like you old farts," he said. "Just let me know when you need a yawn assist and I'll pitch in." He looked at Yukiko. The man stared at Thomas for a moment, snorted in contempt, then shrugged.

"I am a dentist," said Yukiko. "I have an office in West Bluff." He shrugged. "*Had* an office in West bluff. My partner dissolved our business arrangement after a disagreement I had with a patient, who subsequently filed charges and sued."

"You one of those who gas an' grope 'em?" asked Geraldine. "That happened to me once. Dentist in Paducah. Limp weenie. Wasn't much good with a drill, neither. " She bared her rotten teeth and tapped them with a painted and chipped fingernail.

Yukiko averted his gaze from the orthodontic horror. "Can you imagine someone eating chocolate covered peanuts just before coming in for a filling? Hunks of peanut, gobs of chocolate mixed with saliva? Next time he came in he'd just had bleu cheese dressing on a salad. Carrots stuck between his teeth."

"So, what'd you do?" I asked.

"I started pulling out his teeth. Got two of them before the screaming brought my partner."

"No Novocain?"

"He didn't like needles. Fortunate where it happened, really. My partner was right there to put them back in, but the patient would have none of it."

"Dental chair rage," remarked Thomas.

"The fellow ran out into the street and almost got run down by a Hyundai."

"Wally doesn't think much of Hyundais," observed Harvey. "Too light."

"My patient went to the police," said Yukiko, "and I wound up here."

Yukiko looked to his right and Teddy looked up from his chicken stuff. He grinned, displaying upper and lower gaps in his own ivories. "Makes sense. Take out the teeth before you drill them. Saves all that talking, slurping, and bending over." He looked down at his plate. "Well, let's see. Because of heroin I threw away a promising career as a Mafia thug. I've been a bum, I'm currently a Methadone addict, and thanks to my stay here, I've probably been fired as a dishwasher at a diner on the Cross Town."

"Did you mean you were homeless?" asked Thomas.

"No, you little college snot. I was a bum. I do believe, however, that we have a few friends in common. Candy? Little Mary, Big Horse?"

"What—" Thomas waved a hand in disgust at Teddy. "I am no addict."

"Ain't addicts the only ones who *know* they ain't addicts?" asked Geraldine innocently.

"Astutely put, Sister," remarked Harvey.

Teddy laughed. "Sunshine, aren't you the kid who matriculated his roommate out of his third floor dorm window on PCP and then passed out? They woke you up and you freaked and began flattening campus cops? Seemed to be something a little more serious than a sensitivity to shellfish."

"Well, Burnout, I noticed the Silver Line collected your ass up out at the Vadalia Substation for beating some old homeless man near to death."

"He was a bum, too." Teddy pursed his lips and cocked his head to one side as his eyebrows elevated. "Yeah. I did that. You ever seen a new Aston Martin, kid?"

"No."

"Can't call it a car—an automobile. Glossy black with one of those hand-rubbed wax jobs that makes the skin look liquid. Black glove leather interior, tinted windows so it looks like it's driving itself. Man, I'm sitting on something leaning against something down on Fifteenth across the light from the Torrance Building looking at the insides of my head when this Aston Martin pulls up at the light right in front of me. Clean, big, black, beautiful, purring like a great big cat. Guy behind the wheel wearing sharp threads on his back, a big smile on his face. Handsome dude. Two hundred dollar haircut. Drivin' home to someone he wanted to see, I bet." He glanced at me and shifted his gaze to the center of the table.

"That dude was one of the few people on the street right then who was having a really good day. Then here comes this squeegee bum squirting shit all over the guy's immaculately clean windshield, hoping for a hand out. Shit all over that beautiful black Aston Martin. All over the windshield. Spots on the hood, on the roof. Stinking of muscatel. I got out there, pulled the bum off that car, and gave him some instant justice. Shoved that squirt bottle down his damned throat." He looked up at the ceiling for a moment. "Guess I'm still having a hard time with that remorse thing."

"Well, Mafia man," began Geraldine, "I am a woman. That's my job, my curse, and my glory. That's why I got beat up all those years, that's why I raised all those ungrateful brats, an' that's why I took that prune-faced squinty-eyed, bullshit-mouthed mother fucker and—" Geraldine, along with at least half a dozen orderlies, noticed that she was holding her butter knife, edge up in the air, in a gut-thrust grip. She grinned suddenly and put the knife down, gently, upon her plate. "Don't mean nothin'. Take my word for it, though, boys: there ain't nothin' quite like a cheese grater for takin' down a hard on."

Geraldine picked up her spoon. With an upraised pinky, she delicately took a taste of her lemon cake dessert. The rest of the table resembled the Last Supper two seconds after the waiter brought the check. I moved first, facing Harvey. "What about you, Buckaroo?"

Big grin followed by a shrug. "I am an artist with the fingers of Leonardo, the elegance of Botticelli, the passion of Van Gogh, the vision of Dali, and the poverty of Paraebius. My cousin Cory is on the job with the South River Crime Scene Unit, and he took me in to help out with this terrific idea he had about starting up a service that cleans up businesses and homes after bombings, suicides, murders, rapes, and tortures. You ever hear of SceneClean?"

"Sure. I've recommended SceneClean a number of times to families of victims. Very good reputation."

"Yes sir, we gather up the CSU litter, scrape the tissue and bone fragments off the walls, ceilings, and floors, sweep up the maggots, scrub the piss, blood, and shit off everything, fill in the holes, fill, sand, and refinish the bullet holes, replace the glass, refinish and reupholster the furniture, and then give it a shot of good old get-the-corpse-stench-out-of- here air freshener. Word spread fast and now we're doing murders up in Magena, suicides in Copper City, and rapes all over the state."

Harvey looked down at his plate, his gaze searching among the peas and diced carrots. "Sherlock, my cousin told me the company's cleaned up after you a couple of times." He looked up at me. "At the Rizzo brothers car dealership. You know, Rizzo Auto?"

"I think I recall the incident."

"Three dead, one wounded, and the wounded guy was the one who left the biggest mess. That always got me. You'd think there'd be more blood killing a guy, you know, blowing big holes in him."

"You got to be alive to pump that blood onto the floor," I whispered.

"Yeah. That was your blood all over that parts room Cory was talking about, wasn't it? You blew away the Rizzo brothers and then soaked that entire parts room with your blood. SceneClean was paid to clean and repackage the works—even the things that didn't have blood on them. Those were all billed hours paid for by the Battaglia family. Cory said he couldn't believe the guy who leaked all that blood could've lived."

"As a matter of fact, he didn't." A couple of nervous chuckles. I glanced at Harvey. "What about you?"

He looked up, saw that everyone was listening, and looked down at the center of the table. "Yeah. That's called deflecting. Getting the focus off me onto someone else. Very dishonest." He looked back at me. "Remember a kid named Mark Billings?"

"Suicide early last year. Young boy, fifteen or sixteen."

"Fifteen," said Harvey. "Greenwood Academy student. You remember Greenwood Academy, don't you?"

"Yes."

"This was before the Ronnie Petersen shootout. Billings should have been a wakeup call for everyone there, but it was regarded as an isolated incident. Anyway, Mark had a well-off family, nice home in the Heights. Mark got grounded by his parents for smoking pot. A whole week he couldn't go out with his pals and do drugs. Well, one day after school, Mark took his father's twelve-gauge, went into the garage and hacksawed the barrels down to fifteen inches so he could reach, then he sat down on a stool in his parents' bedroom, stuck the sawed-off under his chin, and pulled both triggers."

Harvey looked around at the others. "You know, in the movies, you off yourself with a gun and—pow—all you get is a little raspberry jam squirted on the ceiling and a little trickle of fake blood from one corner of your mouth. The kids think they lay you out in a coffin all dressed up in your Sunday best, your cheeks all rouged, and everybody passes by, looks at your beautiful face, crying now that you're gone and they're really sorry they treated you the way they did. But shotguns don't read scripts. Gases under terrific pressure, high-speed shot, and Mark used both barrels. Held them tight against the underside of his chin. Christ. He inflated and blew off his own head, and that's not just a turn of phrase. His head filled with gas and exploded. A patch of hairy skin from the back of his neck and head were all that was left above his ears —ear, actually. One ear left. Not much good for a viewing."

He leaned back in his chair. "I suppose the MEAs and the rest gathered up what they could find. But SceneClean is meticulous, exacting, and thorough. We don't want the client finding a finger in the cookie jar or blood spatter on the toilet paper. We go over and through everything, millimeter by millimeter, several times. I was the one who found Mark's lips, still attached together on the right side. They were on a bookshelf behind an old paperback copy of *I'm OK—You're OK* by Thomas Harris. Pitiful little moustache he was trying to grow."

"How'd you get here, Harvey?" I asked.

"From the reports, I gather I didn't handle finding those lips very well. The next thing I remember is waking up here full of drugs with two broken hands, no skin on my knuckles, and vowing never to set foot in the real world ever again."

"So now you fill your days making life miserable for Dr. Dan."

"It's something to do."

"Schadenfreude," said Thomas.

"Gesundheit," I answered.

There was a barely audible, choked off cry and we all looked at Yukiko. The dentist's cheeks were wet with tears. He looked up at Harvey and blurted out, "My father. He was a kamikaze pilot."

Thomas's eyebrows went up. "Well? What'd he do? Miss?"

Only one breath of Thomas's horse laugh emerged before the dentist grabbed a metal water pitcher, swung it into Thomas's face, and leaped on the college student. They both tipped over onto the floor as Yukiko experimented with using blunt force trauma in performing tooth extractions.

Two whistles blew, Billy and three other white-uniformed hulks leaped into the fray as the rest of us got up from the table and backed away. As Yukiko was dragged up from the floor in wrist and arm restraints and shot full of drugs, I looked to my right to see a red-haired woman of medium height wearing a plum colored suit with an orange silk scarf around her neck. She had a staff nametag mounted above her left breast pocket, and the name was Amber.

Amber is an Arabic name that means "jewel," and it was almost no distance at all from jewel to Julia. Dark red hair swept up off the back of her neck. Great neck. Deep blue eyes, soft red lips, and a really fine behind. Just enough of a disguise, but no one could hide that behind from me. "It's you," I said, discretely patting her bottom.

The woman looked aghast at me, gave a blast on her whistle, and before she could let loose a second blast, I felt a sap hit the back of my head while beefy angels drove my face into the gray-green asphalt-tiled floor. My arms were buckled into restraints and I looked up from the floor to see Harvey looking back, grinning, and wagging a finger. "Now, that was stupid," he said.

A needle found my arm and it was back on the Goofyland Express.

A FUNNY THING

Images swam in green slime, lights, darks, mushy gray-black things in between the shadows. My ears felt like they were melting and my nose was on fire. By the time I came to and managed to get both eyes open, the universe was made of glass and blinding white beams of light hung with strange yawning sounds. My arms and ankles were in full restraints, neither my wrists nor my elbows able to move. I was balanced, seated in a chair, looking at a big white circular coffee table in the center of which was a box of tissues with an ornate beaded cover. The tissue that was up appeared to be beckoning to me. I wobbled my gaze around, up, and to my left. High on a steel and glass wall was a bright blue hand-lettered sign that read: Dan.

Struck me funny for some reason. "Dan, Dan, he's our man, if he can't do it, no one can," I slurred, making someone else giggle.

"Drool to the left, drool to the right, stand up, sit down, bite, bite, bite!" answered the giggler. It was Yukiko. The dentist was sporting double black eyes.

"You look like raccoon," slurred Thomas, whose nose looked like a beefsteak tomato. We all laughed.

Teddy was sitting in a chair with his back to the mountain. He was next to Leila. Teddy was in full restraints, his head back, his tongue hanging out, his eyes open and exploring other dimensions. Leila was running her lint roller over Teddy's chest, carefully avoiding the drool. Sitting to Leila's left was Louis, sitting back, his arms crossed, glaring at me. The next chair was filled by the mountain of killer Alvin Yuker, also in full restraints but apparently not medicated. Blond hair and lumpy muscles. Big Billy the orderly stood behind Alvin, a brain-breaker police baton in his hands.

Geraldine was sitting next to Alvin keeping up a steady run of unanswered chatter with him. Sitting to her left and my right, Thomas was in full restraints, one eye closed and a fat upper lip to go with his swollen nose.

Sitting to my left was Yukiko, also in full restraints and still laughing at Thomas's raccoon remark. On the other side of the dentist was Harvey, relaxed, smiling, his legs crossed, his hands resting on his lap. It was Half-Satan, Room 333, Dan's corner, and Harvey was grooving on the chaos.

Dr. Dan Walker was ranting at someone. Gaunt guy in whites. Big hatchet of a face, dark sunken eyes, seemed familiar somehow. I couldn't read his nametag.

". . . Come out here for my afternoon group session and half my patients are in restraints and doped up. There are absolutely no positive benefits to drool therapy, Miller! Staff better start getting their acts together, or heads will roll. . . ."

Miller, I mentally repeated to myself as my head began to loll. Miller looked like a young John Carradine. Loved him in *Blood on the Saddle*. No. *Blood on the Sand*. Bullfighting. "Blood on the Saddle" was the singing bears down there in Orlando. Big rat country. Funny bit, those bears. I broke out into song, trying to remember the lines: "There was b-lood on the saddle—"

"—B-lood all around," joined in Harvey and Yukiko. "And—"

"Be quiet!" commanded Dan Dan he's our man. "You and you!" he said. "You and you!" again. I opened my eyes to see the red-faced psychiatrist pointing at me with one hand and pointing at Alvin Yuker with the other. "You and you!"

"Me 'n' him what?"

Leila interrupted Walker's response by saying, "Excuse me for a moment, doctor. My roller needs a refill."

He began wildly waving his hands over his head. "Christ! Could you people possibly become even more obtuse?!"

"Goose goose, we're obtuse," began Yukiko.

"Squeeze a pickle and you get juice," concluded Thomas. More laughter. Damned inspiring, those drugs.

If he ever did transmit the answer to my question about the "you and you" thing, I was in no condition to receive.

Dead silence, moist weight all along my back, a bladder that was under significant pressure. Opening my eyes, the big, fat backwards letter 'L' above me twisted and dipped a couple of times before it resolved into the ceiling of my room. I was in bed, on my back, my tongue as dry as leather. I tried to reach to my face, but my hand was held in place at the edge of the bed by a soft cuff attached somewhere beneath my line of vision. I looked and my other hand was cuffed as well.

"Oh, hell."

Rolling my head to the left, I looked through the window. It was night. I rolled it to my right and looked through the little window set into the closed door. The hallway lights were out, as well. I didn't recall eating dinner or going to bed —or being strapped down in bed. Lifting my head, I looked down at my feet. I kicked off the covers. At least no ankle restraints.

There was nothing resembling a nurse's call button near either of my hands. "Hello?"

No sounds coming from the hall. "Hello? Yoo hoo. Hey! Anybody? I gotta pee."

No sounds at all. Nothing from out in the hall, nothing from outside. No traffic, no jet planes or choppers, no car horns or jackhammers. Impressive soundproofing.

Inflating my lungs, I bellowed as loud as I could. *"Halp!"*

Shaking the wrist cuffs, I determined they were loose enough to swivel, allowing me to get my feet over my head and, perhaps, over the head of the bed. If I could push the bed away from the wall, perhaps I could do a backward somersault and stand on the floor and pee, at least avoiding wetting my bed.

I tried to sit up, but the room began spinning as my stomach prepared to hurl. With my head back on the pillow, I pulled up my knees, but the increased pressure on my bladder drove them back down.

"There was b-lood on the saddle—"

A slight sound, like a whisper. I looked at the door. Someone was on the other side. "Hello? Nurse? Orderly? Glenda the Good?" The door opened silently, an inch at a time. When open a third of the way, a huge shadow emerged from behind it, ducked its head to clear the lintel, then entered the room like a winter storm front. It didn't turn on the lights. I tried to moisten my lips.

The figure stood before the doorway a moment, allowing the door to close behind it, then it took a step and stopped next to my bed. The shadow stared down at me, a slight glitter reflecting from unblinking eyes. "Here's a funny thing," said the shadow, its voice male, deep, and menacing. Then ensued a silence that seemed to last for years.

"I could use a laugh," I prompted.

"See, I was trying out doorknobs—just seeing how big my cage is. Thirty-six doors in this wing open onto the hallway."

"I didn't know that."

"Something else I bet you don't know. Out of all those doors, only two of them are unlocked right now."

"Yours and mine?"

"I guess I can't stump you."

"You got any idea what this is about?"

"Maybe."

The weather front darkened as it leaned forward. "My guess is someone wants you and me to get together, number three-thirty. I know the COs at Books want me dead, but it looks to me like someone here wants you dead, too."

"How do you figure that, Alvin?"

"You know me?" He leaned over and looked closely at my face. "Oh. You're Joe, my groupie. That quack who runs this nuthouse assigned you to be my friend. I'm supposed to be your friend. Hi, friend."

"Hi. What are you talking about?"

Yuker looked around, went to the chair next to the desk, brought it back and lowered himself into it. It groaned beneath his weight and he grunted as though in pain. "Were you sober enough this afternoon at group to remember Walker pairing up everybody?" asked Alvin.

"The you-and-you thing?"

"Yeah. We're groupies, you and me. You're supposed to share your soul with me and in return I reveal to you my complete inner self. As a result of this mutual sharing, we're supposed to cure each other."

"You've been reading the patient handbook, Alvin. What makes you think someone's trying to kill me, as opposed to someone trying to kill you?"

"I'm the one who's walking around and you're the one who's strapped down. Call me crazy, but that appears to give me an advantage."

"If I'm dead, Alvin, that'd be a great excuse to kill you, wouldn't it? No trial necessary?"

Long silence, then Yuker leaned back in the chair. "Groupie, that is first class criminal thinking. Still, there's more of an argument for your death than the doors being unlocked."

I held my knees together. "Like what?"

"Look at the way you're strapped down. You can move your feet. Back at the Book when they strap down a physically able person in the infirmary, they put soft cuffs on the ankles, too. Keeps you from kicking the doc, but also from flipping heels over your head, catching your head beneath your body or going off the end of the bed and getting caught between the bed and the wall, suffocating. It's called positional asphyxia."

"Maybe this is just the way they do it here."

"I saw three other patients on this wing tonight strapped down. They all have ankle cuffs."

"Now that I think about it, Alvin, I was trying to see if I could do just that: flip over my head to get most of me out of bed so I wouldn't pee in it."

"I once saw a guy who died that way. It didn't look fun. You suicidal?"

"No. A cop. Joe Torio."

He leaned in more closely. "Are we connected somehow? I mean before the quack made us therapy buddies?"

"Do you remember Luther Stebbins?"

67

"Luther? Sure. Luther Stebbins and Dale Raye arrested me. Luther and me have been in touch ever since he retired."

"My boss, Capt. Dockery, was partners with Luther after Dale Raye left the force. Stebbins and Raye think you're being set up for the Sloan killing."

Long silence. "I am."

"Capt. Dockery had me put in here undercover to check out a few things."

"Why don't the cops just do a regular investigation?"

"It's complicated."

"I'm a college graduate," said Alvin.

"And I have to take a piss so bad I'm going to be gargling in a second."

"So. Take a leak."

I shook my cuffs. "I can't reach." I nodded toward the nightstand. "Down below. Is there one of those plastic urinal things?"

The big man pushed back the chair, squatted down, a door opened, a bit of clattering, then he reached up holding a light-colored plastic urinal with an attached cap. "Here." He grunted and doubled over.

"Something wrong?"

"Stomach cramps. I get them at night." He shook the urinal. "Go pee."

I shook my restraints. "I still can't reach. So, Alvin. Groupie. Buddy. I have a really big favor to ask."

"Forget it."

"You have an alternative?"

"Get you out of those cuffs. How's that for a plan?" Alvin looked at the restraint on my right hand. "They got a lock on this thing. How much pressure are you under? I could go down to the access door to the nurses sta—"

"Now, Alvin! Now is the time! The other end. Is that strap buckled on below or riveted?"

The big man's head lowered beneath mattress level. "Looped through some kind of metal brace and padlocked." He rattled something down below and said, "Wait a sec."

I heard Alvin grunt, then the bed groaned followed by the snap of breaking metal and more groaning. My arm was free. "Let me get the other one." The big man got up, went around the bed, bent over, and, with a groan and a snap, pulled the left restraint free. Immediately I sprang up from the bed, restraint belts and padlocks dangling, and staggered into the bathroom. Feeling too unsteady to urinate standing, I pulled down my pajama bottoms and landed on the toilet seat like a workaholic hen. Lights flashed as my bladder deflated, relief making me shiver and groan. I was on what seemed like my second quart when the shadow of Alvin Yuker filled the bathroom doorway.

"You're the hangman's son."

"Yeah."

"You took down the Gentleman Killer a few weeks ago. I heard on the grapevine the cop who took down Sunday flipped out and had to be put away. Is that's why they put you in here as a patient? You really are crazy?"

"They put me in here to get your side of the story. I do have a genuine problem or two. That saved making up a bunch of bogus records."

"Why didn't they just throw you in stir with me? As soon as the fifteen days are up, they'll have me filed back at the Book."

"The city doesn't have jurisdiction at the prison."

"State troopers."

"Right. We do have jurisdiction here, though. Also, we took a vote and in our judgment, it makes a whole lot more sense to the other side if you don't make it back to Books at all."

"You mean, if I should happen to get made dead here."

"That would wrap up the murder of Katey Sloan with the least amount of fuss," I said. I stood, pulled up my bottoms, and flushed the toilet as I turned to wash my hands. "Do you understand what it had to take to kill Sloan, ape your pattern, and duplicate your bite marks?"

The big man turned, went back to the chair next to the bed, and dropped into it. He thought on it for a moment, shook his head, and looked at me. "CO's, State cops. City cops, too?"

"That's what it took if it's a frame."

"It is."

I sat at the foot of my bed and looked at the big man, still a shadow in the dark. "Did you kill Katey Sloan?"

"No."

"How would you know, Alvin? According to your testimony at your trial, you don't remember the actual killing of either your mother, Dena Lloyd, or Jolene Gaye. By the way, what ever possessed your attorney to let you on the stand?"

"I did. He couldn't stop me from testifying."

"If you were going to do that, Alvin, why didn't you just plead guilty?"

"I tried. My lawyer, though, he could talk a mile a minute. I couldn't do this, I couldn't do that, the law this, the media that. When the dust settled, I was in court. He was trying to get me off and I had to make sure that didn't happen. The only way I could do that was to scare the jury. I scared the jury."

"Still, when you kill them you don't remember."

"No." A long silence. Yuker held out a hand then let it drop. "I think I got it all bolted down: these thoughts, these feelings. I iron out everything until I don't have any feelings left about anything. Most times I keep the nightmare away. Sometimes the nightmare gets through. I kill it before it grows, though. Reading, exercise, painting, work. But this CO, Katey Sloan, it didn't happen. The shrinks say it takes a certain key to open my lock. Sloan wasn't even close. She was a really good person. And there was something else. You know about Gilbert Kane?"

"The con in protective segregation who OD'd on Valium."

"Yeah. The only ones who had contact with Kane were COs."

"So COs had to have supplied Kane with the drugs."

"That's right. Big stink in the front office. Supt. Cotton wanted answers and we heard Katey Sloan was out to get them. I think she was about to crack the drug operation when she was transferred out of segregation and sent to Arts & Crafts where I was a trustee."

I rubbed my eyes. "Okay, accepting for the moment that you've been framed and Sloan was set up, to research you, set up, torture, and kill Sloan, and get her out of the prison, there would have to be at least three or four COs in the right places at the right times. To set you up for the fall, in addition to the COs, there would have to be someone connected with the Breadloaf/North Valley Division or the Tower—or some one here—to get all the details on your background and pattern. In addition," I said to myself, "someone who could get into the evidence room and copy the casts they made of your teeth that MEA Thornhill used to match your bite marks."

He slumped back in the chair, his head shaking slowly. He let out a sigh, then said, "This is bad."

"Why," I asked.

"The casts never made it through the jury deliberations."

"What?"

"The way I heard it, things got a little hot in the jury room and number four began tossing stuff at number eleven. The casts of my teeth went out the window, and that was six stories down to the street where the traffic turned what was left into dust by the time the bailiff got down there."

"That didn't make it into the records." I tried to squeeze a thought between the drugs. "Did you ever get any dental work done at Books or Parkington?"

"Cleanings, two fillings at Books. Nothing that needed casts."

"Anytime you can remember being unconscious? Under sedation for an operation or something else?"

"No."

"Well, Alvin, if those bite marks weren't made using your casts, and if you didn't make them yourself, then someone must have the original molds from which the casts were made. Do you recall if they were ever entered in evidence?"

"I don't remember." He seemed to stare down at the floor. "Back during the trial, I wasn't listening much. I just wanted to end it."

"Who made the molds?"

"I don't know. Funny-looking guy the cops brought in. I don't remember his name. Dentist from outside. That'd be in the transcript, wouldn't it?"

"Yeah."

"What now?"

"Get back to your room and get some sleep. I'm guessing someone real soon is going to check up on you. If they catch you out of your room, your death, while a pile of orderlies kick the poo out of you, will be regrettable but unavoidable."

The big man stood silently for a moment, then turned his head and looked at me. "Why?"

"Why what?"

Yuker pointed around at the room with his hand. "This. Being here. Taking this risk. I'm just a killer. Why risk all this?"

"There aren't any throwaway lives, Alvin. Not in my corner. Anyway, I owe Al Dockery, Al Dockery owes Luther Stebbins, and Luther Stebbins believes in the big joke."

"Big joke?"

"The one over the entrance to the Supreme Court building."

"You mean 'Equal justice under the law'?"

"A real thigh slapper, huh?"

Alvin got to his feet. "Luther's an old fool in a nursing home."

"That must be the reason."

"What about you, Joe? Where are you with the big joke?"

"Every couple of years I get to see it happen. Maybe this time, too."

"Yeah, but you're a nut in a loony bin."

"You say that like it's a drawback."

Two beats of silence, then Alvin asked, "What do you think about lip-syncing to that Coasters song?"

"What?"

"'Riot In Cell Block #9.' Machine gun? Siren? What do you think about lip-syncing to it for the Turkey Talent Show? Teddy said something about it before he passed out. The whole group could get in on it."

"Are you sure you're focused on the real problem here?"

"First time out from behind the walls in a long time, Joe. New faces, new things to do."

"Like finishing your frame for murder."

"Taking care of that is your job, right? See you in the morning, Joe."

Alvin went to the door, opened it quietly, and slipped into the hall, the door closing silently behind him. I stood, went around the bed, and stopped next to the window to examine the loose ends of the wrist restraints in the light from the outer road security floods. They were nylon-reinforced heavy leather loops made by folding the belts back upon themselves and securing them with padlocks, the wrist loops fleece-lined. I walked around the bed, and took my Maglite from the nightstand drawer. Squatting down, I played the light beneath the bed where the restraints had been anchored. There was a half-inch thick steel brace once riveted to the bed frame at both ends. The rivet's head on one end had been stripped off, the brace bent away from the bed frame, the angle-iron frame itself bowed outward from the force applied by Alfred Yuker's arms.

I tried to pull the head of the bed away from the wall. The wheels were locked. To move the bed only an inch took a considerable effort. If I had been on the bed, the increased weight would have made it almost impossible to move, especially with me weak on drugs, upside-down, the weight of my legs and lower torso on my chest and head, cutting off the air. Positional asphyxia. "Important safety tip," I whispered.

I saw a moving light out in the hall through the observation port. Flashlight. l moved the chair in front of the door, climbed back into bed, plumped up the skinny hospital pillow, put my hands out to the edges of the bed as though I was still restrained, and closed my eyes. As I waited for whoever it was to pass, something nagged at me. An extra wrinkle.

The orderly Dan Walker had been chewing out— Miller—the one who looked like John Carradine. I took my handheld from the top of the nightstand, turned it on and held down the power button until the unit's screen illuminated. Reaching to my dressing, I retrieved the expansion card. Putting in the card, I turned to the SRMHI personnel files. Three Millers in the file, but two were women. The orderly's name was Neal Miller.

Nothing much of note in his file. Thirty-eight, graduated from Vadalia High —where Louis had taught English before the men in the white coats came to take him away. Odd jobs, carpenter, a four-year stretch as a telemarketer working for Right Line Medical Supply, a year cleaning condo chimneys at Breadloaf Ski Resort, then four years as an orderly working at SRMHI. Something else about his face. Whatever it was it was too far away. The more I reached for it, the farther away it went.

The light flashed again, I slipped the PDA beneath my covers, put my wrists out to my sides, and closed my eyes. The light played on my face twice, three times, then it was dark. I waited until I heard the electric door lock switch from open to close. I pulled the PDA out from beneath the covers, got out of bed, and checked the peep hole. All clear. Returning to the bed, I turned to Alvin Yuker's records. I went to the transcript of his parole hearing.

D.O.C., Books State Correctional Facility
3/6/2001,
Transcript, Parole Hearing
YUKER, ALVIN C., 445722

Ch. MILTON: Good morning. Please have a seat. Mr. Yuker. First I'm going to properly identify you for the record, then the board will ask you a few questions, after which you'll have an opportunity to say a few words on your own behalf if you care to do so. Your full name is Alvin C. Yuker, 445722, you were sentenced to fifteen years, and your maximum date is March the sixth, Twenty oh-one. And you've been locked up now for how long?
YUKER: Five years.
Ch. MILTON: Five years. Boy, how tall are you?
YUKER: Seven feet, one inch.
Ch. MILTON: You play a lot of basketball?
YUKER: No.
Ch. MILTON: In the past?

YUKER: Never.

Ch. MILTON: I see. Very well. Please answer Mr. Beiderbecke's questions.

Beiderbecke: You confessed to this murder?

YUKER: Yes.

BEIDERBECKE: Now, this was your mother you killed?

YUKER: Yes.

BEIDERBECKE: How did you feel about that?

YUKER: About what?

BEIDERBECKE: At the time you did it, how did you feel about killing your mother?

YUKER: I don't remember anything about killing her. I remember torturing her, but I don't remember killing her. After, though, I felt bad.

HILLER: Bad? Are you talking about remorse?

YUKER: I don't know.

HILLER: If you felt bad about killing your mother, Mr. Yuker, that might be remorse. I was asking if you felt remorse about what you have done. Killing your mother.

YUKER: No. I didn't feel bad about killing her. Something else.

HILLER: What else?

YUKER: It's hard to say. Killing her was supposed to answer something. Fill something that was empty. It didn't do that. I was even more empty. I would have kept killing, trying for that answer, though, trying to get that fill. That's why I told the judge never to let me go.

BEIDERBECKE: Quite a dramatic flair. Tell me. Why did you kill your mother? (Pause) Did you understand the question?

YUKER: Yes.

BEIDERBECKE: You were an abused child, Right? Your mama put your eye out? She stuck a pin in your eye?

YUKER: It was a nail.

BEIDERBECKE: Is that why you killed her?

YUKER: No.

BEIDERBECKE: I don't know, man. If someone stuck a nail in my eye I think I'd be inclined to rearrange that person's body parts, at least a little.

YUKER: My mother did that when I was nine. When I killed her I was fifteen. My fuse isn't that long.

HILLER: Okay, then, why did she do such an awful thing to you? Why did she blind your left eye?

YUKER: She didn't say.

HILLER: Were there other things she did to you?

YUKER: Yes.

BEIDERBECKE: What?

YUKER: If it's not in the file, I don't talk about it.

BEIDERBECKE: What about all this? These photos? The way your mother died? What you did with the body. Tied her up like this, the burns, bite marks, all this other stuff. The torture.

YUKER: What about it?

BEIDERBECKE: Well, why? If it wasn't her sticking that nail in your eye, then why?

YUKER: I didn't have a choice.

BEIDERBECKE: The judge seemed to think you did.

YUKER: The judge wasn't there.

Ch. MILTON: You were fifteen when you were sentenced, Mr. Yuker. Sent to Parkington until your eighteenth birthday at which time you were transferred here to Books Correctional. This is your first time up for parole. How do you feel now about killing your mother?

YUKER: When I first came to Books, Dr. Keller helped me understand how sick my mother was.

Ch. MILTON: Dr. Mills' report says that you've done a lot of work with him over the months since Dr. Keller died.

YUKER: Mills saw me twice.

Ch. MILTON: He seems to think you've made a great deal of progress toward resolving your feelings of hostility toward women. And you've done a great deal to improve yourself. It shows here that you applied yourself at Parkington, got your G.E.D., you took college courses there, and more college courses since you came to Books. Art courses?

YUKER: Yes.

Ch. MILTON: Excellent. So many young men in your position simply give up. Well, Mr. Yuker, how would you like to continue your education by attending your classes at the university itself? In person.

YUKER: That would be a mistake.

Ch. MILTON: You mean, that wouldn't be a mistake.

YUKER: No. Paroling me would be a mistake.

HILLER: Why is that Alvin? Why do you think paroling you would be a mistake?

YUKER: Nothing's changed. Not in here. Not out in the world. If you let me out, I'll kill again. Dr. Keller knew that. He promised me no one would be fool enough to give me a parole.

BEIDERBECKE: Now, son, all you've killed is your mother. Not to suggest that's a small thing, but we have no evidence to suggest that you are some kind of serial whacko. The psychiatrist has recommended—

YUKER: Are you going to have Dr. Mills do my time when you find out he was wrong? Are you going to put the needle into his arm?

HILLER: Who are you going to kill?

YUKER: I don't know.

HILLER: Me? All women?

YUKER: No. Not you. Not all women. All women don't have that same pull on my trigger. Some do, though, and they aren't rare. I told Mills, I'm not safe to put on the street. Don't you do it.

77

Ch. MILTON: Well, son, I got to admit this is the first time we've heard anything like this. Still, this isn't a hospital and Books really isn't equipped to provide you with that kind of help.

YUKER: What about Squirmhi? The city mental hospital across the canal? Someplace else? I mean it. If you turn me loose, I will kill again and again until I am caught. All those deaths will be on you people.

BEIDERBECKE: Look, Yuker. You're only twenty years old. You have your whole life ahead of you. I know you're afraid of what's on the other side of these walls. We've seen that before and understand it. But what is to be gained by housing you here for another ten years?

YUKER: A lower body count.

Ch. MILTON: I see no humor in this situation, son.

YUKER: Do you see me laughing? Look, I don't have control over this, Mr. Milton. It's like touching a match to a fuse, like getting four when you add two and two. If you let me go free, more women will die, and they will die because I will kill them, and I'll kill them because that's all I can do.

Ch. MILTON: I cannot believe this conversation. Look at the record, Mr. Yuker. You cooperated with the authorities ever since you were put in the system. Your arrest, your confession, helping the police at every step, despite your attorney's attempt to confuse things. You have been an absolutely model prisoner since your first day at Parkington. The youth center's report on you is so glowing, I wish my own boys had report cards like this! Look, son. According to the record, you're only a few credits short of getting your art degree. In the entire five years you have been at Parkington and Books, there has not been a single mark on your record. Are you aware that you're the youngest trustee in this prison's entire history?

YUKER: I didn't know that.

Ch. MILTON: Dr. Mills and the superintendent look upon you as one of their big success stories. You want me to read you their letters?

YUKER: No.

Ch. MILTON: If we aren't supposed to parole offenders with records such as yours, Mr. Yuker, who are we supposed to parole? I know what would happen if we didn't parole you. The next piece of mail I'd get would be from Dirty Bill Marsonak up at DOC wanting to know why I'm turning the State Department of Corrections into a cure for the homeless problem.

YUKER: We are mere leaves caught in regulation's gale.

HILLER: Is that Walt Whitman?

YUKER: No. Carlos Ravines. He took a needle month before last.

Ch. MILTON: Now, Mr. Yuker, is when you get to say something on your own behalf.

YUKER: Don't parole me.

Ch. MILTON: Now, son, we've covered that.

YUKER: Can I appeal? Before I get released?

Ch. MILTON: Well...

BEIDERBECKE: You can file an appeal with the Appeals Board of the State Department of Corrections.

HILLER: I think that's true only if we turn down your parole.

BEIDERBECKE: I believe you're right, Alice. We have to turn down a parole before a prisoner can appeal.

YUKER: What if you grant it? Is there any way I can appeal it then?

HILLER: I may be wrong, but I believe the only one who has standing to appeal a positive decision is the District Attorney's Office.

Ch. MILTON: Look, Mr. Yuker, all this is beside the point. We have five years worth of evidence that proves you can control yourself and conduct yourself along productive paths. I know it's a scary world out there, but believe me, son, it's a lot less scary than it is behind these walls. It's time you grew up. You have your whole future ahead of you. Now, we'll have our decision in a few minutes.

(To Escort) Would you take Mr. Yuker back into the hall?

DISCUSSION: None.

ACTION: Parole granted, effective 7 March 1991, all members concurring.

END YUKER HEARING TRANSCRIPT

They paroled him and six days later they found the bodies of Jolene Gaye and Dena Lloyd. Both Gaye and Lloyd were red headed low-dollar street hookers and had been tied, tortured, bitten, and strangled exactly the same way Lucinda Yuker, Alvin's mother, had been tied, tortured, bitten, and strangled. Both Dena Lloyd and Jolene Gaye had children, and both of them had done to their children what Alvin's mother had done to him.

Stebbins and Raye had taken Yuker down before there were any additional deaths. Yuker had confessed, but his court-appointed attorney had a name and didn't want to let it go. He managed to exclude the confession and went for a trial pleading not guilty by reason of mental defect. Yuker had to confess again, from the stand, to end it. Nevertheless, because of the parole hearing, instead of the death penalty, the judge sentenced Alvin to life without the possibility of parole. As he did so the judge expressed a desire to give the needle to Yuker's parole board.

Something one of the parole board members said about Yuker being an abused child. I indexed to Yuker's medical records. Beatings, bruises, broken bones, and possible brain damage. His mother, the red-headed hooker, rented him out to her clients. As near as the doctors could determine, Alvin had been three the first time she pimped him out. She even used him herself. Three and jammed through a nightmare. One more child aimed like a gun.

I closed the document, turned off the handheld, removed the card from it, and put the handheld back on the nightstand. After hiding the card back inside my dressing, I put my head on the pillow and stared into the dark, thinking about Charlie Matthews, Jay Hellerman, and Nathan Sunday. Three killers addicted to murder, who were also the most gifted actors I had ever seen during a lifetime of watching motion pictures and television. Alvin Yuker seemed perfectly genuine—like he was not acting—which, after all, is the sign of a really great actor.

I rolled onto my side and closed my eyes.

DANCES WITH SQUIRRELS

At a quarter to six the next morning the muffled buzz of the lock to my room being cycled interrupted a nightmare in which Cherie Vitamante was trying to kill me by hurling screaming peacocks down at me where I was huddling at the bottom of a deep icy pit attempting to defend myself by squirting her with big plastic containers of Elmer's Glue. Climbing out of bed, hung over from the drugs, the locks on my wrist restraints clattering, I moved the chair, tried the door, and found it unlocked. Flipping on the overhead light, I went to the desk and opened my patients handbook to the permanent schedule. Five forty-five to six twenty AM, vitals and meds at the nurses station. Make up beds, clean up rooms, then, at seven oh five, gather at the stairwell for the group escort down to breakfast. Then free time or office visits until morning group at ten.

I stepped into the hall and noted that the young woman who had been sitting on the floor beneath the security cameras with her back against the wall was already in her place, her legs folded beneath her, her hands in her lap, her gaze straight ahead. "Hi," I said to her as I crossed her line of vision.

"Hi, yourself," she answered without changing expression or altering her gaze.

Geraldine and some Gilligan-looking guy were the only patients ahead of me by the time I made it to the wing security door to the nurses station. Munroe was on the gate. He let Geraldine and Gilligan through, but stopped me.

"What you got there?" the SO asked, pointing at the leather restraints dangling from my wrists. I held the cuffs up toward him. "Joe, were you placed in restraints last night?"

"Yesterday, I think."

"You were in that fracas down in the cafeteria lunch yesterday, right?" Munroe picked up one of the padlocked loose ends, raised his eyebrows, and let it go. "Well? Let's have it. What happened to these?"

"I really had to go and I couldn't find the call button. Sorry."

"We don't have call buttons."

"Well, there you are."

Two beats. "So, you just pulled these loose?"

"Man, I really had to go."

Monroe cracked a tiny smile, then frowned as he looked at my feet. "Where're your leg restraints?"

"Only these."

"No ankle cuffs? You sure about that?"

"I'm sure I walked to the bathroom and didn't drag my bed with me."

"Who was it who strapped you down, Joe?"

"I'd give worlds to know, but between the drugs and the lumps on my head, I really wasn't paying much attention."

The officer made an "umph" sound. Louis, Yukiko, and two patients from other groups were standing impatiently in line behind me. Frowning, the SO took a key from his pocket, removed the cuffs, and placed the straps on a shelf behind his desk. "Go on into the nurses station, over where those others are lined up, and get your vitals and meds."

"Thanks."

Geraldine was heading the other way as I approached the counter. She winked one of her frog-eyes at me and blew me a kiss, enveloping me in a fog of eau de chum bucket. At the counter a muscular nurse named Carla took my blood pressure, pulse, and temperature, all of which seemed low to me. She also informed me that at noon vitals, she would yank my sutures. Strange way to phrase it, I thought.

The next nurse in line was a tall fellow, blondish, David Bowie-looking face. He was standing at the end of the counter behind a tray crowded with little paper cups filled with water. He was taking pills and capsules in tiny plastic cups out of little drawers set into a rolling cart stacked with dozens of little drawers. I glanced past him to the SO on the East Wing security gate. She was female, about five eight, one-eighty, brown and brown.

The patient in line ahead of me was a sixtyish Andy Rooney look alike from Turkey West named Wally. He was whistling an old Flatlanders tune, "Waving My Heart Good-bye," and smelled of cinnamon. From him, I learned the pill drill: Place pill on tongue, open mouth and show Ed that the pill is, indeed, on the tongue. Take a little paper cup full of water, drink, toss cup into trash basket, then open mouth and show tongue, both sides, to Ed, demonstrating that the pill had, indeed, been consumed.

"If you don't want to take the meds," said Wally in a low voice, "as you drink the water, push the pill into your cup with your tongue, then crumple up the cup and toss it, show tongue, and you're out of there. If you want to save the pill, though, bring a crumpled up piece of paper with you, and after you spit the pill into the cup and crumple it up, keep the crumpled up cup in your hand and toss off the ball of paper, show tongue, and off you go."

"Thanks, Wally. My name's Joe. I'm in Dan's group."

I held out my hand and Wally passed something from his right hand to his left before shaking. "I'm in Nance's group. So, Joe, what do you do when you're not dancing with squirrels?"

"I'm a detective."

"City?"

"Yes."

Big grin. "Really. A violent cop. Who woulda thought. Here on observation?"

"Yes." I nodded toward the east wing security station. "What's her name?"

"Bodak. Heather Bodak. Sort of like naming someone Charity Numbowski, isn't it? She's okay."

"She been here long?"

"As long as I've been here." He frowned as he did a minor mental calculation. "Three months, anyway. Why? You looking for a date?"

"Something like that. So, how about you?"

"For a date?"

"No. Doctor? Lawyer—"

"Wally Spivak, former shoe salesman, former sports store owner, and former convict, currently under suspension as the head janitor at the Smith Building for punching the crap out of a really annoying building manager. Do you know the Smith Building?"

"Of course. It's right next to the Police Park Tower. My shrink's office is in the Smith."

"You're in the Tower? Central Division?"

"Major Crimes."

A frown. "Joe. Joe Torio? The hangman's son?"

"I believe that's my usual tag."

"Hold on. Joe DiMaggio Torio? Your partner was the Gentleman Killer? The guy up on Redshank?"

"That is so."

Wally nodded. "That explains why Dr. Walker tossed us out to take on fifteen-day wonders."

"You were a Dan man?"

Wally grinned and laughed. "I guess it's a good thing you're here. I wouldn't have gotten out of Dan's group any other way. "From what I've seen and heard, Nance is very good. I might even improve." Wally's face became quite serious as he placed a hand on my shoulder. "Even though I was in here, like everybody else in this town, I was obsessed with the GQ killings, and watched and read everything I could get about Nathan Sunday, you, and Julia Powers. That had to be tough, taking down Sunday, and I'm not talking about the wounds."

"Still is rough."

"What did you think of him, Joe? Before you knew he was the Gentleman Killer?"

"He was the best partner I ever had. I really liked him." I faced Wally. "You listed one of your former occupations as convict."

Wally nodded, removed his hand from my shoulder, and moved up in line. "I did three out of a three-to-nine for attempted murder." He took the pills Ed poured into his hand from a little plastic cup, tossed them into his mouth, showed the pills on his tongue to Ed, picked up a paper cup full of water, tossed down the water, then crumpled up the cup, showed empty tongue, and tossed a crumpled up piece of paper into the wastebasket. "Old flame of mine," Wally continued. "Ran her over with my Hyundai."

"I hear you don't much care for the Hyundai."

"Crappy car. Too light. I might as well have used a roller skate. I had to be crazy."

There was a security sergeant sitting at a watch station tucked behind the counter against the far wall. Five screens, five recorders, and the sergeant scanning the screens every minute or so. Two cameras on each hall, middle mounted on the north sides facing toward the ends. The fifth camera was mounted near the elevators and covered the nurses station. The security officer's back was toward me, and I waited until the man looked at the center screen. I waved at the camera, the SO turned, frowned at me, smiled thinly, and waved back. His nametag revealed him to be affiliated with Clan Gomez.

I was next in line. I held out my hand and Ed checked my wrist ID, then emptied a small plastic cup into my left hand depositing there an orange and clear capsule apparently filled with little brown and orange balls. I put it in my mouth, showed tongue, picked up one of the little paper cups of water, tossed down the water at the same time tonguing the capsule into the paper cup. Crumpling the paper cup, I showed tongue and tossed the crumpled cup with its capsule into the trashcan. Ben was already looking at the next patient in line.

Wally was waiting for me, his eyebrows upraised. I nodded in response to the unspoken question, and Wally cautioned, "Don't forget to act a little sedated. You know, shuffle around, mumble, look stupid. If they suspect you're palming your medication, they'll switch you to the suppositories. You don't get to put those in."

"Ooo. Thanks, Wally. Oh, by the way, you know that girl who sits in the hall all the time?"

"Michelle. They call her Doorstop. She's in Wanda's group, but she only takes up chair space, from what I hear. She bites, but she doesn't talk at all."

"She talked to me. Twice."

Wally's bushy eyebrows went up. "No kidding."

"Honest."

"Well, then, Joe Torio, you are one hairy, chest-thumping therapy superstar."

As I passed the checkpoint back into the wing, SO Munroe narrowed his eyes, frowned at me, but said nothing. Neither did Michelle when I passed her, but I waved at her and said, "Hi."

Back in my room, I checked the records of the two nurses, Carla and Ben. Benjamin Baines graduated from Breadloaf's School of Nursing, his first job was at SRMHI, and there he was still at it three years later. Carla Figueres was a Florida State grad, Army nurse, Desert Storm veteran, and on the infirmary staff at Books prison until December a year ago. The security officer at the desk, Maxi Gomez, forty-nine, had been at Squirmhi for sixteen years. Born in L.A., moved to South River in 'Eighty-eight. Police Academy reject for physical reasons: Flat feet.

"Hey, boy?"

I looked up and Geraldine was looking through the observation port in the door. "What?"

"Boy, all us in the snake pit'd like to eat before the undertaker hauls our bones away."

"Sorry." I turned off the handheld, stuck it in my breast pocket, and opened the door. "Here I am."

"Missed you." Geraldine grinned seductively, turned abruptly, and waddled her way down the hall toward the elevator.

"Okay," I muttered to myself resignedly. "She's not Olivia de Havilland."

At breakfast, there were three orderlies and two SOs in the neighborhood as Dan's group ate in oppressed silence. I was memorizing the names of the orderlies and SOs, Thomas was eating with one hand and holding an ice pack to his swollen nose with the other. Yukiko, his raccoon eyes focused on his pancakes and syrup, ate as though he had been starved. Teddy was wincing with every movement as though every bone in his body had been fractured. Harvey couldn't stop chuckling. I looked at the staff table near the cafeteria door, and saw the red-headed floor counselor named Amber sending evil vibes in my direction. I held up my hands and mimed out an apology to no apparent effect.

The pancakes were as dry as cardboard, and Geraldine made some gross comment about used sanitary napkins and left the table early. Contemplating the juxtaposition of flapjacks and feminine hygiene, I got up and left the table as soon as I finished my grapefruit. After a wary SO escort named Keller left me on the third floor, I checked through into Turkey West and walked almost the length of it to my own room, noting that Michelle was not in her place beneath the cameras.

I looked into my room long enough to note that during breakfast my bed had been replaced, the folded sheets, pillow case, and blanket stacked on the foot of the mattress. As I made my bed I pondered that Alvin Yuker had saved my dignity, and possibly my life. The two attempts to kill me, if that's what they were, had cancelled out each other, however. Both attempts required access to staff keys. Crossed wires. Two different persons on the other side, but not working together. But why? After all, I hadn't even gotten started yet annoying anyone regarding the matter of Alvin Yuker.

From behind the doors to Half Satan came the sounds of a television. I walked to the commons, looked through the observation windows, but could see no one. The door squeaked as I pushed it open and squeaked again as I let it close behind me.

Past the double doors, the large octagonal glass-walled space was sectioned off by a number of blue movable dividers into eight areas. From the doors through the central area were tables and chairs, low shelves with stacks of puzzles and board games. Opposite the doors, suspended from the ceiling above another barrier, there was a large screen TV. It was tuned to an episode of *Ground Force* on BBC America. Whatshisface and his crew were somewhere in northern England in the midst of a driving gale attempting to turn someone's patch of dying weeds into Kew Garden.

I looked around and there was no one in the chairs. The four truncated corners of Half Satan were screened off into the group meeting areas, with Dan's group area past the TV to the right. Directly behind the TV screen was a ping-pong table. No paddles. A second ping-pong table was north, tucked in between the Dan group and Nance group areas. Opposite it, on the south side, tucked in between the Wanda group and Mark group areas, was a space with a number of overstuffed chairs gathered around an oblong shaped red maple coffee table piled with magazines.

Turning around and crossing the TV area, I entered the Dan group corner, ten empty chairs surrounding a white circular coffee table. The tissue that had been waving at me from its box's beaded cover was now motionless. The glass walls from that corner overlooked a large fenced in area with an irregularly shaped frozen pond in the middle. There were several circles of gray granite benches, the entire area dotted with budding trees and laced with asphalt paved footpaths. Far beyond the pond was a playing field set up for volleyball. One of the footpaths was just inside the high wire fence that surrounded the park. The fence was topped with triple coils of razor wire and studded with surveillance cameras.

Toward the north, above a line of trees, was Breadloaf Mountain, the thinning southern ski trails obscured by the out-of-bounds broken cliffs and trees called Idiot's Drop. I heard the TV change channels, and the sounds of Delbert McClinton singing about getting hit in the head with a Harley chain.

I looked around the edge of the screen and no one was there. *Imus In The Morning,* however, was on.

I looked into the other areas for whoever had changed the station and saw no one. Mark's group area had a portable chalkboard with the names of emotions on them: mad, sad, glad, and so on. Coffee table with a box of generic tissues, a ring of chairs. Nance's group area was the same. Wanda's group area had it's box of tissues, and was ringed above with cute, fuzzy, little stuffed animals.

Back in the TV area, the skinny wrinkled-up old dude in the fright wig, Wranglers jeans, Resistol cowboy hat, and hubcap belt buckle came on at the conclusion of the song, and went right in on an inventory of someone's character who was in the process of being banned for life from the Imus show. I sat in one of the chairs and watched. I sometimes caught the show on the radio driving to work and had only begun watching it on TV in the hospital after the Gentleman Killer takedown. Good to see a friendly face.

Laura Ingraham was about to come on. Jeff Greenfield and George Will coming up. Promised to be a great show. I glanced around and saw a heavy woman wearing blues beneath a huge, bulky gray cardigan. She was in her late thirties with long black hair, glaring blue eyes, and an expression that made her look like she had been suckled by an electric eel. I turned back to the TV.

"Where's my show? I put on the show I wanted. I was first. I just stepped out for a second to get my sweater. I want to see *Ground Force*. Put my show back on."

"Imus has some great guests coming on. Just a little longer, okay?"

"If you want to watch old Howdy Doody episodes, get a time machine."

"Look—"

"No. You, look." The woman walked up beside me, looked down her nose, and began jabbing herself in the chest. "I don't want to watch that foul-mouthed, right-wing, drugged-out, used up old disk jockey—"

"I didn't know he was a disk jockey," I said as I noted Wally enter Half Satan followed by Leila and Geraldine. The latter two sat together at the back row of chairs. I faced the woman in the gray cardigan. "Just a little bit longer. You'll like Laura Ingraham. She's really nasty—"

"You're that wop asshole cop who killed his partner, right? Torio? I saw that on TV. Your old man still stringing them up down at the prison? Killer? You got the cop body count record, right? Killer? Hey, killer?"

I felt my face getting red, but went for the high road. "Lady, why don't you just button it up, sit your big butt down, and watch the show for a couple minutes. You might enjoy it."

"Big butt?" the newcomer muttered, her own face beginning to resemble a beet. "Big butt!" she roared. *"Big butt!"*

I stood and held out my hands. "I apologize. It was a hasty com—"

Something that sounded and felt a whole lot like a metal folding chair hit the back of my head just as the skinny dude in the fright wig announced great deals to be had on something that would make my lady a hog for my log. I hit the floor, there were restraints, another shot, and it was back on the space lanes to Goofyland.

"You have been here less than twenty-four hours, Joe, and during that brief interval you've been involved in no less than two charted violent episodes." Dr. Walker frowned as he studied the file on his desk.

I slumped in the client's chair as far as my restraints would allow. What a headache.

"Do you have a Tylenol, doc? By the way, what's the matter with the drugs around this place? Everything I got is numb except my headache. And my nose. If you've got a minute and a spare finger, my nose itches."

A tiny sigh from the psychiatrist as he looked up from the file. "I thought we had an understanding. You have very real problems, Joe. If you make a sincere effort at addressing them while you are here, I believe you can do yourself a lot of good. What is your purpose here?"

"Besides getting a Tylenol and my nose scratched?" Walker waited stone-faced. "To see if I need some help, I suppose."

"Do you consider these near-riots you've caused to be some kind of help?" Dr. Walker made quotation marks with his fingers as he said "some kind of help."

"Don't do that."

"Do what?"

"Don't make quotation marks with your fingers. It makes you look like a moron. Look, Dan, I didn't cause any riot. Up in Half Satan, I was—"

"No. Don't call it that. That name is quite anti-therapeutic. Its proper name is Three West Commons."

"Yeah. Well, I guess we've each presented our punctuation and vocabulary preferences."

"Back to my question, Joe."

"I was actually trying to calm things down with that woman when someone hit me on the back of my head—with a chair, I think—which reminds me, I could still use that Tylenol."

"You consider changing the show from what Elizabeth wanted to watch to the Imus show trying to calm down things?"

"I didn't change the station. Someone else did. And Elizabeth, if that's her name, was out of the room and long gone by the time Imus was put on."

"You didn't change it back for her," Walker countered.

"What's your point?"

"I would have thought changing it to what Elizabeth wanted to watch would have been more calming."

"Your mother read you *The Giving Tree* when you were a little boy, right? If you don't mind me saying so, you've got a great future in prison as Big Bubba's best little butt-boy. I just wanted to watch this one guest. Why shouldn't I watch what I wanted to watch?"

"First, Joe, we really don't find the Imus program very suitable for our patients—"

"Not *suitable*. Are you nuts? This is an insane asylum, isn't it? If not here, where?"

The psychiatrist bristled as he leaned back in his chair. "You'll have to help me. What is the attraction to that show?"

"Attraction?"

"Why did you want to watch it?"

"Besides the guests?" I frowned. "I don't know. I usually listen to it on my car radio. Unless I get to hear that cranky old bastard in the morning, I just can't get my day started right."

"That sounds rather dependent."

"Makes more sense to me than that dead weasel you're wearing for a beard."

"We're not talking about my beard."

"I thought I was."

Dan lowered his hand. "Do you listen to a lot of radio?"

"TV, mostly. Not in the car, though. In the car I watch—listen to the radio, when my damned radio is working, but with all the damned potholes shaking—"

"What television shows do you like?" Walker interrupted.

"Old movies mostly. Cop shows. Mostly movies. SpongeBob SquarePants—"

"I beg your pardon?"

"SpongeBob SquarePants. It's like Mr. Potato Head but using a dish sponge instead of an Idaho." The silence lengthened as Dr. Walker refused to ask for an explanation. "Animated. Cartoon?" I gave up. "It is a sub aquatic life metaphor which fills the artistic chasm which opened when Rocky and Bullwinkle left the air. Barnacles? Tartar sauce?"

With a slight gesture, an imperceptibly altered expression, the psychiatrist looked down at a pad of paper on his desk. "Let's talk about what happened in the cafeteria."

"What went on was already going on when that woman on staff misunderstood my gesture."

"Amber is under the impression you were fondling her buttocks."

"Well, I was. But it was a case of mistaken identity."

Big silence. "Case of mistaken identity?" prompted Walker.

"Yeah. I thought it was a bottom I knew well. I was mistaken."

"Who did you think she was?"

"A woman friend of mine."

"By any chance, did you think she was Julia Powers?" I sat back, astonished, and not concealing it. Walker, pleased with my reaction, leaned forward and tapped the blue manila folder. "According to your record, you believe yourself to be in an exclusive relationship with Julia Powers."

"Ye-e-e-s. I'd even go so far as to say I know I am."

Enormous patronizing smile. "Now, Joe, which Julia Powers are we talking about?"

"Are you new in town, Dan? *That* Julia Powers," I answered. "Former cop, head of Hood Semiconductor, Hood Technics, hotels, shipping companies, half a dozen hospitals and EMS services in this end of the state, as well as the Sixteen Stanton Circle Detective Agency."

"You seem to know an awful lot about her."

"Did I mention she is also the love of my life?"

"This is why I wanted you in my group, Joe." Walker leaned forward, his hands clasped together, an enormous smile spreading across his face like an oil slick. "I want to help you and you promise to be a very interesting case."

"I'm in love? That makes me interesting?"

"Tell me, about your relationship."

"Like, what about it?"

"This relationship with Julia Powers. Tell me about it."

"I don't understand. You want a chronological breakdown or the full bump, poke, smooch, and tickle tour? I can sing the words to 'I Got A Woman.' I do the Ray Charles version."

Walker touched the fingertips of both hands together and played spider-doing-pushups-on-a-mirror. "Have you ever actually met Julia Powers?"

The drugs seemed to be getting worse, not better. "Is this a trick question? I worked with her on the Gentleman Killer case."

"Have you ever actually met her in person?"

"Didn't I just answer that? It's kind of tough to carry on an intimate relationship with someone you've never met."

"Joe, this place is full of men and women who have absolutely no problem at all in doing just that."

"You got me there, Dan. Okay. Yes, I have actually met Julia Powers."

"More than once?"

"Whole bunches of times."

"How did you first meet her?"

I leaned forward, reached for my nose, and was brought up short by the cuff chained to my waist. "Doc, let's lose the chains. I'm too full of drugs to attack you, and it's difficult to concentrate on your questions while my nose is being eaten off by the Red Death." Walker's eyebrows rose significantly. "The figurative Red Death."

Walker thought a moment, then got up and pulled a key ring from his pocket as he walked around his desk. "I'm going take a chance and trust you, Joe."

"That's terribly therapeutic of you, old sock." Walker paused short of unlocking the restraints. "Sorry," I said. "It's been a rough couple of days. It tends to make me a little sarcastic. What about that Tylenol?"

"I'll call up an authorization to the nurse's station." The psychiatrist unlocked both of the cuffs and the lock around my waist. He gathered up the chains, placed them on his desk, and sat next to them. When I finished writhing in ecstasy over scratching my nose, Walker said, "You were going to talk about how you met Julia."

"Julia Powers. Well, Dan, among her many accomplishments, Julia is a private investigator, undercover expert, and victim profiler. She was called in to consult on the Gentleman Killer case by Major Crimes. My partner and I were assigned to work with her."

"And you fell in love?"

I remembered my first sight of Julia's Margarita Azzurro in that commandment shattering dress. The image of her dancing at The Score as the Flower, and afterward in the shower—

"You're not going to have an orgasm right here, are you?" asked the psychiatrist, rather petulantly for a care giver, I thought.

"I don't know what you want, man. I answer your questions, but my answers don't appear to fit in with your world-plan."

"This has nothing to do with my world-plan. Did you fall in love?"

"I'm still falling."

Walker held up his hands as though gripping an invisible basketball. "Now, just for a moment, try to focus."

"I'll put my whole mind on it."

"That's what focus means."

"What a wonderful rapport we're having."

Two beats.

"Have you ever actually dated Julia Powers? By that, I mean have you and she ever gone to dinner or a show?"

"Sure." I thought a moment. "We went to shows, some terrific dancing, out to dinner together, and watched a lot of TV in bed as part of our cover."

"It was all job related?"

"Didn't have much time for it to be anything else. I met her on the job and the job ended with me in the hospital. She owns the hospital, though. We've eaten dinner together there every evening since. Breakfast, too. Watched a lot of movies."

"Have you two ever made love?"

"If you've been through my file, you know the answer to that."

"I want to hear it from you. Have you two ever made love?"

"Yes."

"I don't mean in your mind."

"Neither do I, although I do that, too. I have a rich fantasy life."

"How many times?"

I frowned. "I'm not that organized, Dan."

"Do you mean you've done it so often you can't keep track?"

"It's not that I couldn't keep track. I have a handheld computer, after all. I just didn't." I leaned forward. "I'm talking about making love, not whacking off."

"Do you masturbate?"

"Is it a club requirement?"

"Do you masturbate?" he insisted.

I burst out with a laugh and shook my head. "No, man. I'm not being judgmental if you yank the frank, understand, but I can't risk it myself."

"What do you mean you can't risk it?"

"Are you kidding? Julia Powers is in top physical condition, she's a crack shot, has black belts in at least two martial arts, she could bug the Mir space station and impersonate a hat rack if she wanted. I shudder to think what might happen to my hand if it became a rival for my affections."

Long pause as Dan drummed his fingertips on his knee, looked at my file, and nibbled at his lower lip. "What's your annual salary as a detective sergeant?"

"Sixty-two, depending on overtime. I don't think she's after my money, though."

Walker frowned, cocked his head to one side, and tossed his pen on his desk. "Do you have any idea—any idea at all—what Julia Powers is worth?"

"She's worth the universe."

A patronizing laugh at the unexpected answer. "Well, Joe, she's not worth quite that much."

"She is to me."

"I meant monetarily."

"Oh. Well, depending on market bumps and slumps, all added together she's worth about seven hundred million. Before the market went into the dumper it was closer to nine hundred."

One of Walker's eyebrows came down. "How do you know?"

"She told me."

"Why?"

"I asked."

"Why would you ask something like that?"

"I never knew anyone before who owned major industries, a detective agency, hospitals, and an art gallery who also liked me."

"Do you have any idea what it's like to a person to have her kind of wealth?"

"No. I bet you don't either."

Dan reddened up pretty good there. "What I'm getting at, Joe, is the likelihood of a such a person being attracted to someone who pulls down only a thousand and change a week."

"I got to admit, it's my first time."

"My point is that it might not have happened at all. Is it fair to say that you suffer somewhat from low self esteem?"

"That's fair."

"I'm wondering why you don't seem to have any doubts about her loving you."

"You answered your own question, Dan. Low self esteem. I can't afford to question if she loves me. If she does, there's no point, and if she doesn't, the universe ends." I studied the psychiatrist for a long moment, cast my mind back to my records search on Walker, and grinned. "Oh. I get it. You know, doctor, that third eye thing of mine does work once in awhile."

"Pardon?"

"Did you read about that in my file? The third eye?"

"Your facility at intuition. Yes, I read about it."

"My experiences with Nathan Sunday left me with a lot of doubts about it. I think I'm getting back some of my confidence."

"What are you talking about?"

"Yeah, Dan. Sorry. The old third eye is slower when it's dipped in drugs. God, she must've been a knockout. Teen Julia. I can't even imagine. And you, Dan, sat there with your buzz cut and braces hiding behind your three-ring binder, lusting from afar."

Oh, he went red. "This has *nothing* to do with me."

"When you went to school with her, did *you* ever ask her out on a date, Dan?"

"We'll have a chance to work on these things in group—assuming you don't get into any more altercations."

"You never even asked her out, did you. Rejected yourself before she ever had a chance to."

"Another episode like the last, Joe, and I'll have to think seriously about putting you on Redshank."

"Oh no," I yawned. "Anything but that."

Dan opened another file and pushed around some papers. "There's something I need to cover with you. It would've been handled yesterday, except for half of you being sedated prior to afternoon group. There is a patient here—"

"Alvin Yuker, and I am aware that you are leading me off the subject of Julia and her desperate admirer."

"For your information, Joe, to my knowledge Julia Powers didn't date anyone when we were in high school together." He studied me for a second. "Back to Alvin Yuker. I've been asking the other patients in the group what their views are on Mr. Yuker joining the group. He is a convicted multiple murderer and is here for observation prior to being tried for the murder of a

99

fourth person, a corrections officer at Books State Correctional Facility. He would be guarded, but—"

"I thought you already had put him in. You made us groupies. You can't observe him unless he's there to observe, right?"

"There are other ways besides group to conduct observation. I've been having second thoughts. There are women in the group to consider, after all."

"Are any of them red-headed street whores in their early thirties?"

"No."

"Then don't worry about the women, Dan. That's all Alvin Yuker kills, and then only if they have a certain demeanor and do certain things."

"How do you know?"

I smiled. "In between psychotic episodes, I fight crime." I raised my eyebrows. "I read the case reports."

"That corrections officer at Books was neither red-headed nor a prostitute, Joe."

"The presumption of innocence, doc. It's there for a reason. Are we done?"

Dan nodded and pressed a button. As I turned toward the door, I said, "Thanks for taking off the chains."

I opened the door and went into the hall, closing it behind me. The hall wobbled a bit then settled down. My escort, a dark-complexioned orderly named Chase, said, "Tough session, Joe?" Chase was a wiry man with an easy smile beneath a heavy black moustache.

"He took off the chains."

"As Kunta Kinte said, Joe, it's always cool to lose the links."

"Said I could have a Tylenol, too."

"A man of profound mercy."

"I think he went to school with my girlfriend. I ribbed him about it little." I frowned as a thought worked its way through the molasses. "You know, Chase, sometimes I wonder if I'm as smart as I think I am."

"Hardly any of us are," Chase answered, steadying me with one hand and pointing the way toward the elevator with the other. "The only wisdom, I say the only wisdom most folks have is their teeth —Wisdom teeth, that is."

As we rode up in the elevator, Chase chuckling at his lame Foghorn Leghorn impression, I wondered if a man with eight million dollars, a medical degree, a license to practice psychiatry, and a job running a major city institution would be involved in drug trafficking and murder. I made a mental note to check on what the market slide had done to Dan Walker's eight million.

THE DRAGONS

Shortly afterward, Group Dan met in Dan's Corner with Dan. "I apologize for intruding on your morning free-sharing session, but I just wanted to make certain each one here understands to what you have all agreed." He looked at the faces in the circle of seated patients, from Louis on his right all the way around to Alvin sitting on his left. Alvin was the only one wearing wrist restraints, and Billy was standing behind him.

"You have all stated that you preferred to have Mr. Yuker in the group, despite his record—"

"I been talkin' with Marley here," interrupted Geraldine as she poked Alvin in the ribs, "and the way I hear it, his record in the joint is spotless."

"Marley?"

"Jacob Marley," said Thomas with a smirk. "Scrooge's partner? The man in the chains?"

"His record isn't quite spotless," answered Dr. Walker, a patiently pained expression on his face.

"He hasn't been found guilty yet," said Yukiko from the chair on my immediate left. "In fact, none of us have been found guilty of anything yet."

"Actually, Moon Pie," said Teddy, raising his hand and grinning sheepishly, "I have." He let his hand fall to his lap without explanation.

Walker sat back in his chair with an overplayed expression of defeat. "Very well. All of you insist that Mr. Yuker be treated as a regular member of the group?"

Harvey interrupted the mumbled expressions of assent. "Does that include losing Marley's wrist restraints?"

The psychiatrist glanced around the circle once more and said, "Very well. Everyone who is in favor of Alvin

Yuker attending these sessions unshackled, please raise your hand."

Everyone but Thomas and Alvin raised a hand. "Opposed?" No one raised a hand. Dan faced Thomas. "Are you abstaining?"

"No, man. I just don't give a shit." Harvey and Teddy laughed.

Walker nodded at Billy and the nurse took a key from his pocket and removed Alvin's restraints, gathered up the chains, and resumed his position behind the big man. The psychiatrist appeared to struggle with a decision for a moment—again terribly overplayed—and then said, "Very well. It's your group. Do some good work this morning."

He stood, nodded at Billy, and the both of them left Dan's corner, leaving the group to ourselves. Harvey shrugged and said with a smirk, "Well done, Dragons."

"Why 'well done'?" I asked. "They all did exactly what Dan wanted them to do."

"What do you mean?"

"He knows, Harvey."

"He knows what?"

"He knows that when he pushes in one direction, you push in the opposite direction."

"You're saying he wants Marley in this group."

"Buckaroo, the man is the director of this humanitarian institution. If he didn't want Alvin in this group, he would've assigned him to another group."

Geraldine sadly shook her head. "Sherlock, you no fun at all."

After a frowning moment, Harvey raised his eyebrows. "What Walker usually has us do is introduce ourselves and say a little about the specific reasons why we're here, then open it up and wallow in self-indulgence until lunch." He looked at Alvin. "Why don't you begin?"

The big man rubbed his wrists for a moment, then looked around at the group. "My name is Alvin, I'm at Books serving a sentence of life without the possibility of parole. I've been charged with the murder of a CO at the prison. The DA's office sent me here for psychiatric observation. The purpose is to make an insanity plea impossible and line me up for a needle."

"Needle?" asked Louis.

"Lethal injection, Mad Dog," said Harvey.

"Louis."

"Are you insane?" Geraldine asked Alvin.

"Sure," he answered, causing the other members to laugh. He glanced at me. "We're all crazy, right? In my case, though, it doesn't matter because I didn't do it." He looked at Harvey. "Enough?"

"Whatever you want to put out."

Alvin looked to his left at Geraldine. She sat back in her chair and smoothed a non-existent wrinkle in her pant leg. "So, I put a few thumps on the worthless turd I live with, and got into it a bit with the officers who showed to take me in. Could've give me some slack. They know what I been through. The judge he order me in here 'cause he think I got anger management issues." She stuck out her lower lip and nodded. "Maybe I see him after I get out. Talk to him."

While she talked, my gaze was drawn to the box of tissues on the coffee table. Thanks to the miracles of modern chemistry, the tissue peeking out of the beaded box cover was waving at me again. Beaded cover. Yellow beads, blue beads, red beads, and green beads. Tan beads and brown. Organized into little posies. I tried to extract a minor memory or two from the chemical mire. Nance, Wanda, and Mark. Three areas, three coffee tables. Every group coffee table in Half Satan had a box of tissues on it. Therapy often produces tears, so why not provide schnozwad? Have a blow before you go. The box of tissues on Group Dan's coffee table, however, was the only box that had a cover. Damned ugly cover, too.

Geraldine looked at Thomas and the college student began talking about tossing his roommate out of his window, how PCP helped him study, and how much he resented Teddy suggesting that he might have a drug problem.

I stood, motioned for Thomas to continue, and picked up the box of tissues, beaded cover and all. Pulling the cover from the box, I looked inside. In one of the corners was a shiny black oblong: a D1200 miniature remote listening device. Police standard issue. I placed

105

the cover upside-down on the table, pulled my PDA, and recorded the eight-digit serial number.

As Thomas talked, I picked up the box of tissues and the cover and showed the listening device to each person in the circle ending with Louis. Geraldine motioned for me and I held out the box and cover to her. She pulled a tissue from the box and blew her nose near the cover. The individual group members, who had shown expressions ranging from dismay to outrage as they realized they had been bugged, burst out with laughter at Geraldine's blast.

I replaced the cover on the box of tissues, pulled the top sheet through, and replaced it on the table. The receiver for a D1200 was very sophisticated, but it wasn't small. If Walker had one he wasn't keeping it in his office. But there was something he did have on his desk.

I checked the glass walls, the dividers separating the group's space from the ping pong spaces on the east and south sides, the spider plant on the three-tiered white plastic shelf in the northeast corner. I got down on my hands and knees and looked beneath the coffee table. Geraldine and Yukiko, puzzled expressions on their faces, got down on either side of me. We all looked together. Attached to the underside of the table toward the center, was an unsophisticated audio monitoring device. Vintage Radio Shack baby monitor. I stuck my head under far enough to see the ID plate. Another serial number. I pulled out my PDA and wrote it down. Yukiko was frowning. Geraldine was grinning.

Harvey and Louis both came down and had a look, arising with frowns on their faces and looks at each other. Leila went down and checked, then Teddy. Thomas finished his monologue, got down, and looked for himself.

"It is simply a glorious day today," declared Harvey, pressing his hands against the small of his back as he stood. "I find it magnificent, simply superb—especially after being trapped inside all winter long. The sky is a powder blue gossamer blanket, the clouds petite tufts of frosted cotton, and the sun a dazzling golden happy face. Fellow nutballs, according to the patient's handbook, if the group agrees we are entitled to adjourn these proceedings to our ring in the Maplewood out there in Insanity Gardens." He pointed with his thumb toward the park outside.

"Isn't it still cold?" said Leila as she got up from the floor and secured her blue leather bag.

"Nippy, perhaps. Brisk. Bracing. It's nowhere near zero. Most of us have coats and all of us have blankets." Harvey smiled and held his arms open wide. "And it is such a magnificent day. I can't wait to fill my lungs with all that crisp clean air." He looked around at the others. "I really want to meet outside." He turned to Leila. "And you do, too."

"Very well."

"Then, colleagues, let us adjourn these proceedings, advance to our abodes, acquire our wraps, and I shall inquire of the sentry for an escort."

"Cool," remarked Thomas.

THE MAPLEWOOD

As we walked Insanity Path around the south end of still frozen Insanity Pond, Harvey told us the story:

"Before the South River Mental Health Institute, before the Breadloaf Ski resort, before the city of South River, a tiny spring-fed stream wound its way down the southern tip of this mountain, pausing here long enough to form this pond. The early settlers in the area noticed huge ravens frequenting the area and they named the body of water Raven Pond and the stream that fed it, Raven Stream. Then came the city followed by the establishment of the South River Normal School next to the pond.

"The Normal School supplied the city with school teachers until it burned late in the Nineteenth Century. The new teacher's college was built next to the river and renamed South River City College. Later it was moved downstream and renamed East Shore Community College, their football team still retaining the name Ravens."

"Yay, Ravens," said Louis and I in bored voices.

"Thank you, old grads. Early in the new century," Harvey continued, "when the city fathers voted to establish the city wigpicker works, the old Normal School site was deeded to the South River Home for the Insane, which was immediately renamed The Abnormal School by the first inmates. The Home was eventually renamed the South River Mental Health Institute, but Raven Pond, remained Raven Pond until, almost a century later, our Dr. Daniel Walker became the new director. He deemed the name Raven anti-therapeutic."

"Why?" asked Thomas.

109

"The possible pun with the word *raving*, you see? Dr. Walker renamed the body of water Serenity Pond, and landscaped around it this park that he named Serenity Park. The patients immediately renamed it Insanity Pond and Insanity Gardens, the main purpose of which was to get the director of the institute raven— er, raving."

We laughed at Harvey's narration, which, I noted with interest, alleviated the need for anyone to talk about anything until we were outside of our escort's hearing. He was a graying fiftyish security officer named Butcher. Danny Glover with a beer gut. Even so, he was very watchful and looked as though he could take care of himself.

The temperature was in the teens as we passed a shut-down fountain and reached the circle of curved granite benches at the north end of a group of trees a tiny sign identified as "Maplewood." After I checked all the benches, we huddled on the cold unyielding granite slabs in the same order we did in Half Satan, even to leaving an empty place between Louis and Alvin for the absent Dr. Dan. Everyone had coats except Thomas, Geraldine, and Yukiko, and they were wrapped like flood victims in navy blue blankets emblazoned with SRMHI in white. There were only buds on the maples, a crisp blue sky above, and a merciful absence of wind. The escort took South Court Path toward the volleyball court, reached a tree, leaned against it and lit up a cigarette. Butcher was outside all but screaming range, but still within sight of the circle. From where I sat, through the leafless branches of the trees, I could see the west tower of the hospital. A total of three persons on two different floors were looking back.

"Okay," said Harvey looking at me. "I'm guessing that discount crib monitor under the table back in Dan's corner is on Dan Walker, which makes him a two-faced lying son of a bitch as well as an incompetent phony. The bug in the groupwad box, though, looked like a couple of remote listening devices that SceneClean ran across when we tidied up after the OCTF raid on the Scozarri Family four years ago. And you found both of them,

Sherlock, which means you were looking for them. I'd sure like to know what's going on. Anyone else curious?"

I had everyone's attention. Leaning forward, my elbows on my knees, I glanced around the circle. "Okay. You have a right to know. I'm not really a patient here—"

"I'm here gathering research for a term paper, myself," said Thomas.

"And everyone in Books is innocent," said Teddy.

"Well, let me put it like this, Burnout," I said. "I definitely qualify to sit in this circle, but I happen to have an additional occupational agenda."

"What's that?" demanded Yukiko.

"I'm a detective, SRPD Major Crimes. I'm undercover on a case."

Louis stood, stuck the fingers of his right hand inside his coat, and said, "Thank almighty God, citizens, the empire is saved! They have come to rescue me from St. Helena. Bonaparte is free!"

Leila, sitting to his right, said, "Mad Dog, I thought you were supposed to be an English teacher."

"I'm being ironic," he said with curled lip and raised eyebrow. Louis faced me. "You're in a mental institution, Sherlock. I know a guy from Dodo East who thinks he's Elton John, and he's at least got the rhinestone glasses."

"He's got me convinced," added Harvey.

"Well, if he's Elton John, who they got doing the concerts?" asked Thomas.

Teddy leaned forward, his hands dangling between his knees. "Man, you know, it's like Lassie."

"Lassie?"

"The dog. As soon as the current dog goes deaf, dies, or starts licking her butt on camera, they run in the replacement. They got a whole platoon of Elton John clones waiting to fill in."

"Don't make no sense to run in a new one," said Geraldine. "I'd pay cash money to see the old Elton John lick his own butt."

"The point is," Louis insisted, "what case are you talking about, Sherlock? Who are you after?"

"I can't say too much about it—"

"Ongoing investigation," interrupted Alvin.

"Blah, blah, blah," added Harvey.

111

"Do you want to hear this or not?"

"We want to hear, dear," said Leila with a warm smile. "I think what Marley and Buckaroo meant is that we would prefer you to skip the bullshit. You don't have to worry about us keeping your secrets. Even if we don't confuse them with our own fantasies and delusions, no one believes us, anyway. Mad Dog has been talking about a police spy ever since he got here."

"And!" Louis countered, holding his hand out toward me. *"And!"*

Geraldine cackled, reached over, and slapped Thomas's knee. Thomas leaned toward me. "Want to trade places?" he asked.

"Did you recently rush into a burning building and rescue me and my goldfish?"

"No.

"Sorry." I checked to see if Butcher was still holding up that tree. He was. "Okay. It is probable that, to cover up a very profitable drug operation at Books prison, a CO there, Katey Sloan, was murdered." I nodded toward Alvin. "We think Marley is being framed for that murder. To do what we think the conspirators—"

"Yes!" said Thomas. "I knew it! Conspiracy!"

"—Steady, Sunshine. To carry it off," I continued, "they needed staff personnel at Books and in one or more city police divisions. It may involve the State Police and the staffs of one or more hospitals in the city, especially this one."

"Why especially this hospital?" asked Harvey.

"This is where I was sent," interjected Alvin. "Sherlock here thinks that the frame would fit on me a whole lot tighter if I was dead."

Harvey nodded. "It spares them all those embarrassing answers under cross examination."

Louis nodded. "Points the finger away from the COs at Books."

"We have no idea how big this is or who we can trust," I said. "It's liable to be dangerous, and I don't want any of you to get in the way." I described the unsafe way I had been restrained the night before and my late night visitor.

"So, where do we fit in?" asked Harvey.

"You don't. I don't want anyone getting hurt. More than that, the investigation will be time consuming. That's time I don't want to take away from your efforts to get better." I glanced around at the faces. "If that's why you're here."

"Nobody gets better here," said Harvey. "At Squirmhi, if you can't cure yourself, you're doomed."

Nodding at Geraldine, Teddy, and Thomas, Yukiko said, "The four of us are just here under court-ordered observation. Burnout hasn't learned anything new since Nineteen eighty-seven, Sunshine hasn't figured out yet he's an addict, Sister needs to get on with her life, and I just need people to brush and floss before they open their mouths."

"As for me," said Harvey, "if getting better means going out there and choosing between starvation and scraping brains off walls, I'm set right where I am." He looked at Louis and Louis looked at me.

"What about Valjean, policeman?" demanded Louis.

"Who?"

"Don't be coy. Jean Valjean. The gendarmes have chased him relentlessly for years." The man seemed to be growing a French accent as he spoke. "How does he figure into your plans, policeman?"

"I'm in Major Crimes. Jean Valjean was up for a shoplifting beef, wasn't he?"

"He stole a loaf of bread!"

"It's not my case."

"Well," said Harvey as he placed a hand upon each knee, "isn't it nice when everyone is in agreement." He looked at Leila who was rolling Teddy with a fresh sheet. "That leaves you, Dusty. What do you think?"

"Oh," she said waving a dismissive hand. "Catching a murderer sounds much more interesting than anything I had planned."

I held out my hands. "We aren't trying to catch a murderer, guys—"

"Is Dan Baby one of your bad guys?" asked Teddy.

I thought for a long moment. "I don't know."

"What's your hunch?" asked Geraldine.

I frowned at her for a beat. "My hunch is that Walker's okay, but—"

"If Dan's okay," began Thomas, "why does he have us bugged? Isn't it to listen in on what Marley says? Try and get him saying something incriminating?"

"That unit beneath the table goes with the receiver I saw in Dan's office. Why he does it, I think, is because he really doesn't trust his own theories about patients being able to be major contributors to their own recoveries."

"I told you not to read the patient handbook," chided Harvey.

"Who's listening in on the other bug, Sherlock?" asked Yukiko. "The one in the tissue box."

"I don't know. Whoever it is, they have access to top police equipment. I'll bet the bug in the nose blow wasn't there day before yesterday, though. Somewhere within two hundred meters of that bug is a receiver and voice activated recorder."

"Two hundred meters," repeated Louis. "That could put it anywhere in the building or on the south side of the wire."

"That's true."

"Everybody's had a say in this but me," said Alvin. "Do I have a say?"

"Absolutely," answered Harvey. "You are a full member of this group, Marley. Voted in and everything." He glanced at me. "Even if we were manipulated into it."

The big man nodded. "Okay. You people don't know what you're getting into. The ones Joe's been talking about aren't fooling around. They already killed one of their own to save themselves. They want to kill me and it looks like they don't mind taking out a cop along the way. They won't think twice about whacking a couple of nutballs if they think you threaten them. I don't want anybody getting hurt on my account."

"We are adults, Marley," said Leila, "and if we aren't entirely responsible or dependable, we can certainly be stubborn." She held her lint roller out at Harvey.

"Say what you will, we do have that," Harvey said, facing me. "Okay, what's next?"

"If we continue to meet here, I'm guessing this area will be covered by one or more listening devices."

"We can find them, can't we?" asked Thomas.

"If we become obvious hunting down and destroying listening devices, the other side will know we're onto them. That might push them into doing something more extreme. Better we should not let them know. That way we can feed them whatever we want in the way of false information mixed in with our regular therapeutic sharing."

"Cool," said Thomas.

"Definitely cool," agreed Teddy. His eyes, though, didn't think it was so cool.

"If we need to talk without being listened in on, though, what do we do?" Geraldine asked Harvey.

"It's right there in the patient handbook, Sister: Walking sessions. By group agreement, the Dragons can conduct our sessions on the hoof." Harvey pointed and swept his arm around indicating the path that ran just inside the fence. "Boundary Path. We call it the Deadline. There are lots of TV cameras, but no audio pickups. Other paths, too, but those go near other group areas." He looked at me. "What about that?"

"Good. The equipment that would have to be used to pick up what we say on the move is a lot harder to conceal."

"So," said Leila to Alvin, "while we can still sit down and listen, Marley, tell us your story."

Alvin told what he knew from Gilbert Kane's overdose and the drug scene at Books to Teddy playing "Riot In Cell Block #9." After he was done, we settled the next important issue. It was agreed: Dan's Dragons would lip-sync the old Coasters' tune for the Turkey Talent Show. Geraldine would take the lead.

After the session, as we walked Insanity Path around the pond back to the main building for lunch, Harvey came up behind me. "Sherlock, I have a question."

Alvin was thirty feet back on the path talking with Thomas, SO Butcher keeping an eye on Alvin. "What's your question?"

"I'm a bit confused. You have this big top-secret undercover investigation going on and you just spilled your guts to two druggies, four psychos, and a serial killer. Is this a security problem or what?"

"I got a head full of drugs with a judgment to match."
I shrugged. "To tell you the truth, I'm not convinced
we're in any danger. The so-called attempts on my life
could be explained as simple carelessness. The real
investigation should be going on over at Books. That's
where all the hot leads are. The South River Barracks of
the State Police have all the plays in this match."

"Rigged game, though, right?"

"Right."

"Joe, did you see those three persons watching us
from the West Tower?"

"Yeah. Did you recognize them?"

"I couldn't make out their faces, but white-long,
white-short, and gray. One was a doctor, one was an
orderly, and one was maintenance."

As we reached the doors back into the building,
Harvey stopped and rubbed the back of his neck as he
looked around. "Sherlock, I wouldn't be too quick to
dismiss the possible attempts on your life. When they
lock the floor down at night, all the patient doors lock
automatically and automatically unlock in the morning
from the security desk in back of the nurses station. Any
exceptions have to be done individually at the door with
a key. Understand?"

"Yes."

"And those soft cuffs. They're sterilized between uses
and sealed in plastic packaging while they're on the shelf.
Two wrist cuffs, two ankle cuffs in the same package.
Either your ankle cuffs left with whoever strapped you
down, or someone else got into your room and removed
them while you were dopered out. Neither thing
happened by accident."

"Troubling."

"Not half as troubling as this: Your gut feeling is that
Dan Walker is okay, right?"

"Right."

"My gut feeling is that your gut feeling is dead
wrong."

A GOOD ONE

After an uneventful lunch, the entire group under the watchful eyes of three orderlies, I took my expansion chip from my dressing, put it in my pocket, and reported to the third floor nurses station for vitals. I spit my meds into a cup, tossed it, and then Carla took me behind the counter and toward a door past the watch sergeant's station. While she pulled a key ring and searched for the proper key, I noted the row of switches next to the small safe beneath the bank of surveillance screens. Key operated electrically controlled door locks for both wings. There was a sound activated audio recorder that was labeled as recording all telephone calls on the floor, including the patient phones in Half Satan. The watch sergeant had a hands free earpiece and mike and was listening to something through the unit. One of the phone recorders was recording. I looked at the recorders for the security cameras. The LED indicators showed that only three of the five recorders were loaded, both of the East Wing units and the one covering the nurses station. I looked down at Sgt. Gomez: James Woods with a thick black moustache. "Don't those recorders work better when they're loaded?"

Gomez looked up from some papers at me, then nodded at the bank of recorders. "Old equipment. The lights don't work."

I reached out a finger and poked the eject button for one of the recorders claiming to have no tape. Nothing happened. "Bad switch, too, sergeant."

"Don't do that."

"Sorry."

Carla opened the treatment room. Inside the blue and white space, Carla had me pull down the top of my

117

blues and take off my dark blue tee shirt. After removing the dressing and rechecking my record, she said, "It's time to lose the stitches, cop."

"You anti cop, Carla?"

"No. I transferred here from Books about a year ago and that's what cops are called over there—when they're being nice. It's just a name. Hop up on the table. Cop." She grinned slyly.

I moved to the examination table, stepped up, turned, and sat. "What are they calling the COs at Books these days?"

"Keys, covers, grays, Hersheys—"

"Hersheys?"

She smiled as she went to a cabinet and unlocked it. "CO plus CO makes cocoa."

"Got it. Did you know that CO who was murdered?"

"Katey Sloan." Carla shook her head as she opened the cabinet and removed a tray covered by a sterile towel. "I just knew her to talk to on the phone when she was checking up on an inmate she'd sent over to the infirmary. She had a rep among those in segregation, though, for being fair and honest—a stickler for following the rules. One of the cons being treated made a crack about her. He said Katey Sloan was the only person inside who believed in justice. He thought she was a fool. She sounded like a good one."

"How come you made the move here, Carla?"

She shrugged and raised her big black eyebrows. "Philosophical differences. Too many folks over there belong here or in other kinds of hospitals. Inmates and staff both. I like it better working with nutballs who're getting a chance to get better. Like you."

"Is Alvin Yuker one of the folks at Books you're talking about? Who ought to be over here permanently?"

"Are you in Alvin's group?"

"Yes."

"Two things, cop: First, whatever is said in group is not to be repeated outside of group; Second, I don't gossip with anyone about patients here. Especially not with other patients."

"What about Dr. Walker?"

"What about him?"

"Is he okay to gossip about? Do you like him? Is he helping people to get better or is he simply filling a chair?

"You are one big heap of questions, Joe. Must be an occupational thing." She took a few snips with something that looked like cuticle clippers, a few tugs, and it was done, the area cleaned, and a new dressing applied. "This dressing is mainly to keep the occasional leak from a removed stitch staining your clothes. Check it tonight and if you haven't had any spotting you can toss the dressing."

"Thanks. I've had stitches removed a few times—"

"I noticed. Your body looks like a battlefield."

"I'll bring all my future stitch removals to you." I put on my tee shirt.

"Better you should focus on not getting shot and stabbed so much."

"You never said what you thought of Dr. Walker, Carla."

"Noticed that, did you? Get out of here, cop, or you'll be late for afternoon group."

On my way out, I noted the lights on the surveillance recorders. All of them indicated that they were loaded and recording. Sgt. Gomez was not at his station.

Dan's group met in Half Satan. With the listening devices in mind, we played catch with a ball of paper as each shared incredibly personal, revealing, astonishing, and otherwise fictional episodes from our lives. When everyone ran out of material, we went over the lines, singing "Riot In Cell Block #9." When someone from Wanda's group came over to complain about the noise, we took a vote, called an end to the session, and returned to our rooms. In my room, I pulled the orange chair around until it was facing the window. I sat, put my feet up on the windowsill, put the expansion chip in my handheld and called up the murder book on CO Katey Sloan.

Born Katey Lanza in San Jose in 'Seventy-five, her family moved to South River in 'Eighty. Graduated with honors from Roosevelt High in 'Ninety-two. Ditto from East Shore Community College (Yay, Ravens) in 'Ninety-six. Same year Katey Lanza entered the State Corrections Officers Training Academy on Fortieth, next to Books.

Interesting tidbit: While at SCOTA, an instructor, Lt. Adam Stover, entered her room one night and next morning Katey Sloan filed a sexual harassment suit. Suit later withdrawn. She graduated fourth out of a class of sixty. Assigned to Books State Correctional, general residence tier unit, rookie shift, eleven to seven. Excellent performance reviews.

I put in a search, and Lt. Adam Stover resigned from the State DOC two months after Sloan withdrew her lawsuit. "Where are they now?" I made a mental note to find out. Back to the Sloan murder book:

In 'Ninety-seven Katey Lanza married Charles Sloan, a uniformed police officer out of Breadloaf-North Valley Division, three years her senior. Later that same year their daughter Penny was born, followed by the birth of their son, Ricky, a year later. Katey and her husband worked different shifts with Katey's mother filling in as babysitter when overtime called. Down payment on a fixer upper in North Valley, four acres with a view of Breadloaf.

Katey's older sister, Anna Lanza, uniform on the job out of Lassiter Division, on the subject of her sister: "Katey was strong willed, independent, and she had a rock-hard sense of right and wrong." Lots of examples. For instance, she went against the General Population Commander, CO Lt. Robert Wynne, regarding the punishment of an inmate, bank robber Jahir Kamali. Jahir had been tossed in the hole for defending himself from an attack initiated by a shank-wielding Aryan brother named Nevin Connelly. The case was reviewed, Wynne was overruled, Kamali was sprung from solitary and transferred to Rougemont. "I bet Wynne liked that," I muttered. Three days later Katey Sloan requested a transfer out of Wynne's command.

Katey Sloan was assigned to CO Lt. Toshiro Kendo, commander of 'C' Block, protective segregation. She was dropped into the three to eleven shift. A year later, child rapist and murderer Gilbert Kane died of a drug overdose while in his cell. Supt. Cotton demanded answers and Katey Sloan resolved to find them. A message to Supt. Cotton on her findings a few weeks later, then zippo: transfer off "C" Block into Recreation. Only two persons at Books could move her around like that: Supt. Cotton himself and the yard captain, George Candy. Maybe one more with a little paper magic: Cotton's secretary, April Hayes.

Katey's mother, Eve Lanza, on the subject of her daughter: "A wonderful wife and mother. She could find the good in anyone and would go to any lengths to help them become the best that they could be." Heaps of examples. For instance, working on her own with the wives and children of inmates to try and keep families together while their perps did time. After her transfer to "C" Block, she became an advocate to put sex offenders in facility therapy programs, and a pain in the butt to sex offenders who were reluctant to participate, nagging them into treatment. Interesting statistic: one hundred percent of the "C" Block pervs were participating in treatment programs a matter of weeks after Sloan was assigned there. Usual pre-Sloan participation: thirty to thirty-five percent.

Katey's husband, Charles, on the subject of his life mate and the mother of his children: "She was the best." No examples. No transcript of his interview, no notes. I paged through the file to see which State Police detectives were taking responsibility for the investigation. Enrikos Marcilki and Lucy Jones. I didn't know the names, which meant they weren't out of South River Barracks. Since the prison was in South River, why did State Fuzz Command decide that it needed out-of-towners to work the case?

April seventeenth Katey punched in shortly before nine for roll call for her nine to five shift in Arts & Crafts. Before beginning her shift, she left a message with Supt. Cotton's secretary that she had something to report concerning the facility's investigation into drugs and the death of Gilbert Kane. Shortly after ten, Katey received a note from Supt. Cotton to report to his office at three.

After one o'clock, she was in a hall next to the CO assembly area, talking with two other COs, Lois Castro and Thomas Liang, when the phone next to them rang.

CO Castro answered the phone, and handed it to Katey Sloan. "Katey. For you," she said.

In the interview, Castro and Liang said they didn't know who called, but that Katey turned away from them to keep her conversation private. When she hung up she left, not saying where she was going, but saying, "There's something I have to take care of." She seemed angry. "I'm putting an end to this right here and now." She "stormed off."

3:00 PM. Katey Sloan didn't show for her appointment with Supt. Cotton.

5:00 PM. At the regular evening roll call for officers, the Recreation Department Supervisor, Caroline Yotimo, reported Katey Sloan absent. The entire facility immediately went into emergency lockdown, all prisoners confined to their cells. The COs and maintenance personnel combed the prison, going through all of the cellblocks, offices, work, and recreation areas. No sign of her.

"Blah, blah, blah, nobody saw nuttin'," I muttered. "And the next morning, old Gully finds her out at the landfill with enough signs to point to Alvin Yuker and enough additional signs to point at a frame."

I shut down the handheld and put it back in my pocket, stood, and looked down upon distant Books prison. Many journalists who delighted in wringing their hands over "the blue wall" and police cover ups didn't even know about "the fort." I knew about it from Pop and my grandfather and his friends back when Gaspare DeBello was Yard Captain. There were always the old stories, incorrigible cons who died under mysterious circumstances, no CO short an air-tight alibi. This time, though, how much was CO solidarity and how much was culpability? If they truly believed that Alvin Yuker killed Katey Sloan, there wouldn't be any reason to boil up a bogus murder book, and the murder book I had just scanned had more holes in it than Sonny Corleone.

There was a sharp knock on the door, I looked around to see Harvey lean in. "What's up, Buckaroo?"

"Someone to see you, Sherlock. The park's open for visitors, so you can see him there, if you want. It's your father. The hangman? Kind of like death calling, isn't it?"

122

"Not really. Pop runs a landscaping business. All he plants now are grass, flowers, shrubs, and trees."

"Well, sure. Now that he's finished fertilizing the ground."

DEADLINE

Pop and I slowly walked clockwise around the Deadline. He was on my left, wearing tan slacks and a heavy brown fleece shirt that made him look like a bear. He had on his Yankees cap and his voice automatically lowered each time we approached one of the fence-mounted surveillance cameras.

"All those names you talk about, Joe. The ones at Books?"

"Don't forget Katey Sloan's husband. Charles Sloan is out of Breadloaf-North Valley. That's where Yuker was arrested. The evidence would've been moved to the Tower for the trial, Pop, and filed away afterward. Breadloaf/North Valley cops wouldn't have any trouble gaining access, though."

"Detectives," reminded the hangman. "This Sloan is a uniform. Even so, Joe, you think he would be part of killing his own wife?"

"Man kills wife for money? We've never run into that before." I looked at my father's face. That strong jaw, salt-and-pepper hair, he was what Gary Cooper would've looked like if he'd only been five foot eight and fed good pasta. "Sorry. I'm a little frustrated."

"What's the trouble, Joe?"

"All the people I need to get close to in order to get a reading on them are someplace else." I pulled my left hand from my jacket pocket and put it on Pop's shoulder. "Remember the Fort?"

The hangman's eyebrows went up. "Sure. Step outside the wall, say the wrong word, next time a con take a run at you with something sharp, you all by yourself."

"Katey Sloan was definitely outside the wall, Pop. Careers were at stake. Years behind bars. Police house, too. With enough pressure on him, Charles Sloan might even have convinced himself that Yuker did his wife, and to just shut up about anything else that might confuse things. With enough pressure, he might even be an accessory. Maybe he even set her up."

"You think Katey talked to her husband about the job? About her investigation?"

"Sure. The way she was being dumped on and moved around from shift to shift, she'd have to. And my famous third eye is wondering if her husband was pressured to get her off her investigation. Maybe he actually tried. I'd really like to put his toes in the coals and find out how their marriage was going."

"She wouldn't back off and you think the other side took matters into their own hands?"

"Swami has spoke."

After another few steps, the hangman looked at me. "If he was an accessory, Joe, then Charles Sloan knows who killed his wife."

"Either who killed her, Pop, or he knows someone who does know. If I do manage to get something going here, I'm kind of curious who Breadloaf/North Valley Detectives will send to look into it. I already think I know he won't be working for my side."

Past the turn off to Maplewood, the Deadline followed the fence north, the late afternoon sun blocked by the tall pines west of the perimeter road on the opposite side of the fence. Chilly in the shade. At least two of the strategically placed security officers were visible from our present position. One SO was farther ahead, near the west path to the volleyball court, the other just north of the Maplewood grabbing a smoke. On the court, patients were playing the hospital staff to an audience of family members, orderlies, and security officers.

"There's a bench up ahead, Joe. Let's sit. Al gave me one of those handheld things so you can beam over your notes."

"You play any of the games yet?"

"Games? This little thing has games?"

In the center of a group of four irregularly placed oaks, directly across the path from a surveillance camera that was pointed at it, was a granite bench about thirty feet away. As we approached the bench, I said, "Drop something, Pop."

The hangman paused a second, then dropped a white envelope he took from his shirt pocket. I squatted to pick it up. "I'll get it, Pop."

While I was down, I did a quick scan beneath the granite bench. As I stood, I handed the envelope back to Pop. We sat with our backs toward the fence. The hangman stuck the envelope back in his shirt pocket. "What's that about, Joe?"

"It's April. Bugs are starting to come out. This bench is clear."

"Too early for bugs, Joe."

"Bugs, Pop." I pointed at my own ear. *"Bugs."*

"Oh."

I pulled out my handheld and nodded at Pop. "Let's have it."

The hangman balanced his handheld on his thigh, and I had my own handheld aimed at his, beaming over the document containing my notes. "I hope this thing doesn't fry my balls," said Pop.

"I haven't heard of anything like that happening."

"They said radar guns were safe, too, Joe. Now nursing homes are full of old cops dribbling oatmeal down their bibs."

"What do you care if your balls get fried, Pop? Are you and Caitlyn planning on a little bambino? Am I finally going to get that kid brother?"

"We a little old for that. I just don't like fried balls — if they're mine."

"I can understand that."

The hangman nodded at my handheld. "Isn't your charge getting low?"

"A little. I'll plug it in tonight. What about you two getting married, Pop? You set a date yet?"

"Not yet."

"What's your excuse for not getting married this time?"

"You in the hospital, Joe."

"I'm undercover. This is the job."

In the distance, three ravens were sailing the currents just north of the pond, the building blinding peach-white in the afternoon rays.

"What is it, Joe?"

I nodded toward my handheld. "I've got the employment records on these names, Pop, but nothing on them as men and women. If I can't see these folks in person, I need more information." I glanced at him. "Of course, I suppose Dock has the rest of the unit working the other angles. Right?"

"The way Al explained it to me, Joe, the only job you got is to 'put a vibe on Alvin Yuker and a scare on whoever's watching him.' You leave Winnie Hewitt to run down the leads at Books and the other places. You sure Yuker didn't kill Katey Sloan?"

"I don't think he did, but not because of anything I've gotten from him. Yuker is not exactly into self-analysis. Reminds me a lot of Kieff —Nathan Sunday. He's so far removed from his feelings they could be in another person."

"Then why?"

"Bunch of little things. The fact that he's here when he's not going for a mental defect defense—it would solve so many problems for so many persons if Yuker conveniently died here. There are a couple of faces that seem to ring bells. I don't really know."

"Third eye."

"Yeah. What is it, Pop?"

The hangman's unit beeped, he closed it down, and put it back in his pocket. "Joe, I been thinking."

"About?"

"You know, Gaspare, your grandfather. He was Yard Captain at Books. Me, your father, I was a CO at Books. You, my son, are a city police detective." I remained motionless, my eyebrows raised.

"And?"

"Something I notice first back in the 'Sixties when I was a CO."

"What's that, Pop, besides we seem to be in a rut working for the government."

"That's it, Joe. Jobs go in families. Law enforcement, medicine, plumbing, lawyers." He tapped my handheld, now in the breast pocket of my blues. "You must have four or five thousand names in there, Joe, hospital, city, and state employees. Maybe you can high-grade them some by finding out friends, relatives. I bet you find medical personnel at Books with relatives or close friends in police substations, hospitals, clinics, doctors offices around the city."

I was stunned. What a great idea. "Yeah. COs, cops, private investigators, private security. Ward Staples has an uncle in Vadalia Detectives. His brother Harry is a PI. I think his mother was an ADA." I pointed at the hangman's handheld. "Have Dock bring all that to Claire Turner. She's our records Kahuna. If anyone can draw the lines between the right folks, she can. Wait a minute." I fired up my handheld, called up the SRPD personnel records and indexed to Sloan. "Four Sloans on the job with the department." I called up the records at Books. "Another Sloan, besides Katey." I put in a search through the entire hospital records in the city. "Three more Sloans, and that doesn't count relatives of Sloans who go by other names."

"Cousins, school mates, friends," added Pop.

"Yeah. Have Claire do it. I should've thought of it myself, but I'm still detoxing from the cocktails they keep whipping on me." I studied my father for a moment. His gaze was down, his hands nervously fingering the handheld Dock had given him. "Pop, you look very weird. What's going on?"

The hangman studied me for a moment then placed a heavy hand on my knee and squeezed. "This place. I never thought to see you here."

"Hey, Pop, I'm under cover."

"The way it was explained to me, Joe, the only reason your cover works is because your problems are real. Are they real, Joe? Do you need to get out of this? Out of police work?"

"Don't start on me, Pop."

"I'm worried, that's all."

"Pop, you have been worried about me being on the force since I entered the Police Academy thirteen— fourteen years ago."

"And since then you been shot four, five times, stabbed twice, you died, and now you locked up with a bunch of maniacs where maybe the staff belongs to the bad guys, too."

"I never said there wasn't a down side."

He raised an eyebrow. "You make contact with Julia yet?"

"What do you know about that?"

"I asked and she told me she was looking out for you. Said she'd be here. I'm your father. I love you. Sue me."

"My solicitors will get in touch."

"You make contact yet?" Pop insisted.

"I think I know who she is, but I'm not sure. I mean I'm sure she's here. I'm just not sure where." I held up a hand, then let it fall to my lap. "You got anything for me? From Dock?"

"Yes." Pop reached into the pocket of his fleece shirt and handed the envelope to me. "It's already been examined by security here." I opened it, and inside was a lumpy get well card that showed a scene from Dante's Inferno: naked, dismembered disemboweled bodies writhing in eternal agony. I opened it. Inside it said, "The joy is in the journey." The lump in the card was one of those tinny little players triggered by the opening of the card. This one played the music from Fats Domino's "I'm Walkin'." It was signed from Caitlyn, the hangman's prospective bride, my prospective stepmother. As I pried up the pasteboard revealing the tiny player, I saw next to it an expansion card.

"Do you know what's on it, Pop?"

"MCU finally finished scanning it all in, Joe." Pop nodded toward the get well card. "That's all of Nathan Sunday's writings."

I frowned. "I don't get it. Why?"

"Al didn't say."

"This doesn't have anything to do with what we're working on." I nibbled at the inside of my lower lip as I looked at the end of the main building, up at the fenced in open air patio that Redshank had instead of a commons. I thought of Alvin and the human doorstop.

"What is it, Joe?"

"I'm wrong." I tapped the card against my knee. "This has everything to do with why I'm here." I put the get well card into the envelope and the envelope into my jacket pocket. "Two more things, Pop: The director here, Dan Walker. I need Claire to run a full financial breakdown on him. How did the recession hit him? What are his liabilities? Does he need money? If so, how much, and who does he owe it to? The other thing, we have a patient here named Teddy—Theo or Theodore, I suppose. He said something that made me think he might have some connection to one of the crime families—"

"Blond kid, tall, skinny? A junky?"

"That's right."

Pop nodded. "Teddy Toledano. Red Toledano's youngest son. Remember Red?"

"Pop, I was still in high school when Red Toledano caught it. Scozarri family, right?"

"Red was capo back in the sixties. He married one of Don Scozarri's nieces and everybody thought he'd take over the family when the don got what's coming to him." The hangman snorted out a little laugh. "But Red got what was coming to him, first. Teddy was maybe nine or ten when the Battaglias gunned down his father in the Zone. Last I heard, Teddy was living on the street. Always felt sorry for the kid. Maybe he get some help here, huh?"

"Anything's possible."

A chunky-looking man in a gray suit and yellow-and-black striped tie was crossing the grass toward us. He was brown-haired and brown eyed, sort of a fat Charlie Sheen. Behind him walked the John Carradine look-alike orderly named Neal Miller. The orderly pointed in my direction, said something unintelligible to the suit, then turned around and headed back toward the main building, leaving the man in the bumblebee tie looking somewhat lost and nervous.

"Det. Torio?" he called out.

"Yeah?"

"I'm your delegate." He stopped in front of us. "I'm Det. Oran Connor. Homicide. I'm your PBA delegate."

I raised my eyebrows. "The election was six months ago."

"I'm here to talk to you about your medical insurance."

Pop sprang to his feet. "Well, Joe, gotta go. I'll say hi to Al and Caitlyn. Love you. Bye." He bent over, kissed my cheek, patted Det. Connor on the arm, and boogied on down the Deadline, apparently racing Neal back to the main building.

"I'm sorry if I interrupted," said Connor.

"Occupational thing."

"Excuse me?"

"Hangmen never go in for long goodbyes." I pulled the handle on an imaginary trapdoor by way of explanation.

The man frowned as he pulled a wad of insurance papers out of his briefcase. Before he opened his mouth, I could feel my eyes glazing over. Then he opened his mouth. Det. Connor's voice droned on as he explained the provisions of my health coverage, disability insurance, and the rest. After twenty minutes, he began to run down. "Accordingly, the insurance covers just about everything, so don't worry about any of that. And, in the event you have to stay—"

I gave Connor the Stare of Death.

"Bad choice of words. I know you won't have to stay, Joe —can I call you Joe?—Just in case you have to stay, though, your disability benefit will continue until you, uh, die or go back on full duty."

"Joe DiMaggio Torio: Flush in the cracker factory," I remarked.

"What?"

"My coverage will take care of putting my kids through college?"

Confused, Connor looked down at the file on his lap. "I—I wasn't aware you had any children."

"You know, I don't think I do, Oran. I guess I better get cracking, huh? —there's that cracker thing again. Why do you suppose cracker came to mean crazy?"

"I don't know."

"Got it from cracked pot, I bet. A broken head thing."

After staring at me for a split second, Connor put the folder back into his briefcase, placed a brotherly hand upon my shoulder, and said, "Look, there's one more thing—why I came here, really. This insurance stuff is all taken care of. But, there's a little grumbling out there. I suppose you expected that."

"Grumbling."

"I just want you to know there aren't any hard feelings about —you know."

"What?"

"You know. About your partner, Kieffer. About shooting him. Among the cops—"

I sat back wide-eyed, held out my hands, and shook my head. "Man! Whoa! —did you see that? Did you *see* that?"

"See what?"

"Didn't you see that big bag of bullshit fly by my head? Just missed me. Four or five tons if it was an ounce. Damn near broke the sound barrier. With that muzzle velocity it'll probably land out in West Shore. Someone ought to call nine-one-one. The children! My god, the children!"

"What—what are you talking about?"

"Did I vote for you?"

"Beg pardon?"

"When you ran for delegate, Oran, did I vote for you?"

"How would I know?"

"I think I did. My god, I really am in the right place. Talk about delusional. I must've been outside my mind." I leaned forward and fixed Connor with a wild-eyed stare. "It's like going to Fannie Farmer's for an Overeaters Anonymous meeting."

"What—"

"Oran, you are a horse's ass—no reflection on the horse—and you are the biggest argument against organized labor since Jimmy Hoffa."

Connor stood, red faced. "Kieffer was a brother police officer, Torio! Some of us don't feel a lot safer now that there's one less cop on the streets."

"Let it out. Let it all out, Oran. It's okay."

Resuming his seat, Connor lowered his voice, and in a tone of confidentiality said, "You've been around, Torio. You know the score. You want to know how to get this cop-killer stink off you?"

"Even though the cop isn't killed and there's no hard feelings."

"Do you want to know or not?"

"How, Oran? Should I rub tomato juice into my fur?"

"You know this inmate you got here? The one who killed that CO over at Books?"

I blinked my eyes a few times as I mentally shifted gears. He really had surprised me that time. "Alvin Yuker."

"Look, Torio—Joe. We know you're in the same group as Yuker."

"We?"

"I know a few people and they'd be real interested in anything Yuker might happen to say in conversations or in those group meetings. Whatever. Get my drift?" He pulled a small black pocket tape recorder from his jacket and placed it on the bench.

"Who?"

Connor frowned. "What d' you mean, who?"

I picked up the tape recorder, punched the record button, and held it up in front of Connor's face. "Det. Oran Connor, just who is it who is interested in having me, Joseph Paul DiMaggio Torio, record Alvin Yuker's confidential therapy sessions? Why do they want me to do this? What are they prepared to do for me if I cooperate? Reinstatement? Money? Promotion? I'd like the names. Please speak clearly into the microphone."

Conner reached for the tape recorder but I moved my hand out of Connors's reach. "I can't discuss anything, and I have no idea what you're talking about. Give—"

"Connor, you are an alien from outer space, aren't you?" I waved the tape recorder in Connor's face. *"Klatu barada nikto."*

"What?"

"And me without my Reynolds Wrap." I poked Connor's chest with the recorder. "Kieffer's name isn't Kieffer, you moron. His name is Nathan Sunday. Nathan

Sunday is a serial killer. He killed at least five men and women by sticking ice picks in their heads and stirring their brains. He killed at least a dozen more by shooting their hearts full of holes, then he cut 'em up and collated the pieces. As a matter of record, he filled me full of bullet holes and stuck a six-inch blade in my right lung. Does that sound like the blue wall to you?"

"Nothing's been proved in court, Torio, and until that happens, all some people know is you took down a cop. All some other people know is they don't want Katey Smith's killer to get away with it."

"Sloan."

"What?"

"Her name was Sloan, not Smith. And I told Dan Walker that absolute assholes were rare. Well, that just goes to show you everyone can make a mistake."

Connor shrugged, his head cocked to one side. "Look, Torio, like I said, no hard feelings—"

"I can't tell you what a relief that is."

"—If you'll only cooperate on this Yuker thing, we—" He eyed the tape recorder, still recording, and froze.

I suddenly looked at the ravens above the pond. The original three had been joined by a fourth. "Look at those birds. What a life. Sailing around this beautiful mountain focused on looking for something dead and rotten to eat. You want to know something absolutely delicious about my present situation, Oran?"

"Delicious?"

"Something a fellow named Leroy Brown once taught me. I've been thinking about Leroy a lot lately. I ever tell you about Leroy? I suppose not, this being the first time I can recall ever clapping eyes on you, which makes me, again, wonder why I voted for you. I'll never take the right to vote for granted again. Democracy. What a trap for the lazy. Do you think the PBA ought to be privatized?"

"What in—"

"Leroy was a street fighter, Oran," I continued. "Did time for killing a man with his fists. My old man hanged his old man. Pop did such a good job, in return Leroy taught me a few tricks, like how to reach over and in less than a second double chop the bridge and underside of your nose filling your frontal lobes full of bone splinters. It'd kill you instantly, and right now I'm a maniac being held on a violent floor under close observation for chronic paranoia and a murder obsession. I have one hell of a body count, too. I even attacked my captain, and I already have two violent episodes on my record here. Jesus! Is anyone safe? Hell, Oran, the flies won't even be on your corpse before the judge gives me my pass right back here where I can sit on this bench, bask in the sun, contemplate your blood spatter on the granite, and speculate upon your current plane of existence. Now, that is delicious."

"Look, Joe," he said, edging away, "you've completely misunderstood. You—"

I grabbed Connor's wrist, halting his egress. "I like to see you, Oran. I like it a lot. Insurance fascinates me. It really does. Actuarial tables, double indemnity, Fred MacMurray, and I have some ideas I'd like to share concerning the labor movement. I think I should run for office. You come on out and see me again when you can. Hear?"

"Sure. Sure, Joe. Yeah, sure, I'll do that." He tried to move his arm and I pulled on it, drawing him closer.

"And I want you to head on down to the Tower locker room, gather those cruiser apes around you, and tell them that I will be back. Tell them, anyone who thinks I took out a cop instead of a serial killer is just liable to be the cop I really do take out."

"Yes." Connor nodded, I rolled my eyes up, released the man's wrist, and in one jerky movement, Connor stood, stuffed his briefcase beneath his arm, turned, and began sprinting across the grass toward the main building.

"Solidarity, brother!" I called after him.

Out of the corner of my eye, I noticed two orderlies cutting across the grass toward me from the West Court path. One was Billy, the other Chase. I placed my hands on the rear edge of the bench and leaned back on them, facing up at the spotty clouds, fluffs of peach and gray among the blue. I saw the two orderlies looking down at me. "Hi, fellas. What's up?"

"Joe," said Billy. "Surveillance notified us that you might be roughing up your visitor. Isn't that him laying rubber back to the main building?"

"Diarrhea," I explained. "Sudden attack. Just ask him."

"If we could catch him," said Chase wryly.

"You're all out of visitors," observed Billy. "Back to the shack."

"Right you are, officer." I stood, walked around the bench, got on the Deadline, and began following the fence back to the main building, Chase and Billy keeping me company.

GROUPIES

In my room, lying in bed, I looked up Oran Connor on my handheld. Twelve on the job, did uniforms in East Branch and Central, got his gold shield in Vadalia Detectives, assigned to Homicide in 'Oh-one. Divorced, three children, his ex and kids living in San Francisco. Child support running four-fifty a week. I did a search for other Connors employed within suspected institutions, but got discouraged after finding my sixteenth Connor.

I shut down my handheld, swung my legs off the bed, and saw the get well card on my nightstand. I reached to the back of the nightstand and pulled loose the expansion card the hangman had delivered, remembering the sight of Nathan Sunday's first published work painted next to that mural of Nat Turner in the hall of Turner Elementary next to the Seventh Street bridge. We knew about three men Sunday had killed beneath that bridge before he was twelve. My third eye didn't believe that number was even close.

I got up and headed toward the door. It was time to push Alvin toward that edge.

Yuker was in Half Satan, his massive frame stretched out in one of the TV chairs, his attention occupied with SpongeBob SquarePants who, in the company of Patrick, was attempting to bust his driving teacher, Mrs. Puff, out of jail. "You a fan, groupie?" I asked.

"Tartar sauce," responded Alvin, glancing up at me. "Have a seat, barnacle head."

I sat next to Alvin and we both watched to the end of the cartoon. Before the next one came on, Elizabeth entered, her stocky form wrapped in one of the dark blue blankets. The very model of restraint, she pointedly asked me if she could watch what she wanted to watch. I looked at Alvin and the big man shrugged and held out the remote. "I've seen all these before."

"Me too," I said. I looked at Elizabeth. "Whatever you like."

"Thank you." She took the remote from Alvin, punched in a number, tightened up the wrap on her blanket, and sat down in front to watch two men in a boat spin casting into the waters of a large lake.

"Fishing show," said Alvin, straight faced. "I wonder what's going to happen next."

We looked at each other, got up, and moved to Big Chair Country: the south lounge area between Wanda's and Mark's corners. Geraldine and Leila were already in there huddled together in two of the overstuffed chairs close to the cubicle's entrance. Alvin and I sat next to each other at the opposite end of the lounge area, our backs toward the glass. A floor security officer positioned himself at the open end of the cubical, ostensibly watching the ping-pong game in the west cubicle, but keeping an eye on Alvin.

"You've got a tail," I said.

"One of many. I wonder what would happen if they ever caught me alone, without witnesses."

"You're alone every night in your room."

"Yeah, but then they got themselves another Gilbert Kane problem. The only ones who could've done it had to be on staff."

"So if they're going to kill you, it has to be with no witnesses but in an area where other patients have access."

"That's what I figure." Alvin returned the officer's stare until the SO looked away. "Someplace where no one can come if I yell for help." He traversed his gaze until it fell upon me. "And you are my guardian angel."

"Such as I am."

"You might want to think about working out some."

"I let my program slip the last couple of times I was in the hospital. By the way, I never thanked you for saving my life and keeping my bed dry."

Alvin studied me for a moment then said, "You haven't figured out yet that you're here because you're a whacko?"

"I told you, besides being my natural condition, being crazy is my cover."

"That's what they told you, huh? Isn't that how they got you through the door? This is my third time here, Joe. First after I killed my mother and second after Luther and his partner arrested me. I've seen a few things. You wouldn't be the first nut who was told to come in here to fix the plumbing then had the door locked behind him."

"Thanks, Alvin, but I don't need any help fueling my paranoia."

He gave a quick grin. "I'm just yanking your chain."

"What about you, Alvin?"

"Me?"

"Yeah. Don't you have a few issues to sort out, nuthousewise?"

He looked away. "Sometimes bombs are best left to themselves."

"Ever do any work on your arsenal?"

"A few years ago I did some work with the shrink at Books. Mike Keller. A lot of work. He was a rough son of a bitch. Tough as nails. What he called tough love the courts call assault and battery. The cons used to call it the search and destroy school of psychiatry." Alvin shook his head and looked up at the ceiling. "He was a good man. Got me into painting."

"But Keller died," I said.

"Yeah. Keller died." A wistful moment, then Alvin glanced at me. "The next guy was only moving meat through his office. He was the one who recommended my parole. After my conviction for killing Jolene Gaye and Dena Lloyd —well, after that I just stuck myself in my work. You know, painting."

"I saw one of your shows down at the River Song Gallery."

"What did you think?"

"I think you paint beautiful landscapes, animals, buildings."

"I hear a big 'but' lurking in there."

141

"I don't think your heart was in any of the paintings I saw. Your paintings are technically gifted and are layer upon layer, maybe, of what you wish your life had been, and stuff you think appeals to buyers. Considering how many of your works sell, you read the buyers pretty well. According to the art agent Luther works with to handle your stuff, you've put more than three hundred thousand dollars in the hands of your victim's families."

Alvin watched as his right index finger traced figures on the armrest of his chair. "I always doodled, did little sketches and stuff. Dr. Keller saw that and put me in front of an easel with a brush in my hand. He wanted me to take my feelings and put them on canvas. Let them flow. No judgment, no editing, just paint."

"What happened?"

"I tried, Joe. I really did. Four days. During the time I was allowed to devote to painting, I sat in front of an easel and stared at blank canvas, terrified. Finally I did a landscape: made up mountains in back of a made up lake surrounded by made up trees. Put a made up deer in it, too. Maybe there aren't any feelings left."

"You have feelings, Alvin. Terror, for one." I drummed my fingers on the chair's armrests and nodded. "This is his third time here, too," I said.

"Who?"

"Nathan Sunday." I looked at Alvin. "Were you ever here when Nathan Sunday was here?" Thomas entered the lounge area, flopped in a chair to my left, and slouched down, his eyes closed.

"Just this time, as far as I know," Alvin answered. "What about you, Sherlock? You got any feelings? About Sunday? About the Rizzos? About having an executioner for a father? What I know about your story, Joe, you got a few things to sort out, yourself."

"Yeah." I studied my own fingertips drumming upon the armrests. I stopped them. "Want to swap nightmares?"

"Not much point." The big man glanced at Thomas then faced me, his voice lowered. "Everything I've read, Joe, says that once a serial killer starts killing, there's no saving him. He's locked in, lost. Emotionally. Psychologically. I've known other serial killers inside.

They're all numbed out one way or the other. Drugs, religion. The only place I've been able to find is work. Painting those pictures for the buyers, getting that money to the families."

"What about at night?"

"Hell, Joe, you've killed two or three times the number I killed. What do *you* do at night?"

"I asked you first."

Alvin studied me. "Okay. I keep the nights as short as possible. The infirmary at Books hands out sleeping pills by the bushel, but all they seem to do is make it so I can't get out of my nightmare. Work, exercise, meals, more work. I nod off during the day a lot, but those naps are so short a real nightmare can't get into high gear. So, what do you do at night?"

"You mean when I'm not being strapped down, drugged, and murdered?"

Alvin grinned. "Yeah."

"I watch TV: the all-night movies mostly. Tapes of old favorites. Black and white flicks. And I work." I raised my eyebrows. "Nothing like a good murder to occupy your mind."

"Yeah. That's what I always say."

Thomas burst out with a laugh. "Sorry," he said to Alvin. "I couldn't help overhearing."

"What's so funny? I hear you almost killed your roommate running your own flight school. Is he going to sue?"

Thomas shook his head. "No. The PCP I was on I got from him. He's the one who turned me onto it. Said it would help me study." He laughed again. "As if I could remember what courses I'm taking and where the classes meet."

"You don't belong here," said Alvin. "You belong in rehab."

Elizabeth entered the lounge area, still wrapped in her blanket. She stopped in front of where Geraldine and Leila were having their conversation and said to me, "What kind of underpants do you wear?"

"Huh?"

"I just saw a commercial with Michael Jordan and it seemed to be pretty important. Come on. What kind?"

I shrugged. "Haynes briefs. I favor the colored selections." I looked at Alvin.

"State issue boxers. White." He looked at Thomas.

"Fruit of the Loom. Briefs." He looked at me. "I never could resist those singing grapes."

Elizabeth looked at Leila who began laughing. "L.L. Bean thermals until it warms up," Leila answered, "then it's Victoria's Secret all the way."

All except Elizabeth looked at Geraldine. "I want to get in Haynes briefs, too, but Joe's."

As everyone laughed, Elizabeth suddenly faced me. "I wear a thong!" She turned around, pulled her blanket up, and bent over. She had nothing on beneath the blanket, not even the aforementioned thong.

The orderly who had been watching Alvin hastily took Elizabeth's arm, stood her up, adjusted the blanket down over her butt, and quietly led her away. Alvin stared wide-eyed at the spot in space recently occupied by Elizabeth's fundament. "I'm never going to forget that," he said at last.

Thomas, equally wide-eyed, said, "Isn't that what Queen Elizabeth was talking about when she referred to the *annus horribilis?*"

On the way back to my room, I dropped on down next to Doorstop. "Michelle. How was your day?"

"Long day. Every day," she said, her gaze riveted on the center of the hall.

"You like movies?"

"Some."

"Have a favorite?"

Michelle grinned. "*Terminator.*"

"I like that one. Is that really your favorite?"

"No." She turned and faced me. "Ever hear of *Johnny Belinda*? It's really old."

"Sure. Jane Wyman, Lew Ayres, Charles Bickford."

"*Johnny Belinda*," she repeated, nodding once. "My favorite."

I rested my head against the wall. I was about to reveal the title of my favorite motion picture when I felt Michelle's hand hold mine tightly. I looked and she was facing the center of the hall, her eyes open, one lonely tear working it's way down her cheek.

"Favorite," she repeated.

WHEN THE DRAGONS CALL

The next morning after breakfast, while Dan's Dragons were in Teddy's room practicing our act for the Turkey Talent Show, I was on office hours with Dr. Dan. I sat in the client chair, leaning forward, my elbows on my knees. As usual, Dan Walker was scribbling in a file. Without looking up, he said, "I understand you had another incident with Elizabeth last evening."

"We let her watch what she wanted to watch."

"How did you feel?" He looked up at me.

"Feel?"

"How did you feel? When Elizabeth exposed her buttocks to you, what was going on in your mind?"

"You're kidding."

"No, I'm not. When you saw that, what was going on in your mind?"

I looked up at the ceiling. "Well, when I saw that, I asked myself, what would Bill Clinton do."

Dan looked back at the file. "That was a serious question."

"That was an accurate answer."

"You were asking yourself what former President Clinton would do?"

"It seemed the obvious question."

"What is it going to take, Joe, for you to take seriously the reasons why you are here?"

"You taking them seriously would be a start."

The psychiatrist looked up, his eyebrows above his glasses. "I take your problems very seriously."

I pointed at Walker's desk. "Not when you're catching up on your paperwork during my session. I know it's supposed to make you look terribly burdened,

147

Dan, but to be honest, instead of a workaholic, I'd rather have someone who gave a crap."

His face reddening, Dan closed the file, pushed it from him, and leaned back in his chair. "Very well."

"Is this your care giving game face, then? You look as though someone just broke your hobby horse."

Dan's face darkened as he pasted a smile on top of his clenched teeth. "I really don't want to argue with you, Joe. Perhaps I should assign you to another therapist."

"We'll always have that, Dan." I shook my head and held up a hand. "Look, I'm sorry. It's my mouth. I'm still trying to get those drugs out of my system and last night I had a butt stuck in my face and a serial killer counsel me on mental health. If it's that obvious I have problems, well then maybe Alvin is right. It's just that working on my problems seems a little farfetched being subjected to indifferent therapy."

"I apologize for how I might have come across by looking at your file, Joe. However, I am not indifferent to your problems."

"Promise?"

"Where would you like to begin?"

I leaned back, rubbed my chin, and studied Dan. "Okay. I'd like to ask a favor."

"A favor."

"I want to see Nathan Sunday."

"He's in a coma."

"I didn't say I wanted to see him tap dance. I have things to say to him."

"He can't hear you."

"You don't know that. You don't know to an absolute certainty that he is in a coma."

"I don't know to an absolute certainty, Joe, that you are even in my office."

I grinned. "Now you're talking my language."

Walker laughed, chewed on his lower lip, glanced at his desktop, and said, "I don't see any reason why seeing him can't be arranged. Anything else?"

"Yeah. I want to bring Alvin Yuker with me."

The frown returned and grew deeper with each passing second. "Why?"

"I'm not the only one in the joint who could use a breakthrough."

"Yuker is only here for observation."

"Me, too," I countered. "You have all the SOs and orderlies, Dan. You control the locks."

"Serial killers are beyond breakthroughs, Joe. Sunday and Yuker aren't the first we've seen here. The literature—"

"Like getting Lyme disease and SARS, Dan: Someone has to be first. And you still control the locks. What harm could it do?"

"Other than flipping out a serial killer who is stronger than any three orderlies I have on staff?"

"Yeah. Besides that."

"What's Nathan Sunday represent to you, Joe?"

A strange rush of images flashed through my mind—that smile, pancakes, shots ripping through my side, coughed blood on that pristine white blanket. Sunday told me to hate him just before he stuck that stiletto in my lung. I looked up at Dan and shook my head. "Sorry. Went on a little trip there. You ever play sports, Dan? High school or college competition?"

"Skiing, football. Fencing in college."

"You ever beat someone who shouldn't have lost?"

"There's no way to control all of the variables," he said. "Still, every so often the variables line up, impede the stars and help the also-rans over the top."

"Is that a yes?"

The psychiatrist smiled sheepishly. "Yes. Twice I can think of I was owed a big goose egg and walked off with the prize."

"Dan, I figure I am owed one big goose egg. I should be dead. Julia should be dead. Probably a few more couples, as well. Nathan Sunday knew too much about me, about us, about everything to have wound up in that bed on Redshank. You want to know what my problem is, doc: The universe is out of balance."

The psychiatrist hesitated, then leaned forward, picked up the receiver to his phone and punched in a three-digit number. An almost immediate answer. "Ben? Call Alvin Yuker to the nurses station and hold him there until I arrive, okay? Have Billy and Neal stand by. I'll

149

need them to escort for an hour or so." He listened a moment longer, then hung up. "Okay?" he asked me.

"Thanks."

"So, Joe, how do you feel now?"

"Scared," I answered honestly. "Scared to death."

Redshank West looked a lot like Turkey West, down to Norman running his floor scrubber up and down the hall. One difference was that all of the doors were closed and locked, the hall all but deserted. Another difference, at the end of the hall the doors of four thirty-three, currently chained shut, opened onto the roof. Green Adirondack chairs, white tables impaled with collapsed blue beach umbrellas. Redshankers didn't need group space; they didn't do group. In the patient rooms there were no walls separating the toilet facilities from the sleeping area. Somewhere, toward the east end of the hall, someone was pounding on his door. Either that person or another was moaning. I felt the muscles at the back of my neck knotting. Alvin was spooked, too. Dan, Neal, and Billy seemed to take it all in stride.

Sunday was in room four twenty-nine. After Neal unlocked the door, Dan entered first and I followed, stopping at the near side of Sunday's bed. The psychiatrist continued around the bed and began a quick check of Sunday's vitals appearing on the monitor. I noted the soft cuffs on both Sunday's wrists and ankles. There was a tangle of cords, pipes, and wires feeding him food, water, oxygen, and medication as well as monitoring his heart, blood pressure, blood oxy, and respiration. A clear plastic bag a third filled with urine hung low off the side of the bed. Sunday was wearing a wheat colored johnny on a frame that looked to me as though it had lost weight.

Sunday's face. Relaxed, pale caramel skin, eyes closed, his hair grown out partly from his usually clean shaven head and face, a dressing still on the trough my .44 slug had plowed along the left side of his scalp. Another dressing on the side of his neck where the previous round had nicked his carotid artery. The only sounds were from the oxygen feed and monitor, barely audible beeps against background of gentle hissing. I

150

leaned against the bedrail. Alvin, flanked by Billy and Neal, crowded into the room behind me.

"Dan?"

He turned from the monitor. "Yes?"

"Can I be alone with him for awhile? I'll let you know when you can send in Alvin. Can we do that? Please."

The granddaddy of all pauses while Big Dan calculated the angles, weighed the risks, and attempted to divine the purpose. "Very well," he said, nodding at the trio standing behind me. He walked around the bed, and soon the door was closed leaving me alone with Nathan Sunday. I looked down at the man who had gotten tangled between trying to kill me and trying to get me to kill him.

"I thought they'd never leave, Kieff —Nathan. Yeah, I'm here, you bastard, and we're all alone. Are you listening? Can you hear me? Do you understand me?" I looked around at the interior of the room. Video camera mounted high on the wall to the left of the window. Probably a sound pickup, too. I looked back at Sunday.

"After you were shot, when you were down on that stoop, I saw you smile. Julia wanted to know how I knew it was you and I said something about the way you tied your necktie, and you smiled. An ironic little thing, but it was there. I saw it. You heard, you understood, and you smiled. You had enough of a brain left to smile and to stick that damned stiletto into my lung and tell me to hate you. Come on. Give me that smile now, damn you. Let me see you understand."

Gentle beeps and hissing, no change of expression.

I held onto the bedrail and looked around for a chair. No chairs. "You got no juice at all, man. This room is terrible." His automatic blood pressure cuff kicked in.

Time to get to it. "All right, man, what was all that crap you gave me about keeping me alive so we could all go skiing next season. You, me, Julia, and Miriam up on Helldiver doing the drops. You're an emotional chameleon, aren't you, you bastard. What does Joe Torio need? He needs a friend. What kind of friend does he need? And the machine that you are ground out Miles Kieffer so you could set me up for your suicide-by-cop production. And then you tried to scare me off. What was it, Nate old buddy? You wanted an executioner and instead found someone you really liked?"

Releasing the bedrail, I walked clockwise around the bed until I was standing next to the monitoring equipment. "Julia and I pulled your trigger good, didn't we? You were trying to scare me off and we set you off like a damned firecracker. You thought you were in complete control of everything. Control of MCU, us, control of yourself, control of your reality. You picked the players, you wrote the plot, but you never counted on someone like Julia falling in love with someone like me, or someone like me daring to fall in love with someone like Julia. Who could've predicted that? And her Margarita Azzurro, how could you get around that image? Love was the monkey wrench in your gearbox. Messed up the whole thing."

I leaned my forearms on the bedrail and clasped my hands together. "You read my mind, became the partner—the friend—I wanted—needed. That was a pretty valuable human being you became."

His face was impassive, the sound of the oxygen hissing, none of the monitor readings changing significantly. I glanced back at the observation port and nodded. The door opened and Alvin entered, the door closing behind him. "What's this about, Joe? What were you saying to him?"

I nodded at Sunday. "Take a look at yourself, Alvin. Nathan Sunday took his past, his nature, his sickness and denied them all —and he was an expert at it. A graduate of Yale, butchered a few couples, a stretch in here, then a whole new life. Started college all over again. Yay Ravens. Wife, a daughter, a career as a journalist, then an entirely new career as a police officer and detective. But that dragon was never far behind. It caught him, Alvin, and pulled down the whole damned thing. Put him in that bed and it cost a lot of other people, too—those who loved him."

"You're one of them, aren't you, Joe?"

I turned on my handheld, opened the file containing the collected writings of a killer, and handed it to Alvin. "Push that bottom middle button to page down. Pick anything and read it. They were all written by this man."

Alvin backed up against the wall to the left of the door and slid down until he was sitting on the floor, his gaze not leaving the handheld. He was chewing at his lower lip, his eyes studying the tiny screen. He began reading out loud, his voice paradoxically small.

i watch
jeffery during his interview
i watch
john wayne during his interview
i watch
ted during his interview

workaday
we look and sound so good
when we're not
choking
cutting
stabbing
bashing
poisoning
shooting
strangling
and eating people
no wonder they execute us
we look and act like everybody else

what must go on in those jury rooms

well i never did anything like that
and i was spanked plenty
mashing his head against a sink
might have been a bit over the line
but
a little discipline is good for a boy
spare the rod and youll spoil that child
so she patted her boys bottom
stuck an enema hose up his ass
until he was as dry as leather
took a bath with him
scrubbed his penis
sucked him flat

153

and screwed him cross-eyed
for thirteen years
man
that isnt sexual abuse
thats scoring
after all
a boys best friend is his mother
all those voting guilty raise your right hand
well that was painless

hush
we are not a village
my children
we are universes in collision
hush
hush

Alvin stared at the screen, his face pale and drawn. "When did Sunday write that?"

"The year before he graduated from Yale. He took a few weeks off and committed himself here. He was on Turkey back then, his second time." I gestured with my head toward the west. "He wrote a lot of his stuff out there on the roof. The place was special to him."

"Universes in collision," said Alvin. "Am I one of those universes, Joe?"

"That's not my question to answer."

He looked down at the handheld, not seeing it. "I've been making it, Joe. One fucking foot in front of another, focusing on paying back my victims' families, working myself dead tired days, reading nights, leaving myself too damned tired to dream when I do sleep, too damned tired to ask myself why I don't feel anything when I'm awake. But, making it. I get through the day without screaming. What if I poke at this, Joe? What if I poke at it and it all falls apart?"

I looked at Nathan Sunday's face. "Back at Riverside General, Alvin, I was desperately trying to understand about this man here, about his addiction —the compulsion to kill— I used to go to Twelve Step meetings. You know, like A.A. and N.A."

"Yeah. We got Twelve Step meetings at Books. I went to a few." He nodded. "Same reason."

"I don't know if I came out of those meetings with any better understanding of what I went though with this man." I patted Sunday's shoulder, surprised that it was warm. I withdrew my hand. "A guy at the meeting who talked with me said that no matter how bad things are, there are always ways to make them worse. Standing in shit up to your chin is pretty bad—"

"—But you could be standing on your head," Alvin completed. He rubbed his eyes and let his hand slide into his lap. "Those steps are supposed to be a way to rebuild a wrecked life, Joe. That's what they told me. That amends thing they do, it got to me. How do you make amends to the dead, though? I asked Luther about that and he arranged with that art dealer to sell my stuff and get the money to the family members without them knowing where it came from. Both my vics had kids. Doing that work has held me together. It keeps a lid on things."

"I don't think you can keep a lid on this kind of stuff forever, Alvin. Personally, I'd like to see you rip out all those violet mountains and pretty pink flowers and splash your anger, your guilt, your rage, your sorrow, and your pain all over the canvas."

"Why?"

"Art would be a good reason. If you ever took the chains off your paintbrush it would probably torch the skin off the art world's eyeballs." I rubbed my eyes and let my hand fall to my side. "I don't want you to do it for art, though. I want you to do it for me. How's that for selfish? That's my reason, though: Do it for me. By looking squarely at your nightmares maybe I can get the courage to make some kind of move on my own."

Alvin studied me for a moment then pushed himself to his feet. "Is Dan really an asshole?"

"No. He's just like the rest of us: Crazy."

Alvin frowned and focused on a spot in space. "Maybe. If he can get me paints and stuff—even just some charcoal and paper." He held up the handheld. "Can I read more of these?"

"Sure. Keep it awhile."

"Thanks." Alvin got to his feet, walked to the side of Nathan Sunday's bed, stopped and looked down at the man. After a few seconds, he shrugged and said, "Funny."

"What?"

"It's almost time for morning group. Too bad it's a waste of time."

He turned, walked to the door, opened it, and stepped through, the sounds of the mystery patient banging on a door unchanged. Dan instructed Billy and Neal to escort Alvin to Turkey West. As they left, Dan turned, entered the room, and raised his eyebrows. "Was it all you expected?"

"More in some areas, less in others. Thanks for letting me do this."

"I really do care about your recovery as well as the health of every patient in this institution."

"I believe you, Dan. Could you stand a little feedback on your general approach? Just one nutball to another?"

"Of course."

"In the patient's handbook it talks about the self-healing patients can do through productive interaction with other patients."

"Almost word-for-word."

"It's a good theory, Dan. I've seen it work before in Twelve Step programs, other group situations I've been in. Want to know why it isn't working here?"

"What makes you think it isn't working?"

I grinned. "Doc, I'm personally test driving this shitbox. Don't try and tell me it can win the Daytona."

His face went red. "Okay. The results aren't as promising as I had hoped. I thought it was because Squirmhi was—" he grinned, caught out on his own terms. "That this hospital was too prison-like. When I came here it was little more than a lockup. I think most of the patients appreciate the park I put in, as well as the remodeling, the recreation areas, the regular group meetings, but in the end, the recovery rates aren't much improved."

"The place looks fine. That's not the problem."

"What, then?"

"You don't trust your own theories, Dan. You don't trust your patients to want to heal and to help heal others, so they don't trust you, your theories, or what you're doing. It's softer than it was, but it's still a lockup. They're doing time. The group dynamic right now is to do whatever is the opposite of what you want. I've seen you turn it back on them—getting Alvin into the group— but being able to manipulate a bunch of stressed out nutballs isn't much of an accomplishment."

"Why do they resist?"

"Before it was for entertainment. Now it's retaliation."

"Retaliation for what?"

"We discovered that audio pickup fixed to the underside of the coffee table in the Dan group area." Walker's face flushed again, which was all of the admission necessary.

"It was like a backup—"

"Bullshit. Tell me, Dan, are all the groups bugged or just the Dragons?" I took the psychiatrist's next expression as indicating the former.

"Man, I can't be the only patient here who ever looked beneath a table. Look, if this self-healing stuff has a chance of working you need to get the trust of your patients. Without a certain degree of trust in the process, it never works, and man right now your trust tank has nothing in it but fumes. What are you going to do?"

After a long thoughtful pause he slowly shook his head. "I'm not sure." We stood there, listening to the monitoring equipment for a few beats. "Tell me something, Joe. Do you think you have real mental problems?"

"Yes."

"Are they centered in this individual? Nathan Sunday?"

"No. He was a latecomer. In fact, once he gave me some good advice in that regard."

"How so?"

"We were discussing emotional involvement in cases. He said he wanted no emotional involvement at all. My approach involves getting down, in deep, just as crazy as the killer. Feel what he feels so I can know what he knows and want what he wants, collecting all the whys that lead to the wheres. This man wondered how I lasted as long as I had." I glanced at Dan. "I told him, not very well."

"What do they teach you when you're trained, Joe? In the Academy? About emotional involvement."

"Don't get involved. That's what they teach. You have a puzzle to work, pieces of meat to process. They may be right, too. There are only two other cops I know of who did it my way: the first was a State cop named Kirby Flagg who my father hanged for ax murdering his whole family. The second was a Homicide dick named Dale Raye, and right now he's hiding out in a garbage dump somewhere dancing with the seagulls."

"And you're in here."

"Seems to be a pattern."

"Is there some kind of payoff, Joe?"

"Payoff?"

"Why do it your way?" asked Dan. "What's the payoff?"

"I've cracked a lot of tough cases. That's why I get called in."

"What about the payoff; the payoff for you, Joe."

I thought for a moment. "It's a trip."

"Like doing the steeps when you ski, Joe, it frightens you, doesn't it? You can't focus on yourself, your past, or your problems when you have to concentrate on just staying alive."

"What problems are you talking about, Dan? My father having a socially unacceptable job? Never knowing my mother? Being picked on at school? I just described an awfully big part of the population."

"At the risk of encroaching on your third-eye territory, Joe, I'm guessing the roots of your problems are deeper than that." He held his head to one side and looked down. "But you don't have any reason to listen to me." He looked up at Sunday. "Are you done here?"

"Yes."

The psychiatrist walked to the door and held it open for me.

"Are you going to show at morning group, Dan?"

"Will you be meeting outside again?"

"Probably. Are you going to show?"

"I haven't made up my mind."

As we walked the length of Redshank West toward the security access door, whoever it was continued his desperate pounding.

When I checked in at the Turkey Floor nurses station, Carla nodded toward a woman doing some charts behind the counter. "Wanda wants to speak to you. She's one of the group counselors." Wanda was slender, tall, fiftyish, with steel gray hair cropped close, and a mouth that was used to laughing. Very sharp dark eyes and a smooth complexion the color of Hershey's semi-sweet.

"Did I do something wrong?" I asked Carla.

"She's right there. Ask her yourself."

I walked along the counter until I was across from Wanda. She looked up at me and smiled. "Are you Joe? Michelle's friend?"

"Am I in trouble?"

"Of course not." The smile eased. "Do you know about Michelle?"

"I have some guesses."

"I've heard a little about your famous third eye."

"Really."

"So, what are your guesses, Joe?"

"She's been betrayed and all but destroyed. Rape most likely. Repeated. A relative who was a police officer. Role model. Very possibly her father, a close uncle, or an older brother. My money is on the father. I think she became pregnant, was forced to get an abortion, and was told to be a cop's kid, suck it up, and forget about it. Did Michelle kill him or attempt it?"

"Spooky, Joe. Very spooky."

"Which isn't an answer."

"I can't discuss her, Joe. You know that." Wanda studied me for a long time. At last she asked, "Does Michelle know you are a police officer?"

"That was the first thing she ever said to me."

"What?"

"'Fucking cop.'"

She laughed and placed a hand on my shoulder. "I'm glad Michelle found a friend, Joe, but don't forget to take care of yourself, understand?" She walked off and turned into the staff entrance to the right of the nurses station.

WHERE WE WERE

We huddled in our jackets and blankets in Maplewood Circle, the promise of a warmer morning desecrated by an approaching storm front, dropping temperatures, snow to begin in early evening, two to three inches of possible accumulation Teddy reported. He was sitting in Geraldine's old place. Alvin, using my handheld, was paging through the works of Nathan Sunday. Geraldine, in Teddy's old place, was sitting to Harvey's left and was deep into a giggle fest with Leila, who was seated to her left. Leila was lint-rolling Louis. I sat with my hands thrust into my jacket pockets, looking across the circle to Dan Walker's empty place, alternately thinking about my problems, Michelle's problems, Dan's problems, as well as Alvin's.

Louis said to me, "You haven't found him yet, have you, policeman?"

"Who?"

"Valjean, of course."

I shrugged and held out my hands. "No, Mad Dog. As I said, I'm in MCU. The Valjean shoplifting was caught by SVU."

"Special Victims Unit?" asked Harvey with a frown.

"No. Starches and Vegetables." It drew a respectable chuckle.

"I shoplifted a case of Miller's Lite once," remarked Teddy.

"Got by security by drinking it all before you left the store, right, Burnout?" cracked Thomas.

"Who wants to pretend to share this morning?" asked Yukiko.

"Me," said Thomas. He looked across me at the dentist. "Not pretending, though. I'm sorry, Moon Pie.

161

About that crack I made about your father. I was still high and I got a smart mouth. It must've been awful growing up like that and it was an awful thing to say. I'm sorry."

Yukiko stared at Thomas a moment, gauging his sincerity. Then he faced me. "Your father was the hangman at Books?"

"That's right."

"How did you carry that, Sherlock? As a kid, how did you make it?"

"Not real well." I looked around at the faces. "No friends, lots of fights, no dates, the butt of every teacher who wanted to do a rope, hangman, or death joke." I thought a moment, then raised my eyebrows. "That's too easy, isn't it? Short form answer. It essentially means I don't want to talk about it."

"That's right," said Geraldine with a rotten grin.

I faced Yukiko. "Here it is, Moon Pie: I was very lonely, feeling ripped off all the time, full of anger, and occasionally visited with thoughts of suicide. I used to think the world sucked and almost anyone would be a better father than the one I had. Actually, I didn't know how lucky I was. But my father didn't expect to die when he went to work and he hasn't spent the time since feeling guilty about being alive. My father had two concerns: his family and doing his job well. Your father was dealing with bigger things: gods, the end of the universe, and being a role model for a kid who wanted to fix teeth instead of dying in flaming glory."

Yukiko sat back slightly, regarding me. After a moment he looked at the faces in the circle, judging the waters. "My dad was nineteen when he was trained to be a suicide pilot." He raised his eyebrows and slowly shook his head. "World War II. It's like talking about the Civil War. Anyway, the day before my father was to be sent on his mission, Hirohito surrendered. Most of the pilots my dad trained with were already dead, though, their missions completed. My dad was left behind alive. He hauled around this mountain of survivor guilt and depression his whole life, sucking the oxygen out of everything he touched and everyone he ever met, including us, his family. But we never knew why. It was after he came to the U.S. that he married my mom. When I was in the second grade I remember asking him why he came to America. He told me that it was to punish himself. It sounded crazy. We thought he was joking. One time we took Dad to a clinic. He had done nothing but sit in a chair and stare at a TV for days." Yukiko rubbed the back of his neck and shook his head. "We're all sitting in the doctor's office, and the doctor he says to my dad, 'Mr. Ikari, in my opinion you are depressed.' My dad said back, 'No shit, Mr. Moto.'"

We all laughed, including Yukiko. Then his eyes began glistening. "No shit, Mr. Moto. No shit, no treatment, no therapy, no getting better. I grew up with a piece of furniture who went to work fixing radios and TVs, then came home and watched the TV."

"That's where I hid," I said. "Is your father still alive?"

Yukiko rested his chin on his chest. "When the World Trade Center towers went down, my dad, he was retired then. He was home sitting and watching the TV. He sees those horrific images on the TV over and over again. So, all alone with his ghosts, he writes a letter to me and my mom explaining about the war, what he did, the friends he trained with, and what he didn't do. Then the old fool knelt in the middle of the living room rug and tried to cut out his own heart with a damned kitchen knife. *Hara-kiri.* He didn't even know how to do it. God, what a butcher job. He did manage to kill himself, though. Up there now with his ancestors. I'll never forget my mom's face when she told me." He looked at Harvey. "We didn't use SceneClean. My Mom and I scrubbed and cleaned up the place before we called the cops."

"Insurance?" asked Teddy.

Yukiko shook his head. "No. Nothing like that."

"Company was coming," said Geraldine.

The suicide pilot's son nodded.

Long silence, the others in the group feeling for the dentist, reaching outward, being forced to look inward.

"Shouldn't have been like that, right?" said Teddy. "I bet you still miss him, too."

"Yes, I do."

"Moon Pie, you ever see that old Robert Young sitcom, *Father Knows Best?* Some of those others. *My Three Sons—*"

"*Leave It To Beaver,*" added Geraldine.

"*The Brady Bunch,*" said Harvey.

"*Ozzie and Harriet,*" said Leila.

Teddy nodded. "Yeah, all those drug-soaked screenwriters wallowing in what they wished their childhoods had been like. Never forget them."

He was staring at the grass in the center of the circle, a blade or two of bright new green fighting its way up through the brown thatch. "My old man was a Godfather nut. Jesus, those old hoods in his crew. They were all Godfather movie nuts. 'I made him an offer he can't refuse.' Papa Red could recite the meeting of the heads of the families scene from beginning to end."

I held out my hands. "'Don Barzini, I want to thank you for helping me organize this meeting here today,'" I quoted, doing my best Vito Corleone.

Teddy nodded. "Man, you did live your life in a TV, didn't you?" He looked back at the group. "I knew what Papa Red did for the Scozarri family. Before he got gunned down, my mom and I both knew." He held his hand out toward Yukiko, then me, Alvin, then Harvey. "Look at us: Kamikaze pilot, hangman, my old man executed Don Scozarri's enemies, Alvin killed his nightmares, and Harvey charged to clean it all up. Should've been different for all of us." He looked at Thomas. "What does your father do, Sunshine?"

"Drugs, mostly." Thomas shrugged and looked down. "Used to be a musician. Sax. Now he cries a lot and spends his disability check on crack. Fuck him."

Teddy looked at Harvey. "Cop," Harvey answered. Big silence.

Teddy raised his eyebrows at Louis. "And you, Mad Dog?"

"My name is Louis, you prick." Louis took the evil eye off me long enough to look at Teddy. "My name is Louis Gagne, and my father ..." He looked down at the grass, twisted his body, looked toward the pond, and turned back. A helicopter approached from the east and passed south of us. As the beating sound faded, Louis looked up at us.

"My father. He didn't work. Not a regular job. Hardly ever home." He stood, climbed up on his bench, and stood, looking toward the south. "Can't see it from here. The trees are too tall." He faced the group and sat down. "I can see it from my room, though. For a living my father screws little old ladies out of their life savings selling non-existent home improvements. Right now he is in Books. He still has four years to go before he's eligible for parole. He jokes he'll be out of Books before I'm out of Squirmhi. Funny man. Writes me every week."

Louis looked at Leila. Wide-eyed, Leila turned, moved over next to Geraldine, and buried her face in Geraldine's neck. Geraldine put her arms around Leila and waved off the group's attention which then wandered to Alvin. He looked up from the handheld. "Me? I never knew my father. My mother didn't know him, either. She used to tell me my father was a pinhole in a condom." He resumed his reading for a moment, then looked up. "Maybe that's why she stuck that damned nail in my eye." He looked down at the PDA then looked up again. "All right if I read something? Out loud?"

A circle of nodding heads, shrugs and mumbled affirmatives. Alvin read:

the edge
i stand here
eyes closed
arms outstretched
feeling the wind brush my cheek
catch at my robe
tug me this way and that
toward the center of the roof
over the edge toward oblivion

run wind run
carry me there
to
more pointless chatter
down to asphalt certainty

up to clouds and stars
to the possibilities of the unknown

just don't leave me here

Alvin looked up at the circle. "Nathan Sunday wrote that when he was a patient here."

"He didn't like being in Squirmhi?" offered Thomas.

"He wasn't talking about his physical location. He didn't like where he was here." Alvin placed his hand against the side of his head. Using the same hand, he pointed toward Redshank Roof. "He wrote it up there. Balanced on the edge, toying with letting the wind make his choices for him." He looked around at the faces, stopping on Thomas's. "I don't know about any of you, but I don't like the place I'm in."

As we sat in silence, I noticed Louis's eyes glistening.

"Attention, attention," said Harvey beneath his breath. "Wigpicker approaching from the east." All eyes turned toward the path leading from the fountain. A parka clad figure was crossing South Court Path following the twisting walkway toward the Maplewood. As he walked out from beneath the last of the trees, we could see it was Dan Walker. He was carrying what looked like a large cardboard box full of gray metal boxes.

"Good for you," I muttered beneath my breath.

Dan walked into the center of the circle, stopped, and emptied the box on the grass. Nine gray metal boxes landed with a crash. "I'm here to apologize to all of you. I broke the group anonymity rule by listening with this equipment to what you said when I wasn't there. I listened in on the other groups, as well. Let me add that it was without the knowledge of their counselors. I've already apologized to the other groups and their counselors." He looked around the circle. "I cannot tell you how ashamed I am. Either you can improve by sharing your feelings and experiences with each other, or you cannot. If you can, with counselors facilitating between sessions, we'll be able to effectively stretch our scarce resources to help up to two and perhaps three

166

times the number undergoing treatment now. If you cannot," he held out a hand and let it fall to his side, "If you cannot, then what you have experienced thus far is about as good as it can get. In any event, it cannot take place unless we can trust each other, and I have not trusted you. Hence, you have been given no reason to trust me. From now on, there will be no surveillance of patient groups, clandestine or otherwise. I would very much like to continue working with you. Because of my betrayal of group confidence, however, I will understand if you want another therapist. I am so very sorry."

He waited a beat, then he turned and left the circle, walking the path back past the fountain. Teddy faced the group, his expression somewhat bewildered. "What just happened?" He looked to his left at Thomas. "I blinked for a second and the laws of physics changed. What's going on?"

"I don't know, man. Honesty scares me."

"He was so sad looking," said Leila. "Wasn't he?"

"Like he got caught with his fingers in the cookie jar," said Geraldine. She looked across Harvey and Yukiko at me. "You had him up on Redshank, boy. You say somethin' to him?"

"I did."

Yukiko thrust his hands deeper inside his coat pockets and scowled at the grass in front of his feet. "Maybe you should've talked to us before saying anything to Walker."

"He did the bugging, Moon Pie. The problem was his, not yours."

"What about all this stuff about keeping it under our hats so we can feed the bad guys false information?"

"That's still on. There's still the little man in the Kleenex box."

Alvin nodded and said, more to himself than the others, "Dan's problem, and he dealt with it." He looked around at us. "How about it? Do we go for another therapist? In any case, do we work on our problems or just keep screwing around? What about Dan?" He held up his hand. "I say keep him." He looked at Thomas.

"Yeah. Okay." Thomas held up a hand. "Keep him." He looked at me.

"Keep him," I said.

Yukiko agreed, as did Harvey, Geraldine, Leila, and Louis. "Damn," said Harvey at the conclusion of the vote. "If Dan keeps up this shit, I just might have to get better."

Laughter answered Harvey's comment. When we settled down, there was a little cross talk as groupies speculated on what getting better might entail. During a brief pause, Thomas asked, "Think we could meet up there, Buckaroo?" He pointed toward the end of the main building. "Up there on Redshank Roof?"

Harvey looked at the roof and cocked his head to one side. "All they can do is say no." He looked at Thomas. "Want to let the wind push you around some, Sunshine?"

"Maybe. I know I don't like where I am."

Harvey glanced around at the group and said, "Shall I ask, then?" He collected the nods and grunts of assent. "If we get the green light, tomorrow Dan's Dragons meet in the Redshank's nest."

Alvin stood and walked over to the audio monitor and receiver units lying on the grass. One stomp each and they were so much scrap. He looked up at Joe. "Now all we need to know is who is listening in on the really good equipment."

COCONUTS

Afternoon group was taken up with Teddy, Yukiko, and Alvin dragging their recurring memories of being children before their fellow groupies. For Teddy, after his father's murder, it was always a choice of terrors: belong to this family and kill and die, or belong nowhere. "Family is important," said Teddy. "Belonging is important." He looked around at the faces, his gaze resting on me. "What do you do when you find yourself painted into a corner?"

For Yukiko it was a matter of moral cause: Whatever he did or wanted to do was always thrown against his father's standards. "I was painted into that corner before I was ever born."

Alvin had been rented out, raped, beaten, and made his mother's sexual plaything. He remembered anger, fear, sadness, disgust, and loathing from when he was much younger, but he could no longer feel those emotions. His remaining feeling was a dull unattached dread that mostly took the form of nightly stomach cramps.

Later, during visiting hours, everyone on Turkey was allowed to get some exercise and fresh air in the park before the expected snow arrived. Louis, Harvey, and Leila stayed on Turkey to watch the showing of *Galaxy Quest* in Half Satan. Thomas, Teddy, and Yukiko went to get in on a volleyball game in the park. Geraldine, bundled in a borrowed coat and a blanket, sat on the granite bench nearest the main park entrance reading a paperback copy of *Forever Amber*. Alvin and I went for a walk around the Deadline.

"Want to play cops and robbers?" I asked as we crossed the little footbridge that spanned Lower Raven Stream.

"Sure. I'll play."

"Okay. I'll be the cop."

"A real stretch, huh?"

"More than you know. What's your alibi for the time Katey Sloan was murdered?"

"You still haven't figured out you're a patient locked up in a nuthouse?"

"Humor me. From one PM until five, Alvin. Where were you?"

The big man looked up at the overcast, his eyes narrowing. "Twelve thirty is lunch at Chez Toilet—what we call the dining hall. I wasn't responsible for any table duties, so when I was done, I went to PPS—thats—"

"Painting and Popsicle Sticks," I said. "What you call Arts & Crafts. When was that?"

"One. A little after. CO Yotimo was on the door when I got to South House, which was unusual."

"Who's usually on the door after lunch?"

"After she was transferred to the rec department, it was CO Sloan. Yotimo's the Recreation Department supervisor. Hardly ever see her."

"Go on," I urged as we passed one of the security cameras mounted on the fence.

"I did my job, which consisted of checking the classrooms, making sure they have supplies: chalk, paper, stuff like that. Then it was off to the Piddle Palace—Arts & Crafts."

"When do afternoon classes start at Books?"

"One-thirty. By then I was at my easel painting."

"Anybody else in the room with you?"

"No. Where I work is a small room just off the main crafts room. At least three inmates I know saw me go in there. CO Yotimo saw me go in there, too. There's no way out of that room except through the door into the main crafts room. I must've had my vanishing cream on, though. None of them saw me go in or out."

"None of them? What are the inmates' names?"

"Sammy Pike, Kwesi Imara, and Knuckle Mike."

"Knuckle?"

Alvin frowned. "Mike Simpson."

"How long were you in there?"

"Until four-thirty. Then I checked the classrooms for cleanup, made sure the craft area was clean, and reported to A-Block for chow muster. That's four forty-five. After they count heads they herd us down to chow, so by five, I was slopping down."

"Got any way to fill in the holes?"

Alvin stopped, turned, and looked at me. "My alibi is nothing but one big hole, Joe. CO Yotimo says I never showed that afternoon. Pike, Imara, and Simpson back her up."

"Surveillance cameras?"

"Down for the day. Convenient, huh?"

"It's going around." I thrust my hands into my jacket pockets. It was getting much colder. "Are Pike, Imara, and Simpson convincing?"

"My lawyer believes them. Of course, he still believes that OJ didn't do it."

"What do you think the chances are of getting Pike or the others to change their stories?"

"Offer them enough, and they'll say whatever you want. Short of immediate pardons sweetened with lots of cash and tickets out of the country, though, there's no way you can overcome the leverage the COs have on them. One CO on your case can make life in the joint hell. If you got the whole union on you, man, you are fertilizer walking."

"Point taken. Okay. Let's say I'm on the other side. We have to shut Katey Sloan's mouth and hang her murder on someone else, so, out of all the inmates at Books, we pick you to frame. Why?"

Alvin paused, turned to his right, and looked across the pond up toward the mountain. "Why me. I'm a trustee so my movement is less supervised. I had a lot of access to areas denied to the other cons, I spent my time out of my cell in her assigned area, and I do have a history."

I nodded. "Okay. Your pattern, all nicely described in your records, is quite distinctive. Through our relatives and friends in other city and state institutions, we can duplicate evidence and plant it more-or-less undetected."

"Serial killer, too," reminded Alvin. "No loss, no support." He grinned. "Except for a couple of old cops with favors to call in."

I frowned as eye number three provided a belated insight. "Supt. Cotton's secretary. She's a part of this."

"How do you figure, Joe?"

"She was there to queer the first time Sloan tried to give her report to Cotton, then when Sloan's message came to Cotton that second time, his secretary was the one who intercepted it. And who has better access to records, schedules, prisoner and CO assignments?"

"Supt. Cotton."

"True. Something you don't know, though. On his own, Cotton went to my boss to see if there was anything Capt. Dockery could do about what looked like a frame on you. When this gig was first sprung on me, Cotton was there with Dock in my hospital room."

"Supt. Cotton did that?"

"Yeah. He did."

That was something Alvin needed to chew on. At last he shook his head and glanced at me. "Cotton could lose his job. Bringing in city cops to check up on the COs and the State fuzz? They get wind of it, the union'll hang him out to dry."

"Cotton seemed to think the wrong guys were running the investigation. He just wasn't sure who the right guys were." I looked at Alvin. "You're one of his clients. What's your take on Wes Cotton?"

"I'm a convict. My default reaction is to wonder what his angle is." The big man shrugged and thrust his hands deeper into the pockets of his orange jacket and hunched his shoulders up against the cold. "Strict. He's a hard man running a hard place. He's put some juice back into the salvation thing, though. He got the drug rehab program up and running. Education, too." Alvin narrowed his eyes. "He's intervened a few times in CO-inmate beefs to make sure cons up on charges got a fair shake. CO Sloan, too. Think they might believe in that big joke?"

"Maybe."

"What made Cotton think it's a frame, Joe?"

"You must have made a good impression on him, Alvin. Cotton simply didn't believe that you'd do such a thing."

"A serial killer?" His eyebrows arched. "I wouldn't do such a thing?"

"Not just a serial killer, Alvin. You're a man. He didn't believe that Alvin Yuker the man would do such a thing. Cotton has your records memorized. On top of that, there was what Gully Raye found out in the landfill."

"What did he find?"

"They did a great job aping your pattern, Alvin. Of several mistakes, though, the evidence shows that whoever strangled Katey Sloan did it from the back."

His eyes were wide, his tongue darting out to moisten his lips. "In the trial the Medical Examiner said I strangled them from the front." With a haunted expression his gaze darted this way and that, seeing nothing. "I don't think I even want to remember."

I needed for Alvin to back off the nightmare. "What about Yotimo? What kind of person is she?"

Alvin pulled his thoughts back from the edge, rubbed his eyes, and shook his head. "Yotimo. I hardly ever saw her after she was promoted. Before then she was on 'C' Block. You know, segregation. I only saw her coming and going. I never heard any trash on her. Married, I think. Right now, though, I know she's willing to lie to keep the frame on me."

"You know what really pisses me off about this case?" I said.

"What?"

"Good intentions. That's what the other side is banking on. They've got it all lined up: cops don't rat on cops, COs don't rat on COs, helping a buddy has a higher priority than doing the right thing, and you've got to believe the good guys because if they aren't being honest the truth is too horrible to take. On one hand, we accuse you of Sloan's death, bump you off so no one can counter the accusation, everyone breathes a sigh of relief, and goes home. On the other hand, we get someone to flip, he begins pointing his finger, more flips, more finger pointing, and COs, cops, politicians, and who knows who all else go down in flames along with their families."

"Be better all around if I just offed myself."

As we came abreast of the dry fountain, I looked at Alvin out of the corner of my eye. "Are you attempting to be amusing?"

"It's true."

"No, man, it is not true. How about everyone who depends on law enforcement enforcing the law? Will they be better off with you dead? How about those kids you've been putting through school? The children of your vics? How about them? Will they be better off with you dead? What about the people who're selling your paintings? Their families? Will they be better off with you dead?"

"Actually, with me dead, the value of all my paintings probably triples."

"Bad example. But what about Luther Stebbins? What about Gully Raye? The other side still needs to whack Gully if they want to be safe. What about the group? You think you killing yourself is going to help them? And what about me and everyone else in MCU who're putting their careers on the line to clear you? A dead Alvin Yuker isn't going to help us."

"Hey, Sherlock, can I play the cop now?"

I exhaled a sigh of exasperation and shrugged. "Sure."

"Okay, I figure two different people tried to kill you our first night here."

"Two, because they cancelled out each other."

"Yeah. Now, that happened long before you even told anyone about me and this frame you wanted to crack. I figure either you got one hell of a security leak back there at MCU, or you got a couple of enemies here who want to even up some old scores."

Before I could react to Alvin's thesis, we heard a muffled scream. *"No!"*

"You hear that, Joe?"

"Yeah." I ran, cutting the corner over the grass to the Maplewood Path. "There." In a thick group of trees half way to Dan's Circle, a blond boy in his early twenties, a very young Robert Redford, had Michelle up against a

174

tree, his hands busy. Michelle's eyes were open, staring dully at the center of nowhere, her hands hanging limp at her sides. I grabbed the back of the boy's collar and yanked him off her. The back of the blond boy's heel caught a root and he landed on his butt in the wet grass.

"What are you doing?" he demanded.

"That's just the question I was going to ask you. What's your name, squid?"

"None of your fucking business, asshole."

The boy began getting to his feet and I glanced at Alvin. "Could you get his name, groupie? We'll need it for the door prize." I turned to see about Michelle.

"Sure." Alvin pushed the kid back on his ass. "My name's Alvin. You probably heard about me. What's your name?"

"Derek."

"So, what were you doing with this little girl, Derek?"

"She ain't no little girl. She a grown woman."

"Back to my question: what were you doing?"

"She liked it."

I glanced back. "Maybe Derek would like to take a walk. Nothing loud or near the cameras."

Alvin picked Derek up by his arm and placed him on his feet. "Let's take a walk, Derek. I want you to talk to a lady named Geraldine. She's got a sure cure for that woody you're carrying around." He boosted the blond boy south toward the Deadline.

I didn't touch Michelle. She remained leaning with her back against the tree, her arms hanging limp, her eyes blank. "What do you want me to do, Michelle?"

She blinked, looked around, then at me. "Turn around."

I turned around facing the path. There was a little movement behind me. "Okay now?"

I saw Chase escorting a woman in civilian clothes, sharp clay gray suit and matching topcoat, down the path from the direction of the circle. "Okay now, Michelle? Can I turn around now?"

The woman was Lt. Hewitt. "So, Joe, is it okay with your invisible little friend if we talk for awhile?"

175

I turned and Michelle was gone. Winnie nodded at Chase and the orderly waved back and continued south toward the Deadline.

"Where's Pop?"

Winnie pulled her collar up as scout flakes began drifting down through the branches in advance of the main invasion. Her dusky Halle Berry looks seemed rather pale and frozen. "I came instead."

"You guys track down that D1200 unit yet?"

"The bug is out of the State Police inventory. Claire says she can't find out which troop or individual drew it out without bringing in the State fuzz, which risks tipping off whoever it is here."

"It might be worth it just to have a real lead for a change."

"And to point at the bait?" she asked, her eyebrows arched.

"Well, there's that, too."

"We ran a civilian chopper across here early this morning. There's an outer access road that runs around the grounds beyond the trees. On the southwest corner of this road, tucked into the trees, we found a green van. It's within operating range for the D1200. It's State Police."

"I don't get it. You flew the chopper low enough to read its license tag?"

"Orange diamond decal on the roof."

I laughed. "State undercover color of the day?" I shook my head. "We are dealing with some real pros. Are you going to grab them up?"

"No. We need a whole lot more before MCU declares war on the State Police."

We took the path north toward the circle. "Before I forget, Winnie, I need Claire to take a good look at Oran Conner. He's in Homicide. Union delegate. Came out here to get me to carry a wire on Yuker." I pulled the miniature tape recorder from my pocket and showed it to her.

"Conner?" Winnie frowned. "Before my promotion I voted for him."

"Next time, we'll attend the debates."

176

"I'm management now. No next time for me." Hewitt looked down, her lips pressed together.

"Is Conner a relative? Winnie, you look like your dog died."

"It's not that. I want to pull you out of here, Joe. Do you have that reading on Yuker yet?"

"He didn't kill Katey Sloan."

"You absolutely sure?"

"Winnie, I'm not absolutely sure *you* didn't kill Katey Sloan."

"Maybe it doesn't make any difference. How would you like to get out of here anyway?"

That surprised me. "Why?"

"The blue wall, the fort, and the retired Girl Scouts League is about to fall on you. If we get you out of here, maybe we can avoid you getting hung by a half-dozen old school ties."

"What's going on?"

She held her multi-colored knit cap back from her right ear. "Notice how my ear resembles an ashtray? We been burned, DiMaggio. Somehow the brass got on to what we're doing. Our unofficial investigation is now officially unofficial: out of our hands. We are forbidden to interfere in the matter henceforth."

"Henceforth?"

She recovered her ear. "I believe Dock was quoting Chief Harolds."

"Do you know who handed down that order?"

"Claire ran the chain-of-command all of the way up to the governor's office. The complaint is that we are stepping all over State jurisdiction—"

"Which we are," I interrupted.

"—and we are instructed in no uncertain terms to back the hell off."

"You think the cover-up goes that high?"

"You're the one who thinks the governor ought to be doing his laundry at Books." She shrugged. "The cover up could well originate in the governor's office, if not knowledge of the murder itself. To be honest, it smells more like a turf thing, Joe. But the other side is using it."

As we passed the Dan Circle of benches, I asked, "So, what do you want me to do?"

"If you're certain Yuker is innocent, let's pull you, take what we have, and begin raising hell with the state attorney general. Might even be able to work it through the Fed. If nothing else, we can drop it on the media."

"Besides the position this puts Yuker in, we got no names, Winnie. No evidence. A handful of lame leads, the follow-ups of which all lead out of our jurisdiction."

"What about this name you gave your father: Daniel Walker. We ran his finances and he got run over by the business cycle. He's not exactly ready for the dole, but he's down from eight to just under a million net."

I thought for a moment. "No. It doesn't wash if he's still that much above water. I was looking for five or six mill in the hole. It's not Walker, anyway. I have another name, though: Adam Stover. He was a CO lieutenant instructor at SCOTA when Katey Sloan went through the academy. He resigned."

"The one Sloan filed the sex suit against then dropped?"

"That's the one."

"We already tracked him down. He's been in Quantico for the past two months learning how to be a G-Man."

"FBI Academy. Tough to run a drug ring and pull off a murder in another state and keep up your grades."

"Pieces not fitting together, Joe?"

"They fit together great. They just don't happen to belong to the puzzle I'm working on."

"Let's get you out of the storm, Joe, shake the tree, see what falls out."

"That's a great plan if you're looking for coconuts."

"You have a better plan?"

"The usual one: keep annoying people until someone tries to swat me."

Winnie was quiet for a few more steps. "Dock said to leave it up to you, Joe." We crossed the South Court Path and continued walking toward the shut-down fountain. "What's with these circles?"

"Meeting places. Group therapy. The wimpy groups are waiting for warm weather. My group, Dan's Dragons, already meet back there in the circle we just passed."

"It's freezing. You really must be crazy."

"Wait until I tell you about the two persons here, probably on staff, who are trying to kill me."

"What?"

I held up my hand. "It's not as bad as it sounds. To get away with it, they have to rig it so it looks like suicide, an accident, or like other patients did it, which makes it kind of tricky for them."

"Their friends did a pretty good job on Yuker."

"To frame Yuker, they had to bring in too many bodies. You have any friends left in the Department of Corrections? There's a CO named Yotimo and three cons that went conveniently blind around the time Sloan was killed, leaving Yuker without an alibi. They need their shoes pinched."

"They'll have to wait until we have a lot more, Joe. No one in South River PD has a friend in Books Correctional these days."

"Anyway, my current partner pointed out that these guys who tried to kill me probably don't have anything to do with the Katey Sloan investigation. A lot of killers live here, and they all have their own agendas."

"Current partner?"

"Det. Yuker."

"You've got a serial killer for a partner."

"You say that like I've never done it before."

A wry smile cracked her frown. "Right. Back up a second, Joe. What about the other ones who are trying to kill you? Why?"

"Beats me. I was kind of hoping you could run the third floor patients and staff through the computer against my old cases and see if something turns up."

"What are *you* going to do about them?"

"Sleep with my eyes open."

"Brilliant, Joe. Will you swim around my boat the next time I'm on the Amazon trolling for piranhas?"

"What's it pay? I'm saving up to put my goldfish through obedience training."

"Is Julia Powers here to take care of you?"

I looked away, shrugged, and shook my head. "She hasn't made contact yet. Have you heard from her?"

"No, but I'd be real curious what she thinks of your plan."

"I don't know, Winnie. She should've gotten in touch with someone before now. What about her office?"

"Her office won't say. But things come up, Joe. Look, what if you are here all by yourself? Something could've gone wrong with her cover, she could be in a hospital somewhere. What are you going to use for backup?"

"Winnie, Julia is here because she said she'd be here." I frowned and rubbed the back of my neck. "Unless she decided that I needed to do this on my own for some kind of bogus confidence building mental health thing—" The alarm on my handheld vibrated my pocket making me jump. I pulled it out, looked at it, and punched it off.

"You have an appointment?"

"Yes. Practice for the Turkey Talent Show. I'm singing backup in a prison riot." I put away my handheld and looked up at the falling snow. "For now, Winnie, I'm going to stay here. I can't leave Yuker hanging."

"So to speak," she added with a worried smile.

We walked Insanity Path back to the main building,

On my way back from practice in Teddy's room, Michelle was in her place, sitting cross-legged beneath the surveillance cameras. I stopped in front of her. She was staring blankly at the center of the hall, the corners of her mouth down. "Hey, Michelle. My visitor this afternoon was my boss, Lt. Hewitt. Because you sneaked off on me, she thinks I was talking to my invisible little friend." I whirled a finger next to my right temple.

Michelle broke into a smile and covered her mouth with both hands.

"Yeah, that's a riot. Now my boss is measuring me for the rubber gun squad." He pointed at the floor. "Want some company?"

She reached out and dusted off my piece of the floor. Once I was settled next to her, I rested the back of my head against the wall. "Ever small, Joe?" she asked. "In school?"

"I was bullied a lot, Michelle. Older kids punching on me."

"Why?"

"Because they could."

Long silence, looking down at her lap. "I go places." She placed her palm against her forehead. "In here. Since I was little." She lowered her hand. "It didn't work today. I couldn't go."

"I think if you get better, Michelle, it cuts down on your hiding places."

She frowned and looked at me. "What do I do?"

"When I couldn't hide anymore, a friend of my father's taught me how to take care of myself."

"How?"

"He taught me how to fight."

She looked up at me. "Teach me?"

I studied the girl for a moment and nodded. "Sure. I can show you a couple of things. We still have a couple of hours before bed check. Want to see if we can find an escort down to PT?"

"Mommy said fighting is bad."

I rubbed the back of my neck as I thought of Nathan Sunday, of Alvin Yuker, of so many other children. "Sometimes mommies are so wrong they ought to be hit by lightning."

Her eyes filled with tears. After a long moment staring through her tears at the center of the hall floor, she stood up. "Let's go."

Two things crossed into my awareness that night: Michelle was a lot tougher than she appeared and thinking about working out is no substitute for doing it. I slipped into bed that night dreaming of a bathtub full of Tylenol.

OUT ON THE ROOF

At lunch the next day, Neal informed us all that our request had been approved. The Dragons were to meet upon Redshank Roof for afternoon group. Gather at the access stairs next to Half Satan ten minutes before meeting time. After lunch we met there and Neal and Munroe escorted us up the stairs to the fourth floor. On the Redshank landing, there was an additional door to the left that opened onto the roof. We stepped out, the sun squint-bright and warm despite the in-the-shade temperature holding at just above freezing. The few inches of snow that had fallen on the roof during the night were well on their way down the drains.

The roof area was as large as Half Satan, with a new-looking white-painted fence of vertical metal bars inside the edge. In the southeast section of the roof close to the access door, there was a circle of ten Adirondack chairs already cleaned off and dry. Munroe pulled a paperback book from his jacket pocket, sat on a table at the opposite corner of the roof out of earshot, and began reading. Neal went back down the stairwell, the door closing and locking behind him. There was no coffee table, no box of tissues, but toward the southwest, deep into the woods beyond the Inner Access Road, there was the boxy shape of a van parked among the trees. I checked out my chair and helped with the others. No listening devices.

"Yesterday, listening to that thing Sunday wrote," began Thomas after we settled in, "I sort of got the feeling he was teetering on the edge of the roof, teasing the wind to knock him off. With that fence a hurricane couldn't've moved him."

"Nice view, though," said Louis. "I've never been up here."

"When I was here before," said Alvin, "the fence was different. A chain link thing with a couple of gates. They were padlocked, but no problem to climb over. A skinny person could even squeeze between the fence and the gate it was such a loose fit. We had a jumper. That's why the new fence. Back when Sunday was here, he was standing out on that edge. The wall out there is only about twenty inches high."

"So," said Harvey. "What does everyone think of the new Dan Walker? Everybody have office hours this morning?"

"What did you think of him, Buckaroo?" asked Yukiko.

"Deft evasion, Moon Pie."

"Actually, I was intercepting your effort to deflect the focus from yourself."

"You're a quick learner." Harvey grimaced, looked around at the clouds, then leaned forward in his chair. "Okay. No. I don't like where I am. I don't like hiding in this place. I don't like being afraid. I had a big talk with Dan this morning. I told him about Mark Billings and his lips. I told him about all the other horrible things that humans do to themselves and to other humans. You know, it was like a competition out there. We'd clean up after some horror that would look like an extreme of some kind, a mess that, simply by its nature, would say: 'It can't get worse than this,' and you'd kind of adjust to that. You'd say to yourself, 'Okay, if it never gets worse than that, I can handle it.' In a couple of weeks, a couple of days, a couple of hours, though, a new record would be set. We could count on it. Right after Billings, two days, this eight year old kid took his baby brother and laid him out behind the tire of his father's car that he knew was backing out of the garage."

I looked up at him. "You didn't freak out after the Billings thing?"

"No. After that. All of that little boy's guts were squirted out of his anus. Turned him inside out. Everything stayed in his intestines, though. No blood. The kid's brother said he just wanted to see what would

184

happen. There wasn't anything to clean or repair. The mother went berserk. She wanted to know why we refused to clean the scene. We hosed it down, refinished the garage floor, but that wasn't enough. What she wanted us to repair was the past. Next day up in Nelson we're called in to clean up a place where a guy broke into a house to rob it. Mother and four children. He tied them up and cut out their eyes so they couldn't identify him. Not really all that much blood, but how could he not know that their memories weren't in their eyes? You know what that moron said to the media on his way from being arraigned. 'Can't blame me for trying.' That was when I freaked. I punched out my brother, the TV, and electrocuted myself. Why isn't execution by slow torture legal? Why isn't stupidity a capital offense?"

"What's Dan want you to do?" I asked.

"Paint. He wants me to go back to painting. Give my feelings color and put them on canvas."

"Are you going to do it?"

He sat quietly, looking at his hands clasped together between his knees. "For as long as I knew him, every morning, five days a week—sometimes seven—my dad went to work to try and keep the animals from overrunning the citizens."

"Where was he on the job?"

"Down in the Zone. My father wasn't educated, he wasn't even very smart. He'd tell us that, me and my cousin Cory. 'Education,' he'd say. 'If you don't want to wind up with a shithole job like your old man, get an education.' A beat cop. A damned beat patrolman, down there with the whores, junkies, dealers, bangers, bums, and wiseguys. Never made second grade, never got a commendation, got himself flat feet and chronic back pain. Shot down and killed in an alley off of Trask among the trash, used needles, and broken furniture behind a whorehouse. CSU found two different persons' urine on his uniform. They shot him down and pissed on him. He put us both through college, though."

Harvey looked up at the faces in the circle. "He put us both through college and what're we doing? Cleaning up after killers and cops." A bitter laugh. "I miss him. I really miss my dad. I really want to find and kill the bastards who killed him—who pissed on him." He leaned back in his chair. "I really don't want the wind to leave me here."

Alvin nodded. "Dan wants me to paint, too." He twisted around in his chair and looked at the view of Books prison and Soldier Heights beyond. "Dan says I can't deal with my feelings by chasing them off with work, or drugs, or anything else. I need to pick it up, own it, accept it, before I can deal with it. Before I can deal with what I did, I need to own what happened to me. All the things that were done to me. I pushed them off because it's such a cliché in prison. Sexual abuse, physical abuse, brain damage, powerlessness, rage, acting out. The abuse excuse. Dan said it isn't a cliché. It's history. I need to piece it all together and locate the feelings that go with them, if I can."

"Sounds like a big job," observed Louis, his voice sounding hollow.

"Might not even be possible, if the experts are right," said Alvin. "I just make the cut for the definition of a serial killer: three. Once serial killers start killing, they say, they're beyond help. Dan says he doesn't know, himself, but he'd like to help me find out." He smiled. "I guess I have the time. How was your session, Louis?"

"I still don't trust Dan very much. He puts me off when I try to talk about him," he nodded toward me, "and his never ending pursuit of my friend, Valjean."

Thomas made a sucking sound with his teeth. "I don't think you even believe that crap yourself."

"Mad Dog, what did Dan want you to do?" asked Yukiko.

"Aah, he wants me to talk about school, what was going on, my family, what was going on. Here at Squirmhi, and what's going on. There's nothing going on. Nothing to look at anywhere."

"If there's nothing to look at," said Harvey, "then there's no threat. You might as well look at it."

"Why?"

"You'll get Dan off your back, for one thing."

Louis thought for a moment, shook his head, and said, "No."

"'Fraidy cat," said Leila. Geraldine made a sound like a chicken clucking.

"There is nothing to look at!" Louis growled. "Nothing! School is school, family is family! All normal. No problems. Very boring."

"That sounds abnormal as hell to me," said Thomas.

"That from a fucking drug addict!"

Munroe looked up from his book, made sure everyone was still seated and unarmed, then resumed his reading.

Thomas and Louis both were red-faced. Leaning forward, his elbows on his knees, Thomas cocked his head to one side. "Dan recommended sending me over to the rehab unit at Riverside General." Two beats. "I'm going to go."

"What if the court wants you to do time?" asked Louis.

"They have a rehab unit at Rougemont. Dan thinks he can get me in if it comes to that. I'm an addict, Mad Dog, and I don't like where I am. What about you? Don't you want to be a human being again? Go out and teach, go on a cruise, see Paris for real? Aren't you tired being guardian angel to a fictitious character?"

"Oh, boy," said Leila, reaching out to Louis with her lint roller, stopping him as he started out of his chair. "You have fuzz all over you, Louis. Let me get it."

Louis tore his murderous stare from Thomas's face, looked at Leila, then settled back as he shifted his gaze to Munroe, again looking up from his book.

"Sugar," Leila said to Louis. "Dan wanted to talk to me about sugar." She stared at a small white cloud that drifted high above the prison. "Not so much sugar. What I use sugar for." Leila began talking about a little girl who grew up in a wonderful home with loving parents, two sisters for fun and a strong handsome older brother for protection. She was seven when she was snatched out of her front yard, kidnapped, raped, beaten, poisoned, and left for dead by the side of a road in West Shore.

"They said it wasn't my fault. I was told to rake the yard, and that's where I was. It wasn't my sisters' or brother's fault, because they were in the house doing what they had been instructed to do. It wasn't my father's fault. He was down at the office working on a case. He was a superior court judge. It wasn't my mother's fault. As the man's car pulled away from the curb, he punched me, so I wasn't moving. But I saw my mother racing after the car, screaming, shouting for help. It wasn't anyone's fault save Uncle Ralphie, for that is what the man told me to call him."

Uncle Ralphie finished with Leila and her family and was absorbed by the traffic on the Interstate. He was never found, never charged, never punished. Leila's wonderful home, however, was shattered. By the time Leila was ten, her parents were divorced, one sister had run away from home, the other became depressed, suicidal, and eventually took one of those zero mileage tours in her garage with the doors closed. Her older brother wound up doing four years at Books for assault, and when he was released he left town, never to be heard from again. When Leila was eighteen, her mother took her own life.

"Sugar is sweet and so are you." Leila held up an invisible sheet of paper. "She left me a note, my mother: 'Sugar is sweet and so are you.'" She looked at Harvey. "I wish SceneClean could have come in and fixed our past. I wish you and your cousin could climb into my mind, clean up and make the repairs." She looked around at the faces. "For years I hid in clay and glazes and fire. It was a beautiful, sensuous, clever, and exciting universe."

She reached into her blue purse and pulled out a handful of cubical plastic containers of syrup and jellies. "Now I hide behind these. My little soldiers." She looked at Harvey, then me, then around the circle, stopping on Louis. "After I was raped and beaten, I used to sprinkle granulated sugar around my bed at night so I'd hear and wake up if anyone tried to sneak up on me when I was sleeping. Sugar." She held up the containers. "I have these all around my bed, standing guard. They don't even work. Sugar crunches. Corn syrup just draws ants." She looked at Louis. "Hiding doesn't work very well. I think that's what Thomas was saying."

Louis was looking down at his hands, one thumb compulsively rubbing the back of his other hand. "This teacher we talk about," he said, "this mad dog who broke himself into pieces attempting to take these self-centered pot-fried video-brains and introduce them to the treasures—the universes—available to them through the world's literature, only to be called Looey Gag-Me-with-a-Spoon." He grimaced as he saw Munroe put his book away, stand, and say something unintelligible into his hand radio.

Munroe walked over and stopped between Yukiko's and Harvey's chairs. "I apologize for interrupting." He nodded at Leila. "They want you down on Chicken for some tests that Dan ordered."

"Written tests or needle tests?" she asked, her eyebrows raised.

Munroe grinned. "Written. Your escort'll be at the access door by the time you get over there."

"Thank you," she said as she leaned forward and pushed herself up from the chair. She paused for a moment to roll a little lint off Munroe's necktie, then shouldered her blue leather bag and walked to the access door. By the time she reached it, the door opened and she was gone.

Louis leaned back, let out a sigh, and rubbed his eyes. "Every teacher gets one or two during a career. This teacher got one. He had been teaching at a private school down south and moved back to South River to head Vadalia High's English Department. And this kid was in junior English. John. He was like a sponge, absorbing everything this teacher could teach, going outside for more, and bringing it back. And he could write. This teacher couldn't wait to see what the kid would turn in on his next assignment. Can you imagine having a vitally interesting discussion on Voltaire with a sixteen year old kid in a public school? Chaucer? Kafka? Christ, I would've paid the school to teach there."

He stared at the bars of the safety fence. "Voices: young, strong, confident, and so very, very stupid: Hey, kid, you want to be one of us? You want everybody to stop calling you geek? Want to belong? Drink this, weenie. Go on. Show us you can be a man. Drink more. More. Try some of these pills, too. Take a chance." He stared up at the clouds. "Alcohol poisoning. They killed him." He looked at his hands. "Jocks. I only got to beat

189

the hell out of two of the bastards before they took me here." He closed his eyes, his head nodding. "Jean Valjean: he's an idea. A way I think—hope to make it through here. Through life. It gives me a focus, don't you see? A place to put my mind. A place to put my mission, my purpose—my need to have a purpose."

He closed his eyes. "I know Victor Hugo wrote fiction. I know Jean Valjean wasn't real—isn't real." He opened his eyes and looked at me. "You're Joe Torio, not Javert. Of course I know this." His hands formed into fists and he closed his eyes tightly as he teetered dreamily in his chair. "What's the harm? What's the harm? Why can I not have a purpose that isn't guaranteed to fail?"

We talked of other things. Alvin talked about his mother shoving a nail into his eye because he happened to see her naked. He talked about her repeatedly hitting him in the head with fists, vases, a baseball bat, and after she hit him with a brick and he went into the hospital for an operation to relieve the pressure on his brain, she was cautioned that her methods of disciplining bordered on child abuse. She then changed her method: a pair of pliers applied to his genitals. She had been sick. Mike Keller had certainly worked with him on that. Her life hadn't gone the way she had hoped, either. What was left for both of them was an ocean of rage, a switchboard smoking with crossed wires, half persons living half lives, and eventually three corpses.

Geraldine talked about getting free and getting old, and how getting old was taking away the little freedom she had managed to glean from life. She was a grown woman with feelings who had been used up by others, and now that she was free of those who held her down, it was too late. When she would find someone young, someone who was living life, free and full of joy, her jealously made her just want to beat them, tie them up, lock them up, just to show them what they were taking for granted—no, not that. Just to even up the scales a little. Make a little justice.

I talked about Nathan Sunday and how the experience had left me with a great emptiness that threatened to swallow my career, my life, and my love for

Julia Powers, without whom nothing in the world would make any sense. I told them about Gully Raye and Kirby Flagg and how they worked cases—until their rubber bands snapped. I shared that I worked my cases the same way, and that in the back of my head was the constant fear of winding up the same way. I also shared with them that Kirby Flagg was my biological father and that he had ax murdered his entire family, except for me. I was brand new when the blood flowed and in his madness Kirby Flagg had forgotten me.

Teddy closed his eyes, faced the sun, and sat that way, tears glistening in his lashes. One tear streaked down from his left eye making him smile. "Wow. Ain't this a bitch." He leaned forward and rubbed the tears from his eyes. He showed his palms to the group. "Look at this shit, man. Damn. I haven't cried since my old man was whacked." He flopped back in his chair. "People, I'm here to testify that I am a failure at not caring about anyone. You try and cover your ass by not letting anyone get close—no one's got a handle on my feelings. If you leave, if you die, it doesn't matter at all if I don't give a shit. But I care. I tried to burn it out with every drug I could get my hands on, but they don't produce enough. But now I'm in a situation—a bind—I can only survive if I don't care about anyone, including myself. I don't know what to do."

"Can you talk about it?" asked Geraldine.

Teddy shook his head. "Amazing the shit you can step in when you're not looking."

I leaned forward, clasped my hands and rested my elbows on my knees. "You know that question you asked before? What do you do when you find yourself painted into a corner? Is that what you were talking about?"

"Yes."

"Found an answer yet?"

"No. Do you have one?"

"When you're painted into a corner, Teddy, you get out by walking through the paint."

"Sounds messy."

"It is."

LIFTERS THREE

After we came down the access stairs from the roof, Munroe did a head count and left us in front of Half Satan. Harvey, Louis, Thomas, and Yukiko went into the commons to lock in a ping-pong table for the rest of the afternoon, Teddy had an appointment, Alvin gave me back my handheld and went to make a phone call to Luther Stebbins. Geraldine went to the nurses station to check up on her groupie, Leila. I headed for my room to go over some notes when I saw Wally heading the other way. Wally was practically digested by smiles.

"What is it, Wally? You getting out? You win the lottery?"

"Better than either. Nance is on vacation and Nance's Chances have a substitute counselor. We just had our first session."

That woke me up. "Really? What's your new counselor's name?"

"Juliana Strong. She is terrific—what am I saying? She is incredible! I might even improve. My god, is she smart. And a babe. I may never go home again. You never saw such blue eyes or such a shape in your life."

"I just might have, Wally."

Wally patted his pockets then held up a hand. "Oh boy. I need to go to my room. Come on. It'll just take a second." He led the way, whistling that same Flatlanders tune.

"Wally, do you like country music?"

"I hate it."

I said, "Hey, Michelle," to Doorstop as I followed Wally to the low numbers. Michelle continued staring at the center of the hall, but gave me a thumbs up with her left hand. As Wally opened the door to 308 and entered,

I heard crying. I turned, crossed the hall, peeked through the observation window to 309, and the room was unoccupied. In 311, though, Elizabeth was sitting in the chair before her window looking up at the mountain.

I hesitated a moment, then knocked on her door. "Go away," said Elizabeth.

I opened the door. "Did you say okay?"

"No. I said go away!" She covered her face with her hands. "You are the last person in the world I want to see right now. Please go away."

"So, you did say okay. That's great." I pulled the desk chair over to where Elizabeth was sitting. Turning the chair around, I straddled the seat and rested my arms on the back. "I said you have a big butt, Elizabeth. I apologize."

"That was days ago, and I do have a big ass. Big ass, big tits, big belly, big everything. I'm so ugly."

"Unlovable, huh? Went all the way through school with people picking on you, no dates, teachers making jokes. You go to college?"

"Yes."

"Same thing there, right? More subtle, but for all that, more vicious. Lonely, right? Elizabeth must be a pretty horrible gob of snot if all those people hate her. You're sort of a joke God played on the universe, and fairness is just another joke everybody plays on you. So you hide in food, maybe a drug or two, and snap at everyone, rejecting everyone before they can reject you, trying to protect yourself. Who could love a thing like that?"

Her eyes went wide as she put on her glasses. "Who has been talking outside of group?"

"Nobody. Not to me, anyway. I know your story because you're a sister of mine, Elizabeth —do you like to be called Elizabeth?"

"Beth."

"Beth. That's better. Beth, did you know my adoptive father used to be the state hangman?"

She shook her head.

"It's true. Until my father got someone to teach me how to fight, I was the school punching bag, the butt of all the jokes. Who could love a kid whose father

194

singlehandedly filled a graveyard? You hid in food, I hid in the TV. Everybody in this joint is hiding somewhere from something."

"Why'd you come in here, Joe? In my room, I mean."

"Abject guilt. Anger, too. I found myself being consigned by you to that big crowd that is supposed to hate you. I don't like having the people I dislike picked for me. If I'm going to hate them, I want it to be for my own reasons."

"And you don't hate me?"

"No. Maybe I will when I get to know you better. But right now, no."

She studied me for a long time. "Were you lonely in school?"

"Sure. I used to hide in the back of my closet. Played with suicide more often than I've told my shrink." I looked down. "Damned near went and did it once."

"If everyone hates you, Joe, what do you do about the loneliness?"

I frowned as I thought on it. "Somehow I figured out that everyone doesn't hate me." I looked up at her. "Most of the men, women, and children on this planet never even heard of me. And those who have heard of me, well, they don't all hate me. In fact, a few like me a lot."

"Do you have a girlfriend?"

"Yes, I do."

"I bet she's pretty."

"That is such a feeble word, Beth. Beautiful, gorgeous, stunning—they all fall short. Her name is Julia. She's smart. Smarter than me. Richer than me, too. I even suspect she can beat me up."

"No."

"You're right, Beth. Thanks for keeping me honest. I'm positive she can beat me up."

Beth laughed.

"The point is, though, she loves me. I don't know how it happened, or why. Hell, I even found out that my father loves me."

"The hangman?"

"Yeah. You want to know something even more bizarre? I found out that I love him. There's a lot of love out there, Beth, but as a killer I once heard in a Twelve

Step meeting say, 'You can't let others love you until you can love yourself.'"

She burst out with a derisive laugh. "Love myself. Look at me. How am I supposed to do that?"

"Do you know any skinny people you love?"

She thought a long moment. "A number I envy. None I love."

"So, it's not size."

"How do you love yourself?"

"Somebody in the meeting asked the killer that. He said emotions are like muscles: the ones that are used the most get the strongest. I'm guessing the ones that tell you that you're ugly and unlovable look a lot like Arnold Schwarzenegger."

She smiled and then laughed. "The ones that tell me I'm lovable look like Woody Allen. How do I pump him up?"

"Go in the bathroom, look in the mirror, and tell yourself, 'You're okay.' Do it every day for a month."

"That's it?"

"It worked for me."

"But, look at me, Joe. What do I do about that?"

"I was hiding in a TV. The people who can love me aren't in the TV or in drugs or in food. I had to let them find me. Tell me something, Beth. What was that thing in the chair lounge all about?"

"The butt flash?"

"Yes."

She grinned, closed her eyes, and shook her head. "A joke, that's all. I heard that's what Monica Lewinsky did to Bill Clinton in the Oval Office, and the rest is history. I just forgot the thong."

I smiled widely. "Then I was right. I got the joke."

"You were—"

A muffled scream interrupted the moment, then Wally's voice calling, "Joe? Joe?"

I sprang up from the chair, pulled open the door, and saw Wally thirty feet down the hall toward Half Satan. As I reached him, we both heard a bellow come from the open door of room 327. "My baby! My poor baby!"

"That's Geraldine," I said, walking rapidly to Leila's door. When I looked in I saw Leila, apparently unconscious, hanging half in half out of her bed, with Geraldine struggling with holding her shoulders up off the floor. Around the bed and kicked here and there were dozens of white unopened containers of syrup and jelly. A few of the containers had been crushed.

Billy came in behind me and pushed me off to the side as he took Leila, lifted her in his arms, placed her back on the bed, and began a quick check of her vitals. Seconds later he pulled his squawk and called for a gurney and an emergency team. I was feeling a bit helpless until I felt a finger poke me in the back. I turned and it was Wally.

"Grab one of Leila's lint-roller refills," he whispered and quickly withdrew.

I scanned the room, and there were three refills on her desk with more refills in a carton beneath. Next to the carton of refills was a carton filled with a few rolls of waxed paper and another carton filled with letter-sized envelopes. I grabbed a refill, and as I heard the emergency team racing down the hallway, I left Geraldine behind and slipped out of the room. A doctor and two paramedics cursed at Wally as he stood in the center of the hall, looking drugged out, stupid, and unmovable. They pushed the gurney around him and vanished into the room.

"Here's the refill, Wally. What did you want with it?"

Wally pulled a small plastic container from his pocket with a red cap. It looked like a McCormick spice bottle. It *was* a McCormick spice bottle.

"Cinnamon?" I asked.

Wally pointed down at the bit of floor that was between his feet. At first, I didn't see anything. Then, catching a reflection from the light from Alvin's open door, there it was: a complete positive footwear impression made with institutional imitation maple syrup. The emergency team emerged from the room, with Leila strapped down on the gurney. "How is she?" I called to no response save Geraldine holding out her hands as she waddled after the gurney. This time the team had to go around both Wally and me on their way to the nurses station.

"How'd she look?" asked Wally.

"Breathing. Her eyes weren't open though."

No one was watching as Wally bent over and sprinkled cinnamon all over the area between his feet. "Okay, Joe. You can blow."

"Why do you happen to have a bottle of cinnamon on you?"

"Crazy, huh?"

"In a word."

"I like cinnamon. I like it on eggs, I like it on bacon, I like it on potatoes, I like it on steak, I like it on custard and cheese and apple pie. I even like it in coffee. Besides, I couldn't think of anything else that would contrast with that white lint-roller paper." He pointed at the floor. "Blow."

"Why do you think we need to collect this lift?"

"Remember, I was in group with Leila. I know about her sugar soldiers. As soon as I saw someone had stepped in it, I figure two things: first, Leila didn't get that way by herself; second, whoever helped her get that way didn't know anything about her. What's the matter?"

"Nothing. Just feeling inadequate because I didn't think of it first. You sure you aren't a detective, Wally?"

"There are more true crime fans behind bars than anywhere else."

"Go figure."

"Go blow."

Smiling, I got down on my hands and knees and began blowing the cinnamon into the sticky areas and out of the clean areas as Wally went off down the hall. It took four of the sticky lint-roller sheets overlapped and placed face down to completely cover the impression. By then, Wally was back with a sheet of acetate and followed by Beth.

"What are you doing, Joe?"

I glanced up at her. "Getting a lift. Can you think of anything we can use for a roller?"

"What for?"

"We need to apply a heavy, even pressure on the back of this paper."

"How about that lint roller refill."

"Not stiff enough. We really have to lean on it."

Beth used the toe of her left shoe to take her right shoe off of her foot. Using her navy blue clad foot, she stepped on the paper, then lifted her foot, shifted position, and stepped again. After two more times, she put her foot back in her shoe and raised her eyebrows.

"Let's see," I said as I took an edge and gently pulled the lint-roller paper free of the floor. Wally put down a sheet of acetate.

"Where'd you get that?" I asked.

"Off the bulletin board inside the utility room."

I laid one end of the lift on the sheet of acetate and smoothed it out. I picked up the lift and looked at it through the clear sheet. "Perfect."

"And they said all those years in prison were wasted," said Wally.

"Not to mention all those doughnuts," added Beth with a grin. She turned and walked toward her room. "I'd like to stay, crime fighters, but I have a date with a mirror."

"Thanks, Beth," I called after her. I handed the sheet to Wally. "What do you make of that, shoe salesman?"

"Where's your room?"

I led the way to my room and Wally put the sheet on my desk, turned on the lamp, and held the lift beneath the light. "Right foot. New Balance," I said, pointing at the "NEW BALANCE" written across the ball of the foot.

"Nothing gets by you, Sherlock." Wally examined the impression from top to bottom. "They're pretty new. This stipple pattern on the heel is only worn down a little."

"Time wounds all heels?"

Wally leveled a steady gaze on me as he pointed at the lift. "Actually these are the tries that time men's soles."

"Ouch."

"Thank you. Thank you." Wally bowed to an imaginary multitude. "These are cross-trainers," he continued, "size ten, ten and a half." He pointed at the back edge of the heel. "He walks toes straight forward. He might even appear a little pigeon toed." Wally looked at me. "But, this was out in the hall. It doesn't prove anything."

"We ought to be able to fit two more impressions on that sheet of acetate, Wally. Shall we see if there are any impressions left in Leila's room that match this one?"

The floor in Leila's room had been thoroughly walked up by the emergency response team with about a third of the jellies and syrup containers crushed. Among the many we dusted with cinnamon, we found two footwear impressions worth gathering: seventy percent of a right that matched the one from the hall, and sixty percent of a matching left. With Wally standing in for Beth, I lifted the impressions and transferred them to the sheet of acetate. While we were down on the floor, Wally wrinkled up his nose. "What's that smell?"

I sniffed. "Sort of like ether. That's what chloroform smells like." We looked at each other. "Wally, you said you were in Dan's Group before I got here. You were in group with Leila."

"I haven't been lint-free since."

"What does Leila do with the lifts? After she rolls someone, what does she do with the used sheets? Toss them out?"

"Never." Wally blinked his eyes as he looked around the room, then went to her closet and opened it. "They're gone."

"What?"

"Leila's files. She always kept four or five rollers in that big blue bag of hers, and every time she rolled someone each roll got its own sheet. When they were all used and wrapped in their protective covers, she'd come back here, press each sheet onto wax paper, put them in envelopes, and file them in cardboard boxes she had stacked here in front of the window. They're all gone." He looked some more. "So's her blue bag. She used up three or four of those lint rollers every day."

"As an old partner of mine once said, Wally, that's almost a clue." I looked down at the three footwear impressions protected by the sheet of acetate, a familiar feeling of unfocused dread tightening my neck muscles. I looked up at the former shoe salesman. "Wally, can you find a place to hide this?"

"Why?"

"Real soon now someone is going to come looking for it and they are going to rip through my digs with tweezers and a microscope." My eyebrows went up. "Now that I think about it, they'll probably go through your room and Beth's, too. We're all on video."

Wally frowned for a moment, then smiled. "I have a place." He rolled the sheet of acetate, slipped it up his sleeve, and walked quickly toward his room. I stood in the hallway, noted that the west facing camera covered where Wally and I had taken the lift. Beneath the cameras, Michelle was looking back. I walked over and stopped in front of her.

She dusted off my place on the floor. "Thanks." I backed up against the wall, slid down, and sat with my legs crossed beneath me. "Did you see what happened in the hall here a few minutes ago?"

"Things."

"Was there anyone with Leila when she came down from the roof?"

"Big Brother."

"Neal?"

She shook her head.

"Billy?" I held my hand up. "Big Billy?"

She nodded toward the nurses station. "Billy left. Glaze Leila." She frowned as she looked into my eyes. "Gray Death." She jabbed with a finger toward Leila's room then pointed at the sole of her shoe. "Gray Death."

"You saw him go in? That's the impression we got?"

She nodded.

"Who is Gray Death, Michelle? What's Gray Death's name?"

She leaned close to me and whispered, "Jean Valjean."

I was after Jean Valjean. Mad Dog had been right after all. Later, at a dinner of mystery meat au jus, Geraldine informed the group that Leila was still unconscious. The physician treating her, Dr. Mato, suspected a drug overdose. Her condition was reported as "guarded," which drew a cynical chuckle from the Dragons. After all, we were all guarded. Teddy pressed

Geraldine for more details, but she was out of material and patience. She liked Leila a lot.

I frowned at Teddy as my hunch bone began throbbing, forcing me to put off pressing Louis on the identity of Jean Valjean. Louis and Harvey left the table together, followed a few minutes later by Geraldine and Thomas. Teddy was about to leave when I said, "Could you hang back a minute, Burnout?"

With a wary expression on his face, he placed his tray back on the table and resumed his seat. "What's up?"

Yukiko finished his bread pudding, washed it down with the remainder of his coffee, and left Teddy and I alone at the table. "I had a feeling you wanted to talk," I said to him.

"A feeling."

"My boss calls it my third eye. I call it a hunch. Under both tags it's gotten me many arrests, five commendations, and damned near killed four times. Every now and then it points me in a direction I can use."

"Third eye, huh?"

"Yes."

"I know you're a cop, but are you undercover or a real patient here?"

"All of the above."

"Damn it, that was a serious question."

"That's the best answer I have, Burnout. I'm mostly undercover, but I'm dragging my own baggage train." I frowned and measured the likelihood of being able to convey an understanding of my predicament when I wasn't certain I understood it myself. "Look, Teddy, I use a kind of insanity as an investigative tool. Maybe it's just that conclusions come to me at a faster rate than the awareness of what goes into reaching those conclusions. I sometimes feel things and the things I feel can be useful. I let myself become, in a way, just as crazy as the guy I'm looking for. It can be tough on the belts and bearings. Does that help?"

"Man, I can't talk to a cop. The wiseguys would freak."

"It's all right. I'm *omerta* qualified."

"What are you talking about?"

"The Gentleman Killer. One of his victims was Vince Polizzi. Vince's father, Don Scozarri, seems to think he owes me because of that."

"Vince Polizzi is dead?"

"Yeah. Tough to keep up with the news looking at the insides of your eyelids."

Teddy smiled wryly. "Well, goomba, *amico intimo*. Walking through the paint; I guess I need to know how messy is too messy."

"Why don't we drop the metaphors."

"Yeah." Teddy slid his tray to his left, crossed his arms, and rested his elbows on the table. "What do you think of Alvin?"

"Alvin?" I pondered a moment and shrugged. "He's smart, talented, he's got a lot of courage, a sense of humor, a sense of right-and-wrong that somehow managed to survive this load of history and pain he's carrying. He's struggling to become a better person and do the right thing, and he might have saved my life. I like him."

"And he's a serial killer."

"Yes."

"You've killed more people than Alvin has, haven't you?"

"I have."

He wanted to ask something. Teddy broke eye contact and stared at the green plastic salt and pepper shakers. "Two years ago, Joe, maybe three, I used to shack out in the old abandoned Reston Steel plant on Seventh. Me and maybe ten other bums off and on. I killed a man there. Sandy. That's all he was ever called. Young guy, mean bastard. We were fighting over a blanket I'd stolen from another bum. Sandy got me down and tried choking me, I gave him a push and a kick in the chest, and he went over a railing and down three stories onto the floor of the rolling mill. Broke his neck."

"What did you do?"

"Nothing. Didn't even notice he was gone. I took my new blanket, my smack, holed up in my corner and rode the needle. I don't know how long I was there. A day. Three. I ran out of stuff. By the time I was back in the world, they were taking Sandy off in a body bag and cops were all over the place."

"And you didn't know anything."

"I really don't remember. I needed to get my head right. Hauling dead bums out of that mill was getting to be a regular thing for the cops. Nobody pressed me on it." He shrugged, unfolded his arms and rubbed his eyes. "Anyway, I spent the next couple years in a fog, woke up one day in detox over at the Fellowship Center, and decided to try going straight. After detox, I went to meetings, washed a lot of dishes, kept busy and out of trouble." He glanced up at me. "A few days ago a guy's waiting for me in the alley behind the diner when I bring out the garbage."

"He have a name?"

"Not that he was willing to share with me. With those clothes, he had to be a cop. He had a piece. Anyway, he wants me to commit myself here for observation on a certain day. He said that he knows I killed Michael Sands—that's Sandy. I'm a murderer, and unless I want to put in fifteen to life in the Book, I should do what he says."

I kept a steady gaze on Teddy. "He wanted you to smuggle in a miniature tape recorder in your boom box."

"Yes."

"Then he wanted you to record everything Alvin Yuker says."

"You are a fortune teller, aren't you?"

"What're you going to do, Teddy?"

"This guy knows where I am, Joe. I got no cards."

"Have you recorded anything yet?"

Teddy nodded. "Everything. Nothing incriminating, as far as I can tell. Personally, I don't think Alvin killed that CO. They can take his voice off the tape and doctor it, though. Make him admit to anything."

"It's been known to happen."

"I still have the cassette. No one's come for it yet."

"What'd this guy look like?"

"Five ten, maybe. Blond, kind of shaggy. He leaves on a couple day's growth of beard like a fashion statement. Makes him look like a derelict. Wears his piece on the right. Gray eyes. Smirky mouth."

I rubbed my chin thinking that Teddy's visitor didn't sound like Oran Connor, PBA delegate with a deal. "Let me talk to someone I know, Teddy. That paint might already be dry."

"I'll do whatever I need to do, Joe. I don't want the wind to leave me where I am, either."

"Tell me, Teddy, can you play along for awhile?"

"You mean if that guy shows and wants his recorder back?"

"Yeah. Don't tip him off. Play along and keep me posted. Okay?"

"You got it."

"You might want to wipe that tape. Smack that recorder around and say it got broken."

"Cool."

I leaned back, regarding Teddy.

"What?"

"The squeegee bum and the Aston Martin: Did that really happen?"

"Why?"

"I'd kind of like to think it really happened."

Teddy smiled sadly. "It happened. That's how I got myself in here. How much trouble am I in?"

"The big challenge right now for all of us is to stay alive. We'll sort out the small stuff later."

Teddy nodded as he pushed his chair back, stood, and took his tray to his colleagues at the dirty dish window. I sat for a moment thinking about wet paint, a murderer I had seen executed, a face, and a murderer in the making—not a serial killer. A serial killer wannabe.

As I left the cafeteria, I caught myself whistling a tune. I continued until I realized it was the same Flatlanders piece that Wally had been whistling. Yee-haw.

GO FISH

The investigation of the Leila incident took place in Wanda's corner of Half Satan. I was called in after Thomas and Yukiko. I sat all the way south, my back toward the lights of the city, a detective seated on either side of me. Det. Nina Haddad of Breadloaf/North Valley Division sat to my right. She had close-cropped black hair, deep dark eyes, and full lips. Mid-thirties. She wore a loose-fitting gray suit with a dark purple scarf around her neck. Her partner, Det. Harry Cotter, sat on my left. He was blond, freckled, gray-eyed, intense, and barely thirty. A little raggedy around the edges, he was experimenting with the stubble look and was clad in denim with a blue-checked sport jacket and wore his shield clipped to his belt. Southpaw. Wore his shoulder holster beneath his right arm. A smirker.

Two uniforms stood guard in the area in case the crazies freaked. The uniform guarding the entrance to the group area was a balding pink blob named Getz who had enough hash marks on his sleeve to open a diner. He had his back on the doings, keeping an eye on the outside. The other uniform sat in one of the group chairs, closest to the entrance, slumped down, his arms folded, his gaze fixed on me. Late thirties, black and brown, six one, pale winter skin. His nametag read: Sloan.

"So your name is Joe Torio," stated Det. Cotter.

I looked at the man. "Yes."

"And where do you live, Joe?"

"You're kidding."

"When you're not in here."

"Fifteen Ninety-nine Pike."

"Occupation?"

"Detective."

"Det. Sgt. Torio from Major Crimes?" asked Cotter.

"The same."

Big frown on Cotter's face. "Really? Gee, I'm sorry. What're you in here for?"

"Observation." Another long silence accentuated by unasked questions. I looked at Cotter. "At Riverside General I jumped Capt. Dockery and engaged him in a bout of fisticuffs after he brought me a box of chocolates with soft centers. He knows I can't stand soft centers." I tapped my fingernail against my teeth. "Bad for the ivories."

Long silence while Cotter and Haddad exchanged meaningful glances. "I understand Leila is in your therapy group," said Cotter.

"That's right."

"Does she have a history of using drugs?"

"I don't know. What was it, by the way?"

"What was what?" asked Cotter.

"What drug?"

"We found a set of works. What was left in the syringe tested positive for heroin."

"Find any of her prints on the works?"

"No."

"Did that tell you something?"

Cotter frowned. "What do you mean?"

"Well, do you think she wiped down the syringe after shooting up?"

"You suspect an attempted homicide?"

"Don't you?"

"I think we'd better ask the questions," said Cotter. "What happened when Leila left the session up on the roof?"

"Munroe, the security officer who was escorting the group, he got a call on his squawk. He said to Leila that she was scheduled for a written test down on the first floor, an escort would meet her at the access door, she got up, went to the door, it opened and closed behind her."

"Did you see who met her at the door?"

"No."

"That was the last you saw of her?"

"No. When I returned to the third floor I heard Geraldine cry out for help and ran into Leila's room. I saw her then. One more time out in the hall as the EMS team rolled her away."

Cotter glanced at Haddad, who said to me, "I understand you were in her room after she was removed."

"Before, too."

"Why was that?"

I twiddled my thumbs for a moment, noting that Officer Sloan had not shifted his gaze from my face once since my session had begun. "I heard one of my groupies cry out, I went in to see what was wrong, but I was just in the way. I left after Billy showed up."

"After she was removed from her room, why were you in there?"

"I wanted to make some footwear impression lifts."

All of the cops laughed at that, including Sloan. "Why would you want to do that?" Haddad asked.

"In this place, who can say? My guess is I wanted to lift the impressions before they were obliterated by foot traffic."

"What Nina is asking," interrupted Cotter, "is what was your purpose? Why get the lifts at all?"

"I had reason to believe that the impressions were made by someone fleeing from Leila's room."

"The impression that was out in the hall? That could be anything."

"Is that the way it looked on the tape?"

Cotter's face remained impassive. "There was no tape. The unit malfunctioned."

"Do tell."

"Why did you go into her room the second time?"

"The sticky stuff seemed to come from Leila's room. That's why we went in there: to see if we could find impressions that matched the one we found in the hall."

"Did you?"

"We certainly did."

"This is bullshit," interrupted Sloan. "They can't use that in court. Chain of evidence. Besides, the guy's a nutball, Cotter. He's a patient in a mental institution."

I looked at Officer Sloan. "A voice crying in the wilderness," I said to Haddad.

"May we see the lifts you made?" she asked.

"I'll have to consult with my colleagues about that," I answered. "After all, it is an ongoing investigation."

"Asshole," muttered Sloan.

I stood and held out my hand toward Officer Sloan. "Pleased to meet you, Asshole. I'm Det. Sgt. Joe DiMaggio Torio."

Sloan got to his feet, Getz turned and gave Sloan a disgusted look. "Sit down."

Reluctantly, Sloan sat.

Haddad's fingers drummed upon her knee. "What made you think that anything was suspicious?"

I shrugged and resumed my seat. "Geraldine screaming, Leila out cold half out of her bed, and her syrup containers squashed were my big tip-offs."

"Do you know of anyone who might have seen the assailant leave Leila's room?"

"No, unless SO Gomez was watching the monitors."

Cotter, he of the smirky smile, leaned back and asked, "Are there any questions you think we ought to be asking, detective?"

Page one forty-seven, Mensieger's *Practical Interrogation*. Not getting what you want? Perhaps the subject will reveal himself given the illusion of controlling the interrogation by being given the opportunity to ask the questions himself. Throwing in the "detective" was a grace note designed to entice me through insincere respect.

"Sure," I said. "I have a couple of questions." I thrust out my lower lip and nodded slowly as I steadied my gaze on the uniform in the chair. "Sloan, is your first name Charles?"

The uniform sat up straight. "That's right."

"Did you help kill your wife, Sloan?"

"What . . ."

"Or did you simply set her up and then participate in covering up her murder? Is that what you're helping to do now? Are you covering up her—"

It took hardly a second for Officer Sloan to leap out of his chair, launch off the center of the coffee table, and land in the middle of my chest, the chair collapsing beneath our combined weight. The back of my head smacked against the glass wall and the concrete floor in rapid succession. For some inexplicable reason, my unconscious default went straight to the executions of Larry Collins and George Pruitt.

Tiny little room. The witness box. No air. Guacamole green.

Collins went like a good little soldier. The judge said die, and Larry Collins had never in his life disobeyed a judicial order. Pruitt had never willingly obeyed one. He pissed himself, and fought, and screamed, and cried, and begged, and pleaded. I couldn't tear my gaze away, my heart skipping beats, thinking that a condemned man ought to get it standing or at least sitting upright. But Pruitt didn't care that he was getting the feelgood exit. Whatever his shitty little life had been, he preferred it to the unknown. *As Pruitt's chest stopped moving, I felt myself gasping for air.*

Insanity for a tool, getting just as crazy as the killers, using the whys to point the way to the wheres. Once they're caught, though, it's not over. They never do quite leave. I'd been looking through their eyes too long to be able to cut it off for a mere execution. *Dock had introduced me to his wife, Ellie, after we had been riding together for a month. "This is Joe DiMaggio Torio, babe. He rides nightmares."*

Just before I opened my eyes and began dealing with the mother of all headaches, I remembered Officer Sloan's highly polished shoe as it landed on the coffee table just before his weight landed on me. The shoe had landed next to the group's box of tissues. This time, however, Group Wanda's box of nosewad had a cover over it, cream-colored, quilted, with a sprinkle of tiny red hearts. The bugs were multiplying.

There was the smell of old fish.

I opened my eyes. I was in bed in a treatment room. A face was withdrawing from mine, the aroma of chum bucket filling my sinuses. Geraldine's face came into focus.

"Aw, shit, Geraldine. Did you just give me mouth-to-mouth?"

Geraldine grinned, stuck out her tongue, and wiggled it. My hands flopped around until I found the call button. I pressed it, conservatively, thirty or forty times before the nurse arrived fifteen seconds later. The nurse was a Carol Channing replicant named Gretchen.

"Can I get you something Joe?"

"A five-pound breath mint and a gallon of Listerine. Stat." Gretchen left the room, laughing. I looked at Geraldine. "How is Leila?"

She held up a thumb and grinned. "Just fine, sweet pants. Just fine. So are you." Before I allowed my headache to drive me back to sleep, I checked to make certain neither wrists nor ankles were restrained and Geraldine was out of the room

UNCLE RALPHIE'S LEGACY

The next morning in Dr. Walker's office, I sat in the client chair while Dan talked on the telephone with Dock. After a heated discussion in which Dan invoked patient anonymity, trust, treatment integrity, fairness, truth, justice, and the American way, the psychiatrist banged the receiver in its cradle and faced me with a less than serene countenance.

"Very well, Joe—Det. Sgt. Torio. Your Capt. Dockery confirms your story. You are here undercover, officially or unofficially—that wasn't clear—attempting to clear Alvin Yuker of the murder of that corrections officer, who also happened to be the wife of that policeman you provoked last night. As an ostensibly sane person, would you mind telling me what it was that possessed you to accuse Officer Sloan of killing his own wife?"

"It seemed like a good idea at the time."

"There was actual thought involved in that decision?"

"Believe it or not." I leaned forward, placed my elbows on my knees, and rested my face in my hands. "I wanted to see Sloan's reaction."

"I see. What did you deduce from the reaction you received?"

"He has really quick reflexes and a short fuse. He wasn't in on the killing, but he's carrying a heap of guilt about it. It's possible he was the failed carrot bearer who first approached Katey Sloan to back off her investigation. In any event, he's under pressure to maintain the cover-up." I looked up at Dan. "He's torn by it. Two kids to support by himself. Whoever it was who waved that old blue school tie at him probably has something on him, or threatened to boil up something, that would cost him his shield and maybe even buy him some hotel time. If blue wants to frame you, it's damned hard to wriggle out."

Dan seemed to exchange his angry expression for one of interest. "Alvin Yuker, a case in point," he said.

"Indeed. Sloan's under lots and lots of pressure, Dan. I kicked him to see if he would pop. He popped."

"This third eye malarkey Capt. Dockery attempted to describe is paramount to fortune telling."

"True. I might just be full of crap."

"I believe I just said that."

"We still have our wonderful rapport, Dan."

"I don't approve of any of this, detective. It violates the trust of every patient in your group—"

"They all know."

"They what?"

"They know what I'm doing here. I told them all about my job on my second day—just as soon as we could get away from your eavesdropping equipment. By the way, we found another bug in the tissue box. Very sophisticated stuff."

"A listening device?"

"Yeah. Police issue. We figured it wasn't yours, which leaves the question: whose bug is it? Current theory in the group is that it belongs to the same folks who framed Alvin Yuker."

Long silence, heavy thinking, Dan absorbing the implications. He glanced at me. "Your group. I'm curious to know what their reactions were when you told them all this."

"I'm not certain anyone really believed me. I gather I'm not as convincing as the fellow who thinks he's Elton John. But, in general, they hold that everybody ought to have a hobby. They still think I'm crazy and that I should work on that." I shrugged. "Can't argue with them."

"Really."

I reached out a hand and tapped a finger on Dan's desk. "Look, Dan, you want to see my third eye at work?"

"Okay," he answered warily.

"Dig this. You are an adult who is insecure, tense, and with a very responsible, demanding, and frustrating

214

position. Here is where you work. You have got to have Tylenol in here."

Dan pulled open his center drawer, took a bottle of generic acetaminophen and placed it on the edge of the desk nearest me. Turning around in his chair, he opened the door to a tiny refrigerator and took out a can of Dr Pepper. "Here. Wash it down with this, if you can stand it."

"Dan, everybody is wrong about you. You are a great healer." I took the can, opened it, tossed down two of the white oblong tablets and took a drink. "Thanks."

"Are you sure you're all right?"

"The emergency room doctor down on Chicken—"

"Dr. Pinot."

"Yeah. She said no concussion or fractures. My brain got sloshed a bit. Headache for awhile. It should go away, although I am kind of curious what it would be like going a whole day in this place without getting drugged or beaten senseless." I went back to holding my face in my hands. "Dan. Mind if I ask you something about Leila?"

"You can ask. I might not be able to answer."

"You can answer this." I looked up. "All those preserved and filed lint roller sheets of hers: Where are they?"

Two beats. "According to the police, there were no files in her room." He angrily raised his eyebrows. "They do think her being shot up with drugs was suspicious."

"They went that far out on a limb, did they? Look, Dan, Geraldine told me, between mouthfuls of Listerine, that in her room Leila had four good-sized cardboard boxes filled with files. Other patients have seen them, too. When Geraldine went into Leila's room and found her almost dead, the boxes were gone. I think it's possible that they have been removed by someone who believes that something in one of those boxes incriminates him."

"I don't know what to tell you."

"What about the surveillance tapes for Turkey West?"

"No signal, according to Sgt. Gomez. Nothing but snow. He said it was a loose connection on the recorder. Loose connections do happen."

"I'm sure his defense attorney will make that argument. Where are Leila's *other* files?"

"What other files?" He looked singularly guilty.

"Dan, baby, when Leila would go back to her room, each used lint roller sheet would be detached from the roller, placed face down on a small sheet of waxed paper, slipped into one of her envelopes, then the envelope marked and filed in one of her boxes. Okay, follow the math: fifty-six sheets per roll, roughly three refills per day, that comes to one hundred and sixty-eight filled envelopes filed per day. That's almost twelve hundred a week, almost five thousand a month. One of those boxes can only hold five hundred envelopes, five boxes to a carton, that's twenty five hundred. Four cartons, that's a maximum of ten thousand envelopes—almost two months worth of current files. And how long has Leila been here? Thirty months? Let's say that the four cartons that were in her room are gone forever. Fifty or sixty cartons are still unaccounted for."

Dan's gaze dropped to his desktop. "More than that, actually. Once the envelopes are filled, you can't get five hundred of them back in a box. In addition, when she came here she brought a number of boxes with her. She needed a more-or-less clear room in which to reside, so I had most of the cartons put into storage down in the basement. We worked it like a bank. If she wanted to look at one of the cartons in storage, she had to turn in one of her current boxes."

"How many cartons are in storage?"

"Over a hundred."

I rubbed my eyes. "If she had four cartons, that'd cover at least a month, maybe two, so whoever tried to kill Leila got the ones covering Katey Sloan's murder."

"Maybe not." Dan began pushing through the papers on his desk, found a note, then turned to the two-drawer filing cabinets lining the wall to his right. He pulled a very thick file from a bottom drawer and looked into it. "I believe Leila drew those four cartons out the second day you were here." He studied a paper. "Yes. She deposited four cartons and withdrew four. The previous deposit was five weeks earlier." He looked at me, his eyebrows arched. "The sheets from the past five weeks are in the storage room."

The packed cartons filled three quarters of a locked windowless basement room illuminated by twin neon lights. Envelope cartons, refill cartons, cartons for wax paper, and piles of envelope boxes. "That is a lot of lint," I said with just a touch of awe.

"You can see why we couldn't allow her to keep all this in her room."

"I'm glad you hung onto it, Dan, but what I don't understand is why."

The psychiatrist stared at the stacks of cartons with the hapless expression of a skier with a blown knee checking out a mountain range buried in champagne powder. "I've never before seen obsessive-compulsive behavior manifest itself exactly like this." He touched one of the boxes, slid his fingertips along an edge, and faced me. "I had hopes of studying all this, preparing a paper perhaps, but—"

"—But who has the time?"

"Indeed. And I ran into something of a brick wall."

"What wall?"

"All these envelopes are coded."

"What do you mean?"

Dan picked an envelope box at random, opened it, picked an envelope out of the middle, and partially pulled the envelope behind to mark his place. "I can't associate any of these to when they were taken, who they were taken from, nor what meaning any of them have to what was going on in Leila's life at any particular moment." He handed the envelope to me. "Take a look at that."

I looked at the envelope. In tiny, faint, handwritten letters, the following:

```
ENRTT
EPOWH
TMTOI
HAHTS
ITEHW
RWROA
TAOUS
YNFSC
TDBAO
HAINL
RSLDL
EGLAE
ERYNC
BOADT
YUTTE
LPTHD
EAHRA
IRREP
LEEER
AAEFI
GRTRL
IOHOS
LOIME
BMRTC
ETTHO
RHEEN
TREBD
```

"You're kidding, Dan. This isn't a code. Look." I traced the columns vertically with my finger, right to left. "'This was collected April Second, Two thousand and three from the brother of Billy at three thirteen PM at Wanda's group area, Room Three Thirty-Three by Leila Gilbert.'" I frowned and looked at Dan. "Does Billy have a brother?"

"Yes. But, how could you read that? Right off."

"How come you couldn't, Dan?" I lowered the envelope, put it back in its spot, and replaced the lid. "Okay, look. Doctor. You want to communicate with the nutballs in this place? You really want to help them?"

"Psychiatric advice from an admittedly neurotic police detective?"

"Consumer surveys are done all the time. You want to help these people?"

"Of course."

"You're never going to make it happen by waiting for them to get their heads on straight enough to use your language. You have to be willing to climb into their heads and look at the world the way they see it—not objectively: actually. Walk a hundred miles in those kinky boots. Speak the language they understand. Get just as crazy as they are. Do you know about Uncle Ralphie?"

"Just what was in Leila's file. That was the name she used to identify her kidnapper."

"No, that was the name her kidnapper-rapist used to identify himself. Notice how the writing on that envelope makes no sense standing up? You've got to make that envelope lie down before it speaks. She was lying down when she was raped, and I'll bet you two doughnuts against your medical degree that Uncle Ralphie had a lot of lint on his clothing. Lint that was transferred to Leila's clothes. I don't think she helped much with the identification of Uncle Ralphie, she was made to feel guilty about it, and when her rubber band finally snapped, she wanted to make certain that no piece of lint ever again went without a name. You know how to read these things now?"

"Yes."

"Then give me a hand, Dan. I need to find all of the envelopes that cover from right before Katey Sloan's murder up to the present. Let's hope that Leila filed them in order."

Mike Ijumaa, the CSU liaison to Major Crimes, stood in the parking garage beneath the East Wing, his beat up black Ford Focus behind him. He still looked like Eddie Murphy in a bad mood, this time wearing faded black sweats over a pair of lurid purple pajamas, evidence of his day off. After Dan placed the third carton in the back of the car, I placed the last box next to the other three and closed the hatch.

"Mike there are between three and four thousand carefully preserved lifts in these boxes. Just as soon as is possible, without letting anyone in authority know you're doing it, I need to know what's on them."

"No problem. That should be a snap. You want me to drive the report over in a dump truck? Tomorrow okay?"

"If it takes a dump truck, Mike, that would be fine. Tomorrow would be terrific."

"Irony goes right over his head, don't it?" he said to Dan.

"A different drummer," agreed the psychiatrist.

"Ought to stop beating that drum with his head is what I'm saying. What am I looking for, Joe?"

"I don't know. As often as Leila cleans off everyone, you'll probably find a lot of similarities in there. Names, lint, food particles, skin cells, loose hairs. What we're looking for is in there, though. At least it is in the opinion of the guy who almost killed our collector to get it back."

"What about this business of not letting anyone know I'm doing it? You want to tell me what that's all about?"

"You don't want to know."

"Great. What about Dock?"

"You can talk to him about it. Winnie Hewitt, too. No one else, particularly not with anyone connected with the State Police."

"Who is going to pay for it, then? Whose account gets the paper? MCU?"

"You have my personal marker."

Mike threw up his hands and headed to the driver's side. "How can I lose?" Looking across the roof of his car at the psychiatrist, he added, "Save a bed for me, Dr. Walker. I see some bad paper and a major commitment coming my way." He climbed into the driver's seat, slammed the door, coughed the Focus to life, and drove from the garage up to the fresh snow in the East Wing parking lot.

"Now what?" asked Dan.

"Now I go back to Turkey West and we wait. Oh. Last night did Cotter and Haddad interview everyone in the group?"

"Everyone they asked to interview."

"Who didn't they ask?"

"Alvin and Teddy. Is that significant?"

"Oh, yes."

"Now," said Dan, "can you answer something for me?"

"Sure."

"Joe—detective—"

"Joe is fine, Dan."

"Very well, Joe. Between my discussion with Capt. Dockery, reading your file, and what you have shared with me, what Capt. Dockery called your third eye is, essentially, why you consider yourself crazy. Is that right?"

"Actually, I consider everyone crazy. It's just that, thanks to my run-in with the Rizzo brothers followed by the Gentleman Killer, my confidence was shaken." I raised a hand and rubbed the back of my neck. "No. My confidence wasn't shaken. You can't shake what you don't have. My conception of the universe was shattered. I was frightened. For once it wasn't the kind of fear that drives me. Instead, it just made me want to hide."

"You appear to have improved."

"Joe Torio gets back his groove." I thought a moment, grinned, and said, "You're right. And as a friend of mine once said, that makes you one hairy, chest-thumping therapy superstar. Are you going to be at group this afternoon?"

"Up on the roof?"

"In the Maplewood. The bombs are dropping on the wrong people, Dan. Somehow I've got to get those sights trained exclusively on me. I don't want anymore of the groupies getting hurt."

After a lunch of toast, salmon, and peas swimming in a nauseating pink cream sauce, I went back to my room to find it thoroughly tossed, and not very carefully reassembled. The bed was made, but made differently—sloppily. The jacket in the tiny closet had fallen to the floor. The pillow case was not even all of the way on the pillow. After checking the room for bugs, I stepped into the hall, walked over to Michelle and slid down next to her. "How's business, Michelle?"

"Lint lady?"

"The doctor says she'll be okay."

"Good."

"Did you see anyone go into my room?"

She looked into my eyes. "Look at PDA?"

"Sure." A little surprised, I took the unit from my pocket. "What do you want to see?"

"Nathan Sunday."

"You heard about that?"

She nodded.

"The card's in there. There's a lot of it. Would you like to keep it to read for awhile?"

She smiled. I showed her how to turn it on, punch to the Sunday document, and get around in it. "So," I said, "anybody in my room?"

She nodded. "Jean Valjean," she said.

"Really? Mighty spry for a fictional character."

Michelle hid the PDA between her legs and stared straight ahead, her expression lifeless.

"Michelle?"

She jabbed my left arm slightly with her right elbow and continued to stare at the floor. I leaned the back of my head against the wall and waited as Norman passed pushing the automatic floor scrubber around us. Norman had brand new Reeboks on his feet. A startlingly clean white pair with red and blue decorations. In fact his walk did look a little pigeon toed. As Norman passed, Michelle leaned to her right and whispered, "Jean Valjean."

A WALK IN THE PARK

Afternoon group in the Maplewood. The overcast
was joined by a warming mist that was working its way
toward pea soup grade fog. We were huddled on our
respective benches: Jackets and blankets with Dan
wearing his yellow and tan parka. Leila's place was
conspicuously empty.

"The ones covering up the murder of Katey Sloan are
beginning to panic," I said. "We aren't dealing with
psychos or pros. We are dealing with working stiffs who
thought they could buy more of the things they want for
themselves and their families by looking the other way
and getting just a little dirty. They supplied drugs to
captive addicts, took their money home, put steak on the
table, an SUV in the garage, and bought Bunky his
Nintendo station. Then came Katey Sloan, a woman who
thought the oath she took meant something. She not
only wouldn't look the other way, she began looking for
those who *were* looking the other way. They had to shut
her down."

"Nobody likes a cop," said Teddy, "especially other
cops."

I nodded. "Exactly. I'm betting Katey Sloan was
offered a substantial carrot to drop her personal
investigation. When the bribe didn't work, she was
probably threatened. When that didn't work, she was
isolated while the conspirators set up their frame on
Alvin. They arranged for it to be possible for Alvin and
CO Sloan to have been in the same place at the same
time, then they killed her. They are pros in their own
fields, but they aren't professional criminals. They made
some dumb mistakes. When they realized that, they

panicked and started pulling in others to help cover up the mess."

I looked around the circle at the faces. "They need to make this all go away. To do that, Alvin needs to be regarded as the murderer of Katey Sloan. The easiest way to do that right now is to kill Alvin here, make it look like suicide or frame a Squirmhi patient for killing him." I held out my hands. "Enter Dan's Dragons who have nothing better to do with their time than to tangle assholes with a murder and drug distribution conspiracy." I nodded toward Leila's bench.

"Leila is paying the bill. Fearing that something she had collected on her lint roller might incriminate someone, whoever it was sent in an accomplice to confiscate Leila's collection. It looks like what they did was to wait until we met up on Redshank Roof to sneak into her room and steal her files. Leila had a test, however, and left group early. Since she had to take a written test, she dropped by her room to get her reading glasses. She walked in, bumped into the other side, and they panicked again. They slugged her *and* dosed her with chloroform. Then they shot her up with heroin, enough to kill her, they thought. Along with that they planted a set of works."

"Which means they blew it again," said Harvey. "Leila never did drugs."

Louis faced me. "Sugar soldiers. We all know about her sugar soldiers. But the stranger stepped on them and you got the footprints."

I nodded. "That's right, Mad Dog, and we got some excellent lifts. The main problem with Leila's collection and the lifts we took from her floor is that they are both useless in court."

"Why?" asked Alvin and Dan simultaneously.

"With the evidence we have, a first-year law student could get Ted Bundy off in his street clothes, simply because of the sources."

"We're crazy," said Thomas.

"Damned right," said Yukiko.

"What about your big third eye?" demanded Geraldine. "How come you can't mind read these killers?"

"Good question. I don't know the answer."

"Joe," said Dan. "You told me that your gift—insanity—enables you to get into the minds of killers who have less than sane reasons for killing. Looking for the whys."

"That's right."

"Is the difficulty you're having here because these killers are protecting their pocketbooks rather than attempting to fulfill psychotic needs? They're too sane for you?"

The group laughed but I pursed my lips and thought on what he said. "Maybe." I looked at Alvin. The big man was looking at the grass between his feet. I closed my eyes but the only image looking back belonged to executed murderer Larry Collins. Why Collins? George Pruitt put on the more dramatic show, but it was Collins's face that kept looking back. Something the hangman had said—

"Is swami contemplating something he'd like to share with the rest of the class?" asked Harvey.

I was about to say something rude when the annoying ring of a cell phone shattered the moment.

"I apologize," said Dan as he pulled his unit from his pocket and punched it on. "Yes?" As he listened he unconsciously got to his feet. "Have the police been notified?" A pause, a glance at me. "I'll be there as soon as I can." Shutting down his phone, he said, "Beth and Wally from Juliana's group have both come down with drug overdoses. Wally is dead."

Beth's room and Wally's room both had been taken apart and the ones doing the demolition hadn't even bothered to keep their passage a secret. Beth had been taken to University Hospital. Just like Leila, Beth had been slugged, chloroformed, and then shot up with heroin. Respiratory and cardiac complications, however, required the move to BU's ICU. Wally's body was down on Chicken in the Squirmhi morgue, awaiting the Medical Examiner. As the afternoon mist thickened, the team of Cotter and Haddad from Breadloaf/North Valley Detectives made another appearance, this time without the support of Officer Sloan. Replacing Sloan was another uniform, Officer Kyle Bannerman, a big beach blondie who looked like Steven Seagal on peroxide.

The interviews took place in Dan Walker's office. In the outer office, under the watchful eyes of Getz and Bannerman, I waited with the rest of the Dragons who hadn't been questioned: Thomas, Yukiko, and Geraldine. When the detectives were finished with Wally's and Beth's new counselor, I scanned Juliana Strong as she left the room. A cloud of curly black hair, very red lips, dark smoky eyes. No sign of recognition.

As she passed Geraldine to leave the room, Geraldine grinned at me as she mimed patting Juliana's bottom.

Det. Haddad poked her head out of Dan's office. "Joe?"

I got up, followed Haddad into the office, and sat in the client chair.

"As I understood from our previous session, Det. Torio," began Cotter from his seat behind Dan's desk, "your footwear impression lifting team consisted of you, Wallace Spivak, and Elizabeth Foley."

"Not from my session, you didn't."

"I beg your pardon?"

"As well you should. Is this bumbling incompetence you exhibit simply a put on to instill a sense of false superiority in your subject, or is it the real thing?"

Det. Haddad, seated in a chair to Cotter's right, turned her face away.

"You got some mouth."

"Well, at least you didn't say it was real purdy."

"What are you talking about?"

"Deliverance? Forget it, banjo boy. It is the real you. So much for my celebrated third eye." I looked at Haddad. She was still hiding her face. "Shall I tell him or will you?"

She turned back, a suppressed smile making her look like she was chewing on a live salamander. "I believe Joe never mentioned the names of the ones who helped him make those lifts, Harry."

"Of course he did." A deep frown thinned to a defensive pout. "Someone did."

"And that's a Crimestopper," I said.

"What?"

"Dick Tracy. My rather crude way of indicating that I believe that you have stumbled upon an important investigative point." I looked at Haddad.

"He's curious who gave you that information," she said to Cotter. I nodded my thanks.

"You know better than that, Torio. It's an ongoing investigation."

"Is your name really Harry Cotter? Like at Hogwarts?"

"That's Potter."

"Your name is Harry Potter?"

Cotter got up. "Perhaps you'd be more comfortable talking with Nina." He left the room just a little wild-eyed.

"He's not a sensitive type, is he?"

"He has his moments."

"What would you like to know, Nina?"

She studied me for a second. "The lifts you and your colleagues took from the third floor hall and from the floor in Leila Gilbert's room: do you know where they are?"

"No."

"Are you certain?"

"Absolutely."

"Do you think they have any value to this investigation?"

"They're worth killing for, apparently."

"What do you know about Wallace Spivak?"

"Wally." Whistling that stupid Flatlanders tune. How to avoid the meds. How to save up the meds, which was what Wally had been doing. "Not much. He took time out to explain things to a new guy. Used to sell shoes and he used to do time. Head janitor at the Smith Building. Sharp guy. Knew a lot about feet. He should've been a detective."

"Do you think he told anyone what you three did?"

"Any number of persons could have seen us. The surveillance cameras had us covered, as well, but they appear to have come down with the flu."

"There was something wrong with the recordings?"

"What were the chances of that? Boy, I never saw that coming."

Long thoughtful pause. "Sarcasm aside, Joe, you suspect someone on the security staff is involved?"

"I wouldn't want to jump to any conclusions. We could wait until Gomez mails in his confession from Brazil."

"Did Wally do drugs?"

A pause. "Yeah. I think he did." I frowned. "He used to palm pills at meds. I assumed he was saving them up for either use or barter. Did he get it the same way as Leila and Beth? Heroin?"

"No. It was Oxycodone. It was prescribed for him, but not in the dosage that killed him."

I looked through the office window at the fog. Sonofabitch. Wally had been celebrating.

Nina leaned forward in her chair, her large dark eyes studying me. "What do you think is going on, Joe?"

"Okay, detective. I think a murder took place at Books to stop the investigation of a CO-run drug operation there possibly led by former SCOTA instructor, Adam Stover. Considering the cover he's getting, it's more likely that it goes higher on the food chain than that. In any event, as part of the cover up, the conspirators tried to hang the murder on Alvin Yuker. It was a flawed frame, the wheels began coming off, and they, and all their friends in the Fort and on the Blue Wall are panicking, striking out at anything that might implicate one of their own. That's what just hit Leila and Beth."

"And Wally Spivak?"

"I'm not sure."

She leaned back in her chair, a wary expression on her face. "Explain something to me, Joe. Cotter and I have been out here twice investigating three possible assaults in a mental hospital's violent section where such events have been a daily occurrence since this building was erected. We shouldn't even be here. These are symptoms, not crimes. Yet you want to tie all of this in to the murder of CO Sloan over at Books, which, again, is outside our jurisdiction."

"Things hardly ever are what they appear," I answered. "You said it, yourself: why are you here? Think someone at Breadloaf/North Valley Division might be connected?"

"Absolutely not."

"Spoken like a true blue brick in the wall."

"Very well." Det. Haddad's gaze seemed to be occupied with a thought, then she faced me, thought again, and raised her eyebrows. "Did you know Arif Rida is my father-in-law?"

"Mr. Rida? The candy man? Mr. Rida was my dentist's mortal enemy." I frowned. "Which of his sons did you marry?"

"Ahmed."

"No kidding."

"Seven years ago. We have a little girl, Luciane. She just began school."

"Ahmed's at Lassiter Division, right?"

"He's just been moved over to SWAT."

I nodded, got up, walked over to Dan Walker's desk, and began poking among the papers and desk items.

"Ahmed told me how you helped out his father when he got jammed up by airport security a few months ago. He and Rais are grateful."

"They each gave me a call." I continued searching Dan's desk. "Big hunks of chocolate in a suitcase register on screening machines as plastic explosives. Important packing tip." I found what I was looking for, glanced at Haddad, and pointed at the desk. Hidden between Dan's magnetic paperclip dispenser and a pile of patient files was the familiar black shiny oblong of a D1200 remote listening device.

After examining it, Haddad faced me, her eyebrows raised.

"Well, Nina, I helped Mr. Rida because of all the peanut turtles and chocolate-dipped almonds he slipped me under the counter over the years." I turned the unit over, noted the serial number, and turned it back. "Stuffy in here, isn't it? Visiting hours are still on. Want to go for a walk out in the park? It's a little foggy, but a nice walk will help me work up an appetite for the evening repast."

"I'd like that," she said.

At the door to the outer office, she told Getz, Bannerman, and Neal that she and I would be going out. She had to make a pit stop at a restroom, and I went back into Dan's office to wait for her. I stood with my back against the doorjamb, trying to sort out what to do. Bannerman followed me in and pulled the door to the outer office shut behind him. He turned and looked down at me.

"Do you know who I am?"

I glanced at the big man's chest, then up at his face. "Do you have on the correct nametag, officer?"

A frown; a look down. "Of course."

"Then I know who you are."

"I bet you don't know Chuck Sloan is a friend of mine."

"Actually, I do."

Another visage of confused Officer Bannerman.

"You just told me," I explained. "You're not staying on the job in hopes of making detective, are you?"

"You got a smart mouth. You're going to find out why I'm here, stumpy. I wanted to deliver something personally on behalf of Chuck and his family."

The fist came at my face surprisingly fast, and equally surprising, I instinctively dodged the blow with time enough to appreciate the multiple cracking sounds as Officer Bannerman's fist crumpled between the force of his well-developed muscles and the corner of the concrete-filled steel doorjamb. Bannerman cried out, grabbed his right wrist with his left hand, and almost sank to his knees.

"Want me to get a doctor, Bannerman? There should be one on duty, although he's probably only a psychologist. He can't fix your hand, but he can help you to accept this event as a life lesson rather than as a self-reprimand."

The door opened and Geraldine stuck her head in and looked around. After noting that I was all right, she looked at Bannerman hop around the room. "Now that's what my old man did after I got him with that cheese grater, though he was holdin' somethin' else."

Neal pulled the door open all the way, pushed Geraldine aside, and looked at Bannerman. "Officer?"

Officer Getz followed Miller in. "Bannerman, what in the hell are you doing?"

When he didn't get a response, Getz looked at me. "What's the matter with him?"

"Like the rest of us, Officer Getz, he's mere flesh and bone doing the best he can in a hard, hard world." I waved my hand at Neal. "Come on, Neal. Det. Haddad and I are going for a walk in the park."

HE'S NOT HEAVY

Nina and I walked the Deadline anticlockwise, north past the fenced off section maintained for Redshank and Buzzard patients, then west, following the fence through the trees north of the pond. There were only a few patients in the park. Because of the mist, we were out of sight of the main building.

"What's going on?" I asked her.

"That's what I was about to ask you."

"You first."

Nina Haddad smiled as she looked down at the path. "We're here investigating cases that aren't even cases. While I'm interviewing men and women who can't tell me anything, my partner is off doing something else. Unspecified."

"Unspecified?"

"At the very least, we're attempting to mortar our stretch of the blue wall."

"At the most?" I asked.

"I don't know. There have been enough meetings in smoke-filled back rooms—excluding me—at the Breadloaf/North Valley Substation to put Ronald McDonald in the White House. The unsaid agenda that oozes out of every knothole in the house: pull together to protect cops."

"Kind of makes you wonder what the cops need to be protected from."

"I'm not in this to hurt cops, Joe."

"That's not why I joined, either." We walked in silence for a few steps, then I asked, "Where are you with the big joke?"

"Big joke?"

"Equal justice under the law."

233

She stopped and faced me. "These days persons who look like me depend upon it not being a joke."

I nodded. "So, what about hanging a murder on an innocent man if it would get off a few cops and COs and avoid a lot of official embarrassment?"

"Joe, I'm not in this to let murderers escape, either."

I looked toward the pond, the fog obscuring the far shore, the water black between the shore and the remaining ice. "I'll start. Nina, I'm in here undercover and off the books trying to make sure neither I nor Alvin Yuker get killed before the real killers of Katey Sloan get revealed. I stuck a stick in the hornet's nest, trying to attract the attention of someone flippable, and Leila, Beth, and maybe Wally paid for it."

"Yuker is my house's star collar."

"Nothing about this can change that. But someone is trying to hang the Katey Sloan killing on him, as well, and that murder belongs to someone else."

"Do you know where the footwear impressions are, Joe? I went over those rooms. The way they were tossed, I don't believe the lifts were ever found."

"As I said, they won't carry much weight in court."

"I understand. I also understand that the ones who are snipping off all those loose ends really want those lifts. As worthless as they may appear, I'd love to put them overnight in a locked filing cabinet in an unoccupied room within view of a carefully focused video camera."

I smiled. "Now, that is first class thinking. Do you believe those lifts stink enough to draw the right brand of flies?"

"They will if this conspiracy you blame for everything really exists. Do you know where the lifts are?"

"I gave them to Wally to keep, and he didn't tell me where he put them." I studied her eyes for another second. "Wally used to sell shoes, Nina. He knew an awful lot about shoes, feet, and walking. If you get down to the hospital's morgue and find his shoes, my guess is you'll find those lifts trimmed and placed beneath the inserts in his size twelves. Now, I'd like a little favor in return."

"What?"

"The casts of Alvin Yuker's teeth were destroyed during the jury deliberations. I'd like to know if the original molds made by the dentist were ever entered into evidence, and if not, where are they?"

"You're thinking that the bite marks on Katey Sloan's body were made from casts from the original molds?"

"That's what I think."

"Are you certain that Yuker didn't kill Katey Sloan?"

"About as certain as I ever get. The guy who left those footwear impressions, by the way, is on the maintenance staff here. His name is Norman Cote. Unless he is totally stupid, he's gotten rid of the shoes by now. Earlier today I noticed he had on a new pair. Do you think Cotter planted that D1200 on the shrink's desk?"

"I'll be sure of it if he gives me a hard time for going on this walk with you. I'll let you know what I find out about those dental molds." She frowned. "If I get a nibble on those lifts, Joe, who do I approach?"

"Capt. Dockery or Lt. Hewitt at MCU. No one else. This is a career croaker, Nina. Mind the shadows, walk between the winds, Ninja detective."

"This from the one-man band and fireworks display. Watch out for yourself, Joe. If what you believe is true, it would be damned convenient if you and Yuker killed each other."

I paused. "Yes. That D1200, by the way, is the second one of those units I've seen since I've been here. The other was in the Dan Group area. It may still be there. We haven't disturbed it. MCU traced the serial number to the State Police inventory. The one on Dan Walker's desk has a serial number one digit higher than the one in the Dan Group area."

"Let me have the number," she said, pulling her own handheld out of her inside breast pocket.

I recited the numbers, she wrote them down, and, after giving me her home and station numbers, she put the handheld back in her pocket as she looked at me. "Take care."

I watched her as she faded into the mist walking back down the Deadline toward the main building.

Officer Bannerman's fist came to mind, and my nagging guilt about letting myself get out of shape during the previous few months moved me into the dangerous land of good intentions. I actually had thoughts of putting in a bit of a run. Past where the Deadline crossed Upper Raven Stream, a path led to the left, following the stream until it emptied into the pond. There the path teed into Insanity Path, which followed the pond's shoreline. Start small and work your way up. I turned right and decided to stretch out at Sonny's Circle, across from the still-frozen pond's north shore.

Sonny was one of the Turkey East counselors. Seated on one of the benches was an overweight boy in his late teens or early twenties, a red jacket over his blues. He was looking to his right up into the woods, then behind, then left, then right again.

"Hi," I greeted.

The boy started, faced me, and grinned. "Lost." He waved a pudgy hand at the mist. "Can't see. Lost."

I crossed the circle until I was standing in front of the boy. The boy's eyes weren't exactly vacant, but they never seemed to look at anything for any length of time. His gray eyes looked crossed and his tongue looked too big for his mouth. His hair was brown and cut close to his scalp. "Where's your escort?"

The boy laughed and smiled with his whole face. "Where is your escort, Joe?"

I raised my eyebrows and grinned. "You got me. My escort is probably back at the main building keeping warm and wondering where I am. You know my name. What's your name?"

"Paul. My name is Paul and I'm twenty and a half years old."

I sat next to him. "So, Paul, how come you know my name?"

He nodded. "Days ago. I ask my brother and he told me. Seen you visiting. Here. Your father, too. Your father's name. Nicolo Torio." Paul frowned with his whole face. "Hangman, huh?"

"He used to be a long time ago. He owns a landscaping business now. Who is your brother? Is he a patient here?"

236

Big smile and then Paul lifted a hand and pushed my arm. "You tell a joke. My brother is Billy. You know Billy?"

"Divine?"

"Billy Divine. That's my name, too. I'm Paul Divine."

The sample lift that Dan had pulled from one of Leila's boxes down in that storage room: From the brother of Billy. I nodded as the question of why a skilled nurse would take a big whack in pay to be an orderly at a nuthouse faded into the mist. "Your brother loves you a lot, Paul."

He nodded and looked down at his hands resting in his lap. "I know." He frowned. "I go stupid and both brothers go in here. Not fair. Don't know why I can't get better. I try so hard." Paul leaned over and rested his head on my chest. Tears were running down his cheeks.

I put a tentative arm around Paul's shoulders. "I'm sure he knows you try."

A huge white figure started to materialize out of the mist, and by its size, it had to be either Billy or the abominable snowman. I shook the boy's shoulders. "Look who it is."

Paul looked up. "Aw! Billy! Hi, Billy!" He dried his tears on the sleeves of his jacket.

"Hi, kid." Billy, his face carrying a very worried expression, stopped in front of the bench. "You okay, Joe?"

"I'm fine."

"How about you, Paul? You okay?"

"Okay, Billy."

"You got away from me in the fog, didn't you? What'd we agree on when we come on out here?"

"I stay. Right next to you, I stay." Paul looked across the pond into the center of the mist. "I went in the fog. I forgot just for a second." Paul faced me. "I love fog. I want to get lost in fog, Joe. Like in dreams. In fog is being awake in a dream. I'm not ugly in fog. I'm not stupid in fog. Nobody can see me. I can't see the world. I can be anything. The world can be anything."

"You're not ugly and your not stupid, Paul," said Billy. "You think I hang out with ugly stupid people?" He looked at me. "Do I?"

"Never," I answered.

Billy pointed toward the bench. "Stay there, kid, okay? I want to talk with Joe. Stay there. I mean it."

"Okay, Billy."

I patted Paul's back, stood, and followed Billy a few paces away toward the path. Billy stopped and looked down at me. "Are you sure you're okay?"

"Yeah. I'm fine. I just saw him on the bench and he said he was lost. We had a chat."

"He got away from me. I can't believe how much ground he can cover in a minute. I don't want to use restraints on him, but maybe on days like this I better."

"Well, you found him. He's okay. What's the big deal?"

"Four years ago, Joe, remember up in Nelson? The zoo?"

"No."

"The gorilla that was killed and mutilated? The two keepers who wound up in intensive care attempting to stop the killing of the second gorilla?"

"Oh."

I turned and looked at Paul Divine, sitting hunched over, his hands in his lap, his lips making a boip-boip-boip sound, his knees bouncing up and down, his eyes again searching the mists for his wonderlands. A poet and dreamer, but not a gorilla fan.

"Joe, what's going on?"

I looked at Billy. The big man's face looked worried. "What do you mean?"

"The scuttlebutt is that you're doing undercover to clear Alvin Yuker. Seems to me like it's not much of a cover if everyone knows about it, unless you're trying to get someone to make a move on you."

"Then, again, Billy, I just might be another Filbert in the bowl."

"Yeah." Billy glanced at his brother, nodded at him, then faced me. "Whatever it is, Joe, you got a mojo working against you. Carla's the one who pointed it out to me. She's seen it at Books, I saw it in the Navy. I bet you seen it in the cops. A word dropped here and there, a couple of comments, subtle little signals letting everyone on staff know that so-and-so's got the mark on him and when the hammer falls, be out of the way. You do know the Half Satan phones are monitored, don't you?"

"I heard."

"Security on each floor monitors the patient phones on that floor while the calls are being made. The staff phones aren't monitored, but there's no way you can get to them."

"Thanks. You know who I should be looking out for?"

"Here's where it gets tricky, Joe. You can't tell who's pushing and who's just passing it along. I've heard things from some of the security staff, maintenance staff, and medical staff. Munroe, Tucker, and Gomez. Norman— the guy who pushes the floor scrubber. Carla, of course. Chase, and Ben. Even a couple of the doctors. I don't know if any of them are in on anything, Joe, but I do know the word is getting around. Not just on you. On Alvin Yuker, too."

"Thanks."

"You know, Joe, you really had me fooled. You do crazy good."

"We're all crazy, Billy. They just haven't finished labeling all of us."

BEWARE, JAVERT

After walking Billy and Paul back to the main building, I asked Neal if it would be all right to do a little running in the park before I came in. Neal checked his watch, looked out into the thickening mist, then nodded and went back to his magazine. "Think you can last a half hour or so?"

"I think so."

"Where are you going to run?"

"Just around the pond. Start small."

Neal nodded and turned back to his magazine. "Knock yourself out."

Bones cracked and muscles protested at the Bette Circle as I stretched out for the first time in months. The skin felt tight over the healed wounds in my left side, but no sharp pains. What hurt the most was where Sunday had stuck me. Maybe he'd scraped a rib with that stiletto. I stepped off jogging clockwise around Insanity Path, wondering if I'd be able to circle the pond without stopping. The shoes I had on weren't ideal. Barely fifty yards from where I started, still at the south end of the pond approaching Wanda's Circle, I could already feel it in my lungs.

"I've got the stamina of a soap bubble."

Past the Fountain Path turnoff, I jogged up the west side of the pond, around the shallow little cove and out onto the peninsula in the center of which was Mark's Circle. Around the circle, off the peninsula, right around another little cove, then I was on the north shore of the pond, approaching Sonny's Circle, the backs of my legs screaming.

Up ahead was the group of trees surrounding the footbridge that crossed Upper Raven. As I came abreast

241

of Sonny's Circle, I stopped, bent over, and rested with my hands on my knees, wheezing out the theme from *Rocky*.

I thought I saw a very wide figure standing on the footbridge, then a fold in the mist drifted in front of the bridge, grays fading into grays. The sounds of someone running behind me. I turned to see another gray figure approaching. The one who had been on the bridge was now almost out of the trees, coming toward me.

"Uh oh." It looked like the other side had solved its Gilbert Kane problem.

I moved off the path toward the circle and both of the gray figures moved north of the path, across the patches of snow on the wet grass. Running north I would eventually be trapped with my back against the fence. Maybe the video cameras would get a couple of snaps of my assailants before I went down, always supposing the tapes were recording. I could slug it out where I stood, but if those gray figures in the fog were staff orderlies armed with muscles, chains, and drugs, it would be hopeless. I looked toward the pond, its mostly frozen surface fading into the fog.

"Okay." I turned, crossed the path, and ran for the pond. Past a lone bench and the tree that shaded it, two steps in arctic water between the shore and the ice, then I was on the ice, sliding my feet across it's slushy surface, the sounds of ice cracking beneath me making my muscles tense. In a moment I was out of sight of the shore, hoping I was still going south, when I heard a double splash and a curse behind me. One of the gray figures was on the ice with me. Close. The time for sliding along had expired. I began a half-run, half-slide across the ice. As I heard the second figure splash in the water and get on the ice, I landed with my left foot on a particularly thin spot and went through up to my hip. One of the pursuers landed on me, the force of his descent driving my face into the ice, and through it into the dark waters beneath.

Hands on my throat. It didn't make any sense. Why try to strangle someone who was under water and couldn't breathe anyway? As quickly as the numbing cold awakened me, it began making everything dreamy and slow. I felt like a fly caught in molasses. I tried to kick the man in his nuts, but my foot moved so slowly whoever it was avoided the blow. Just before I went blank, I felt the face of my assailant, made a fork of the index and middle finger of my right hand, and drove my fingertips into the person's eyes. He screamed. The man wasn't holding onto my throat anymore. That was a plus. I wondered if I was still under water and if it mattered—if anything mattered. So cold.

A wistful place, that ocean of soft black cotton. Warm, too. No cold, no pain, no concerns, no issues, no tasks left to do. I swam in it, remembering it like an old friend from when my heart had stopped. Just as I was about to launch my new exploration of the universe, it began withdrawing from me, growing cold, rough, and gray.

I saw Collins getting the needle, the lights in the witness room were dim, the lights illuminating Larry Collins bright. Collins couldn't get his breath. I turned away for a second. Just for a second, and there were faces in the room. Faces.

A face.

Light gray laced with black branches and twigs. My backside cold, my nose, too. My chest and ears wet and warm. I touched what was on my chest, and it was smooth, warm, skin like, but thick. Around my head were arms: thick, warm arms—arms that had no bones—

I opened my eyes, the hideous warm thing squatting on my chest, its arms around my head—no legs—some kind of giant two-legged sponge insect—

I screamed and fought with the creature, fighting to free myself from its hideous embrace. Hands pushed me back down. "Joe? Joe? What the hell's the matter with you?"

I opened my eyes to see a very wet Geraldine looking back. Her awful teeth bared in a hideous grin. "Ah, hell, God. Take me now. I don't care anymore." I looked again at Geraldine. Her breasts were down about five sizes. I allowed my gaze to behold once more the two-armed sponge monster.

"Hi, Honey Bumps," she said.

"Julia?"

"You were breathing so I put my Geraldine bazooms on you to keep you warm while I worked on Louis."

"Louis—Have you, I mean, since the bus?"

"Yes."

"Why didn't you tell me you were you?"

"I practically molested you on the bus. Dropped lust hints every chance I could ever since. I figured you were really into your part, so I hung back until you got in over your head, so to speak."

"I was really holding out for it being the new counselor, Juliana."

"I thought you'd go for that look. My Margarita Azzurro disguise all over again, right?"

"Hubba hubba."

"I noticed you didn't pat her bottom."

"I'm getting superstitious about bottom petting." I sat up. "What did you do to your breath?"

"I thought you liked sardines."

Louis was on the grass, curled up in a fetal position, silently crying. "Louis. Why?"

"Need you ask, Javert?" said Julia.

"He doesn't even believe I'm Javert."

"Actually, he does. That little speech he gave in group about his mission being a little reality he created for himself is just a piece of people pleasing: trying to get the group off his back."

"He really believes I'm Javert?"

"Yes."

"How is he?"

"He's okay. Help me back on with my bazooms. It's going to take all night with my hair dryer to dry these things out."

I held my hand to my breast pocket. "Oh, hell. My PDA." I raised my eyebrows. "That's right. Michelle has it."

"That Michelle?"

"Yeah. She wanted to read some Nathan Sunday."

I stood and picked up the foam rubber appliance. Looking at it I said, "How come they didn't pick up on the rubber during your physical?"

"I haven't had a physical yet. For some reason the physician keeps putting it off." She grinned widely, displaying those amazingly rotten dentures.

"Go figure."

Julia's back was toward me and she had lowered the top on her coveralls. As I reached around her with the foam, I kissed her bare shoulder. In a trice, Geraldine's face, those horrendous teeth grinning, looked over her shoulder and said, "Hi, hot pants."

"Tartar sauce. Hold the sardines."

Louis moaned on the grass and I turned, squatted next to him, and shook his shoulder. "Louis? Can you hear me?"

"I hear you," he answered weakly.

"Good."

"You poked me in my eyes."

"Just as hard as I could." I grabbed his collar with both hands, dragged him to his feet, and growled in his face, "You are crazy, Mad Dog! Your brain pan is full of bedbugs!" I shook him like a rag. "What the hell were you thinking? So help me, if you hurt me and make it so I can't ski next winter, not only will I catch Jean Valjean, I will throw him into the deepest darkest dungeon in Paris along with that priest, his family, his dog, the entire population of that village he was mayor of, and every fucking rat in the Paris sewer system! Killing me is not okay. You read me, nutball?"

Louis stared at me for a long moment then lowered his eyebrows. "You're going to jail the *rats*? Now who's insane?"

I released Louis's collar. "Okay. Maybe I overstated things a bit. But it still goes, Mad Dog. Killing me is not okay."

"What are you going to do, Javert?" asked Geraldine, bazooms attached. "Give him a time out?"

I glared at Louis. "What if I stick you back in that pond with one of those granite benches on your chest to hold you down?" I let my breath out and took Louis by the arm. "C'mon, man. Let's go in. It's cold out here." The three of us walked Insanity Path through the mist toward the Upper Raven footbridge.

"Why didn't you just let me drown?" asked Louis.

"Javert is a cop, Mad Dog, not a murderer. It's not the deep but the Château D'If for you."

Louis frowned. "That's Dumas."

"Sacre bleu!"

JUST VISITING

When the three of us got back on Turkey, Neal eyeing our soaking wet clothes, Norman was just bringing his floor scrubber from the east wing over to the west. He glared at us as we left wet footprints on the hall floor. A new group of patients condemned to observation were being oriented by the Wanda Group leader. I went to Michelle's now vacant place beneath the cameras, slid down, and sat on the floor, my legs crossed beneath me. I stared at the opposite wall, listening as the floor scrubber came closer and closer. It stopped four feet from where I sat. "You got to move, Joe," said Norman. "C'mon. Your little buddy took a break and it's my chance to do this piece. And look at the wet spot you're leaving."

I faced Norman and wiggled my finger for Norman to approach.

"Look, you got to move. Lots of floors to do today. Be nice and sit on the other side. As soon as I pass, you can come back and mess it up."

I continued wiggling my finger. Norman glanced behind himself, looked again at me, grimaced, put the brake on his machine, and walked around it, stopping in front of the human obstacle. "C'mon. You got to get out of the way."

I held up my hand and Norman took it to pull me to my feet, but instead I grabbed Norman's hand, twisted it around, and bent it back, driving him to his knees. "Have a seat, Norman. Here. Right next to me."

"The security officers'll be here in ten seconds. Let me go."

I pulled him down to the floor into Michelle's old place. "I doubt it, Norm. Did you know this is the only

247

spot in the hall not covered by the surveillance cameras? It's a fact. Ten feet in any direction and you're on TV. Right here, though, the eyes are blind."

"What about the wing SO station?"

"Take a look. It's on the other side of your Zamboni machine, Norm." I increased the pressure on Norman's wrist.

"I got it, I got it! What do you want?"

"A lot of folks have been getting hurt on this floor, Norm. You notice that?"

"That's got nothing to do with me—"

"Oh, I think it does."

"No one has a thing—"

"Gomez took care of that, did he?"

Norman's mouth hung open.

"Not a poker player, eh Norm? We know. You aren't safe, Norm. We know all about the whole thing and your part in it. Understand? I am one crazy bastard who already has a body count some put into double digits, so one swab jockey more-or-less isn't going to make any difference."

"What—what's this got to do with me?"

"Look. However this thing shakes out, Norm, I don't want anyone else getting hurt. Understand?"

"I don't know what you're talking about."

"You'd best figure it out." I maxed the pressure on Norman's wrist, making him cry out.

"Okay! Okay! I hear you! I hear you."

"If anyone else gets hurt, Norman, I'm coming after you. I'm not just a cop. I'm a crazy cop. I can do whatever I want to you and get away with it, and you don't want to find out what I can do to you. If you're between a rock and a hard place, forget about the cover-up and go to ground, boy. Take off, run to Brazil, fly like a little bird. If you're going to stay here, though, make certain everyone you know understands that no one else gets hurt. If anyone else gets hurt, we're all coming after you."

"All?"

"Every killer on all five floors, Norm. We know each other. We had the meeting and made the agreement this afternoon. Anyone else gets hurt, for whatever reason, we all go after you. *With our teeth!"* I clacked my teeth together "Got it?"

"Yes!"

"Now, where's Michelle?"

"Who? Doorstop?"

"Why isn't she here?"

"It wasn't my turn to watch her."

"She better not be hurt."

"If she is, it's got nothing to do with me."

"If she's hurt, Norman, it's got everything to do with you." I bared my teeth and clacked my jaws together several more times, taking a snap at Norman's nose. I released his hand, stood, and went to my room to put on dry clothes. There my PDA was waiting for me in the center of my bed next to a tiny cinnamon teddy bear with one articulated arm raised in thanks.

Pop showed for the last hour of visiting. We walked clockwise around the Deadline, past the Maplewood, past the bench where we had stopped on his previous visit, past the West Court turnoff up to a group of oaks in the northwest corner of the park. Due to a rising wind the fog was thinning, the late afternoon sunlight giving the remaining mist a surreal glow. We stopped and sat on a bench screened from behind by a row of trees.

"You look all fresh and clean, Joe."

"I just got back from swimming."

He nodded and looked up at the sky. "I got a question."

"Shoot, Pop."

He looked at me. "Are you really crazy, Joe?"

"Thanks, Pop."

"I mean, bringing this Nina Haddad in? Especially if you think her partner is involved? That's not smart."

"If you're going to give a guy enough rope to hang himself, Pop, you can't be stingy with the hemp."

"You brought this Dr. Walker in, too?"

"Yes. While we're at it, there are the patients in my therapy group and a couple of others, too. Right now it's all over the institution."

The hangman shook his head. "I know you don't play cards, Joe, but if the other guy knows what you got and he knows what he got, you can't bluff."

"I win anyway, Pop, if I have the better hand. If I stay in, that is."

"You should live so long."

"Well, that is the plan. What do you have for me?"

"Mike Ijumaa's report."

I was stunned. "What? How?"

The hangman grinned. "Mike said he'd get you."

"What? You mean there is no report? Great little kidder, Pop. I'm hanging out here off the end of the yardarm and you and the tweezer man make with the comedy."

The hangman tapped his handheld with a finger. "I got his report," said Nicolo. "All but the DNA. He said that's going to be a few days more."

"Again: How?"

"You know Mike teaches at the State CSU Academy. He put three classes on those lifts as an assignment, divided the lifts among eighty-four students, and, what he say, 'unleashed the dogs of science.' Ready to receive, *Enterprise?*"

"Yeah. Beam me up."

While the two handhelds had robot sex, the hangman said, "Mike wants you to know that he flagged the reports that looked important. One in particular. It had a hair Mike says matches Katey Sloan's. He said it had a root. That means they got DNA, right?"

"Right, Pop. That envelope have a name to go with the lift?"

"Hawk. Like the bird. It was dated a couple days after Sloan was killed."

My handheld beeped, and Pop tapped up another event. "I also got Claire Turner's report on who knows who."

"Great."

"She says it's pretty sketchy." While the beaming proceeded, the hangman looked at me. "Julia make contact yet?"

"She certainly did."

"Good." He smiled. "You like her disguise? I remember you like her Margarita Azzurro a lot."

"I'll dream about her Geraldine for years." The handhelds beeped signaled the end of the beam event, and I punched mine off and stuck it in my pocket.

"How's your head, Joe?"

"Inside's doing better than the outside. I think this was a good idea, Pop: putting me on this job. I got to get a few things off my chest with Nathan Sunday, and I've gotten involved with some other humans—gotten out of my own head. I'm getting my confidence back. The guy who runs this place might even know what he's doing." I squeezed his arm. "I'm okay."

"I worry about you."

"Remember what Aunt Cella said about worry."

Pop nodded. "Worry is a way to tell God not to help because you're going to take care of it yourself." The hangman stood, placed his hand on my cheek, and patted it once. "We never did much church after Cella died."

"I was grateful." I stood. "Come on, Pop. Let's get you out of here. Look. The fog's almost all gone."

"I feel better now Julia's here."

"Me too, Pop." I put my arm around his shoulder and squeezed. "Me too."

After saying good-bye to Pop at the door, I looked at Geraldine sitting on the bench next to the main entrance reading her copy of *Forever Amber*. She scratched beneath her left breast and said, "You got some cookies from your papa, there boy?"

"Why yes, you sweet old thing. Come on. I'll share them with you."

I helped her up and we crossed the grass over to Insanity Path. We walked up the east shore of the pond, checking out Mike Ijumaa's lift reports. Mostly they were as expected. The same name would produce a monotony of similar lifts: fibers from the blue coveralls, blue blankets, the person's individual jacket or coat; hair predominantly the liftee's, but occasional contributions from that person's fellow group members and even group facilitators. Skin cells from dandruff and from winter dryness. Bits of institutional tissue, occasional gobs of mucous, and a menu of food crumb and dribbles.

"This is the one Mike Ijumaa flagged as having a hair possibly matching Katey Sloan's. It's a perfect visual match, the DNA is working. Number nine thirty-one, processed by CSU trainee Mike Dugan. Fibers: cotton, brown. Skin cells: human. Hairs, nonhuman: rabbit, white. Hairs, human: black, two different sources; blond, one source (similar to Katey Sloan sample). Wood dust, adhesive, two different paints, plaster, heavy grease, and cigarette ash."

"Working man," said Julia. "Maintenance."

"Not at Squirmhi, though. Squirmhi maintenance wears gray." I looked up, frowning. "How many body shops, machine shops, hospitals, and cleaning outfits in the city use brown coveralls?"

"Books Correctional and the SRPD, for two," she answered.

I read out Leila's ID on the lift: "'This was collected April Twenty-third, this year, from the Hawk at ten twenty-six AM in the hall before Room One Fourteen by Leila Gilbert.'"

"The Hawk?" she asked.

"Leila never puts down actual names. Only memory jogs. The lifts from Harvey were called 'Scene.' The one's from Wally were called Foot. Hawk who? Hawk what? What's room one fourteen?" I scanned through the file titles. "No one named Hawk, first name or last. Chicken hawk, goshawk, red-tailed hawk."

"Isn't there a white-tailed hawk?"

"I don't know. Cooper. There's a Cooper's hawk, isn't there?" I punched up Claire's who's who on the handheld and put in a search. "Crap. Between the peedee, the prison system, and the city's hospitals there're eleven Coopers."

"How about Swainson?"

"Swainson?"

"Out west. Swainson's Hawk."

I did another search. "You sure that isn't Swanson? I have three Swansons."

"Swainson." She spelled it out.

"No Swainsons."

"Isn't one-fourteen the staff lounge?" asked Geraldine.

"We'll pass it on our way back to Turkey. Let's check it out." I looked at her. "Do you know what happened to Michelle? You know, from Juliana's Group?"

She grinned with all those rotten teeth. "I sure do."

"You want to share that with me, you horrid old crone?"

"Why, Joseph Paul DiMaggio Torio, you could turn a girl's head with talk like that."

"So?"

"It's a surprise—Look, Joe."

I looked where Geraldine was facing and saw Butcher, the security officer, over on the grass keeping an eye on Alvin. Alvin was standing between two facing benches looking down upon a young woman who was seated on one of the benches. She had bright red hair, black slacks and an apple green jacket. She was in her twenties and was a dead ringer for the crime scene photos of Jolene Gaye. "Uh oh."

I stepped off the path and walked across the grass, Geraldine following, until we were standing on either side of the big man. "Hi, Alvin," said Geraldine.

Yuker was trembling, his hands actually shaking. His breath was coming in shallow little gasps. "What's happening, Alvin?" I asked. "Are you okay?"

Alvin opened his eyes and looked down and to his right at me. His eyes glistened with tears. "Hi, Joe."

"What's going on?"

Alvin glanced at Geraldine, closed his eyes tightly, and nodded toward the young woman. "Know who this is?"

"No," said Geraldine. "Why don't you introduce us?"

"She's Jolene Gaye's oldest daughter. You know. One of the women I killed."

The young woman stood and faced Geraldine, then me. "Are you friends of Alvin's?"

"Colleagues," I answered.

"Just a couple of passing loons, dear. I'm Geraldine. He's Joe. What's your name, darlin'?"

"Pauline Gaye. I'm a student at BU's School of Law." She looked from Geraldine to me.

253

"We're fifty percent questions and all ears," I said.

She was strong when she told us, all of her building blocks carefully pointed, the reconstruction almost complete. After years of trying, Pauline Gaye had tracked him down, the murderer of her mother. That's not who she had been seeking. She had been looking, instead, for the person who had paid her and her sister's way though Lanford Academy, the tutors, the therapists, her way through Breadloaf University and law school, and her sister Angela's way through Dartmouth.

It had been frustrating, as investigations go, but as thin as it was, the paper trail was there. Eventually it all came down to a seven and a half dollar receipt for a tube of titanium white that had to be backordered, and was accidentally sent directly to Books prison. That was when she found out that her benefactor and her mother's murderer were one in the same.

"Now that you've found him, what?" I asked her.

She was silent for a long time, her gaze fixed on the cliffs of Idiot's Drop high on the mountain, the last threads of mist being pulled free by the wind. At last she began speaking, her voice quiet but still strong. "My mother was a prostitute. She used to sell my sister and me to her clients. For fifty dollars you could do anything you wanted to a little girl seven years old. Really turned on those old drunks. For another fifty, you could get her five year old sister thrown in. Dressed in sexy clothes, drunk, drugged, fondled, beaten, raped—whatever." She was whispering, the memories making her momentarily small. Then she stood and held back her head.

"And then one night, like an answer to our prayers, it all went away. Mother went off to work, my sister and I hugged each other and waited for her to show up with another monster for us to please. The next thing we knew the cops came through the door, along with a Human Services case worker, and took us away. We slept on clean sheets that night. We had a hot breakfast the next morning. We were sent to a foster home that afternoon. For years, my sister and I didn't know why. No one would say what happened. It was like magic."

"When did you find out?" asked Geraldine.

"I started looking things up when I was in eighth grade. Newspaper archives showed that our mother died rather horribly in room four-oh-eight at the Egypt Hotel down in the Zone. The pictures in the *News* were very graphic. Torture. Strangulation."

She looked at Alvin and he had turned away, the sight of her apparently unbearable.

"I suppose Social Services and our foster parents wanted to protect our young sensibilities." A bitter smile stole across her face. "No one really understood how therapeutic it would have been for us to watch Mother be put to death. But, all we were told was that our mother had gone to Heaven, which really pissed us off. Her clients went elsewhere to do their business, so we weren't raped and beaten anymore, and someone was paying to put us through Lanford, the most expensive private school in the state. Paying for therapy. Paying for pretty clothes, college. Our foster parents, wonderful couple, eventually adopted us. But I had to know who it was who had paid all of the bills. As it turned out, it was the same person who had gotten us away from that woman."

Alvin looked sick enough to die. His eyes were closed, his body still shaking. For a man detached from his feelings, he seemed to be registering a heap of them.

Pauline looked up at the big man. "You know, Alvin, I found the daughter of the other woman you killed. Her name is Belinda Lloyd. Her mother didn't rent her out to her clients. Instead, her mother used to do the raping and beating herself with a chair leg. Now Belinda is in West Point. She's going to be an Army officer. My sister Angela is going to be a mathematician. Right now I'm trying to make up my mind between the D.A.'s office, the FBI, and private practice."

"I didn't kill her for you and your sister," blurted Alvin, pushing away the life preserver he thought he was being offered. "I didn't kill Dena Lloyd for her daughter."

"I know."

"I didn't kill any of them to save anyone but me."

"I know. I've read everything about you and your case, Alvin. I even own two of your paintings." She reached up and placed a hand on his wrist. "I wonder what you would have become if someone had murdered your mother when you were seven."

"Pauline, I want you to know I didn't kill Katey Sloan. I didn't kill that CO."

"I never thought you did." She stood, went up on tiptoe, kissed Alvin's cheek, took his arm, and led him toward Insanity Path. "Can we come and visit you? We all want to."

They walked into the distance, Pauline asking about the charges against him, about his appointed attorney, and about his finances. It looked like Alvin Yuker's real court defense in the matter of Katey Sloan was getting under way. Butcher followed a few paces behind them, his hands clasped at his back. I looked at Geraldine, and Geraldine's inner Julia was leaking from the eyeballs. I held out my arms, drew the horrid old crone into an embrace, and held her.

"You big marshmallow," I said.

"Something to think about, officer," she said.

"What's that?"

"I can't think of anything more calculated to trigger Alvin Yuker than the sight of Pauline Gaye."

"But, it didn't work," I said.

"True, but aren't you curious how that invoice made it all the way from Books prison into Pauline's possession?"

"You think the other side drew her in here?"

"If Alvin got killed while guards tried to protect Pauline, I wonder how many sighs of relief would rise from the city. I don't think the other side cares at all who or how many get killed in their cover up." She leaned back and frowned at me. "What?"

I glanced back at the building then at Julia's Geraldine. "I was thinking that if many more officers and public servants get pulled into this cover up it might reach a kind of critical mass of invulnerability."

"Too big, too important, and too many to be brought to justice?"

I nodded. "As far as I know, they never hanged a lynch mob."

ONE LAST POKE

That night, the group was in Teddy's room rehearsing our act for the Turkey Talent Show. Geraldine was in the easy chair before the window taking the lead vocal, backed up by Harvey, me, and Yukiko from Teddy's bed. Louis was on air siren and Alvin on air Tommy gun, both of them sitting on Teddy's desk, which had been pulled next to the window. Teddy was on air drums sitting on his desk chair to Geraldine's right, and Thomas played the sash to his bathrobe in lieu of a sax, standing between the head of the bed and Teddy's desk. Our backup singers went through the minimally choreographed moves we had devised and named "The Squirmhi." We all went through our parts three times with Teddy's boom box shaking the walls, and at the conclusion of the third run, we laughed and applauded ourselves. We had the sync down.

"Show time tomorrow morning at ten," announced Harvey. "We go on third. Break a leg, figuratively speaking."

We talked about nothing for a bit, no one really wanting to end the fun, the backup group eventually settling back on Teddy's bed. Louis pulled out a peace offering for me, an unopened can of Dr Pepper. It was a little on the warm side, but I appreciated the gesture. There was a moment of silence that grew to the point where I was about to excuse myself and go to bed, when Harvey glanced at me and asked, "Where are we with our case?"

I glanced at Geraldine then looked around at the faces. "We have a hook in the water. A lot of worms are getting beaten up, but the only real nibble we've gotten so far was connected with another case." I glared at

Louis for a moment and Louis went red and faced the window.

"What have you got on your handheld?" asked Thomas. "I saw you and your father beaming notes at each other."

I pulled out the PDA and looked at it. "Leila must have rolled someone near the time Katey Sloan was murdered—someone connected with either the murder or the cover up."

"That's why she was hurt?" asked Yukiko. "Someone figured to cover his tracks by killing her and grabbing her files?"

"Yes." I thought for a moment, nodded once, and said, "It turns out, though, that the files covering the dates near Sloan's death weren't in her room when she was injured. They were in a storage room down in the basement. I sent those files off with a criminalist I know, and his report was one of the things my father brought. The other thing was a document from our records wiz, Claire Turner. Among corrections, police, and hospital employees, who is related to whom. My father has this theory that occupations go in families. Maybe the people here who are in on the cover up are related somehow to the ones at Books who are in on it."

Yukiko held out his hand. "May I look at the CSU report?"

I reached across Harvey and handed over the PDA. "The file that's flagged in there, the one called Hawk, is a maintenance type. The lift Leila took off him picked up a hair that is similar to Katey Sloan's. DNA will make sure, but that's going to take awhile."

"Who's Hawk?" asked Harvey.

"Unknown. Leila filed nothing under real names. Instead she used memory jogs. You were 'Scene,' for SceneClean." I looked at Louis. "Her name for you was 'Guardian.' My best guess is that Hawk isn't on staff here. The lift was taken in front of the staff lounge down on Chicken. He could have been a staff visitor."

"Does that mean that this Hawk is the killer?"

"Maybe."

"Brown cotton fibers?" asked Yukiko, reading off the PDA screen.

"Yes. Maintenance at Books and the SRPD use brown coveralls. Hawk's got paint, grease, wood dust, pet hair, and plaster on his coveralls, which makes him either in maintenance or a real slob."

A chuckle ran its way around the room until it was interrupted by Yukiko. "That isn't plaster."

I leaned across Harvey and looked at the PDA screen. "There." I pointed at the place. "Dihydrated calcium sulfate. That's plaster."

"Not with this consistency," said Yukiko. "You plaster up your walls with Dihydrated calcium sulfate with a consistency of one hundred. This has a consistency of thirty to thirty-two."

"Gypsum cement," I said.

"That's right. Dental stone." Yukiko raised his eyebrows. "Have you searched these names for Hawk?"

"Yes. And for Byrd, Swallow, Jay, and others. No luck. Dental stone. Crime scene techs and cops use it for making casts of foot impressions and tool marks. It could also be used to duplicate Alvin's bite marks using the original molds. This has got to be our flip-bunny. If he didn't have a direct hand in killing Katey Sloan, he at least knows who built the frame on Alvin."

Alvin stood, stretched his back, and resumed his seat on Teddy's desk. "Did giving those footwear impression lifts to that one detective turn up anything?"

"No. I don't even know if she found them, much less used them for bait. I just guessed where they might be. If her partner tried to steal them, she hasn't called to let me know."

"Jesus," said Thomas. "No evidence that you can bring into court because we're all crazy, and what evidence we do have we either can't attach to anyone or for all we know, you gave it away to the bad guys."

"These tasks are being performed by professional detectives on a closed course," remarked Teddy. "Don't try this at home."

"Funny," said Louis staring down at the floor.

"What's funny?" asked Alvin.

"Different names for the same thing. Like in England they call Jell-O 'jelly,' but they call jelly 'jam.'"

"I'll be darned," said Thomas, making a show of yawning.

"I once taught senior English in a military school in Georgia." Memory seemed to make his attention drift. "Brilliant kids. Interested. Respectful. I was there for three years. Wish I'd never left. Who the hell needed to be English Department Chair at Vadalia High."

Big silence. Alvin looked down at him. "And?"

"Who's who?" Louis glanced at Alvin then leaned back against the wall. "In certain areas of the south, do you know what they call dragonflies?"

"No, Louis," said Teddy. "What do they call dragonflies?"

"Skeeter hawks. Dragonflies attack mosquitoes, you see. Search on the wing, catch one in the air, just like a hawk goes after a jay."

"What's your point?" I asked.

"Leila's originally from Alabama, Javert. Didn't you know that? Not much of a detective."

"I confess. How else has Valjean eluded me all these years?"

Louis reached out to Yukiko for the handheld, and once the dentist handed it over, Louis took the unit, punched up a document, put in a search, smiled, and showed it to me.

I read it. "Byron Walsh? On the maintenance crew at the Breadloaf/North Valley Substation?"

Louis nodded. "That's Jean Valjean's cousin. Norman Cote? That's his cousin." He smiled widely at me. "His nickname is Skeeter."

Later, in Geraldine's aka Julia's room, I sat in her easy chair and rubbed my eyes. "Between Thomas's case summary and Louis's big breakthrough, I'm beginning to wonder what I'm doing here. I feel less and less that taking Nina Haddad in was a good idea. Damn, I wish I had a cell phone. The house phones are monitored—by the same team that can't keep the video surveillance recorders working. I really need to talk to Dock."

Geraldine unbuttoned the front of her blues, bumping and grinding to her hummed rendition of "Night Train," her layers of rubber jiggling repulsively.

260

When she was unbuttoned all the way down to her crotch, she bent over, reached in with her right hand deep between her legs, and came out with a cell phone. She held it out to me.

I took the unit from her with two fingers. "Do I want to know where you where you were keeping this?"

"Right cheek. Inside, high."

I cocked my head toward the door. "Keep an eye out."

As Geraldine went to the door, I punched in the number for Nina Haddad's home. Three rings then her answering machine kicked in. I didn't leave a message.

I called the Breadloaf/North Valley Substation and was connected with the detective squad. Nina Haddad was not in the bullpen and no one knew where she was. Cotter was not available, either.

I punched in the number for MCU. Claire Turner caught the call.

"Joe, I have a little addendum to that who's who file. It just came in." She sounded worried.

"What?"

"It's a nurse on your floor. Benjamin Baines?"

"Yeah."

"Do you remember Paul Baines?"

I felt pin pricks all over my body. "The old wino with the new Beretta."

"Paul Baines is Benjamin Baines's father. I don't know if it has anything to do with the case you're on, but I thought you ought to know."

"That'll help me sleep nights."

"I'll get Dock."

"Uh." I sat down on Geraldine's bed, facing the window.

"What is it, Joe?"

"You know Ben? The one who hands out the meds?"

"Yes."

"He is Paul Baines's son."

"That Paul Baines?"

I nodded.

"Bummer."

"Joe?"

I turned back to the phone. "Yeah. Dock?"

"You all right?"

"Getting better all the time. Look, we might have an ID on that lift with the blond hair: Hawk?"

"Is this a land line?"

"No. Julia smuggled in a cell phone."

"Good. The name that goes with the lift: Let's have it."

"Byron Walsh, aka 'Skeeter' Walsh. He's on the maintenance staff at the Breadloaf/North Valley Substation. He's a cousin of one of the maintenance people here at Squirmhi, Norman Cote. It's a pretty sure thing that Cote tried to take out Leila Gilbert. That plaster that was detected on the lift: according to my expert, that's dental stone. Walsh either made the casts that put those bite marks on Katey Sloan's body or handled the gypsum cement."

"Your expert?"

"A dentist. His father was a pilot."

"I bet this Walsh destroyed both the molds and the casts he made," said Dock.

"Probably. He doesn't wash, though."

"That's always a plus."

"You hear anything from Nina Haddad yet?"

"Not since her first contact. By the way, she said you were wrong about where those lifts were."

"She didn't find them?"

"No."

"I can't raise either her or her partner. What do you think about bringing in Charles Sloan and Ahmed Rida for sweat sessions."

"The other side knows we were ordered off the case, Joe. We risk tipping our hand for nothing."

"If Nina is good people, we need to look out for her, Dock. Put Winnie Hewitt and Stan Brooks in the sweat house with Chuck and Ahmed. Bring in Lt. Trask, too, and shake IAB at them. Put the screws on. These guys have to crack sometime."

"You're throwing wild, Joe. Look: this whole thing is caught on a stump. Nothing and no one is moving and I think they're being professionally advised not to move. If they just sit tight and do nothing, they're clear. Even if the frame on Yuker doesn't hold, it'll still look

like Yuker got away with it rather than that someone else did it."

I exhaled a breath of frustration. "Try and track down Nina Haddad, Dock. She has a daughter, too. Luciane. She's in school. See if she's safe."

"Should I call you if I get anything out of those two cops or track down Nina Haddad?"

"Yeah." I looked at Geraldine. "This phone have a vibrator?"

"Yes."

I gave Dock the number and cut off the call. "As long as the other side does nothing, they're safe."

"You are obviously not being annoying enough, Joe."

"That was what I was thinking. I have a minor flipper. Teddy was put in with a wire to get Alvin. From Teddy's description, it sounded like Cotter was the one who pinched him into doing it. Let's see what Cotter's ammo looks like." I punched in a number for my old place at the Cold Cases desk. The oldest cop on the force answered.

"Det. Nelson, Cold Cases."

"It's your old partner," I greeted.

"At my time of life, kid, I don't have old partners."

"What are you doing at the desk at this hour, Cab? Haven't you got a home?"

"Chasing down some new leads on an old case. How are you doing, Joe? You still in Psycho City?"

"Just elected mayor."

"Congratulations. What can I do for you, your honor?"

"Cab, there was a killing two or three years ago at the Reston steel mill. A homeless guy named Michael Sands, aka Sandy. Where's that case?"

A few keystrokes. *"Cold, but popular, apparently. For some reason, Breadloaf/North Valley Detectives called it up several times over the past month."*

"What's the status?"

"Most recent review shows no activity, no new leads, no changes."

"Is Theodore Toledano on the list of suspects?"

Pause, keystroke. *"He was questioned, but not charged. No arrests. The cops on the case had nothing and apparently didn't give a crap. Why?"*

"I'm checking out a possible blackmail on Toledano."

"Is this Red Toledano's boy? The junky?"

"The same."

"Well, if someone is trying to hold this over Toledano, it's a waste of time. We've got nothing. For what it's worth, no one wants Mike Sands's killer. He's cross-listed here as the prime suspect in the Shanty Murders."

"The guy who was killing all those bums?"

"That's right. Kill you for a blanket, a pair of sox, half a pint of sneaky pete. Chances are, if your boy killed Sands, it was probably self defense."

"Really. One last thing, Cab: Was the detective who called up the case named Harry Cotter?"

"And DiMaggio hits another one out of the park."

"Thanks, Cab. Go home. Get some sleep."

I punched off and wiggled the cell phone at Geraldine. "Here. Stick this . . . put it back where it belongs. Keep it on buzz. If Dock tracks down Haddad, he's going to call."

As she replaced the phone in her butt foam, she said, "I see gears turning, lovey. What are you thinking about?"

"Two things. First is that blond hair lifted off Skeeter. There's something wrong with that—something that doesn't fit."

"What's the second thing?"

"I'm going to call Dock again." Geraldine began reaching for her butt. I held up my hand. "Let's use one of the Half Satan phones."

"Going to give that old hornet's nest one last poke?"

I nodded.

We entered Half Satan and, after a warning from Van, one of the night orderlies, that it was getting close to bed check, I moved toward the phones. Geraldine sat at a table and began leafing through an old copy of *Women's Sports & Fitness.* Thomas was on the other phone, grunting in low tones. At another table, two patients from Mark's group were winding up a cribbage game. Michelle and two of her groupies were watching a movie, Danny DeVito's *Matilda*. Michelle was actually laughing. I leaned my shoulder against the wall and punched in the number for Dock's cell phone.

"What?"

"It's Joe again, Dock." I said it slow and slurred. Thorazine man.

"What's up?"

"You remember Adelaide, Dock? Luther introduced us."

Two beats. *"Adelaide. Yeah, I remember. What's she got?"*

"She just gave me some information that will crowbar the lid off this whole damned thing. I got at least two of them dead cold for being involved in the cover up and at least one of them for the Sloan killing. I'm certain all these birds will roll all the way to the top."

"Think it will hold up in court?"

I smiled. "A two year old kid could take the evidence I'll have, prosecute these birds, and get them all the needle. We've broken the frame on Yuker, Dock. Names, dates, places. A little work on these guys and we'll have the whole thing."

"Who are they?"

I paused and counted to three. "I can't talk right now, but remember the name Neal Miller, Dock. I like him for the killing. Gotta go."

"When do you want to get together?"

"Visiting hours tomorrow. I should have it all together by then."

"Four o'clock. See you tomorrow."

"Okay."

"Stay low, Joe."

I hung up the receiver, turned to my left, and saw Thomas standing there, staring at me, his mouth hanging open. "Something wrong, Sunshine?"

He glanced around then looked at me and said beneath his breath, "Man, you got to know these phones are bugged."

"And your point is?"

265

Thomas's eyebrows went up. "Well, it's just this choice you've voice-mailed to the bad guys, Sherlock."

"What's that?"

"Get out of Dodge, eat a gun, or feed you one."

"Actually, that's a fairly precise appraisal of the situation."

I looked at Geraldine. Without looking up from her magazine, she said, "Listen to all them nasty old hornets buzz."

LEMONADE

The next morning at the nurse's station, after Carla took my vitals, I moved to the next line. I noted there was a new face behind the watch sergeant's desk. Gomez was off. This one was male, late forties, black and brown, the hair gathered back in a high-end pony tail unsuccessfully attempting to cover up a growing bald spot. He must have lost weight or borrowed his uniform. It was too big.

Yukiko got his meds, tossed them down, and showed tongue to Ben. I was next. Ben seemed to be concentrating on his paperwork. "Good morning," I said.

Ben glanced up. "Hi."

"Ben, do you know who I am?"

The nurse looked back down at his papers. "Yeah. I know who you are."

"I'm sorry about your father."

Ben smiled wryly without looking up from his papers. "Lots of people named Baines in this city, Joe. What makes you think that was my father you killed?"

"You mean, besides the snotty tone in the question you just asked?"

He grinned. "Yes. Besides that."

"I got a detective named Claire who works records like a crime scene. If she says Paul Baines was your father, Paul Baines was your father."

"So."

"I just wanted to say I was sorry."

"You already did that."

"I was at your father's funeral. You weren't. Why is that?"

Ben turned to his left and said to Carla, "Can you cover me for a couple minutes?"

"Sure."

Ben gestured for me to come behind the counter. As I followed Ben through the door, I checked the new security officer's nametag: Parsons. Parsons didn't look back. None of the Turkey West recorders were even on.

Ben led the way into the treatment room and through it to the floor staff lounge area. Three easy chairs, a coffee table and a table with a coffee maker and works on it. "Cup of coffee?" he asked.

"No, thanks."

Ben flopped in one of the chairs and pointed at another. Warily, I sat in the indicated place. "Joe, I loved my father. He was my hero from before I can remember until, when I was thirteen, he was driving drunk, ran a red light, and my mother died. He was silly, happy, entertaining, fun. When we buried my mother, it got through to me that he was also irresponsible and dangerous. Over the next couple of years, what was left of my mother's insurance, his job, our furniture, our house, everything went to buy more booze, more drugs. Long before you killed him, my brother and I were into the system. We were a little old for foster care, so we stayed at Fairview Center until we were eighteen."

"How was it?"

"Now you ask."

I felt my face flush. "At the time, Ben, I had lawyers, civil rights groups, the media, and Internal Affairs all over me. On top of that, Human Services made it very clear that you and your brother wouldn't want any contact with me. In addition, I was ordered by the D.A.'s office not to have any contact with you or any of your relatives. What was I supposed to do?"

"I guess it sucked all around, Joe. For you, for me, for my brother. Orphanages suck. That's how it was." Ben looked at his own finger scratch at something on the arm of his chair. "I only want to know: Did my father really try to kill you?" He looked up at me.

"Yes. I don't know where he got the gun. We couldn't trace it. I don't know why he came at me. Because of some other things that were going on at the time with the OCTF investigation into the Battaglia family, the stink raised because I killed your father was terribly convenient for Nicky Batts. I was pulled off of everything during the investigation, which left the Battaglia investigation going nowhere."

"You think the Battaglia's hired my father to hit you knowing he'd get killed?"

"It's only a desperate guess, at best. Me groping for reasons. I haven't found anything at all to back it up."

"It wouldn't have been hard. Promise him a bottle and he'd have tried brain surgery." The nurse sat forward, rested his elbows on his knees, rubbed his nose, and shook his head. "If you hadn't done it, someone else would have, or he would've done it himself. You didn't make us orphans all by yourself."

"You did quite a job, putting yourself through BU's nursing school."

"Thanks. Every now and then I entertain this fantasy of paying off my student loan sometime before I turn eighty."

"What about your brother?"

Ben smiled. "He's in rehab at Riverside General. He's a drug counselor."

"You're not going to say something about lemons and lemonade, are you?"

Ben stood and held out his hand. I took it and we shook hands. "Good luck, Joe. I've put this ghost to rest. I hope you can, too."

I checked my guilt tank and it was still half full. Time. It always takes time. "Oh. I never got my meds."

"That's okay, Joe. I can shitcan your Thorazine by myself."

Instead of morning group, the Turkey Talent Show was being held in the center tower auditorium down on Chicken. Dan's Dragons were seated in the front row near the side stage entrance. All of the patients at Squirmhi who could be reasonably trusted not to mess themselves or commit assault, suicide, or homicide for an hour and thirty minutes were in the audience, a solid row of orderlies standing along the back row of seats. Here and there, seated with the patients, were relatives of patients and members of the hospital staff. I looked and Pop was seated in the left center aisle four rows back. I waved and Antoinette from Admitting and Amber of the fine behind joined the hangman in waving back.

While I pondered my meeting with Ben Baines, a fanfare was played on a piano backstage. Dan Walker came out from between the blue velvet curtains wearing a tux that fit him like his DNA. He welcomed everyone and introduced the first act. The curtain rose on Nance's Chances, recently renamed Juliana's Jewels, Wally's and Beth's old group. Four men and three women, with the stunning Juliana herself standing in and playing one of the two guitars. One of the Jewels, a man named Garth, announced, "This one is for Wally and Beth."

They began with the riff from that Flatlanders tune, "Waving My Heart Goodbye," but Wally, indefatigable foe of country music, had reworked the lyrics just a bit.

> *Standing in the station*
> *Only masturbatin'*
> *Waving the trains good-bye.*
> *On their way to Philly*
> *Whackin' on my willie*
> *Givin' me the eye.*
> *Poundin' on my penis*
> *Guess it came between us*
> *Time to say good-bye . . .*

There was more, but the additional verses were lost in the laughter. I was sure Wally would've loved the performance's reception. As Juliana's Jewels concluded and took their bows to thunderous applause, Wanda motioned to Harvey from the side stage entrance. The Dragons got up and filed into the wing next to the stage. Teddy was there with his boom box, and as Dan introduced the next act from Wanda's Wanderers, I said to him, "I checked out your Sandy problem, Burnout. Don't worry about it."

"You sure?"

"Whatever's left is between you and your shrink. Has the man with the wire gotten in touch with you?"

"No."

I frowned as something subliminal caught my attention. "What'd Dan just say out there?"

"I don't know. Why?"

"I thought I heard him . . ."

One of Wanda's Wanderers, an elderly woman who looked strangely like Madonna, sat down at the upright piano that had been wheeled out and began playing something that sounded like a simple children's song—something you'd find in an ancient how to play the piano book. Five other members of the Wanderers, all women, stood in a line behind Old Madonna, and added their voices, humming a harmony of the simple tune. It was kind of beautiful. Then Michelle came out wearing a beautiful white dress scattered with little blue flowers. I glanced at Geraldine and her inner Julia was looking quite smug.

Michelle stood in the center of the stage close to the footlights. She said, "For Joe." Then she sang in a voice sweet, soft, and clear:

> *Traffic go. Traffic stop.*
> *All must heed the traffic cop.*

Michelle turned her head, looked back at me, and continued.

> *When I'm grown, I shall be*
> *Just as fine a cop as he.*

She sang it again, her voice stronger, and the scene smeared as my eyes filled up. I felt a finger poke my shoulder and I turned and saw Geraldine standing there, hand on foam rubber hip. "Now who's a big marshmallow?"

"It isn't that." I sniffed and looked around at the others. "How are we going to follow two dynamite acts like that?" I said, wiping the tears off my face with my palms. "We're going to get killed out there, guys."

After Dan's introduction, the Dragons went on, siren, machine gun, and drums. Geraldine and the Jailhouse Nine Minus One did just fine. Dedicated to Leila.

□

On our way to lunch, Dan, back in his usual long-and-white, plucked me out of the group for a talk. The others continued down Chicken Run toward the Trough.

"Great job on the show, Dan."

"Thanks. Joe, I wanted to let you know that I'm pulling Louis from the group and sending him up to Redshank."

"Why?"

"He told me he tried to kill you."

"Treatment setback, huh?"

"What I want to know is why you kept this to yourself."

"It was between him and me—actually, it was between him and the relentless Javert." I looked at Dan. "Me tattling wouldn't have changed anything. He told you on his own?"

"Yes. And you're right. That represents change: current and possibly future." The psychiatrist smiled with a puzzled expression on his face. "He said something about not wanting the wind to leave him where he is. It's the second time I've heard it from one of the Dragons. What does it mean?"

"It's from something Nathan Sunday wrote. It means Louis wants to get better."

"Can I get the full text of that?"

"Do you have a PDA?"

"Yes. Back in my office."

"Next time we get together I'll beam you over the lot. Leave plenty of room. It's a trip through the mind of an incredibly brilliant, incredibly twisted, killer who wanted nothing more than to be something else. Have you gotten an update on Leila or Beth?"

"They're both out of the woods. Conscious, but they don't remember anything about what happened."

"Damn." I thought for a moment. "Did cops from Breadloaf/North Valley do the questioning?"

"Yes. Det. Cotter ran the investigation."

"By himself?"

"No. They both insisted on having a nurse in the room. Why?"

"Nothing."

He frowned at me for a moment, unanswered questions poking the insides of his skull. "There was something else." Dan reached into the side pocket of his long-and-white, and held out his hand. On his palm were two keys. "Louis turned these over to me. They're staff master keys for the doors and for the restraints. From the serial numbers on them, these were reported lost by a staff member three days ago."

"Who reported them missing?"

"Ben."

"Benjamin Baines? The meds nurse?"

"Yes. From a report that Luke Munroe turned in, I gather that you were in bed restraints with only wrist cuffs."

I nodded. "You figure Louis did that? Opened my door, sneaked in, and removed the ankle cuffs? Then went and opened Alvin's door?"

Dan frowned. "Don't you?"

"Who is on record for putting me in restraints that night?"

"Neal and Chase. They both confirm that you were put in a full set of restraints, including ankle cuffs."

"Where did Louis say he got the keys?"

"He said he doesn't remember. He also said he doesn't remember how long he's had them."

"Sort of just found them in his room?"

Dan smiled. "What's your third eye make of that?"

"It wasn't one person who both removed the ankle cuffs and left Alvin's and my doors open, Dan. Swami has spoken."

"Why?"

"While I was trying to figure out how to do a somersault in bed so I could pee on the floor instead of in bed, Alvin came into my room and rescued me."

"That explains how the restraints were torn free."

"The point is, Dan, the two key events cancel out each other. If I'm supposed to kill myself through positional asphyxia, why send in a killer who might just interfere with the execution of Plan A?"

"Logic isn't the big seller around here, Joe. It might not have made any sense for Louis to have done both, but that's according to what makes sense to us. Louis, by his own admission, is in a different reality. He may have done both with no contradiction in his mind. Where does all this leave your investigation?"

I studied the psychiatrist for a moment, noting in particular the wing's surveillance cameras. These cameras had sound pickups. "Actually it's in pretty good shape. There are a few loose ends to neat up, but once I get together with Capt. Dockery this afternoon, the trap will shut."

"You sound very confident."

"I am."

"It sounds like that bait you're dangling is meant for me," he said very quietly.

I fixed my gaze on Dan's eyes and replied just as quietly, "It's not meant for you, but spread it around anyway."

The psychiatrist nodded, "When your investigation ends, I suppose you'll be leaving."

"I miss my goldfish."

"I don't know if you know this, Joe, but you're having quite a positive effect on some of the patients here."

"Yeah. The ones who haven't been hospitalized or killed."

Dan brushed off the self-deprecating comment. "Did you see Michelle at the talent show? In front of the entire unit? Singing? Dedicating her song about a cop to a cop? She's talking now, participating in group, taking an interest in her recovery. You had a big hand in that. Elizabeth—"

"Beth."

"Yes. Beth. You struck a real chord with her, Joe. She told her group about your mirror suggestion. The report from University is that the first thing she asked for when she regained consciousness was a mirror. And Alvin. Psychiatry says Alvin is a wall of resistance, a lost cause. He and the legal system agree. You tell him to work on his stuff, and he's working on his stuff."

"Stuff? Don't you mean issues?"

"No. I mean stuff. Have you seen the charcoal drawings he's been doing the past couple of days?"

"No."

274

"Powerful. He's been doing them at night, and I've found tears on more than one of them. Harvey, Thomas, Yukiko, Teddy, knowing you has changed them all for the better." He smiled and nodded. "I count myself among the ones who have benefited greatly from knowing you, Joe. At lunch, Alvin wants to ask you a favor." He winked, patted my arm, turned, and walked toward the elevators.

Quickly through the serving line, I sat at the table and began on my salad as Alvin dug into his chocolate ice cream. I talked across Geraldine. "Alvin, Dan cornered me out there. He said you wanted to ask me something."

"I did some sketches. I was up until four o'clock drawing. Would you look at them?"

"Sure. I'd love to."

I turned and faced Harvey. "Buckaroo, are we meeting up in the nest for afternoon group?"

"Yes."

I nodded and faced Alvin. "Let's get together at the bottom of the access stairs in front of Half Satan after lunch."

Alvin smiled, finished his ice cream, and got up from the table. As Yukiko and Teddy got up to leave, Geraldine faced me. "What'd Dan want?"

"I think he wants to offer me a job. Thinks I have a future in the mental health field."

"You'd be good, boy. You'd be real good." She scratched beneath her right breast. "Wouldn't be happy doin' head work, though."

"Why?"

"Don't get to shoot people doing head work," said Thomas. "Not as a regular thing, anyway." He grinned, got up and left the table, followed by Harvey, leaving Geraldine and me alone.

"I would be a great therapist," I said.

"I'd get on your couch any old time, sweetmeat."

She blew me a kiss, I automatically winced, then raised my eyebrows when the expected blow of dead fish failed to materialize. "What happened to Chanel Chum?"

"I simply cannot face another sardine. I fear that aspect of my persona has been Listerined into oblivion. Your call last night draw a nibble?"

"Nothing yet. Maybe I wasn't sufficiently convincing. I might've thrown a couple of sparks in the oxygen tent, though. Out in the hall, we were right under the cameras. You wouldn't believe how confident I am of an early arrest."

She faced me. "Maybe the other side decided to stop using amateurs. Did you notice that Norman didn't show for work today?"

"Yeah. I gave him a little caution about patient safety."

"What if he runs?"

"Norman's not a pro. Right now, he's at home, looking at his swimming pool, his large-screen TV, his new furniture, his new wife, trying to figure out how to keep them all. I'm betting the only answer he and his associates arrive at involve my eradication. New man on the security desk this morning. Parsons. I don't have him in my PDA."

"A ringer?"

"Not exactly a tailored uniform. Hiding his face, too, instead of watching his surroundings."

"Want me to call Claire?"

"Yeah. Did Dock buzz your butt yet regarding Haddad?"

"Early this morning. She and Cotter are officially on vacation. So is her husband and daughter."

"I could never get off on a day's notice like that. What kind of deal they got over in Breadloaf/North Valley? I'm senior detective in MCU and I can't get off on only twelve hours notice unless I'm shot."

"Dock put Winnie, Brooks, and Staples on tracking down Haddad and her family. Either Cotter and Haddad have both gone to ground or Haddad is tied up somewhere with a mouth full of socks."

"Or dead. No trace of her daughter?"

Geraldine stood and picked up her tray. "Keep a happy thought. Cops all hold up their part of the blue wall, Joe, but they all watched the Westerfield trial, too. Dead little girls tend to make juries obsess about needles."

HIGH CRIMES

Later, as I approached the bottom of the access stairs, Parsons was leaning against the wall, his arms folded. The door was blocked open. "Waiting for Dan's Group?" I asked.

Parsons nodded, checked his watch, and shrugged. "Still early."

"I'm meeting another patient."

"Alvin?"

"That's right."

Parsons pointed toward the stairs. "He already went up. You can go ahead if you want."

"Thanks."

I was actually three steps from the Redshank landing before the great third eye finally kicked in. I stopped dead and said beneath my breath, "'Welcome to my parlor,' said the spider to the fly."

I turned and took a step down when I heard a metallic click reverberate off the concrete walls of the stairwell. Third floor door locked. I went the rest of the way down, tried the door handle, and knocked on the immovable door. I looked behind me and was facing a wall of concrete block. Turkey was as low as the stairs went. My skin prickled as my tongue went dry. "Well, what have we learned today, Joseph?"

Leroy Brown's training kicked in and I did a quick inventory of what I could use for weapons, while I muttered, "'So' Dock says, 'How would you like to get out of that hospital bed and go back to work, Joe? Get out of your head, make some new friends, have a few laughs?'"

The jumpsuit and joggers, by design, left me somewhat weaponless. There was a lump in my side pocket. I reached into it and pulled out Oran Conner's miniature tape recorder. I weighed it in my palm and decided it was too light to weight a fist. It had other uses, though. I pushed the record/play buttons and said into the sound pickup, "Tell Pop my will is in my desk safe. I want to be cremated and my ashes thrown into Capt. Dockery's face." Leaving the recorder running, I replaced it, and buttoned the pocket.

"Oh, let me guess," I said out loud as I turned and climbed the stairs. "Who am I going to see when I open that door?"

I worked up some spit, moistened my lips, and took another step. "Faces, Neal. Faces."

Another step.

"I was going down for the third time out there in the pond, and I saw faces. Remember when Larry Collins got it?"

I stopped on the Redshank landing. The door was cracked open a couple of inches. "Sure, you remember, Neal. Larry was getting the feelgood juice and I turned from his face for a split second and I saw yours. Neal Collins. You're Larry's brother. You changed your name from Collins to Miller."

I placed my hand on the metal door to the roof, warm from the western sun.

"This is a red letter day for you, boy. You've gotten back at everyone, now, haven't you? The cops, the prison, the squirrel house here, and even the cop who took down your brother and his partner. Nothing goes away from this one without a bad smell."

I waited but the only sound was the wind. "Well, Monty, let's see what's behind door number one."

I kicked the door to the roof and stood back. It swung open, banged as it hit the doorstop, and came back part way. Seated, facing me in a wheelchair, was Nathan Sunday, eyes closed, head forward, mouth hanging open.

"Wrong again," I whispered to my third eye as I stepped onto the roof. The sap hit me on the back of my head. I twisted as I went down. Two faces registered before the fade to black: Neal Miller and Harry Cotter. Neal closed in and he had a syringe in his hand. Back to Goofyland.

□

"Want to see what's on the other side?"

Major wooze, the universe once again made from Jell-O, the prospect of having to get into a drug program hovering before me, should I live so long. I opened my left eye, my right eye apparently glued shut. My left cheek was against the tiled deck of the roof. Lifting my head slightly, I wiped my right eye with the back of my hand. It came away bloody. My face felt like it was asleep but there were sharp pains from my ribs. Someone had worked on me rather enthusiastically while I was unconscious. But drugs, too. I was grateful for the inconsistency. I lifted my head up from the tile a few inches and wiped my eye again. It opened. Sunday was still in the wheelchair. All I could see was the back of his head. There were dribbles of blood on the tiles from in front of the access door, around Sunday's wheelchair, to my present location. "Another Torio SceneClean challenge," I slurred.

"Funny man," said Cotter. I felt the toe of someone's shoe nudging my leg. I pushed myself up a little farther, gingerly looked over my shoulder, and saw Cotter sitting behind me on the edge of one of the picnic tables. Neal was to his right on the south side of the roof. The orderly had a ring of keys in his hand and was opening the gate in the safety fence.

"Want to see the other side, Joe?"

"That's okay." The universe's pitch and yaw gyros seemed defective. Unstable horizon. Jell-O planet.

Neal glanced at me. "You ever read some of the stuff Nathan wrote out there on the edge, Joe?" he asked. "The wind grabbing at his clothes, pulling, pushing, making his decisions for him?"

"I did, Neal."

"You afraid of heights, Joe? Your file says you are."

"And you're good with records, aren't you, Neal."

"Big skier dude like you. Scared of heights. How does that compute?"

"The slopes I usually ski on are a bit more gradual than falling out of a building. If you've got boots, poles, and skis to loan, though, I'll give it a try. Snow pack looks a little thin, though."

The orderly suddenly pulled open the gate to the safety fence. "C'mon, funnyman. Let's look at the scenery."

I tried to think of a comeback, but my brainpan was full of butterflies.

Cotter's hand dropped on my shoulder. Neal walked over to the patient in the wheelchair. "Well, Dr. Dan," said Neal, "I thought Nathan could use a little sun. You had him taken off the respirator yesterday and he seemed so much better. Old Nathan here looked as though he was going to be just fine sitting there, but I guess he just came out of his coma. Go figure." He took the key ring and put it in the pocket of Sunday's robe.

"So, what is this, Neal?" I said. "Nathan Sunday overpowered you, took your keys, opened the fence, and tossed me over the side? Then, what? He lapses back into his coma or does he jump himself?"

"It's that remorse thing, Joe. He's filled with it. You and Alvin know all about remorse. Right?"

"Alvin?"

Neal nodded toward the open gate. I turned my head and could see a body lying on the other side of the fence, next to the edge, just inside the low masonry wall. "So, Sunday is going to attack both of us? Weak, a hole in his head, and that catheter still up his joint? You ever have one of those things stuck in you, Neal? Nobody goes into a fight with that kind of handle on him."

Neal frowned for a split second, then smiled. "Well, let's face it, Joe: Nathan Sunday is one crazy son of a bitch. You ought to know. You're the one who shot him in the head."

I looked at Cotter. "You're going to risk it all just to help this psycho cover up your connection to a drug ring? Felony murder? For the conspiracy, you face maybe three years, if that. Hell, you could deal your way into a walk. Felony murder gets you the needle."

Cotter shook his head. "No, Torio. The only option that allows me to keep my shield and keep the money flowing involves you, Yuker, and your old partner here doing some bungeeless jumping."

"Bungeeless jumping. Pretty good, Cotter. I like that. What about Nina?"

"What about her?"

"She's your partner, asshole. What'd you do with her?"

Cotter pointed toward Nathan Sunday. "Wasn't he yours?"

"Is Nina all right. Her husband? Her daughter? Or are you as big a psycho as Neal and just wiped out everybody?"

"Terrible how people are taking the law into their own hands these days. A good American family, both parents on the job protecting and serving, risking their lives every day to keep the city safe, taken out by some home grown vigilantes simply because they have Arab names." He smiled. "Think that'd be hard to sell?"

Cotter slid off the edge of the table and looked down at me. "You and Nina heading off into the park. That was cute. Let me tell you about the jam you put her and her family in, Torio. Unless they can get their song in tune with ours, they are worm meat. Proud of yourself?"

"A lot prouder than I am of you. Detective."

Cotter pulled back his foot and kicked me hard in the thigh.

The drugs weren't that good. I cried out and held up a hand. "You know, when Doc Kratzer looks at me on that autopsy table, it's going to be kind of suspicious if it looks like I got tossed over the side twenty or thirty times before I died."

Cotter shrugged. "Nah. I'm guessing the investigation is going to show that you and Yuker got into it pretty good before Sunday knocked out Neal and tossed you and Yuker over the side."

The corners of my mouth went down as I nodded. "I got to admit, Harry, that touches all the bases."

I looked at Neal. The orderly came over, stood in front of me, and said, "I can't tell if you're an undercover cop playing a crazy or a crazy playing an undercover cop. I'm not even sure you know."

"Actually, Neal, I'm the real Elton John."

Neal smirked. "Either way, Elton, I'm probably going to get a commendation for getting myself knocked silly trying to save you from these two serial killers. It's just lucky that Det. Cotter came up here when he did to question Yuker. He saved me from Sunday just in the nick of time."

"I think I saw that movie. Which one are you? Larry, Moe, or Curly?"

"Trying to drag out the patter, Joe? Waiting for the rest of your group to arrive?" He grinned and looked up at Cotter. "Show him."

Cotter grabbed me by my collar, pulled me to my feet, and dragged me over to the west side of the roof. He pressed my face into the bars of the safety fence. "No sudden intakes of air, Torio. You try to cry out and I'll snap your spine."

Past the pond, beyond the fountain, in the Maplewood, the group was there, most of it, some of them seated. A gray-haired woman with very shiny shoulders was taking her place. Leila was back. Dan was there looking at his watch. Geraldine was there making jokes with Teddy.

Neal came up on my left. "Aren't those last-minute schedule changes a bitch? I guess you and Alvin didn't get the memo." Neal grabbed my hair and pulled my head back. "You've been quite a nuisance, Joe. You have no idea how much trouble you've caused."

Cotter let go of me and my knees sagged. I could still see the Maplewood. Dan and Geraldine got up. Geraldine was looking toward the roof. They were followed by Harvey, Louis, Yukiko, Thomas, Teddy, and Leila. I pointed with my head. "More trouble coming, Neal."

"Jesus," said Cotter.

Neal glanced in the direction of the Maplewood, his eyebrows climbing. "Let's get it done."

"I can't be here," said Cotter. "Let me get clear first. Understand? Let me get clear first."

I wobbled my gaze around until I was looking at Cotter. "So, you're talking to someone, you hear the screams, and run up here just in the nick of time to save the day."

"Fuck you, too, Torio."

"What wit, such repartee." As Cotter's footsteps faded, I sagged until I was being held up by Neal's grip on my blues. "I hope I didn't offend."

"Nothing's going to matter in a second." Neal pulled me to my feet.

"The attempts on Leila and Beth are on Norman, right? What about Wally Spivak? You killed Katey Sloan, Neal. That we know about. We have the evidence."

The orderly's eyes went wide. "You don't have a thing."

I couldn't help but grin. "Hair out of place. By the way, these are excellent drugs. Simply fills me with giggles. From your private stock?"

"What are you talking about? What's out of place?"

"Yeah. See, why would Norman meet his cousin Skeeter down in the staff lounge, I asked myself. Doctors, nurses, therapists, orderlies. What would a couple of grubby maintenance grunts in filthy coveralls be doing in the staff lounge? Stick out like a pickle in a shortcake."

Neal said nothing.

"So, why would Skeeter be anywhere near Books or Katey Sloan, for all that matters? He's at the Breadloaf/North Valley station. I can't think of a single cover he could use to get into Books. He had access to the original dental molds and made the casts, though. Used the measured bags of Castone and water they have already prepared for making casts of footwear and tire impressions. That's all Skeeter did, except for delivering the casts to you."

"Why to me?"

"I bet the maintenance staff here has it's own little rec area down in the basement. Coffee pot, fridge, a few old chairs with the springs sticking out. If Norman was his contact, the meet would've been down in the basement. But at ten twenty-six the morning of the twenty-third, old Skeeter was standing in front of the staff lounge where he met you. Mr. Locard took over from there."

"Who?"

"Edmund Locard. The Locard Exchange Principle?" I turned and faced Neal. "Whenever two objects come into contact with each other, a transfer of material from each to the other occurs."

"What are you talking about?"

"What'd you two do, shake hands? A manly hug? When you and Byron Walsh met in front of the staff lounge after Katey Sloan was killed, Skeeter's coveralls picked up something from you. Exchange principle. It was a hair."

"So what?"

"Well, you see, the hair was one of Katey Sloan's. Remember when your special expertise was needed? Because you had access to former patients' files and thought of yourself as some kind of mental expert on serial murder? Remember that woman you tortured to death on the Twenty-first? Her name was Katey Sloan. While you were burning holes through her skin, she left a hair on you. Then you gave it to Skeeter. Skeeter gave it to Leila, Leila gave it to Dan, Dan gave it to me, and I gave it to Mike Ijumaa, our CSU man over at Major Crimes. Mike took it to the CSU Academy and his munchkins peered through their microscopes, and right this very minute that hair is being DNA tested. If you start running this very second, you just might make it off the mountain before the bulletin goes out on you. You might as well run if Ahmed Rida's family dies. The only deal you could get involves an arm full of needle."

"You're all bluff, Torio. Those lint sheets have all been destroyed."

I laughed out loud. "Oh, man, I can't make this stuff up. Two days before Norman grabbed her boxes, Leila exchanged them for four other boxes down in the storage area. Hair today, gone tomorrow—"

Neal put his hands around my throat and began shaking. "You don't want it easy, do you, fucker? You're just going to keep running your mouth until I have to make it hard."

I laughed at him. "Look at you, man! What a fucking amateur. You sneak around at night, opening doors, manipulating victim look-alikes in to see Alvin, and you're their expert on setting up a serial killer to take a fall outside his pattern. You don't have the slightest idea what makes Alvin tick, do you? Look how you're holding me. You can't choke me. Not with me looking at you, you can't. No matter how important it is. There's a crazy old bum out on the landfill that saw it first. The ligature marks on Katey Sloan's neck were broken in the back. You strangled her from behind. Alvin always strangles his from the front so he can watch their anguish. You're too squeamish for that, Neal. I got your older brother a ride on the spike, and you still can't strangle me from the front. You haven't got it in you. That's why, right now, your name is all over Katey Sloan's death."

Neal's eyes were glistening. His voice came at me, low and strained—almost a growl. "I was there, standing next to you, when my brother died, when they pumped that poison into his arm, I watched you, Torio. I watched you as my brother died! You didn't feel what I was going through! You didn't notice me at all!" He threw me down on the deck.

After a coughing fit, I was on my hands and knees. "My god, Neal, how self-centered can you get?" I looked up at him. "That was an execution. It wasn't about you. It was about your brother."

Neal pulled me up by my collar and leaned my back against the fence. Four-five inches on me, eighty pounds. "You work out, huh, Neal."

"A lot."

I brought my right knee up into his scrotum, then drove my foot down on top of the arch of Neal's left foot as I shoved my left thumb into his right eye. The orderly bellowed, grabbed the front of my jacket and swung me around, my back slamming into the solid steel bars of the safety fence. Dark spots hovering before my eyes, I jabbed the knuckles of my left hand into the center of Neal's voice box. Loose from the orderly's grip, I reeled toward the wheelchair trying to reach the access door.

A familiar weight hit the back of my head, I began falling toward Sunday. Before I touched down the black spots overlapped and I never did feel the landing.

Silence, a gentle breeze, a chill, life in a jar of thoroughly-opiated molasses. I opened my eyes—both this time—saw concrete, tar, fine gravel, and a Jell-O housefly cleaning its wings in anticipation of a fulfilling and exciting season eating shit, spreading disease, and making maggots. *Introducing our newest gelatin flavor: Housefly!*

I was face down in the drainage gutter on the edge of the roof, my body in the shade leaning against the low masonry wall.

I pushed with my left hand against the wall and flopped over on my back. Nothing seemed to be shattered. I gently flopped over again and pushed myself up until I was on my hands and knees. Gravely surface. Using the low wall for support, I slowly climbed to my feet and stood weaving on the edge. The masonry wall was only a little higher than my knees. A sudden gust rocked me forward then pushed me back. The drugs covered up a lot, but not my fear of heights. I backed against the fence and grabbed onto the bars.

Quiet. Deserted. I looked around the edge, back on the other side of the fence. Neal wasn't there. Alvin was still out cold in the gutter on the other side of the gate. I looked through the fence again. Nathan Sunday's wheelchair was on its side but Sunday was nowhere near it. I looked around at the otherwise unoccupied roof.

"I'll be damned, he did it," I said. "Sunday escaped."

I staggered back from the feelings: horror mixed with a strange sneaking pride, shame at the pride, weariness at what it would take to get him back.

Great. To solve one garden variety murder and drug ring I managed to help unleash once more world's cleverest most vicious serial killer. While I was mentally mulching that, I began wondering where Neal was. What had happened to Cotter?

There was a shout from below. I turned, let go of the bars, got on my knees, and cautiously worked my way over to the wall. Placing both hands on it, I looked over the edge as the vertical drop sucked at my phobias. Lots of lawn down there, bisected by the access road that circled the park outside the Deadline fence. A bridge where Lower Raven Stream went beneath the road. Halfway between the building and the bridge were two bodies. One wearing short and white; one wearing short tan and nothing. The short and white was Neal Miller. The other was Nathan Sunday. I gripped the top of the wall, remembering those lines from Sunday's "humans."

☐

> i wonder
> if i am the answer
> to anyone elses question
>
> there can be nothing so sad
> if i am not

He gave up his escape, his final triumph over authority, to be that answer. For me. Perhaps that *was* his final triumph over authority.

A security cruiser, its blue Christmas tree lights flashing, was pulled up on the inner access road east of the bridge. A security officer squatted next to Neal, tried for a pulse. She looked up and saw me looking down at her. She pulled her squawk and put in a call.

I turned, pulled myself along the wall, moving on my knees, until I was next to Alvin's head. I turned about, slid down, and sat in the gutter. It was wet. Still a little snow left on the north side of the wall. I checked Alvin's pulse. Strong. I leaned back against the wall and stared through the safety fence at the empty wheelchair. "Thanks, partner."

The access door opened and Teddy stuck out his head. "Joe? Alvin?"

"Over here, Teddy," I called. "You better get out of here. Call security. Someone's coming back with a gun."

"Joe?" Geraldine came out of the access door behind Teddy. Footsteps clattered in the stairwell, then Cotter shoved Geraldine aside and leaped out holding his gun, two-handed stance and everything. Immediately following him were Dan and Munroe.

"Keep back, please," Dan said to the others.

Cotter froze, realizing that Neal was not there.

"What's happening?" Alvin asked quietly. "Where's Neal?"

I pointed with my thumb over my shoulder toward the short wall. "Sunday took Neal over the edge. Right now Cotter's trying to come up with a story that won't get laughed out of court."

"No kidding?" Alvin struggled up part way, looked over the edge, then flopped back in the gutter. "That's weird. So what's going on?"

"Couple things left to sort out, Alvin. By the way, if things don't work out so good for me, make sure the tape recorder in my pants pocket gets to Geraldine. Okay?"

"Her?"

"Yeah."

"You know, that's what I can't understand, Joe. Something I meant to tell you." He rolled over, swung his legs around, and pulled himself back so that he could use the wall for a head rest. "Can't understand it."

"What's that?"

Alvin opened his eyes. "Wow. These are killer drugs, aren't they?"

"I hadn't noticed. What were you going to tell me?"

"Oh. You and Geraldine. Is it a perv thing?"

I grinned. "Look at her, buddy. She is the woman of my dreams. Anyway, how could you tell we're an item? I thought we'd kept it pretty well hidden."

"You and her hugging in the park. Little whispers watching TV. The Imus show. Coming out of her room late at night. It was gettin' downright repulsive. It's not like you're ugly—"

"You two! Freeze!" shouted Cotter from the gate. "Freeze and shut up!" He had both of us covered with his weapon.

"What'd he say, Joe?" laughed Alvin.

"'Sneeze.' I said, 'You two sneeze.'"

"Aaaa-chooo!" went Alvin. I joined in. We were sneezing and laughing so hard, we were killing ourselves. More footsteps clattered up the access stairs, then a boyish voice shouted, "Drop the gun! Put the gun down!"

Not moving his aim, Cotter turned his head. I squinted and looked through the fence. There was a SRMHI security officer I'd never seen before standing thirty feet in back of Cotter, holding a gun on him. Dark kid, slender. Really shiny black shoes. The security officer also sported the classic two-handed pistol stance.

"Look at that." I wobbled my head around and looked at Alvin. "It's good to see so many taking firing range discipline so seriously."

"Our tax dollars at work—"

"You two shut up!" commanded Cotter.

"Put down the gun!" the security officer repeated.

"I'm on the job, man. I'm a detective, SRPD."

"I don't care who the fuck you are, Jack. I just watched you kick the shit out of one of our patients, and nobody gets to do that but us! Put down the gun."

"If he was watching us on TV," said Alvin, "Why it take so long to get here? We was beat up some time ago."

"Coffee break, Alvin. Union thing—"

Cotter fired his weapon over our heads. "Shut the fuck up!"

"Sorry," we both muttered.

"You all right, boys?" shouted Geraldine.

"Just so we don't have to stand, move, talk, or think," I called back.

Alvin shook his head. "These are great drugs. I wish Neal'd told us what they were before he took off."

"Took off!" I repeated, both of us helpless with laughter.

"Shut up! Shut up! Shut up!" screamed Cotter, trembling, shaking his gun, suspended between giving it up and going for broke.

"That's enough," said Geraldine as she hitched up her breasts. I jabbed Alvin's shoulder. "Hey. Get a load of this."

"What?"

"Just watch Geraldine."

Everything was frozen for a split second, then Geraldine began running at Cotter's back. When she jumped, her well-padded body arched gracefully through the air like a pirouetting hippo, twisted about, and smacked a good stretch of jogger sole upside Harry Cotter's head. The detective dropped like a load of wet wash and as he touched down, his gun went off, the slug chipping out a hole in the masonry between Alvin's head and mine. We both looked at the spot. Alvin studied it for a second, then looked at me. "Girlfriend definitely got her freak on," he observed. Then we both collapsed in laughter.

Geraldine cleared Cotter's weapon, the security officer began cuffing him, and a very confused Dan followed Geraldine through the gate. "Are you two all right?" she asked.

More laughter from us. Of course, right then the recipe for institutional potato salad would have had us in stitches. While Dan struggled with helping Alvin get up, Geraldine helped me get to my knees. I turned and rested my elbows on the edge as I looked down at so much of my recent past. A second security cruiser, and two SRPD cruisers had joined the first vehicle. I could see Dock's car and the team from MCU coming in from McClay. The ME's black van was coming up Fortieth. I heard the cuffs going on Harry Cotter's wrists as I looked at Neal's body.

"Penny for your thoughts," said Geraldine with Julia's voice.

"A multimillionaire ought to be able to do better than that."

"Supply and demand, honey bumps."

I smiled and nodded at the bodies on the grass below. "I was thinking of that thing you hear in therapy every now and then: I may be finished with the past, but is the past finished with me?"

Dan came over, but before he could say anything, Geraldine opened her blues, pulled off her tits, and handed them to him. "Here, honey. They're beginnin' to chafe me a mite," she explained. Then she took out her teeth, turned, and kissed me.

LAST GROUP

We met in the Maplewood. The sun was warm, the temperature up into the low forties. Dan was attending, his parka open. I was in my usual place wearing the jeans and jacket in which I had arrived. Julia, wearing her blond hair up, her blues replaced by a deep ochre pant suit, sat in Geraldine's old place. Leila was seated in a wheelchair next to her bench. On Leila's bench, by special permission, was Beth. On Louis's bench, by special permission, was Louis. Sitting next to Dan on his bench, by special permission, was the mystery SO who had saved the day: Arnold Phelps.

On the payroll less than two weeks, that day Phelps had been a last minute fill-in for Security Officer Moe Tucker, Redshank sergeant-in-charge. The reason Phelps filled in for Tucker was that Tucker had been delayed in traffic at the Fortieth Street Bridge. His delay was compounded by his unfortunate remark to the uniformed police officer who pulled him over for reckless driving in a highway construction zone. Tucker worked his mouth, the police officer shifted into high prick, he ordered Tucker out of his car, which was subsequently searched.

The search netted approximately a hundred and twenty thousand dollars worth of prescription downers, Tucker didn't have a prescription, which resulted in his arrest. This prompted the security officer to work his mouth some more, which prompted his interrogators from Breadloaf/North Valley Detectives to make a point of showing Tucker just how big a prick a true professional can be. The new and relatively uncorrupted detectives who caught the case had a devil of a time finding a phone that was free for the call to which Tucker was entitled. The end result of this set of circumstances was that Tucker was not manning the Redshank security desk when he was supposed to be and neither Neal Miller nor Harry Cotter had been notified of the change.

Phelps knew nothing about Neal Miller's pharmaceutical or homicidal interests, and would have objected to them had he known. When he took his post at the back of the Redshank nurses station that morning, he had actually checked to make certain that all the floor surveillance cameras were working, and that the recorders were plugged in, connected, loaded, operational, and running. What's more, he even watched the video monitors and had seen much of what Neal and Harry had been up to.

He saw Harry Cotter's nine millimeter and determined to attend the upcoming altercation with something in his hand beside his palm. The watch sergeant's pistol, however, was kept locked in the station's safe, which Phelps had never seen opened. A call to the duty officer to find out the combination and raise the alarm, two tries entering the combination in the old tumbler lock, then the gun, a Colt .38 Special, needed to be loaded. The ammunition, at least, was the right caliber and next to the gun. The keys to the padlocked chains on the doors to the roof and to the door to the roof access landing, however, were at the Breadloaf/North Valley substation on Moe Tucker's key ring, which was in a brown paper envelope in a locked personal effects locker while Tucker remained in the holding cage.

Phelps took the elevator down to the third floor, ran to the west access gate, where he picked up SO Munroe, ran down to the end of Turkey West, where SO Munroe duked it out with SO Parsons while SO Phelps ran up the access stairs to the roof and held his weapon on Det. Cotter. Adequate and just in the nick of time.

It rolled up rather quickly once Dock convinced Harry Cotter that his chances of avoiding a needle lay along the path of maximum cooperation. With the information Cotter supplied, Officer Ahmed Rida's new friends at SWAT closed in on the caretaker's house in

Avon Gardens Cemetery, where Ahmed, Nina and their daughter Luciane were being held. They were released by their captors, Officers Sloan and Getz, their captors then taken into custody themselves, along with Homicide Det. Oran Conner.

At the same time, at Books prison, four corrections officers, two maintenance personnel, and Supt. Cotton's secretary were placed under arrest. At Squirmhi, SO Sgt. Gomez, SO Parsons, two other security officers, the assistant purchasing supervisor, and, at his home, Norman Cote, were taken into custody and additional charges filed against SO Sgt. Tucker. Norman Cote had been found watching *Law & Order* reruns, popping Valium, and singing "Duke of Earl."

At Breadloaf/North Valley Substation, Skeeter Walsh was arrested, and up in Copper City the alleged brains of the drug distribution ring, former CO lieutenant and newly graduated FBI special agent Adam Stover was arrested, which led to more singing, and more arrests, much of which was still left to do. Many "No comment" comments coming from the State House.

The Dragons were much impressed. It was Harvey, though, who pointed out that, between police officers, corrections officers, Squirmhi security officers, and the FBI agent taken down, I probably had the department record now for the number of law enforcement officers taken down in the line of duty. All that was left was to exchange goodbyes which, when completed, would leave me free to tie up my last loose end.

Louis had big monsters to face, and thanks to "the swim in the pond" he had with me, he had been brought to face them. Leila was attending her first group session without a lint roller. Her part in catching a killer seemed to relieve her of the necessity of naming every piece of lint in the world. She was working in clay now and promised to send me a finished piece. The next morning, with court agreement, Thomas would be off to Riverside General's chemical dependency unit. No criminal charges. His roommate from Breadloaf, casts, crutches, and all, would be joining him there.

Yukiko, once his father's standards of what is and what is not important were sufficiently extricated, planned to investigate a career in forensic dentistry. "I think knowing there's a good chance my patient will be either buried, jailed, or executed will do worlds toward maintaining my serenity." He thanked me for the suggestion.

Harvey was back to painting and he had notified his cousin Cory to get another man. Teddy had talked to Cab Nelson at the Cold Cases desk, an investigator from the D.A.'s Office had taken a statement, and it looked as though the D.A. was going to decline prosecution for both the death of Michael Sands and the assault on the squeegee bum. When Thomas got on the Silver Line to Riverside Rehab, Teddy would be going with him.

Alvin was leaning forward, his elbows on his knees, staring at the grass. "I don't know what to say. One way or another, all of you got into this thing to break the frame they had on a killer." He looked at us all. "Lots of different reasons, I suppose, but all I can say is, I'm grateful." He leaned back, his hands on his knees. "I only wish Wally hadn't been killed. I never even met him, but he died trying to help me."

"He died because he popped himself to death, Alvin," said Beth. "They had him on Oxycodone because of his back. He used to save up his pills and then pop them all on special occasions." She smiled sadly. "He said it was like playing chess, but staying two moves ahead." Beth slid off her shoes, picked them up, took out the inserts, and removed the trimmed lifts of Norman's footwear impressions. "He was very happy about his hiding place and wanted to celebrate." She looked at me. "Are they of any use, Joe?"

"They've already been useful, Beth. They didn't take the wheels off the wagon, but they sure panicked the driver." After the lifts had been handed counter clockwise around the circle, I took them and looked at Alvin. "Addiction took out Wally, Alvin. It wasn't because he helped you."

"Doesn't make me feel any better about it."

"It wouldn't. What are you going to do?"

"Back in the joint for me. Capt. Dockery said I'm being moved to Rougemont Farm." He smiled. "Didn't want to place temptation in the path of my old bunch of COs. I can paint new pictures there. Work on getting a new head." He nodded at Dan. "One depends on the other." He looked at the group. "I'm adding Katey Sloan's kids to my payment thing. They're all alone now. Pauline Gaye says she'll help Luther set it up."

"Alvin," said Harvey, "It's still life without the possibility of parole."

"I'm a killer, Buckaroo. Besides, I got a roof over my head, a place to paint, full medical coverage, dental, and all the beans I can eat." He grinned. "Van Gogh would've cut off his other ear to have my deal."

Dan looked around the group, then faced me. "Good luck, Joe. I know I speak for the entire group when I say there'll always be a place for you here."

Everyone laughed except Leila. She looked very sad. Dan turned to her. "What's the matter?"

"Geraldine. Where is she?"

Julia leaned over and said in her Geraldine voice, "Leila, honey, I'm right here."

She looked at Julia, her face in smiles. "Oh, Geraldine! You clean up good!"

After packing, I lifted my duffel bag, left the room, and turned down the hall. As I approached Michelle seated in her usual place beneath the cameras, she dusted off the floor next to her. I dropped the bag and sat down, my back against the wall.

"You leaving, cop?"

"Yes. How about you?"

"Someday."

"You mind if I check in on you every now and then? See how you're doing?"

"I never had a visitor." She nodded and looked at me. "That would be okay." Her eyebrows went up. "I know all the words to Wally's song."

"No kidding? Standing in the station, only masturbatin', waving the trains good-bye?"

"That's the one."

"I'm in no hurry, Michelle. Let's have it."

295

And we sang.

THE RETURN OF BATMAN

Early the next morning, Gully Raye sat in his perch high in the pumpkin pine overlooking the north end of Nile County's Sanitary Landfill near Nelson. From the treetop he could see the landfill's working face, the topsoil mountain crusted with gulls, and the appliance dump. Beyond the north greenbelt, across the Interstate, cast in powder blue by the distant haze, was Diamond Lake. It was a better view than the one at the Collier Landfill in South River. Better quality refuse, too. They only ran the compacter three times a week. Plenty of picking time. Only three other pickers, too, and they kept to themselves.

Gully faced the east to catch the rising sun when he noticed something down near the working face. A figure. Man. Medium height, black and brown, jeans and a tan jacket, hiking boots, and a Yankee's ball cap. He sat on the edge of a cut bank, the exposed red earth beneath him almost black in the early morning shadows. His legs were hanging over the edge and he was leaning back on his hands like he was at the bottom of the Grand Canyon taking in the view.

Gully climbed down the branches of the huge tree, slowly, deliberately, not shaking a needle. Once on the ground, he moved silently east, along the paths, deep into the greenbelt. Dangerous to go to his new shack. If they had found him, they'd be waiting there, too. All his food, his warm clothing. Pausing in a thicket of alders, he squatted and pulled off his rucksack. In the bottom of the bag was Little Dog Morgan's Colt .32. Gully took the safety off and left his backpack behind. Leaving the thicket, he continued along the paths, darting from shadow to shadow until he had worked his way around to the north greenbelt. Creeping south, he looked out of the woods. The figure was still sitting in the same place on a lone patch of grass above the cut.

"I talked to your Aunt Adelaide," the man called out without turning around. "She sent me to let you know it's all clear."

"What's her name again?" demanded Gully.

"Adelaide, although she pronounces it Luther."

Warily Gully moved out from the protection of the woods, his gun trained on the man's back. "Who are you? What's your name?"

"Joe DiMaggio Torio."

"The hangman's son?"

"Yes, indeedy."

"I have the clippings. You took down the Gentleman Killer." Gully stood on Joe's left, looking down at him.

Joe grinned. "What's happening, Gully?" He nodded at the gun.

Gully put the safety back on and put the Colt back in his pocket. "Sorry." He lowered himself down and sat next to Joe. "Did you clear Alvin Yuker?"

"He's cleared. A lot of fine people over at the South River Mental Health Institute did most of the work." Gully looked puzzled. "That's where Yuker was undergoing observation."

"City jurisdiction," Gully noted. "How bad? How many?"

"We haven't shaken them all out of the trees yet. A dozen or more. There's a rumor the governor is going to appoint a special prosecutor before he grabs his own flight to Brazil."

"Any cops?"

"Four that we know of."

"That's bad."

Joe nodded his agreement.

"I know about your partner—the Gentleman Killer. He's out at Squirmhi."

Joe looked down and stared at unseen images. "He died saving my life. Yuker's life, too."

"You ever wonder what goes on in their minds, Joe? Serial killers?"

"All the time, Gully. All the time."

"Do you ever get there?"

"A peek here, a peek there." He glanced at Gully and smiled. "I don't know if I could take anymore than that."

Gully paused for a long anxious moment. "Are you here to bring me in?"

"No. Besides bringing you the all clear," Joe pointed toward the gulls on the topsoil mound, "I came to watch the show." He reached to his right, picked up a plastic grocery bag full of stuff.

"What show?"

"I want to see you dancing with the gulls. You know there aren't any gulls at the Collier landfill anymore? Luther says they all followed you here."

"There's a reason Luther's in a home." Gully frowned and squeezed the pockets of his coat. "I don't have enough yet."

"Here." Joe emptied the bag. There were twelve tins of sardines and two boxes of small Milk Bone Dog Biscuits.

Gully carefully examined the tins one at a time. "These sardines are still good."

"They were donated by someone who has sworn off sardines for life. I don't much care for them either. What about you?"

Gully smiled widely as he took the sardines and dog biscuits from Joe. "They'll love these. I can dip the dog biscuits in the sardine oil, too. Open the tins. I'll get 'em to fly."

As Joe began opening the tins of sardines, Gully stood, reached to his pocket with a wide sweeping gesture, and by tens and hundreds the gulls launched themselves into the air. In seconds Joe and Gully were in the center of a screaming gray and white twister, Gully Raye turning slowly in the center, his grinning face to the sky.

▢ ▢ ▢